The Lives and Times of Bernardo Brown

BOOKS BY GEOFFREY HOUSEHOLD

NOVELS

The Third Hour	Watcher in the Shadows
Rogue Male	Thing to Love
Arabesque	Olura
The High Place	The Courtesy of Death
A Rough Shoot	Dance of the Dwarfs
A Time to Kill	Doom's Caravan
Fellow Passenger	The Three Sentinels

The Lives and Times of Bernardo Brown

AUTOBIOGRAPHY

Against the Wind

SHORT STORIES

The Salvation of Pisco Gabar
Tale of Adventurers
The Brides of Solomon and Other Stories
Sabres on the Sand

FOR CHILDREN

The Exploits of Xenophon
The Spanish Cave
Prisoner of the Indies

The Lives and Times of Bernardo Brown

by Geoffrey Household

AN ATLANTIC MONTHLY PRESS BOOK

Little, Brown and Company/Boston/Toronto

FIRST AMERICAN EDITION

T 01/74

Library of Congress Cataloging in Publication Data

Household, Geoffrey, 1900–
    The lives and times of Bernardo Brown.

    "An Atlantic Monthly Press book."
    I. Title.
PZ3.H8159Li3   [PR6015.07885]   823'.9'12
ISBN 0-316-37434-2   73-13724

ATLANTIC—LITTLE, BROWN BOOKS
ARE PUBLISHED BY
LITTLE, BROWN AND COMPANY
IN ASSOCIATION WITH
THE ATLANTIC MONTHLY PRESS

Published simultaneously in Canada
by Little, Brown & Company (Canada) Limited

PRINTED IN THE UNITED STATES OF AMERICA

Contents

The Lives and Times of Bernardo Brown

1. Zita

HE SPOKE tenderly of the youth he had been as if there were no connection through the navel string of the years, as if age had come upon him in a sudden access. This painstaking description of a former self grew night by night from the hotel terrace like some lusty shrub forcing up the paving slab laid over its roots.

"This wasn't a hotel then," he said. "Fifty years ago it was the villa of — well, a poor widow I suppose one might call her."

It was difficult to imagine Bernardo Brown in the nineteen twenties. So little evidence was left beyond laughter in the eyes. His body must always have been strong and stocky; now it had become a bit roly-poly, but then it would have bounced upright when it hit the ground. Features, precise and clean cut, could not be resurrected; to prophesy how a young face will change is far easier than to guess what an old face once was. Subtraction helped. Take away the bags under the eyes, the spaniel jowls under the cheeks, and it was possible to see

3

the deep hollows where a few white bristles escaped the razor as fine lines on a pale tan which had deepened to mahogany and at last reverted to the present sandiness of color and texture. Yes, he could have been a very good-looking boy of more than middle height with dark-brown, wavy hair. No doubt the full, mobile mouth was then alive with that inner amusement which the gray eyes still retained.

Guesswork could reach no farther, but always he must have held the promise of the highly civilized European he was. He looked like a fine type of businessman from the Basque Provinces, cunning, candid and kind. One could not tell whether he was British or Spanish till he spoke. Then his English — a rather old-fashioned, careful English — left no doubt that it was his native language.

"What beat me was that anyone could think I mattered," he said. "There's nothing more patrician than royalty, nothing more plebeian than police — yet both were alike in being self-confident and after me, a plain, respectable shipping clerk. Contented, or near it. Who the devil is ever contented under the age of thirty? One wants more money for less work, and some sort of freedom which one can't put a name to. Still, I was far from wanting freedom to travel over half Europe with no more than small change in my pocket and all of them intent on talking to me."

His father had been a bowler-hatted foreman at the big Bilbao shipyard: one of the skilled emigrants common in days when Glasgow, Belfast and Newcastle were still considered to be the world's nurseries of craftsmen. In order to marry the daughter of a deep-sea fishing skipper he had turned Catholic — or at any rate sufficiently Catholic for the port of Bilbao. The sole result of the union was Bernardo.

He was educated by Jesuits who saw in him a possible theologian, for he had a precocious interest in doctrine and languages, ancient or modern. They had already begun to add Hebrew to his Greek and Latin when they decided that scholar he might be, but priest never. In fact he was being punctiliously diseducated by his father once a week or so. Pious responses during the day. Wellsian machine-socialism at home. This disconcerting process gave him the ironical detachment of a mature actor under cover of which he could build his own morality. Looking back, he didn't think it was wholly beneficial; he felt too much of an observer, set apart from his fellows. But it was by no means bad training for an outlaw.

His education was completed by a business course in London and a desk at a shipping office, so that the lines of his future career were more or less settled when in 1918 his parents, eager to see him again, were offered free passage on a newly built ship being delivered to the British Government. She was extinguished by two torpedoes in the Western Approaches. Bernardo, now that both of them had gone, could never quite accept his father's country as his only home. He returned to Bilbao as Number Two of his firm's local agency. Not bad, he said, at the age of twenty-four.

So there he was in July 1925, a shipping agent with good prospects and bilingual — or rather better if one counts fluent French and a classical education — but without any special interests except girls, the sea and the mountains. He was inclined to underestimate the young Brown. Tastes have to start from somewhere and be formed.

It was on a Sunday, after sunset, that he found himself at Lequeitio, having walked twenty-three miles across country from Bilbao alone and sometimes singing his way over the hilltops — no doubt bilingually. He intended to return by an elderly bus which left at ten, God willing and assuming that prospective passengers could be routed out from the taverns. He never did return, at least not from Lequeitio.

"The beach below this terrace was just as it is," he said, "except a lot cleaner. No ice-cream cartons. No desolate French letters. Close under the wall would have been a very private place to take your girl if you had one. In those days in the north of Spain no girl would have been out after dusk with a man. And look at them now!"

So he had been by himself, wandering along the beach below the villa which was now a hotel. It was at the bottom of a roughly rectangular bay. The left or western side was occupied by the little town and its fishing quays, with the narrow entrance to the harbor in the northwest corner. The eastern side was closed by an old causeway, covered at half tide and nearly awash at low, which led to a sparsely wooded island. Beyond the causeway was the river running out into the Atlantic over a sand bar.

The shore along which Bernardo Brown had been walking was empty except for a dinghy moored in the angle of the causeway and the beach. He supposed that somebody was shrimping or searching for clams. He ought to have considered, he said, that anyone engaged in so lowly an occupation would not have possessed a boat with an engine in it. But why give the boat a thought at all? The night was softly overcast and velvet black. He was silently padding over the sand, dreamily content between his hills and the sea. A pity he had not been singing.

When he was nearly beneath the villa, he heard a shout, running and a scuffle above him. A suitcase was dropped over the wall, instantly followed by somebody who picked it up and ran for the moored dinghy. Somebody else on the terrace fired shots into the darkness. One seemed to hit the fugitive who staggered and recovered; another passed very close to Bernardo's ear, destroying all possibilities of calm calculation.

He dropped flat on the beach and heard the dinghy begin to

putt-putt off into the night. It was challenged from somewhere beyond the causeway. When there was no reply and no attempt to return, a fusillade of rifle fire was aimed — presumably — in its general direction, sending an occasional ricochet howling down the beach.

What Bernardo did then was, he admitted, the act of a terrified lunatic. He could have boldly shouted at the top of his voice that he was on the beach and that people should look out where they were firing; he could have stayed where he was, crouching under cover of the terrace wall until the excitement died down, or run along the beach and up to the nearby town square. He instantaneously rejected the lot. Whether he stayed or ran, he risked being grabbed as an accomplice and compelled to spend a night in the police station.

The trigger-happy pair of the Civil Guard — he had recognized their challenge — had now stopped spraying the water around the sunken causeway with their carbines and were probably closing in on him. Civil Guards pullulated around the slums of Baracaldo where the Bilbao steelworkers lived and plotted their republic, but had little business among the seaside villas of the well-to-do; so the pair must, he thought, have been lying in wait for a gang of smugglers or burglars.

He wriggled quickly down to the edge of the sea, tied his shoes round his neck and took to the water, careful not to make a splash. A dripping, squelching passenger on the last bus would arouse only laughter. Someone with a skinful of the dark Rioja wine always fell in off the quay.

There he stayed with a toe on the bottom, trying to decide from lights within the villa and lights moving towards it when it was safe to swim for the nearest steps. He wondered what the man in the dinghy was up to. If he had not been caught at his work, whatever it was, he must have intended to chug straight out of the harbor and into the freedom of the Bay of Biscay. He might still be able to manage it. Telephone communication with the harbormaster or coastguards was bound to be slow.

Bernardo was congratulating himself on having done the right thing in an emergency — always a satisfying experience for youth — when a powerful acetylene lamp fizzed on the terrace and threw a beam across the water which picked up his face before he could dip it under.

Someone yelled, "There he is!"

And there he was. Nobody bothered to fire at him from the terrace. He was caught. He could count on reception committees on the beach, at the shore end of the causeway and the quayside. His only chance was to swim straight for the island and hope to reach it before any boats put out after him.

"I meant to run across the island and dive into open sea on the other side," he said. "God, I was in a stew! I was much more frightened of wading ashore with my hands up than all the unknown risks of surf and currents."

So he struck out for the island, swimming underwater whenever the beam looked like picking him up. His plan seemed futile as soon as he was committed to it. A boatload of police could cross the narrow harbor entrance and arrive on the western shore of the island before he could reach the southern.

Still, these things take time, especially on a Sunday night. When he landed he had the island to himself. In the darkness it appeared sufficiently overgrown to conceal him, but then he remembered how small it really was. His best bet was to try to get clear away along the sand bar at the river mouth wading or swimming through the edge of the surf. What absurdly worried him, now that he had broken contact, was that he would be late at the office.

To his surprise he heard an engine and made out the dim

outline of the dinghy close to the tumbled rocks where the end of the old causeway rose from the bay; it was bumping against the boulders, out of control with the propellor still turning over. The pair of the Civil Guard seemed to have just arrived at the other end of the causeway. Presumably they had hurried over to the villa after assuming that the criminal had escaped and then had also noticed that the engine was running but not moving away. They were now trying to wade over to the island, slipping on the seaweed, splashing into unseen pools and doing a poor best to keep their curses from echoing through the night. Bernardo Brown said that never since that night had he heard such vivid abuse of the Holy Family. Being recruited from men of unquestionable devotion to the Church, the Civil Guard had all its technicalities to play with.

There was a body lying on the bottom boards of the dinghy, whether dead or unconscious he did not know. What leapt to his mind was that if he could drag or float the boat over the causeway he was clear. Given enough fuel in the tank, he need not even worry that he had missed the last bus.

The engine was an old-fashioned, reliable, single-cylindered Kelvin. He threw out the clutch and waded about looking for a passage. The pair were some two hundred yards away and there was never any doubt of their position. One was complaining of what God and the limpets had done to his backside and the other had lost his carbine. Meanwhile Bernardo found a helpful slope with two linked pools beyond it and quickly manhandled the boat over the causeway, attracting only shouts and wavering torch beams which had not the range to reach him. It was amazing, he said regretfully, what a sturdy but quite ordinary fellow could accomplish in youth without suffering more than a few aches next day.

He was over and away. The bar at the river mouth which

9

was taking the force of a restless Biscay swell caused some peaks in his continuous chart of panic — not so much from the breakers as the hollows between them which slammed the dinghy on the sandy bottom. However, he got through and headed straight out to sea. When Lequeitio was well astern he turned west and closed the coast — or where he hoped the coast would be. He could handle a boat but knew nothing about navigation.

He was also much occupied by the corpse. When he tried to revive it or bandage it or do whatever decency required, he found that it had bled to death. A bullet low down between the shoulders had pierced something essential, probably a main artery. The bottom of the boat and the thwarts were still all sticky with blood in spite of the water he had shipped in crossing the bar and the frantic bailing when he was over. While attending to his passenger he had paid little attention to the tiller, let alone the stars.

The tank ran dry before dawn, and he was left rocking in a faintly phosphorescent blackness. He had planned to make the Guernica River during the night and to beach the boat in some quiet marshy creek on the left bank from which he could easily walk to Bilbao. As it was, daylight showed him that he was miles from the coast. He could only recognize the high bluff of Cape Machichaco.

Well, he had at least a pair of oars. For the moment the worst risk was that a fishing boat might pass close and see the corpse. He propped it up as if it were squatting on the bottom boards and supported the lolling head in a credible position by means of the suitcase jammed firmly between a thwart and the engine housing. He hoped that the dead man would pass as a lazy fellow fast asleep while his companion rowed.

It was a long pull. By midday, blistered and very thirsty, he was rowing along the iron-bound coast with not a hope of landing except in the little fishing port of Arminza or on the beach at Baquio. He could of course have thrown his idle companion overboard but intensely disliked so drastic a solution; the dead should be found and identified even if nothing else could be done for them. Anyway the boat was pickled in blood. He was bound to be questioned whether or not the villages of the coast had been warned to look out for him.

The only remotely possible landing place he could see was at the foot of a rock fall which centuries of Biscay rain had smoothed into a climbable gully. Outlying black boulders appeared in the suck and vanished in the swell like hungry whales. He would have been very glad, after all, of some help in sight, but there was only a fishing boat steaming north, sometimes a dark rectangle higher than his horizon, sometimes showing only a speck of funnel and a plume of smoke. If its skipper spotted the boat at all, he probably assumed that some daring longshoreman was profiting from settled weather to drop a few lobster pots close under the cliffs.

Bernardo rowed hard for the rocks, hurdling one on a breaking crest and smashing broadside into the next. A third sea left the sinking dinghy precariously balanced on a longer reef beyond which was more sheltered water. He dived in and swam ashore on a triangular beach of huge pebbles, followed at intervals by the oars, the rudder and the forepart of the dinghy; the stern half, weighed down by the engine, had been rolled off into deep water by the tremendous backwash, and the corpse hurled into a pool where it was floating among seaweed. When Bernardo had drunk his fill of the fresh water seeping down from the gully he had at last leisure to consider his position.

Absent from the office and not at home? Well, a good, believable excuse would have to be invented. Corpse and boat? It was unlikely that either would ever be found. Would it be known that two persons, not one, were in the boat? That also seemed unlikely. The pair could not know that the wanted man was dead; they were bound to assume that when he ran his boat into the causeway he had taken to the water in a panic, but had swum back again after being picked up by the searchlight and finally heaved the dinghy over into the river.

So Bernardo could stroll home without a care provided there was a way to be found up the cliff which appeared to have plenty of ledges and chimneys between the perpendicular crags. He felt some compunction at leaving his late passenger in the heaving seaweed to be eaten by crabs and dragged him up the beach — if one could call it a beach — where he lay curled up and safe from anything but the spray of high seas.

It was not easy to spot the gully which had been so obvious from the boat and ended somewhere among the great boulders which towered over him. He scrambled up them and was then faced by a climb so monstrous that it would only have been attempted by an optimistic young man with no alternative. It was more than doubtful that he could ever get off the beach again in one piece, and even if he could there was nowhere else to land.

He worked his way up the gully, sometimes taking the broken rock of the sides, sometimes digging toes into the slippery mud. At the head of the fall he was relieved to find jagged rock. The cliff was climbable, and a slip would only carry him down to his starting point with nothing worse than skinned hands and knees.

The easiest route was out to his right. He was extremely careful to take no risks and to concentrate on every step and handhold. This absorption in the very immediate future was too successful. When he stopped on a ledge to consider the way off it he nearly fainted then and there. Below him was no saving gully but a sheer drop into the sea with a pair of planing ravens emphasizing the vast emptiness of the air.

So back in a cold sweat to the cracks and chimneys. Now again he had the gully beneath him, though so far beneath that it would break him up if he crashed into it. To his left was a steep arête which he climbed by the suicidal method of tufts of grass. The top was so narrow that he could totter to rest with a leg in space on each side of it. Below the outer precipice of the arête white streaks of foam wrote Arabic from rock to rock; on the inner side was a deep cleft where he might remain alive if not too badly hurt but would certainly remain forever.

The arête ended in a buttress which an experienced rock climber would, he assured himself, find as easy as a ladder. What about the cliffs of Kanchenjunga? To hell with ropes! Great care was all one needed. Bernardo clung to it, half circled it, zigzagged up it, forcing himself to ignore the sheer drop beneath which was now nearing the full four-hundred feet.

He reached a bit of a platform the size of a tea table and again rested. He could not see what was above him, but at least grass, bushes and a large clump of sea pinks were protruding over the edge of something which might be a terrace or might be the top. The last twenty feet of loose stones embedded in earth were vilely unsafe but held fast. He was up though still not quite home and dry, for he had arrived on a vertical slab of hanging cliff which might fall that day or stay put for a hundred years. However, one had only to drop into the fissure which separated the slab from the rest of Spain and scramble up the other side. The gradient of the solid land when he reached it was about one in two, but with enough gorse and shrub to catch him whenever he slid on the short, too smooth turf. Then at last the slope flattened and his eyes could rest on the green Vizcayan countryside, miles and miles of it with nothing perpendicular until one came to the crags of Mount Gorbea in the distance.

It was over. He dropped on the grass, welcoming the sun after that clammy, north-facing cliff while he got his breath back and the muscles of arms and legs gradually stopped their involuntary quivering. When he stood up and shook off whatever mud and dust would leave his wet clothes before setting out on the simple walk back to Bilbao, he saw somebody observing him through binoculars. A ruined wall which must once have kept sheep and cattle from straying too near the edge ran up and down well inland from the line of cliffs. The man was standing on the highest visible section of wall, a quarter of a mile away, from which he would have a view of a considerable stretch of coast.

It was disturbing to be examined through binoculars, but Bernardo decided not to arouse suspicion by running away. After all he had nothing to explain; he could well be taking an innocent, meditative walk along the cliffs.

The man lowered his glasses and strode decisively down the hill towards him. He carried himself well — a proud, athletic sort of chap with a bald head, in spite of appearing in his early thirties, and a clear, sunburnt complexion etched with deep lines.

"Not so common as today," old Bernardo said. "Now, there's a change for you! Any European with a good, ruddy tan was almost certainly engaged in agriculture."

Features and coloring were not those of a Spaniard. He put down the stranger as a foreign visitor walking for his pleasure and likely to sympathize with anyone doing the same. The man looked as if he ought to have a knapsack on his back, but evidently preferred to keep toothbrush and spare socks in his pockets which bulged.

"What were you doing down there?" he asked Bernardo in bad Spanish, waving a hand at the sea.

That was startling. The utter destruction of the boat could not have been seen, nor the beach, nor his climb, but there was no hope of denying — against those powerful binoculars — that he had rowed a boat in to some sort of landing place.

"Catching lobsters."

"And your companion?"

"What companion?"

"I have been watching you for the last two hours."

"Oh, that one!" Bernardo answered as casually as he could. "He's down below at the foot of the cliff."

"And where do you come from?"

"Baquio."

"You are not dressed like a fisherman."

"Man, can't one fish for pleasure? Yesterday, I remind you, was Sunday."

"Good! Then let us walk to Baquio where you can identify yourself."

"But I can't leave my companion down there."

"Your companion is dead, friend. Did you kill him or was he shot at Lequeitio?"

Bernardo Brown threw out his palms in a gesture of incomprehension. It did him no good. The foreigner pulled one of the bulges from his pocket, ordered him to link his hands behind his head and searched him thoroughly, taking his wallet in spite of Bernardo's protests. Twenty-five pesetas, his address book and the signed photograph of a strip dancer who had performed a month earlier at the Bilbao music hall were no great loss, but his identity card was. For the first time he experienced the feeling, later to become familiar, that he had lost all personality in a world no more controllable than a dream.

"And now his suitcase! Lead the way!"

"But look here!" Bernardo shouted. "There is no path!"

"Then how did you get here?"

"I climbed."

"The cliffs are unclimbable. Don't waste my time with lies! We will go down the way you came up."

Bernardo began to object excitedly and in detail, but was cut short. The man had reason on his side. The cliffs were indeed unclimbable; therefore there was a practicable path, and Bernardo must know it as well as the discreet landing place.

"No nonsense, and lead the way!" the stranger repeated. "I remind you that if I kill you here no one will ever know."

That was very true. It also cut the other way. Bernardo put the thought out of his mind which was normally peaceable and introverted. But unless this lunatic stopped insisting on his goat track, smugglers' path or whatever he had in mind before it was too late, the leader was surely going to die, and the follower probably.

"It's incredible what a man will do for money when he is used to heavy doses of the stuff and can't live without it," old Bernardo said. "Of course at the time I knew nothing of his character and his motive. I just saw a reckless nihilist with one idea in his head. He never considered the risk that I might be telling the truth, only the physical risks. Every criminal takes those. What about gangsters as ready to face a tommy-gun as any devoted soldier? And the risk this well-muscled tough was prepared to take was not, from his point of view, at all unacceptable. The route down to the landing place was hair-raising all right. He knew that. But if I could do it, he could."

The first part, down through the steep furze, was easy enough. At the edge it was difficult to see what was below, and Bernardo was far from sure of the exact point at which he had returned, as it then had seemed, to life. He worked his way along the border between turf and eternity until an outward curve of the cliff brought the clump of sea pinks into view. That at least marked the top of his route. He could also see from this angle exactly what he had climbed and nearly went over the brink with vertigo. It had affected him only once when clinging to the face.

The menace of that automatic or revolver — or perhaps half a pipe for all he knew, having concentrated on the black hole at the end — followed him all along the edge a safer twenty feet above him. There was nothing for it but to prove to the fellow that no way down existed. He lowered himself into the fissure behind the half-detached crag. That bit, worn by foxes or a very daring bunch of sheep, really did look like a path, and his companion remarked "I told you so" or words to that effect.

He scrambled up to the top of the crag, closely followed. To climb down from there onto the table-sized platform demanded more courage than anything else in all his life. He would have clung weeping to his insecure handholds if it had not been for the worse threat above. However, once again he found his feet standing on the buttress.

From above there was no certain indication that this little platform was the absolute end of the possible. A broad ledge, just below, curved away inwards until it narrowed to nothing. Bernardo had never before noticed it, for his climb had been up the sheer side of the buttress clinging to cracks, eyes blurred by sweat and terror. The man looking down from above could not help noticing it. The beginning, the inviting beginning, of this ledge presumably confirmed his certainty that a path existed, though he did not much care for the way down to it.

"You came up here?" he asked. It was an exclamation rather than a question.

Zita

"I did," Bernardo answered. "This is it."

He could accuse himself of nothing more, and he hoped his reply could not be considered murder. Anyway it was the truth. So far as there was a route, this was it. He had already explained that descent was inconceivable.

He even told the fellow, whose questions were beginning to sound hysterical, where to put his feet — correctly, too. It was the big pair of binoculars which did it. Hanging on the man's chest they did not allow him to get closely balanced against the face of rotten rock. He tried to swing them behind him with his right hand, and the slab which was the hold for his left hand pulled out.

Bernardo returned to the top, his palms slipping with sweat on those lightly embedded stones. He was trembling but beyond fear. The prolonged scream had emptied him. It grew lower in pitch like a jet engine as it increased its distance. He refused to let his eyes follow. The sound of the impact made it certain that the body fetched up on rock, not in water.

He cleared out as fast as he could feeling perfectly safe, safe as in the womb. It was the effect of contrast. At one moment he had been doomed to certain death; at the next he was a free man with nothing on his conscience. Being convinced that he could not be traced through any of his movements, he hardly gave the future a thought, never considering that the movements of others might have some bearing on it. Young men who tend to be introverted make very bad criminals.

What the bald-headed foreigner had been up to was easy to guess. He didn't fall from heaven, so he had to be an accomplice. He might have been in the woods behind the villa and heard the firing, or he might have waited for the arrival of the dinghy further along the coast. The boat was too small for anything but a short voyage out of the harbor and into darkness.

18

When the burglar, or whatever he was, did not turn up at the landing place he was clearly in bad trouble. If he had been arrested or killed, that was that; but if he had escaped he might be anywhere — perhaps wounded, perhaps with an empty tank. So in the morning his partner decided to watch the open sea from several headlands where mile after mile of coast was visible. It was long odds against spotting a drifting boat but his hunch had paid off — or would have paid off if not for his obsession with a path up the cliff.

"My reconstruction was not far out, but the older I get, the more I see that speculation should be kept for bedtime," Mr. Brown said. "What I ought to have been thinking about was plain boy scout stuff."

Well, he was not. A little slinking from cover to cover, a bit of hiding behind field walls to let people pass, and he would have been all right. But there he was with this exaggerated feeling of safety, kicking up the red dust on a by-road as he tramped towards Bilbao and the office. And so he walked slap into another pair of the Civil Guard lounging along in search of the rare evildoers among the Basque peasantry.

Bernardo had not fully realized the effect of his appearance, for he was still too occupied by the man inside the clothes. They were of course heavy with dirt and sea water and flapping against him. Even if the pair had not been warned to keep eyes open for anyone who might have secretly landed from a boat, they would have stopped him to find out if he needed help.

"How did you get into that condition?"

"Fell in."

"Where?"

The only place behind him — omitting Lequeitio — where he could reasonably have fallen in was the fishing port of Bermeo, so he chose it.

"What were you doing there?"

"Sleeping on the quay."

"Identity card, please."

Bernardo made a show of looking through his pockets and exclaimed that he must have lost it. He gave a false name and address. He said that he had got drunk in a tavern, missed his bus back to Bilbao, spent the night on the quay, rolled over into the water and was now making his way home.

What time was the bus? What tavern? Who were his companions? Was the fishing fleet in or out? He wriggled on the hook and was proved to be lying. He would have come straight out with all the truth if it had not been for the extra corpse somewhere at the foot of the cliffs. He was very much afraid that nobody would believe the bald-headed foreigner's obstinate insistence on a path till it was too late.

The pair put on an unusual solemnity. No triumphant jokes. No coarseness or knocking about. Bernardo assumed that it was because he was a respectable middle-class citizen; that much was evident from his clothes and shoes in spite of their disreputable state. One of them set off at a military pace to Bermeo and a telephone. The other marched his prisoner away from the road into the shade of a clump of dwarf oaks where they could see and not readily be seen. It was all very exceptional. The pair rarely separated. Normal practice was to bring in a suspect together.

A couple of hours passed. Bernardo was wet, shivering, hungry and longed for a drink. There was hardly any conversation to while away the time. His escort refused to answer questions and — more surprising still — seemed to think it his duty not to put any.

About five in the afternoon a large, black limousine cruised slowly along the road. The guard stood up and signaled to it. When it stopped, his companion jumped from his seat alongside the chauffeur, threw open the door and stood at the salute while a resplendent major of his corps got out, followed by a tall civilian in an obviously expensive suit of dark but sporting English tweed. All three walked up to the oaks where Bernardo was being so discreetly detained.

"Is this the man who was interrupted in his disgraceful attempt?" the major asked in fluent French, his Spanish accent sounding as if it were played on steel with cracked drum sticks.

"No, no! That's not him," the civilian answered pleasantly. "The fellow who broke in was slimmer with fair hair."

He gave an impression of geniality. There was no hint of criticism or disappointment in his voice. His bearing was easy and distinguished. He wore a soft, dark-brown moustache which matched his eyes and was neither the toothbrush then in fashion nor the luxurious, soup-straining growth of an older generation.

"You are sure?"

"Nothing like him!"

"Then may I go now?" Bernardo asked, also using French which seemed to be the agreed language for this incident. "I am hungry and I need a bath and a drink. If a man can't have too much wine on a Sunday evening without being run in for it, I ask with great respect: Where are we?"

The civilian laughed.

"Come back with me and we'll soon put that right," he said.

The major of the Civil Guard seemed doubtful, but gave way to the other's casual air of authority. Warm hospitality, the tall civilian insisted, was a duty. It was most desirable that there should never be any ill will at all among the local inhabitants.

The pair continued their patrol. The major was dropped at

his front door where there was an inordinate exchange of compliments. Bernardo, though well accustomed to lengthy strings of Spanish politeness, was impatient with so much artificial nonsense in French. At last surrendering to physical exhaustion he sank back on the cushions of the car and did not listen. The position might have become clearer to him if he had. While the car purred off to the villa and he was alone in the back with his aristocratic companion, who appeared to be courteously avoiding any personal questions, he was vaguely aware that he was expected to know something which he did not.

They entered an annex on the landward side of the villa which appeared to be some sort of guest suite occupied by his companion. He was given a stiff brandy and soda and the use of the bathroom. A valet took away his clothes to be dried and brushed, and laid out for him shirt, underpants and a superb dressing gown of padded silk with a fur collar.

When he re-entered the living room he felt more like himself — a cheerful self very tired after, say, a football match — but shy at his own gorgeousness. He was immediately put at his ease by the unconcern of his host and by a small table placed at the open window, gay with bottles of sherry and four different varieties of the delectable shellfish of the Basque coast.

His rescuer said, "A more serious meal will be along in a few minutes. If you will excuse me, I shall only join you in these. I have to dine later with Her Majesty."

"Her Majesty Queen Ena of Spain?" Bernardo asked.

"Her Majesty the Empress Zita," the other replied.

Bernardo, too astonished for manners, asked who she was. He had supposed — so far as he had given it a thought — that the villa beneath which he had been strolling till bullets started to fly about belonged to some wealthy industrialist or perhaps was the summer residence of a Madrid politician.

There was no reply. The lips under the fur-like moustache became for a moment more grim than genial. The slight awkwardness was banished by Bernardo's evident appreciation as dish by dish his scratch dinner appeared. He remembered the menu exactly, since he had not eaten for nearly twenty-four hours and the meal was of outstanding delicacy: *foie gras en gelée*, a superb red mullet and a dish of small, round pancakes with scraps from paradise sandwiched between them. Retrieving his manners halfway through the second wine, he remarked that his reception was like something out of the Arabian Nights.

"I am enchanted that you should find it so," his host answered. "But didn't the traveler then have to tell his story? I know you are not the man who entered this villa last night, but the face I saw in the water was yours."

"It was," Bernardo admitted. "And it's very kind of you not to tell the police."

"Not kind at all. I intend to have the truth out of you before they get it. First, who are you?"

"My name is Bernardo Brown and I work in Bilbao."

"English? They all thought you were Spanish."

"My mother was."

The man immediately deserted his rather formal French and broke into perfect English with a slight accent.

"Good God! What the devil is an Englishman doing mixed up in this?"

Bernardo outlined his story and then expanded it under close interrogation, coffee and brandy. His questioner, who introduced himself as Count Istvan Kalmody, never lost his courteous man-to-man approach, but Bernardo had no doubt at all that he could be ruthless if it suited him.

"Now, why didn't you run for it instead of taking to the water?"

"It didn't do the other fellow any good."

"You think it was my shot which got him?" the count asked with a shade of pride as if he had bagged a fine duck in the last glimmer of the evening flight.

"It looked like it."

"And when you were handed over to me, didn't it occur to you that you might be safer with the Civil Guard?"

"Of course it didn't! How should I know about Zita — Her Majesty, I mean. I still don't."

"I thought you were bluffing when you said that the first time. If you are not, you appall me, Mr. Brown. Only five years, and you, a very civilized young European, have forgotten!"

Bernardo searched his memory for headlines read long ago in the daily rush to Leadenhall Street. He recovered a few of them then and there and the rest later. In November 1918, Karl, Emperor of Austria and King of Hungary, abdicated. In 1921 he made two incautious attempts to regain at least the crown of Hungary. Czechs, Romanians and Yugoslavs were having no more Hapsburgs on the Danube, and the Hungarians themselves were not so fond of the family that they would risk invasion for Karl's sake. So he retired to Madeira where he died, and King Alfonso of Spain established his widow, Zita, in Lequeitio.

"Such an unlikely name!" old Mr. Brown remarked. "Empresses ought to be called Maria or Sophia or Matilda or something like that. But she was still Empress of Austria-Hungary to anybody who cared. Quite harmless people, both of us! There had I been walking along the sands without a care in the world, and there was she in the villa above me mourning her husband and the lights of Europe."

No wonder a permanent patrol of the Civil Guard had been on the road to the villa! Not that poor Zita was in any danger of assassination — it was just that King Alfonso, a genial and hospitable fellow, was determined that nothing should disturb the melancholy peace of his distant Bourbon-Parma cousin.

She was never mentioned in the local papers. Citizens of Lequeitio of course knew all about her, but Bilbao had hardly heard of her existence. Bernardo had once seen a party of frock-coated passengers on the little toy train from the French frontier and assumed that they were going to the funeral of some foreigner. He never dreamed that they were Hungarian magnates loyal to their ancient monarchy and on the way to kiss the hand of their queen.

He apologized humbly and meant it, ignorance seeming a greater crime to the young than to the old. He thanked Count Kalmody for believing his story and asked — no doubt clumsily — if there were any way in which he could show his gratitude. He was also eager to know what had caused all that excitement on the previous night.

The Count replied that it seemed to be simply an unsuccessful attempt to steal Her Majesty's property. She had something worth stealing for the first time in six years, and the burglar must have known it.

"He was taking an awful risk with you around, wasn't he?"

"Crowned heads in exile like routine, Mr. Brown. From half-past nine to half-past ten Her Majesty reads an improving book aloud to her faithful servants. Obviously the man knew that. I wouldn't be surprised if he had spent an earlier evening having a good look round. What he didn't reckon on was that I should be spending a few days at the villa to see how Zita was getting on and — failing a direct command — I refuse to be read aloud at. I caught him just when he was sneaking out to the terrace with a suitcase. Nothing is missing, so I was in time to stop him filling it."

"It was not empty," Bernardo said.

"Well, now you mention it, he did seem to me to be running a bit lop-sided. What was in it?"

"Just clothes, I thought."

"You didn't look? No curiosity?"

"Not enough to fiddle with locks. I wanted to get home."

"Where do you think he was going in the dinghy?"

"Not far. One of the beaches to the east and then over the frontier by land."

"What makes you say that?"

"Well, he didn't look as if he belonged here."

"You're very observant, Mr. Brown. We had a moment's conversation before I realized he had no business to be in the villa. I addressed him in French since I speak no Spanish. His replies were so idiomatic that they left no doubt of his nationality. Can you make any guess where the other, your fellow alpinist, belonged?"

"Not Spanish or French. Might have been a German but I don't think so."

"Describe him to me!"

"Sunburnt. Built like a light-heavyweight. Not much over thirty but already bald. Deep lines running down to the corners of his mouth. Mad blue eyes."

"My God, Bobo!"

"Bobo?"

"Heir to a Russian grand duke, but don't let that bother you! The Romanoffs will all be thankful to be rid of him. Dubiously claims to have sabered dozens of Communists in the Civil War. Lived on stolen diamonds. When they ran out, sold himself to the Czechs and Romanians to do their

26

dirtiest jobs — with their French friends looking the other way. He's above high-tide mark, you think?"

Bernardo, feeling slightly dizzy with this shot of memory in his brandy, said he was sure of it.

"Then we're in trouble, Mr. Brown. How about reconstructing his movements? He'd have waited all night at the rendezvous arranged with his fellow agent. Then at dawn — Do you agree? — a look at the open sea and any likely beaches. Only when he had drawn a blank would he have tried the headlands west of Lequeitio. How do you suppose he moved around so fast?"

"Must have had a car."

"And where is that car now?"

"Oh, lord!"

"Exactly. Deserted and standing by the side of a road somewhere very near the cliffs."

"But the police couldn't guess where to look for him."

"Well, I know where I should try first — at the edge of the precipice. And perhaps find some footprints where you say he thought there was a path?"

"No footprints, I think. At least not where anyone could get."

"And then, if the sea is calm tomorrow or the next day, I should take a boat along the foot of the cliffs and I should find both bodies with your wallet and identity card in Bobo's pocket. It's going to look as if you killed both of them."

"But, damn it, you shot one and the other fell!"

"Assuming you didn't give him a push. But possibly you didn't. It's only in war that you English are at your best. That goes for the Spanish half, too. Why the devil did you pull Number One up on the beach?"

"We had shared the boat for so long. And for all I knew

he might only have been caught with his pants down by somebody's husband."

"That remark is not in the best of taste, Mr. Brown. Where's the suitcase?"

"It went down with the boat."

"Think again!"

"Look here, my lord! You can't climb a cliff carrying a suitcase. And what's funny about that?"

"I am laughing because I have to like you. Nobody in England ever calls a foreign nobleman 'my lord.' They just say 'count' or 'baron.' "

"Do we? I didn't know."

"Damn it! If only there were just the original body, Alfonso would be able to fix it."

"Alfonso?"

"The King of Spain. Don't tell me you haven't heard of him!"

"Couldn't Bobo sort of join the party?"

"Mr. Brown, this is going to be difficult for you to understand. In these days whatever my country does is wrong. We are guilty of starting the war though we voted against it. Because we governed minorities speaking other languages, it's now considered right that they should have independence and govern Hungarian minorities. We are guilty because we won't take that lying down. And, worst of all, we are guilty of being the only civilized nation in Eastern Europe."

"I think we all feel rather sorry for you in England," Bernardo said.

"Oh, in England! You don't even know where Hungary is without looking at a map. But the French do and their allies do. If they can pin a crime on us, they will. Who assassinated two harmless tourists in Spain? The Hungarians of course! The gangsters of Europe!"

Bernardo protested that he was surely exaggerating. The count, ignoring this squeak from the tennis club, asked — more to himself than his guest — why and for what Bobo had been employed.

"We can rule out bombs and common burglary," he said. "What's left? Compromise her and us in some way so that the bloody newspapers have a stinking, international scandal to play with? I don't see how, but I'll bet that is what they were after. And they have got it, though not in the way they intended. Perhaps you can be of great help to us."

"If I can, I will," said Bernardo stoutly.

He had a pleasant vision of being received by Her Majesty and invested — if that was the right word — with some ancient and magnificent order, third class.

"Well, corpse number one gives us no trouble. A thief tried to break into Her Majesty's villa, perhaps mistaking it for a richer establishment. He was challenged by the Civil Guard and shot, but managed to escape. Finish! That's all anybody knows."

Bernardo pointed out that the bullet in his body would probably be different from those fired by the carbines of the Civil Guard.

"A most intelligent remark," the count said. "But I am sure instructions will be given that the Civil Guard bagged him whether they did or not. Now have some more brandy and shut up while I consider that tourist who fell down the cliff. Suicide? Bolshevik assassins? An interest in gulls, if gulls nest there?"

"Ravens do."

"Ravens then. In any case this tragedy which happens yearly on all savage coasts has nothing to do with burglars, Hapsburgs or Hungary. Obviously there must be a connection between the two bodies but no one knows what and their employers won't talk."

"But my identity card is in Bobo's pocket," Bernardo objected.

"I was coming to that. And Mr. Brown will be recognized by his description as the chap who had been in the sea and was walking to Bilbao. I cleared him — casually and convincingly, I hope — of the attempt on the villa. I shall never mention that I saw his face in the water. But Mr. Brown, if he is available, will be arrested and perhaps tried. The law is the law. And, worse still, Bobo was about fifth in succession to the throne of Russia.

"Tomorrow or the next day that intolerable major will call here and ask me what I did with you. I shall reply that I offered you a bath, fed you and turned you loose with apologies. Inevitably you are going to be suspected of murder, but that has nothing to do with the Empress Zita."

The more Bernardo considered his story, the more unlikely it appeared. He could not even decide whether it was better for him to have been seen in the water or whether Count Kalmody should keep quiet about it.

"I think I could clear myself, you know," he said nervously. "Spanish justice is slow and I might spend a long time in jail and lose my job. But the British consul would help and I'd be all right in the end."

"We should not be so lucky and found guilty of God knows what barbarities. And so, Mr. Brown, I cannot allow you to be interrogated. You must cease to exist."

"But you can't! I mean . . ."

"My dear chap, that sort of thing starts east of Hungary! What I propose is to save you from all this absurd embarrassment and let the Arabian Nights carry on instead. You're a young man. You'll have the time of your life as my guest."

"Wouldn't you be taking a big risk if you hid me here?"

"I should indeed! However, I possess a remote and beautiful estate. The Romanians have stolen half of it, but a lot remains. What do you enjoy? Horses? Shooting? Girls?"

"I don't know much about horses and shooting."

"You shall learn. Just girls wouldn't be good for you."

2. Magda

"ONE SELDOM heard of kidnapings in those days," said Mr. Brown. "It was a very rare crime. And look at it now! Political extremists hard at it, and any poor sod they collar is damn lucky if he doesn't get his throat cut! They all take themselves too seriously. Vulgar impatience — that's the trouble with them. One should always find time for manners. Myself, I had nothing to complain of, nothing at all except a bit of a headache."

Count Kalmody had shown him his bedroom, locked the door and gone off to dine with Her Majesty whose peaceful retirement Bernardo had embarrassed. He was certain that there would be no mention to her of his plebeian presence under her roof, and that amused him. Inevitably a shade of exhilaration was mixed up in his general alarm. Kalmody, he suspected, did not wholly believe him and would believe him even less if he ever had an opportunity to examine that cliff, but for the moment relations were cordial. The window offered a way of escape onto a lower balcony. He was not tempted, for escape was only going to land him in Bilbao police station. His future was so plainly unpredictable that there was no point in fussing about it. Being still hungry, he sat down to the refreshments which were laid out on a delicate mahogany table at the foot of his bed.

Bernardo woke up to find himself in a small but comfortable basket chair enclosed on three sides by a windscreen. Beyond the windscreen was the back of the driver. It puzzled him that there was no passing scenery. He sat up and looked over the side of the car to see the road. There wasn't any. Some five thousand feet beneath him was the sea.

"Hell! Must be an airplane!" he said aloud.

A voice behind him asked if he was feeling all right. He turned round. In another basket chair behind him was a man in his fifties or so with a shock of white hair and a grin on his face.

"You've woken up too soon, young fellow. Istvan reckoned you wouldn't start eating again till midnight. What an appetite!"

"Where are we?"

"Coming down to refuel. That's Italy over there."

Even allowing for ex-empresses, Bernardo could not make out how his Arabian Nights magnate had materialized a flying carpet in the course of half a night. He asked where they had started from, expecting that he would not be told. Far from it. His talkative companion shouted a flood of information into his ear.

"Pasajes. It's Istvan Kalmody's plane. Very handy if he wants to call on Zita, or Alfonso asks him to stay at San Sebastian."

"But why a seaplane?"

"Because he can take off from Lake Balaton and come

down wherever the pilot can spot a bit of water. He says you never know whether a field is flat enough till you're standing on your nose."

"What happens if there isn't a bit of water?"

"There always has been so far. Istvan came down on the Seine once and bloody nearly took the top off Notre Dame. Got away with it, too! The French just said it was one of those Hungarian magnates again and fined him enough to make sure he'd take the Simplon Orient Express next time. That's Mussolini's naval base of Spezia below us. God, what a clown!"

"Who?"

"Mussolini. Wants Hungarian friendship and thinks Kalmody is important. So he lets him refuel here. I have to ask you not to leave your seat, but is there anything I can get you?"

"Whatever you think best. Coffee, or can I have a drink?"

"We'll chance it. Zita's tame doctor told me you should have another pill when you came round. I shouldn't think it would do any harm to take half a bottle of white Tuscan with it, well cooled. It's going to be hot on the runway."

The plane bounced twice, splintering the oil-streaked mirror of the Mediterranean, and came to rest on a submerged pontoon which was then winched clear of the water. Escort and pilot strolled over to the command block shimmering in the heat and left Bernardo alone except for two armed guards who remained at a discreet distance. There was no object in appealing to them. He had no passport, papers or money and could not even prove who he was without reference to Bilbao. His clothes had gone and the dressing gown had been exchanged for a furred flying-coat. It never occurred to him that he had become a non-person. His sense of identity was strong for a young man in his early twenties.

The pilot returned with the fuel truck, and ten minutes

later his companion appeared with two glasses and a bottle of champagne in a bucket of ice. Bernardo observed that Hungarians — to judge by the two he had met — were given to lavish hospitality.

"It was all I could find that was cool. Let's have it in the shade of the wings."

Bernardo climbed down to the ground. The pilot protested loudly.

"It's only that he wants me to put this cigar out. Nothing to do with you. Cheers!"

"Cheers! How well you speak English!"

"English governess, Lord help her! And when that didn't work, Eton."

"But you are Hungarian, aren't you?"

"My name is Sigismond Pozharski. Polish originally. But anyone who wanted to be Hungarian always could be. The most liberal-minded nation in the Empire!"

"Suppose they didn't want to be?"

"Well, then they weren't and had no rights at all — simple! I say, we shouldn't forget the pill."

It was large and orange-colored. Bernardo's reluctance was obvious.

"Zita won't let you down," Pozharski assured him. "Here's another one! I'll take it myself just to give you confidence. Pills never make any difference to me. Then we'll finish the bottle and have a pee on the tail."

The two references to Zita without any handle struck Bernardo as irreverent.

"You live in Her Majesty's villa?" he asked.

"God forbid! I live in Madrid most of the year and San Sebastian in summer. So Istvan could whistle me up in half an hour. Zita is a second cousin of mine. Wrong side of the blanket of course. My grandfather was, I mean. Bourbon-

Parma, Romanoff, Hohenzollern, Stuart — you mention it, I'm related to it. A natural choice for delicate missions, if available. This pre-war tumbler, Bernardo, arouses happy memories. I used to ask the maitre d'hotel to fetch me one from the kitchen. I wonder if I can still do it."

He threw the empty tumbler high in the air and neatly caught it upside down with the champagne bottle. The bottom of the tumbler exploded upwards. The rest of it formed a jagged crown around the bottle's shoulder. Waving away the startled pilot, mechanics and guards, he took Bernardo's arm and led him down the ramp to the tail of the plane.

"Well, I can understand you would want the Hapsburgs back," Bernardo said.

"Not in a hurry. Nothing can ever be the same again as in dear old Franz Josef's day. So we must just forget it and see that chaps like you don't rock the boat through no fault of their own. That's a splendid stream you've got there. Lucky young fellow!"

Bernardo Brown remembered that at that point Zita's pills, combined with champagne, crumpled them up like a pair of opera hats. He presumed that pilot and mechanics hoisted them into their basket chairs.

When he woke up, the plane was pitching violently over the hot plains of Hungary. The movement did not affect him; indeed he was beginning to feel eager for his next meal and wondering what it would be. Behind him he heard snores, then a long silence was succeeded by an explosive retch.

"You all right?" he asked, turning round.

Pozharski was staring down into space.

"My blasted false teeth! No time to get a hand to them! They could put some poor chap's eye out if he's looking up at us. Hell and damn, I hate eating pap!"

Bernardo, roughly calculating height and speed, reckoned that Pozharski's teeth would probably land on the esplanade of the most westerly Balaton spa. The pilot flew high over the full fifty-mile length of the lake, its shores dotted with parks and yellow beaches of little holiday resorts, and spiraled down to land on the edge of marshes near the lonely north-east end, then taxied up a wide shallow channel between high reeds towards a cottage and a wooden jetty.

There were only two persons to observe their arrival — a ferryman paddling out from the jetty in a punt and the chauffeur of a dark blue Daimler with two heraldic, coronetted falcons on the door panel. Bernardo saw little point in a clandestine landing when the plane must have been seen from all the police stations of Lake Balaton. Being now accustomed to the freedoms and privileges of a primeval jet set, he assumed that Kalmody was as subject to customs controls as any of his fellow citizens but that no questions were asked if he broke laws decently and with tact.

The blue Daimler rocked over a farm track which served nothing but the jetty and a few vineyards, and then headed east across the Hungarian plain with the power and indestructibility of a steam locomotive. It seemed to Bernardo a rich but very naked countryside in which the white villages, though not so mean as the streets of hovels on the rolling Spanish plateau, lacked the welcoming solidity of the Basque coast. Government was more obtrusive than in Spain, every little town being dominated by the neat rows of windows in some small but imperial public building.

Any moving vehicle left a towering thundercloud of dust behind it through which little could be seen in daylight and nothing at all in the gathering dusk. The chauffeur seldom reduced his speed, confident that the road would be empty or that, if it wasn't, the obstacle would be softer than the car. There was one splintering crash which he ignored. Pozharski made no move to stop him.

"Only the wheel of a cart," he said. "Serve him right! At this hour peasants should be drinking, not on the road."

The surface suddenly improved and for mile after mile the headlights showed a ribbon of black tarmac passing through forested hills. Dim village lights could be seen up the side tracks but there was no town to justify the existence of such a highway.

"Istvan's father built it to link the estate with civilization," Pozharski explained. "He meant to have a private railway but after your Edward VII talked him into motor cars he settled for a road. All done by the tenants and horse rollers!"

They ran through a noble eighteenth-century gateway with the coronetted falcon of the Kalmodys surmounting each post, and up a long avenue of evergreen oaks. The mass of the house ahead, a long rectangle cut from the stars, was suddenly speckled with lit windows along the line of the ground floor. As they drove into the courtyard Bernardo's impression was of a troop of wheeling cavalry and wide steps lined by footmen.

"Who on earth do they think I am?" he asked.

"Just a guest sent by the count — which means he has to be respectfully received. For all they know, I might be escorting the President of the United States."

"I hope I shall have an interpreter."

"Yes, of course. Nepamuk, the steward. He'll be in charge of you."

Pozharski disappeared into some private world of his own, leaving Bernardo to be served with dinner in lonely state except for a butler who spoke a little French and was eager to know his tastes in wine, and Nepamuk who remained standing but at once assumed an air of intimacy.

He was a Slovak, tough and strong in spite of a gross belly, who spoke fluent English with a whining Cockney accent. Bernardo disliked him on sight and saw that it was always going to be difficult to get rid of him and his pretentious obsequiousness. Nepamuk was not only in charge — whatever that might mean — and indispensable, but he was an insistent chatterer repressing the smiling and intelligent Hungarian butler and ingratiating himself by dreary reminiscences of London and pubs. It appeared that Nepamuk, father, had worked in the embassy kitchens and made enough profit out of suppliers to return to Hungary, where Nepamuk, son, had jumped up a class and spent some years as a tax collector before entering Kalmody's service.

For the moment Bernardo's inner self was busy as a machine; excellent food and drink were pumped in and the energy required for polite human contacts came out. But he never could forget the uneasiness of the faintly lit procession to his room. It still turned up in his dreams — a glimpsed immensity of doors and staircases and corridors with a few respectful wraiths, male and female, faceless and sinister, with whom it was impossible to communicate.

When his valet and Nepamuk had gone, the silence was too overpowering for sleep. The Kalmody palace had become an underworld, full somewhere of the half-living. He sat by the open window listening to far-off sounds of horses stirring in the stable wing and unfamiliar cries from the boundary between parkland and woods of which only owl and fox were certain. Though sleepless for most of the night — Zita's pills had already ensured enough — morning and a cold shower restored curiosity. His day began with the reappearance of the valet who shaved and dressed him, accompanied by Nepamuk as interpreter. He did not mind being dressed, since a choice had to be made and fitting supervised among armfuls of clothes and footwear, but he objected to being shaved and demanded a safety razor. There was not, Nepamuk said, such a thing in the house; it would at once be obtained. He wondered what they made of his arrival without any baggage. Perhaps political refugees were not uncommon and Kalmody's retainers were trained to ask no questions.

Pozharski was at the breakfast table dealing with a remarkable pap of eggs beaten up in apricot brandy. He was cordial as ever but anxious to be off at once to his Budapest dentist. He had hoped, he said, to stay for a few days to settle Bernardo in.

"But you'll find it very simple, dear boy. You can do anything you like — absolutely anything just so long as you use a bit of tact and common sense. Istvan has the local police in his pocket and they wouldn't dream of bothering any guest of his. But you don't want to make it too hard for them, so keep out of the villages! And I'm afraid you'll have to put up with Heinz Nepamuk. An unpleasant fellow — but he helped Istvan to get his estate back from the Communists in 1919."

"Was it difficult?"

"Distasteful rather than difficult. It's all forgotten now. I just mentioned it in case you find Nepamuk a little truculent. He has his orders, but keep him in his place!"

Bernardo asked how much Nepamuk knew.

"Only that you got mixed up in some royalist plot in Lequeitio. Good enough for these backwoods, but most unlikely. Zita couldn't tackle anything more complicated than getting a niece into a nunnery."

"How long do you think I'll have to stay?"

"That depends on what goes on in Spain. Are they going to be sensible when they find those two bodies? Leave it all to us and don't worry! Istvan will look after you when all's clear."

"But look here, Mr. Pozharski, I'm not an international criminal!"

"Oh, all the best people are international criminals. Think of poor Bobo! Well, now I'm off. Try the bacon! Best in the world."

So that was that. Bernardo for the moment was overwhelmed by depression. These Hungarians were not the ghosts; he was. But it was no use gibbering. Somewhere in this emptiness one must come upon familiar human society.

His guide through the underworld turned up as soon as Pozharski had driven away. Nepamuk evidently considered that the royalist intriguer would be fascinated by the past glories of the Kalmodys and conducted him round the house with the pomposity and little jokes of a peak-capped courier. Armor. Furred robes. The library. The gold-inlaid chamber pot used by the Emperor Franz Josef. The bedroom of Edward VII when he was Prince of Wales. Bernardo asked what entertainment — beyond boar hunting — had been provided for His Royal and Randy Highness. Nepamuk pretended to be shocked. He said that one did not crudely provide such entertainment; one waited until the gaze of the distinguished guest fell upon a bit of stuff that appealed to him. One also ensured beforehand that the bit of stuff and its parents had no objection which could not be squared by a suitable reward.

A heavy mausoleum of a house it was: furniture, paneling, tapestries, the lot. But one could imagine it with all the French windows open on a summer morning or every chandelier blazing at night, full of gaiety and the peacockings of rich and idle youth. Bernardo asked if the count had no family. Yes, but they were all at Biarritz, and after that would come Paris and Budapest. They would not return till Christmas.

He felt some sympathy for the Kalmody family's absences from their too overpowering house; but when at last he was outside in the sun, passing through the Italian garden, the English garden, the avenues and the splendid stands of ornamental timber, he wondered how anyone who could afford such beauty could ever bear to leave it.

"And while they are away you are always in charge, Mr. Nepamuk?"

"Of the business interest, I am. Chancellor of the Exchequer, you might sye."

Influenced by Nepamuk's barrow-boy English, Bernardo wondered how much he managed to slip into his own bank account. Yet when speaking his own Magyar language the steward was invariably cold, dignified and exacting. That much was clear without understanding a word he said. The respect paid to him was extreme. He received it without warmth, and whenever Bernardo genially stopped to talk he felt that the translation of his remarks never reproduced their tone. One couldn't call the Kalmody employees submissive or servile, but in Nepamuk's presence they divested themselves of all personality. Possibly the right pigeonhole in which to place him was as an incorruptible feudal retainer who would stick at nothing to prove his loyalty.

In the stables, where the steward's only authority was to sign the checks, he formally presented Mr. Kovacs, the Master of the 'Orse — a gallant old boy with a grin under his immense moustache who loosed off the few English greetings which he knew, asked no questions and patted Bernardo as if he were a promising two-year-old appearing out of the blue by order of the count.

The domain of the horses had a warmth and democracy of

its own to which Bernardo at once responded. The paddocks, the stallions, the brood mares under the shade of great trees — all seemed to him to represent a proper use for money. A self-perpetuating beauty had been created, and men served it proudly. He asked if he could be taught to ride. Of course! With pleasure! How extraordinary that an Englishman could not ride!

Nepamuk translated the last remark with a shade of contempt which had not been there in the original. Thereafter Bernardo got along cheerfully with noises and sign language, leaving the steward trailing behind unless appealed to for help. His stable vocabulary was in any case limited to about as much as could be picked up while talking to the driver of a four-wheeler in a London pub.

In a far paddock Bernardo's eye was caught by three splendid ponies who seemed by their build and coloring — two duns and a pinto — as foreign as he among their fellows. When they came to the white rails he spoke to them with the Spanish endearments which he normally used for animals. The response was marked and immediate.

"The master of the 'orse wants to know what you are speaking," Nepamuk said.

"Spanish."

Kovacs was delighted to the last hair of his moustache. He had always maintained, he boomed, that horses were as human as himself, and there was the proof of it. Spanish was their language.

He shouted for Perico. A lean man, somewhat more golden in complexion than the sun-browned Magyars, left his barrow of hay and lounged over to the group. He answered Kovacs in oddly accented Hungarian out of the corner of his straight horseman's mouth. Then he addressed Bernardo in Spanish.

"Yes, from the North," Bernardo replied. "And you?"

"From Argentina."

"What the devil brought you here?"

"Because there are people with more money than they know what to do with."

They went at it with the complete abandon of two exiles. Kalmody had bought three of the best polo ponies in Argentina and their groom with them. Perico had now been two years on the estate, first with a special interpreter, a Spanish-speaking Jew, and then on his own when he had learned some of the language.

"They treat you well?"

"Yes, and the horses too. For these Hungarians there is little difference between us."

Before Perico could develop that double-bladed remark, Nepamuk interrupted, disquieted by the fact that there was someone else to whom Bernardo could talk. The master of the horse told Nepamuk — so Perico said — to shut up. Mr. Kovacs was a man of one idea at a time and he was listening to the foreign language as if it preserved mysterious secrets of the Tartar past.

"The old one says that here is your home," Perico translated, "and I am to teach you to ride."

A week passed in which Bernardo was easily able to accept his prison without bars. Perico's lessons put some points of reference into blank space and gave him a sense of live action so that on waking each morning he could ignore the overpowering lushness of his confinement. He was also satisfied with himself, for he had found a sport at which he could be more than competent. His understanding of the animal, mounted or not, was quick and instinctive. All he had to learn was to impress upon it who was boss. That had been very good for his character, old Bernardo said; up to then he had always lent himself rather than commanded.

Magda

Perico became an intimate friend, neither of the two having any other. The result of his quick-fire comments was to turn the whole place from the incredible into a human society. Perico's description of Kalmody fitted the man with whom Bernardo had spent a single evening. He was impulsive, generous and popular when he was on his estate. But that was seldom. Meanwhile servants and tenants were left to the mercies of middle-class zombies of whom Nepamuk was typical. Their obsession was that the abyss between themselves and the peasants should remain impassable.

Perico's invective did not extend to Kovacs, whom he admired. Kovacs, he said, was half horse and worthy of any grandee's carriage. It was a vivid sketch of the old boy's massive, springy bearing, gray forelock falling over his forehead and yellow teeth in a long face. The master of the horse stood no nonsense from Nepamuk, shooing him off when he insisted on attending lessons. The steward need not have worried, for Bernardo never rode outside the park. He still had in his ears Pozharski's question: Are they going to be sensible? The Kalmody palace was exasperating, but a lot better than Bilbao jail.

He was of course widely known to exist, but Pozharski was right in telling him that a guest of Kalmody had no official being so far as the police were concerned. Nepamuk must have offered them some explanation. Whatever it was — too ardent admiration of Zita or a suspected case of leprosy — it had been accepted. Bernardo's own story to Perico was that Kalmody had snatched him out of Spain when he was in trouble with the law and had good reason for it. Perico showed no curiosity. Everyone had friends tangled up with politics or the law. One did not discuss the matter till help was required.

Refreshed by open air and the society of the stable block,

45

Bernardo began to hope that the traditions of hospitality which governed the visits of royalty might be extended to his own bedroom as well. The steward was impervious to hints, nor had any Edwardian bit of stuff appeared — apart from a couple of chambermaids whose mischievous eyes and ripe-apricot complexions made him curious as to what the technique should be in dealing with so many voluminous petticoats.

Perico was sympathetic but had no suggestions. The few wives and daughters in the stable cottages were highly respectable, and he himself had had no success at all. There was a satisfactory whore in the nearest town and a couple of semi-professionals in a Kalmody village. He was ready to take the risk of fetching one of them over to the hay barn if Bernardo was really desperate and would finance the transaction until his friend was in the money again.

Money was the tactful chain which prevented any break for more liberty. Bernardo had the best of food and wine, horses to ride and every comfort of a rich recluse, but not one penny in his pocket. When he complained to Nepamuk that he ought to be able to hand out some tips, especially to Perico and his valet, the steward replied that he had only to say the word and it would be done. The Kalmodys themselves never had any money when they were at home; they couldn't be bothered with the stuff.

An exaggeration to keep him quiet, though there might be some truth in it. The steward was their private banker. He kept the cash and issued it against receipt as and when needed.

"But, Mr. Nepamuk, suppose one of them suddenly brought a girl home and hadn't any money, what would he do?" Bernardo asked frankly.

"Not 'ere, Mr. Brown. Never! One of them summer 'ouses."

"Well, wherever it was, he'd want to give her a present. Or would the valet do it?"

"If 'e was in attendance, Mr. Brown."

The picture delighted Bernardo. The respectful retainer presumably tucked you up in bed and you left the rest to some form of irrevocable Kalmody credit.

"You may 'ave complete confidence in the count," Nepamuk added. " 'E knows what 'e's abaht."

That was vaguely hopeful. Bernardo would have given a lot to see the telegrams and correspondence passing between the count and Nepamuk. Possibly they were waiting to see how discreet he was before providing further domestic comforts.

One evening after thunder had rolled across from Romania washing the sky a paler blue and the dusted trees a darker green, he rode back to the house with the master of the horse. Like a couple of friendly animals they were on the best of terms with no need for any talking beyond exclamations in each other's language. Kovacs had somewhere picked up most of the words of an infuriated British horseman — tone accurate, vowels all wrong. Bernardo corrected and explained, a forefinger to the sky for "God," a thumb to Kovacs' ample seat for "bugger." On arrival at the open front door he saw an unusually formal tray of drinks laid out at the far end of the hall. He gestured to Kovacs to hand over the horses and come in. The master of the horse was, he understood, grateful and honored.

Kovacs was an inspired peasant who had risen to groom and from groom to his present dignity. It was always dangerous to drink with him if one had anything to do afterwards, for his cheerful neighings, though remaining formal, invited more and more cordiality. Bernardo, as a result of training in Vizcaya, was able — just — to keep glass for glass with him provided the process was slowed down a little. While hard at it, he vaguely watched through the open double doors the table being laid in the dining room — two places and a lot more silver than usual. For Nepamuk? But Nepamuk took his meals in his apartments. Then was the butler assuming that Kovacs would stay for dinner? That did not seem to conform to the traditions of the house, but no doubt the butler's experience could be trusted. He slipped out to ask him. If Kovacs was going to be about for the next three hours, consumption of apricot brandy had better be cut down at once.

"For the master of the horse, Lajos?"

"For Madame la Baronne."

"Who's she?"

"The daughter of the count."

"When is she coming?"

"She is here."

And nobody had told him a thing! Arrangements must have gone wrong because his return was much later than usual. Kovacs had also seen the second place and had no doubt that it was not for him. He patted Bernardo's shoulder to show that they were equals, bowed to show they were not and cleared off. Bernardo shot upstairs crudely yelling for his valet and found him of course already in his room with a velvet dinner jacket laid out on the bed. A quick bath left him fairly sober — which, strictly speaking, he was not — and he beat the baroness to the hall by three minutes.

She came sailing down the stairs in a long dress of crimson brocade with a high collar; it fitted her as closely as a swim suit and ten times more romantically. Bernardo had been expecting some large, pink-faced noblewoman, either sporting or religious. This astonishing creature with dark-brown hair and eyes as near violet as made no difference was in her middle twenties and the most devastatingly poised and finished young woman he had ever set eyes on. At that age he had not, he remembered, had the experience to distinguish between female beauty and female ensemble. He was not sure that he could do it yet.

Alcohol inhibited any inferiority complex. He bowed gallantly over her hand, not kissing it because he was uncertain of Hungarian customs.

"I must apologize for not being here," he said. "Nobody told me you were coming."

"I didn't know myself when I would arrive. Just sometime. How are you getting on in the Arabian Nights?" she asked in near perfect English.

Her father must have repeated Bernardo's impulsive phrase. Perhaps it had amused both of them.

"Bored, baroness. But now I think I must have rubbed the lamp without knowing it."

One up for drinks with Kovacs! She spotted the compliment, smiled with merry eyes and immediately drooped long lashes over them, as if Bernardo's gaze were too fervent. It probably was.

"What have they told you about me?" she asked.

"Nothing at all. Lajos just said you were here, and Nepamuk never warned me."

"Oh, Nepamuk! The only bearable thing about him is that he can keep his mouth shut. What did you think of his English?"

"I wish I spoke Hungarian as well."

"Such a polite prisoner! Do you know that everyone likes you?"

"No. How can anyone like a ghost which can't speak to them? I don't even know your name."

"Well, I used to be Magda Kalmody," she said. "But now I am the Baronin von und zu Pforzheim."

She pronounced her title in stilted German, underlining her Magyar disrespect for mere Austrian aristocracy.

"And you know my story?"

"Only that you were the witness to one of my father's wilder pot shots in defense of Queen and Country and that he felt you'd be better out of Spain till it all blew over."

That was one aspect of the truth and simple enough by itself to be convincing. Bernardo did not elaborate it.

"Something of the sort," he admitted.

She took the head of the table with Bernardo on her right. When he had been alone Lajos and a footman were in attendance on him. He now realized that this lavish service was merely the ordinary routine for bachelors. Magda rated full uniform for Lajos — which made him look as if he had just dismounted from a horse on a chilly evening — and an extra footman, plus formal poppings-in and poppings-out of the housekeeper whom Bernardo had seldom seen. She was presumably acting as a jack-in-the-box chaperon.

The first flash of sympathy could not be developed under many eyes so that he was compelled to be on his best behavior. Excitement helped rather than hindered. It was essential to convince Baroness Magda von What's-his-name that he was a possible companion before opening up other possibilities.

She questioned him about what he had been doing in Spain. Bernardo promoted himself to shipping manager and launched into his love of the country. No, he didn't know any of the grandees she mentioned. She replied that they were a stuffy lot and not up-to-date.

"Everybody knows that the English manufacture their gentlemen, and very well," she said.

Bernardo let that pass, allowing it to be thought that some imperial public school was responsible for him. For a few seconds the dreamy detachment of good wine took over and he observed his performance with satisfaction. What the hell *was* responsible? Spain and his mother for manners; the Jesuits for quick reaction and the ability to hold his own in any society; his father for dignity; a year at a Polytechnic for the unimportant skills of earning a business living which any fool could pick up in the course of it.

Over the coffee she exclaimed, "All this is such a bore. Give me the twentieth century!"

That was comforting. One was always entitled to be optimistic when young women started to purr about the twentieth century. Certainly she was determined to show her disapproval of the Kalmody style of living. There had been a puzzling impatience in her attitude to the family retainers, which sometimes gave an impression of dislike for the person rather than the system. Bernardo was surprised to discover that the Spanish half of him was on their side.

"I am a socialist," she announced.

Those lovely, flashing eyes, dark blue now rather than violet! He adored her fire and sincerity, though she was the most improbable socialist he had ever come across. Socialists were his dear iron-workers in Baracaldo. Still, they might not be the only kind. Somebody had to deal little by little with all this colossal, wasteful wealth.

Meanwhile this exquisite example of conspicuous consumption — probably dressed by one of those Paris names seen in print and forgotten — had demanded from Lajos her father's best cognac. It was the first time Bernardo had seen a woman drink brandy; after sipping his own he could not take his eyes off the brown and gold of hair and glass, and the red brocade provocatively outlining those imperious young breasts.

After dinner the long vistas of the garden beckoned, where the pyramid moon shadows of cypress and Irish yew fell across the gravel walks. Bernardo was now in the delightful state when he would have accepted Eden as plain fact and advised the Almighty — with genial respect — how to run the place. He was aware that Magda liked him but had no idea, being still young enough to suppose that seduction was the prerogative of the male, how to initiate slap-and-tickle with a Kalmody. One couldn't just grab the flower of Europe and any soft meetings of hands seemed provincial.

The problem was solved by his own genuine emotion as she stood, half turned away from him, with one hand flicking moss from the underlip of a stone urn. The Bilbao cabaret provided a precedent; there too you could not touch but you could certainly express enthusiasm and a lot of good it would do you. What he thought of her poured out of him, sounding no doubt exotically emotional since his passion had slipped into Spanish ringing with the native melancholy of unattainable desire.

It was far from unattainable. The response of arms and lips was gloriously unexpected. He hurled an unknown someone's dinner jacket over a scattering of dry leaves and lowered onto it the red dress and its contents. Or was it a mutual collapse followed by the most artistic show of reluctance he had ever imagined? And that was saying something. Kisses interminable, evasions, returns. No and no, and finally the cry, "You should help me to be faithful."

Bernardo felt a tinge of conscience — not much, but enough to let the moment go since the future was reasonably assured. It was plain that fidelity to the baron was a matter of six square inches; you could do what you pleased anywhere else. Considering the storm of physical and romantic excitement which she was capable of arousing, it was improbable that all lovers had been as manageable as himself.

It was time to return to the house and be seen in public.

Lajos asked if they had any further commands for him, shut the French windows and said good night. Magda went upstairs, leaving him in the vast emptiness of the hall. He could not follow. For one thing, her maid was already curtsying to her on the landing; for another, he had no idea where her room was. This was hell. Far too many people, and unfamiliar conventions. It occurred to him for the first time that he did not even know who turned the lights out and when. One might have to explore those convenient summer houses of which Nepamuk had spoken.

As soon as his unnecessary valet had been dismissed he tip-toed out of his room and listened to the silence of the empty passages. Somewhere at the end of the long gallery on the south side of the house he heard footsteps. The rustle of petticoats suggested that it was not Magda but her maid. The maid did not return, and unmistakable sounds revealed that Magda was having a bath not very far away. He chose a window seat in the gallery and waited, more to catch a last glimpse of this astonishing creature than in any hope. There was a soft light for every ten yards of the gallery which had never been lit before. A Kalmody could not be allowed to search for a switch.

She came out of the bathroom and looked up the gallery. Bernardo felt slightly embarrassed at his own affinity to a tom cat sitting patiently on a wall. She seemed to feel none at all, giving the impression that she was completely in command of a quite natural situation. She came to meet him and leaned forward, holding his hands, to give him a little-girl good night kiss. This time he did grab. It was the bow of wide, red ribbon on top of her head which did it, making it impossible to consider her as wife, baroness or anything but an adorable poppet in a filmy dressing gown. She clung to him as he carried her into his room, soft and tremulous in orgasm

53

and deliciously pretending to be ashamed of it. No, he could never forget a moment of that first night, for his experience till then had been limited to purely physical enjoyment or the unsatisfactory sentimentalities of youth. She left him exhausted and unavoidably in love, running the arrival of that damned valet pretty close.

She insisted on absolute discretion in public — not too difficult since they spent more time in private — but the affair must have been obvious to the whole establishment. All behaved, however, as if Bernardo and his baroness existed on some ethereal plane, continuing like priests to perform monotonous service without questioning what they were serving.

Old Kovacs was the most unconcerned of the lot, seeming to consider the affair as natural as the successful covering of a favorite mare. He did not of course comment, but always looked as if he were about to put an arm round each neck and walk between them to some bucket bubbling with his own strength-giving mixture of black beer and hot corn mash. Bernardo was beginning to feel he could do with it. Day and night, the park, the summer houses, bed, variations of arm-chairs and the drawing room floor — he had long since lost count of all but the most ingenious few which aroused ecstatic protests and therefore had to be repeated. Magda's own original contribution was gramophone accompaniment. He had known her disconcertingly to stretch out a white arm and wind it up so that the record should not run down before Bernardo did.

Nepamuk had handed over his beaming prisoner as if there were perfect understanding between himself and Kalmody's daughter. He never questioned any decision of hers except on one occasion when she insisted on sending out for a gypsy band to show Bernardo their Hungarian music. Her response to Nepamuk's hesitation was startling. Bernardo's red-ribboned girl was transformed into a statue which spoke fast and tonelessly with set face. When Nepamuk raised his obsequious head, Bernardo ventured a quick glance of sympathy. It was returned by an insolent stare putting him in his place as an outsider.

He did not entirely desert the Kalmody stables. Sometimes when Magda had flickered down the gallery to her own room and the fresh morning was an invitation, he would slip out of the house, take a salami sandwich — plus the inevitable tot of brandy — with the master of the horse and join Perico.

Their former intimacy was strained. Bernardo put this down not only to the loss of a companion but to Perico's frank disapproval of Magda's horsemanship. She rode flamboyantly without any consideration for her mount which she would bring back to the yard in a lather of foam and with staring eyes.

"You should not hold it against her," Bernardo told him. "It's that she lives in towns and has no patience."

"I have nothing against her, friend, except that to her we are dirt, the horses and all. I have never been in Spain. How are the grandees there?"

"Far worse than here. They let their people starve."

"But speak to them as gentlemen?"

"Of course."

"Listen, friend! You are wasting your time and are too decent a fellow to see it."

"Not a word against her, Perico!"

"Good, man, good! Take it that I have said nothing!"

Bernardo returned to the house in a Castilian mood of fury; he would have laid his hand upon the hilt of his sword if he had got one. The reasonable Englishman then took over. What offended Perico was after all very natural in a girl brought up to such splendor. But how magnificently she had declared herself a socialist! He was sure that she herself, so warm and eager, could have no idea of the effect she produced. If only they could live long together, he would help her. That "if only" was, he knew, a wild bit of daydreaming on a par with the cheerful fantasies which had occupied him on the Lequeitio beach and just as full of risks. All the same he maintained stoutly to himself that this was the only woman for him if ever he could return to prosperous life.

There were still a few more days of paradise before the occasion for his help arrived. They came back from an evening ride to find Kovacs waiting in the palace courtyard to take over the horses. He was slightly flushed with liquor, and Bernardo instinctively understood why he was there in person. In an access of affection he had come to do the menial service of a groom: a parade, as it were, of his homage and loyalty. He allowed himself some too genial remark. He might have commented on the fact that the horses had hardly been ridden at all, as indeed they had not. Magda savagely reprimanded him, and he turned his back. Later on he sent down Perico instead of one of the usual boys to lead back the horses.

After dinner when Bernardo was alone with Magda in the vast, chintzed drawing room, where he seemed to himself no bigger than the Dresden china shepherd preposterously tootling a flute on the mantelpiece, he asked what Kovacs had done.

"He must be retired, and I told him so. He'll be well looked after."

"A tragedy for him to do nothing!"

"He does nothing anyway for half the year."

"But that goes for all of them."

"Then they are better back in their villages. Once a peasant, always a peasant, Bernardo."

"What about your socialism?"

"That is politics and has nothing to do with it. If this country wants the lower classes to be contented, it must care for them properly. But that does not mean that I can't tell Nepamuk to dismiss an impudent servant."

"You leave that kind of thing to Nepamuk?"

"It's what he is there for and he likes it, so why not?"

"I wouldn't turn Nepamuk loose on anyone."

"Peasants only respond to kicks, Bernardo. You cannot treat them as equals as you do that groom."

"Perico is not a peasant. He is a friend."

"Please forget that you are the son of a dock laborer! If I can, you can."

What was the use of saying that a foreman shipwright was not a dock laborer? He was alarmed at the gathering storm and exclaimed that he wouldn't care if her father was a bootblack and that with all the future in front of them . . .

"Don't worry about the future! My father will certainly set you up in some little business."

Mr. Brown, looking back on it fifty years later, forgave her. His Magda — possibly slaughtered in her late and still beautiful forties, possibly a distinguished old lady doing her best with poverty — had no doubt felt it her duty to disillusion him, but she need not have been so cruel.

"I thought we loved each other," he said miserably.

"Oh, what's the good? What's the good? Yes, Bernardo, you were the perfect choice."

She left him without a kiss or another word. He hoped that in the morning some burst of tears or invective would explode the quarrel and leave peace when the smoke had cleared, but meanwhile there was plainly going to be no sharing of bed or waiting in the gallery.

Bernardo lay awake till the small hours, at first resentful then bitterly blaming himself for impertinence in daring to criticize her and folly in dragging up the social disparity between them, of which, as likely as not, she had always been more conscious than he. The silence of the great house at last soothed him into deep sleep. He never even heard the car leave; he did not know she had gone until the valet brought him a note and at once retired. It said nothing except that she was never coming back and that he should forget her. He clung to his only scrap of comfort: her cry, "What's the good?" It had no more meaning than her puzzling revelation that he had been chosen, but her remembered emotion preserved him from the agony of utter despair.

The days of hot sun emphasized lonely monotony. Inside the house he could not mistake a change of mood, though hidden in the mist of an unintelligible language. There was obvious relief that Magda had gone and yet a shade of disappointment that no one was left to serve except the stranger. His status as the lover of Kalmody's daughter should have been immensely enhanced. It was not. He sensed only a warm, unspoken pity.

Nepamuk was more casual than before. He no longer gave the impression of obeying the count's orders with regret; he was more like a prison warder patronizing his favorite, and exacting conversation with that persistent whine for which in London one could feel affection but which was exasperating, when isolated among the emphatic birdsong of the Magyar language, as the saw in the timber mill when the wind was the wrong way. Bernardo took refuge from it in the stables. Even there Kovacs and Perico were inclined to limit their conversation to saddlery. The week was desperately long until Sigismond Pozharski turned up with a new set of teeth and a smile more incorrigible than ever.

Melancholy was difficult in his presence. He never gave time for it, snapping up Bernardo, radiating geniality and trotting with him round house and estate as if he owned them. Even the difficult Perico admitted that Pozharski was a good fellow — too good, for if he really did own the place he'd never get much of an income out of it. Nobody would be afraid of him.

At dinner that evening, with Lajos relishing his new customer, Bernardo said he had heard that a landowner couldn't make money unless his peasants were afraid of him, that they only responded to kicks and what did Pozharski think about it?

"Perfectly true, dear boy, if you want to regiment them into efficiency. Look at Russia! But the worst possible way if you want devotion. Istvan knows that. Magda doesn't care. Your own interest in people she called slumming. Of course under the circumstances she was a bit on edge."

"You have seen her?"

"Just a word in passing."

"What did she say?"

"Smiled like Mona Lisa and said somebody ought to cheer you up. So I came over. What upset her?"

"I didn't like the way she treated Kovacs and others. It would serve her right if they talked."

"They won't. They are too loyal to the family. Were you ever actually caught at it?"

Bernardo felt he ought to ask: Caught at what? But Pozharski so evidently knew more than he should.

"Er — no," he said, blushing slightly.

"Want to be cured?"

"If you mean what I think you mean, no!"

"Europe, my Bernardo, is paved with the solid granite of hearts once broken by her. Dear Lajos, we are going to need some of the 1870 Tokay if you would be so good."

"But she is so very genuine."

"She can persuade herself of anything, dear boy. She could fill all the boxes of the Nemzety Theatre and have even politicians weeping the starch out of their shirt fronts."

"That," said Bernardo, "only shows that she is all woman."

"It does indeed. Now, an intimate question! Did you notice that she took no precautions?"

"I wondered. But she isn't fertile, the poor darling."

"O dear God! The theatre in tears again! Bernardo, didn't I once tell you that my specialty was delicate missions? To my personal knowledge Magda lays enough eggs to win a prize at a poultry show and is always abominably careless with them."

Bernardo was tense with anger. This was all a lie — a crude attempt to make him lay off forever a generous, emotional girl who was in love with him and could not allow herself to be. He murmured something about her marriage.

"Marriage, yes. Well, that's just the lead we wanted to carry on the cure. Try the Tokay! It's out of this world. Now, Pforzheim is a very worthy fellow, conscientious and extremely wealthy — a point which Magda has never overlooked. Not a breath of scandal since her marriage. One sinner who repenteth and all that. But Pforzheim carries some nasty stuff in the family. He shouldn't breed and he won't. Duty to God and man. On the other hand, an heir, eh? So, as you're an admirable chap, don't exist and aren't here, Istvan told his daughter to run down and look you over."

"She didn't spend long looking," Bernardo said bitterly, for this revolting story at last made sense of that "perfect choice."

"Well, there's a compliment for you!"

"Does her husband know?"

"That is a matter between him and his spiritual adviser and we will not inquire. Pforzheim is a good Catholic of princely generosity to the Church. But he is not likely to have a long

life, and both the first and second heirs are Baptists or Bud-
dhists or something. So one can see that Rome might take a
fatherly interest in the matter of the succession."

"I wonder they didn't choose you for the delicate mission."

"So do I sometimes. But Magda and I know each other too
well. However artistic my performance, she would at once have
detected the lack of spontaneity."

"You dirty old bugger!"

"That, dear boy, is exactly what I was trying — with rather
less coarseness — to express. No better than that stuff out of
a bottle when you come to think of it."

Such intolerable geniality! One might as well try to be angry
with the devil.

"What stuff out of a bottle?" Bernardo asked wearily.

"Latest thing in Vienna. Artificial insemination they call
it. Chap gives his offering to nurse. Nurse pops it over the
screen. Doctor delicately intervenes. Could have done the job
himself without all the fuss, I always say. Magda wouldn't hear
of it — said it was disgusting and boring and ran to Daddy."

"I am told he may be good enough to set me up in a small
business."

"God, you must have stung her on the raw! You didn't
bring up the question of her socialism, did you? A small
business indeed! A big one or complete repudiation of you —
that's Istvan!"

"How are things in Spain?"

"Sticky. But I'm not quite up to date. All I know is that
Zita has been writing to the Pope. You haven't bumped off a
cardinal by mistake, have you, or anything else that will take
a bit of fixing?"

"I haven't bumped off anyone, Mr. Pozharski."

"You need practice. That's what it is. Pity the partridge
season isn't open yet."

He never knew how to take Pozharski. This descendant of imperial bastards did not seem to care whether a chap was innocent or guilty, as if the question were of no importance compared to good manners and the ability to accept with casual unconcern whatever life sent up from the basement. It was a civilized attitude for which there was a good deal to be said, provided one had friends, position and especially money.

Bernardo was without any of them and could get no useful advice out of Pozharski who pointed out — as Nepamuk had — that the Kalmodys seldom carried cash and that he had only to ask for whatever he required. Quite true and on the face of it reasonable. Yet the real motive for keeping him penniless was obviously that he should not be able to escape. Bernardo had the tact not to say it and so make matters worse by showing that he had escape in mind.

Pozharski, though more than double his age, was at least an amiable companion, staving off his melancholy by trivialities and a remarkable standard of what a meal should be in content and conversation. But when Pozharski had gone back to the clubs and chandeliers, there was nothing left except the memory of Magda. The cure had not worked and — considering his desolation — could not work. He was more in love with her than ever, persuading himself that in spite of her original motive she too would be unable to put him out of mind and that sometime, somewhere unspecified, both would try to meet again.

"I suppose we would all like our youth back if we could have it," old Mr. Brown said. "Yet the suffering was far worse and enjoyment not that much keener. They say these young lost souls take to drugs because they have too much imagination. Quite wrong! It's because they haven't any. I could kid myself that she would take me back if she had to pick me out of a Budapest gutter. Unbelievable!"

But even that romantic gutter was impossible to reach without money, an identity and a passport to prove it. He was shut up with his emotions and no way out. A very likely definition of hell. And he could well have landed down there in good earnest via the estate graveyard if it had not been for Nepamuk.

On his daily visit to the stables he was greeted with unusual eagerness by Kovacs and Perico. A policeman had bicycled over that morning to demand Perico's residence permit which had never been renewed. Perico was worried by the man's severe formality though insisting loudly that there was no need to worry since the police did whatever the estate told them to do. That seemed to Bernardo too vague a phrase; he asked who actually dealt with the police. Nepamuk.

It was difficult to get exact details. Perico's Hungarian, while adequate for the routine of the horses, was not up to translating into Spanish Kovacs' explanations and resentment. It appeared that the master of the horse had already tackled Nepamuk who pretended to know nothing. Bernardo must short-circuit him and appeal directly to the count. Kovacs reasonably assumed that he must have influence, being a friend of the family and on the best of terms with the Baroness Magda.

On his return to the house Bernardo remembered Pozharski's advice to keep Nepamuk in his place; he decided to play the superior and summon the steward from his office. He explained the anxiety over at the stables and asked Nepamuk to fix it, pointing out that Perico was someone to talk to.

"It's me you 'ave for company," Nepamuk answered.

"And very welcome," Bernardo said politely. "But when

you are busy I am sure the count would not object to my talking to Perico."

"Sure, are you?"

Well, no, he wasn't. It could well be that Kalmody had forgotten all about Perico when he assumed that Bernardo would be limited to Nepamuk or to swapping a little kitchen French with Lajos. This was not going to be an easy interview. Nepamuk hardly bothered to conceal his lack of respect under the usual obsequiousness. It sounded as if he were jealous, too.

"Sorry, Mr. Brown, but we can't 'ave 'im 'ere no longer."

"Orders from the count?"

"I don't wait for orders when I sees what the family interests are."

"But Kovacs wants to keep him."

"That's why I 'as a short word with the police."

"It's a dirty trick. Perico doesn't know anything about me."

" 'E knows you're in trouble and no bloody guest."

"I shall appeal to the count."

"Know 'is address?"

"No, Mr. Nepamuk. But naturally I have a way of getting in touch with the baroness."

"You 'ave, 'ave you? But she don't like Perico no more than what I do."

So much for bluff. Bernardo was helpless. Even Kovacs would not risk having Nepamuk as an enemy. How had he dealt with the peasants who seized the estate in 1919? Everyone must know but not a soul mentioned it. Nepamuk was like the devoted chief of police of a dictator, and Kalmody tolerated him. He could put right the worst of Nepamuk's injustices whenever he came home and get the credit for it.

After Bernardo's evening ride the following day, he remained with Perico instead of resigning himself to the melancholy of the house. As soon as the horses had been delivered to a stable lad, Perico fussed over his precious Argentine ponies. It was his pride to keep them as if there were likely to be an international polo tournament the following week, though in fact Kalmody had never got nearer the game than a passing enthusiasm and half a dozen lessons at Hurlingham.

Perico did not think there was enough good grass for them, the paddocks being brown and dry in the blazing Hungarian summer, and decided to fetch sweet, new hay from a group of stacks out on the plain. Bernardo walked with him over the stubble and sat on a hand-cart entertaining him with anecdotes of Basque character while Perico forked down hay. Such memories of his freedom a bare month earlier kept his mind off Magda, though only the externals of the past — sea, mountains and friendship — seemed desirable in a world where she had not existed.

The group of stacks, a thatched shelter, a well and a vast manure heap formed an island in the plain cut off from the house and its gardens by a belt of chestnuts. On the other side were miles of stubble, the faraway, white walls of a Kalmody village and, beyond it, the blue line of Transylvania and the foothills of the Carpathians. It was impossible not to be momentarily at peace in that isolated depository of handouts for horses.

The sun was setting when he saw Nepamuk emerge from the line of trees coming towards them from the direction of the house, not the stables. Presumably he had news for Perico or was anxious about his prisoner's absence at an hour when Bernardo should have been helping himself from the table of drinks at the end of the hall. The steward stumped across the paddocks with his usual air of a self-important government official, turning about to close gates as if on parade and continuing his march to the stacks.

Ignoring Bernardo except for a nod, he stopped five yards from Perico instead of walking up to him and sharply beckoned to him to approach. He spoke at length and slowly so that Perico might understand. It was like listening to a couple of talking statues: Nepamuk commanding, Perico disregarding bad manners and occasionally responding with the coldness of a Spaniard standing on his rights.

"He says I have no permit to be in Hungary and that I cannot work here," Perico explained. "I've no objection but he must pay my fare back to Argentina."

Bernardo repeated this in English, and thereafter both of them used him as interpreter.

"Nothing abaht that in 'is contract, Mr. Brown."

Perico insisted that there was, but added that he would not mind taking another job until the count came home.

"No, 'e can't."

"What is he to do then?" Bernardo asked.

"Go and eat 'orse turd for all I care."

Bernardo was so angry that he translated this exactly.

Perico took two steps forward and let Nepamuk have it in Spanish. Roughly speaking, he had been born in a brothel where his mother had brought him up as a bugger boy and taught him to steal from their joint customers as he did to this day from the count. Bernardo passed all this on with relish and at the full speed of a United Nations interpreter, adding a few personal details when he could not immediately jump on the English equivalent of the fighting language of up-country Argentina. Nepamuk slapped Perico's face, still with dignity as if he were an insolent peasant of the estate.

Bernardo grabbed his friend's wrist as the knife blade glowed red in the last of the sun.

"Careful, Perico! What you like, but not that in a foreign country."

"What I like? Good, then! What I like, and I go forever."

Perico jumped back for his pitchfork and lunged at Nepamuk, stopping an inch from his broad stomach.

"March! Or it goes in."

Nepamuk appealed to Bernardo, assuming that he must be on the side of property and stewards, just or unjust. Bernardo was not. His personal loathing of Nepamuk did not really count, for at that time he was still a mild-mannered fellow who could not approve of violence as an expression of dislike. What did count was his resentment of the indecent power of the man over these cheerful, kindly people like Perico and Kovacs. In the case of the latter the true culprit had not been Nepamuk, but Bernardo was in no mood for distinctions. He was finally revolted by the whole set-up — no money, no identity, no freedom and then being used as a Kalmody stallion.

"You'd better march. He means it," Bernardo answered.

There was no arguing with a bloodthirsty groom from South America and a political prisoner who was himself a possible assassin. Nepamuk marched, pricked onwards by Perico through the line of stacks to the manure heap.

"Down on your knees!"

Nepamuk obeyed, turning to Perico in the belief that he was being forced to apologize.

"Other way round! Crawl in, bastard!"

"I can't."

"Use your hands! Dig! Dig!"

This time the prongs went through the seat of Nepamuk's breeches. He screamed and dug until the steaming trench was four feet deep.

"Now get a halter from the shed, Bernardo, and tie his hands and feet!"

Bernardo did so, shocked at himself for departing from good English neutrality; he had not intended to interfere so long as Perico confined himself to humiliating the man. But he was conscious now of an overwhelming sense of release. Damn what might happen afterwards! At least it would mean change — a coming to grips with something solid instead of sitting through a nightmare of frustration.

When Nepamuk was trussed up, Perico exchanged the pitchfork for a dung fork and dug the trench further into the heap. He dragged Nepamuk up to the end of his excavation, set him on his feet and threw back the manure so that he was completely covered except for head and shoulders. He might try to roll and wriggle himself clear but would stop in a panic as soon as he realized that he risked burying himself.

"How long are you going to leave him there?"

"Tomorrow sometime the gardeners may come out for manure. No one is likely to come from the stables."

"He'll be heard yelling in the night."

"No. It's too far. And with all the owls hooting — just one more of them! When will he be missed at the house?"

"When his man calls him in the morning. He's often out at night and doesn't need to tell anyone where he is going."

"That gives me time to get clear."

"Where are you off to?"

"The frontier." Perico waved a hand at the dusk gathering over Transylvania. "A good horse and I am there in an hour. Friend Bernardo, I have enough."

"I have enough, too. But what can I do without clothes or money?"

"Clothes? What more do you want? You're dressed like a prince in those boots and breeches. And money — I have my savings and we share them. If both of us go together, everything is much easier. Wait by the track through the stubble over there till I have seen Kovacs. I shall be back with horses when I can."

The night fell quickly. Across the plain were the faint lights
of the village and through the trees he could see the harsher
light over the door of the Kalmody palace welcoming back
the guest who would not return. Perico had been quite right.
At a distance of quarter of a mile Nepamuk's cries were
muffled by the haystacks, and there was nobody but himself
as near as that. Any wandering peasant would take the
ethereal, persistent wails for those of a long-eared owl drifting
in search of rats or a young partridge.

He was alarmed at his choice, but Perico seemed to know
what he was about; and afterwards somewhere there would be
a British consul. It might even be easier to get in touch with
him when jailed by Romanian frontier guards. Better Romanians than Hungarians! Nobody over there was going to bother
him about cliffs and Kalmodys and the Empress Zita. A
frontier was a frontier was a frontier.

Perico was back in an hour quietly walking three horses,
saddled and bridled, along the verge of the track. Bernardo
recognized the led horses as two of Kalmody's black half-
bloods, famous in the district. The third was a working hack
for general duties. Perico was wearing the black horseman's
cloak of the count's retainers, splashed with the coronetted
falcon, and had brought another for Bernardo.

They set off across the empty fields, by-passing the nearest
village. On the way Perico, very pleased with his cunning,
explained the three horses. Success had depended, he said, on
whether Kovacs had or had not done his last round of the
stables.

He had gone straight to the master of the horse and asked
leave to ride into town and stay the night. That was at once
granted, and he took a glass in the parlor while Kovacs jovially
speculated on how he proposed to spend his time. As soon as
Perico discovered that his boss would not do his stable round

till after supper, he said that he had just saddled two horses for
Mr. Nepamuk and Mr. Brown and that they had been secretive about their intentions. It could be that Bernardo was
going to meet the baroness and that Nepamuk was unwilling
to let him out of sight.

"So now when he finds three horses out he'll think he knows
why and will tell the house," Perico added. "We have all
night and much of tomorrow before questions are asked."

They stopped well before the outskirts of the compact
little town and jumped the tumbled stones of a ruined, white
wall into the cover of a cherry orchard. Bernardo was to wait
there with the two black horses while Perico rode openly
through the streets, left his own mount in the stables of his
usual inn and then walked back to the orchard.

Bernardo had another long and nervous interval in which
to consider the incalculable risks of what he was doing. Though
impressed by Perico's daring and ingenuity, he felt that the
Argentine had no very precise idea of European frontiers
especially when the two opposite sides were hardly on speaking
terms; a fugitive from justice could not just ride, as in the
Americas, from emptiness to emptiness across a line which
existed only on a map. He was tempted to return to his luxurious prison and rescue Nepamuk on the way. About all that
stopped him was longing for Magda. Whatever the way to
her was, it could never be through the Kalmody palace.

It was after midnight when Perico appeared, for he had
slipped back into the open country through side lanes taking
great care not to be recognized. The pair then rode for the
frontier easily reached by an empty road still in the Kalmody
lands which before the war had stretched far into what was
now Romania. Perico had never had reason to explore the
boundary and had seen little more than a wide belt of no-man's

land which the count, disgusted at being expropriated by mere treaty-makers, had left derelict to keep Romania out of sight, hearing and recognition. There were plenty of tracks and dirt roads — far too many of them — which had once connected village to village and were now blocked by barbed wire and palisades of tree trunks with scrub growing on the surface of the road as freely as in the once-cultivated fields. In the darkness they were soon hopelessly lost. The only certain way for horses was the beaten path along the wire made by patrolling frontier guards.

At one road block the coil of wire had been slightly flattened and Bernardo suggested that they should jump it, though God and the Romanians alone knew what was beyond in the silent night. Perico refused.

"The count and Kovacs have treated me decently," he said. "I will not steal their horses. If we take them into Romania it is certain they will never see them again."

He was unwilling and illogical. He would not take the horses, yet he was conditioned not to set out into the unknown without them. He pointed out that they had no wire cutters and that even if they managed to scramble across they had not the time to get clear of the frontier before morning. They were arguing far too loudly, and the question was quickly settled by a short burst of rifle fire from the Romanian side which cut the leaves from the bushes and sent them galloping back to safety; it also ended all chance of following the track along the wire, for Hungarian patrols as well would be alerted by the firing.

"We are not smugglers and we don't know how to do it," Perico said furiously. "This has to end in blood."

Possibly. But why not try what respectability would do? Bernardo remembered that in a former life he had been a shipping and forwarding agent. There was little he did not know about frontiers and their officials from the commercial angle.

"What is the nearest station where trains cross the frontier?" he asked.

"Nagyvarad. About fifteen kilometers to the north."

"Let's go! There is always a chance."

It was no use trying any cross-country route. If they were to reach Nagyvarad before the sun, they had to stick to the roads, follow sign-posts and risk being held up and questioned by gendarmerie. It was the devil that they had no papers, Bernardo said.

"I have my passport and an identity card which shows that I work for Kalmody. Now that Nepamuk is in the dungheap no one else will dare to say that a Kalmody groom has no right to be in Hungary."

"And my story?"

"Look, Bernardo! In this country so much depends on how one is dressed. It will be clear to everyone that you are of the upper class. And since they like Englishmen, say what you are! You have no need to carry a passport. I am only taking you to the station to meet a friend."

They met nobody, so that the story was never tested. Bernardo considered it in silence as they alternately walked and cantered their horses. It seemed to have possibilities. If Perico was right, the name of Kalmody might work wonders even at Nagyvarad.

It was nearly dawn when the road led them up over a first shoulder of the Transylvanian foothills, and there immediately below them were the files of harsh lights over the frontier station. A long train of wagon-lits was waiting to enter Hungary, its windows all dark, and dim pools of light at the doors of the coaches showing the occasional busy customs officer and armed, idle sentry. On the opposite track was a shabbier, third-class train facing Romania and spilling peasants onto the platform. Under the arc lights of the yard Bernardo could see packed freight trains without locomotives. To his practiced eye it looked as if Nagyvarad, once of little importance, needed a lot of development before it was large enough for international traffic. As it was, the yards were jammed solid, and the only hope for the unfortunate importer waiting for goods week after week at Budapest or Bucarest would be to visit the frontier station himself with a pocketful of bribes.

"Perico, do you think anyone at the station would know these are Kalmody's horses?"

"Man, look at our cloaks and the coronets on the saddles! At least the stationmasters and the police will know."

"Then leave it all to me! Here I am at home. I am an Englishman and a friend of the count, as you said. You are his trainer under Kovacs and sent to interpret for me, which may not be necessary. At an international station enough people speak French. And this is our business. We are expecting two English mares which the count has bought from Romania. We are afraid they may be stuck in the yards without food or water."

"But how will that help us?"

"I don't know yet, Perico. We must wait till we see our chance."

They rode down the hill and trotted into the paved court of the station. Barracks, stations, government offices, they were all the same: simple and dignified oblong blocks with regimented lines of windows, imposing under the Empire but now, after long war and near bankruptcy, shabby and with peeling plaster.

Old Mr. Brown laughed at the memory of their arrival with a shade of pride in his youth.

"We must have been a fine-looking pair. Beautifully mounted and — apart from language — so obviously belonging to the ancient, traditional Hungary. A breath of fresh air in that *milieu* of trains and internationalism and grubby customs officers. And there was Perico demanding the stationmaster as if he were a Nepamuk or better!"

The stationmaster came out of his office and saluted the two cloaked riders standing motionless in the courtyard. He spoke fair French, and Bernardo dismounted and launched into his story with a geniality he had not felt since Bilbao. The stationmaster personally took them to see the yardmaster, who was certain that there was no horse van in his yard. And, if there had been, of course the horses would have been fed and watered.

"Could they be in the Romanian yards?" Bernardo asked.

Well, that was possible. What could one expect of Romanians? They would let the mares die in their box and eat them afterwards.

"Can we go and see?"

"If they let you," the yardmaster answered doubtfully. "I will do my best. Meanwhile leave your two noble horses with us."

It seemed time for a token of gratitude. Bernardo suggested to Perico that they should slip him something.

"No. These Hungarians, even the little officials, are different to the rest of us. They do not take bribes."

"You speak Romanian?" the stationmaster asked.

"That was Spanish," Bernardo answered. "The count's trainer comes from Argentina."

"Well, over there they all speak Hungarian — not to us, but they will to you. And here is something that will please them! You should call this town Oradea Mare, not Nagy-varad."

The Romanian yardmaster was a surly, unshaven func-tionary whose dislike of Hungarians — at any rate when well dressed or neatly uniformed — was pointed. He was offended at the suggestion that there could be horses in his yard un-known to him and refused to take the responsibility of allow-ing Bernardo and Perico to see for themselves. The Hungarian yardmaster tactfully reminded him that nobody could lose by doing favors to a Kalmody, and at least persuaded him to pick up the telephone.

A young Romanian lieutenant — of army or security to judge by his sky-blue-uniformed air of contempt for com-merce — came belted and booted into the office. He spoke excellent French, and Bernardo was able to take over. The name of Kalmody made no impression. What did the trick was Perico's Argentine passport. The lieutenant had never seen one before.

"Where are your horses from?"

Bernardo said they were from Bucarest, which was the only Romanian town he knew by name.

"They may be at Arad."

"We have asked at Arad and they told us to try here."

The lieutenant turned on the yardmaster with a show of military impatience and led them smartly out of the office.

"I told the fool to look through his papers again," he explained to Bernardo. "I will show you the trains myself."

Very amicably they did the rounds of three separate trains in the sidings, Perico dutifully stopping to examine any cattle truck which might possibly contain horses.

"And you like Hungary?" the lieutenant asked.

"Frankly, no! It is a joy to be here speaking the French of culture with a Latin brother."

"But you are English."

"My mother was Spanish, lieutenant. I can see I should be happy in your country."

They sentimentalized over the Latin brother tucked away from all the rest of the family on the Black Sea.

"Ride over when you wish! Ask for Lieutenant Mureshanu!"

"I shall be delighted, and have my passport with me next time. Now tell me, my lieutenant — in other countries it would be in order to give a little present to the yardmaster for his trouble, but here I am not sure."

"He'd take it all right. None of us are well paid."

"Then might I ask you to give it to him?"

"With pleasure, monsieur."

It was hard to know how much the goodwill of an officer was worth. Bernardo had no idea of the value of Hungarian pengös, never having handled any. He only knew what Perico's weekly wage was and gave Mureshanu twice that. The sum was most graciously received.

A sound investment it seemed on general principles, but there was less chance than ever of getting rid of the lieutenant or, now that it was full light, of hiding in the busy yard. As the three walked along the passenger platform, Bernardo asked if any more freight trains would cross the frontier that morning.

"There should be one from Bucarest in about an hour."

"Then we will go back and have some breakfast and come over again if you allow it."

"Have it here on the station. That will save trouble. I will come and fetch you when the train is due."

Coffee, rolls and eggs were all excellent, and Bernardo, who was very hungry, was on the whole prejudiced in favor of Romania. Perico, however, was demanding action, any sort of action, and alarmed that they should waste time by a casual breakfast.

"Suppose they find Nepamuk?"

"If they do, it will still take time to find us. And now that everyone has seen us with the lieutenant we can wander about without question."

He asked Perico to pay the bill and to change some money into Romanian lei. Meanwhile he watched movement on the station. He knew that he was far less daring than Perico, much more ready to resign himself to fate. On the other hand he had, he thought, been doing rather well by lending himself to whatever turned up. That local train was still standing at the platform, now with a locomotive at the Romanian end. Having discharged one load of passengers — who had had to cross the frontier on foot with their bundles and take another train on the Hungarian side — it had now received a new load. Police and customs officers had finished with it, and it was due to start at any moment.

He had to be patient during long minutes while Perico changed money.

"Walk slowly down the platform," he said. "Don't hurry even if the train starts. And let's leave our cloaks on the chairs to show that we are coming back. It's too hot to wear them anyway."

They crossed the line behind the train and very casually walked up the other side of it until three wagons hid them from observation. An empty first-class compartment was opposite and the door was unlocked. In an instant they were inside and under the seats.

The train obligingly started immediately and then stopped outside the station. That was the worst moment of all. They were sure they had been seen; and no fairy story could be convincing enough for even Lieutenant Mureshanu to save them. It then reversed and a comforting bang showed that something had been picked up at the tail of the train — probably the three wagons on the next track. When the engine began to chuff-chuff with some purpose, they rolled from under the seats and looked out of the window with all the assurance of ticketless first-class passengers who could not be caught till the next station.

"Where is it going?" Perico asked.

"Man, even if they told us we'd be no wiser."

3. Sanctuary

THE UNKNOWN country was rolling, wooded and restful to the eyes after the brown Hungarian distances, but intervals for satisfying curiosity were too short. The slow train stopped everywhere and sometimes at a nowhere without visible reason for a station, compelling them to dive back under the seats. At one remote valley halt their compartment was invaded by a family of Romanian peasants — two trouser legs of grayish white frieze, four pairs of white woolen stockings, two small bare legs, all with shoes made from old tires — who were immediately ordered out by a screaming guard. So far as one could guess, it was their first journey by train, and either classes of travel were unknown to them or they could not read numbers. They obeyed, but not so humbly as in Hungary. The guard locked the door. Thereafter Bernardo and Perico risked remaining on their seats so long as peaked caps showed no sign of walking up the platform at the stops.

Soon after midday they clattered into a town where ticket

collectors and controls were certain. Sounds suggested that the train was emptying. No other passengers arrived. This was evidently the terminus. Since the platforms on both sides of the line were busy and there was no chance of leaving unobserved, they stayed under the seats in very anxious peace until the train was hauled off onto a siding. They left it cautiously, hoping that Lieutenant Mureshanu and his colleagues had not guessed where they had gone. The cloaks on the chairs and the horses in charge of the Hungarian yardmaster must be a strong indication that Kalmody's trainer and his distinguished English friend were still in Nagyvarad, shopping, visiting or waiting for banks to open.

It was a fully imperial little town into which they strolled. Zita could have been received at the town hall or university with all the proper medieval ceremony rather than blowing a kiss — if she did blow kisses — at a ragged line of peasants and paper flags. They bought a map from which it appeared they were in Cluj in the heart of Transylvania. Perico's Hungarian was accepted without question or resentment.

At lunch Perico was unusually thoughtful, staring at the map which was spread over the café table with a bottle of wine on the Ukraine, and the Danube winding round Bernardo's glass at the opposite corner. Bernardo thought for a moment that Perico could not read a map, for their next move was immediate and obvious — directly to Bucarest where there would be consuls and at last the relief of fitting into a familiar world whatever might come of it. But Perico shook his head, brooding over lines and colors as if they represented a journey of the spirit instead of a neatly rounded Romania.

"This!" Perico said, tracing with the point of a fork a winding railway, which Bernardo had never spotted, up over the high Carpathians and down into the province of Moldavia where it joined the main line from Bucarest to the north.

"But why? It's a long way round."

"I will tell you, dear friend, when I am sure. This could be farthest of all from the Nepamuks and railway guards — the bastards without heart or courtesy."

Bernardo did not argue. Perico was so generous in sharing his money. That give him the right to decide where they should go. He also had the right to make his own way to whatever world he foresaw. Bernardo's own world could wait.

Back at the station Perico bought two tickets only as far as the Moldavian junction. Bernardo had no objection, for it was common sense not to waste money when it might be wiser — at any rate for himself — to jump off the train and disappear. During most of the journey Perico either slept or was silent. Bernardo was too fascinated by the rushing water and supposedly wolf-haunted darkness of pines to do more than doze. He had never before seen the primeval forest of Europe.

They arrived in the dusk. There in old Romania Hungarian was no use, but the stationmaster spoke a very little French.

"Ask him about the trains to north and south," Perico said.

"There is a train to the north in an hour and at midnight to Bucarest. What are you thinking?"

"That Russia is not far away."

"And what the devil has that to do with us?"

"I am going there."

"They'll shoot you at the frontier."

"I don't believe it. I know the patter — a little of what must be said to them."

Bernardo protested that even if he could quote Lenin and Karl Marx by the yard they wouldn't let him in.

"Why not go back to Argentina where men are equal?"

"Who says they are equal? Do you think there are no

peaked caps in Argentina? And besides I do not like the sea. I tell you I am going to Russia. Come with me!"

Bernardo was appalled by the mere thought. After all he had been a businessman in a small corner of capitalism which worked efficiently. He was prepared to go a long way with socialism — his father and Spain had seen to that — but not so far as complete rejection of the Europe he knew and enjoyed. He reminded Perico that he had admitted Count Kalmody treated him decently.

"But he should not exist. The wastefulness of it all!"

"Yes. But it saves them from unemployment such as we have in England."

"I tell you I am going to Russia."

"You won't last long, Perico. Hammers and sickles — you can't use either. What will you do?"

"Horses. A trainer, a captain of Cossacks, who knows? Man, if they don't shoot me on sight there is no risk. I have a passport and it will show that I escaped from Hungary. The worst they can do is to turn me back to Romania. And then the Romanians will let me stay when I tell them I was ill-treated by their enemies."

That gave Bernardo his excuse. Without a passport it was lunacy to try to accompany Perico. He felt guilty, for Perico — considering his ignorance of frontiers — should not be allowed to try alone. The map showed a single blocked bridge over the Dniester. The only other way to Russia was to swim the river if it was swimmable. There would be searchlights to pick out a head in the water and machine guns to open up on it. Bernardo had had enough of that. Capitalism, socialism, friendship — none of them were so compelling as his vision of the Dniester in the dark.

The North Express clanked and hissed to a stop. They embraced, and Perico mounted the steps of a third-class coach while the stench of snoring peasants escaped, almost visibly, past him. At the last moment he took out half the money he still possessed and stuffed it into Bernardo's pocket before he could refuse.

It was as if luck or Bernardo's nerve had disappeared with his companion. He left the station and shuffled through the warm dust to a communal well where he sat on the coping wholly occupied by memories of Magda and the dreamlike quality of the last twenty-four hours. As usual he was quite unconscious of his appearance.

A brown-uniformed policeman materialized out of the night, saluted respectfully and was evidently asking who he was or if he needed help. Bernardo, drowsy and careless, made signs and noises to indicate that he had just arrived on the train from Bucarest.

"Otel? Bagajul?"

The smiling policeman's meaning was plain. He was eager to show the distinguished foreigner in boots and breeches a bed for the night and to arrange a porter for his baggage. It was Bernardo's second experience of Romanian helpfulness — genuine but seldom excluding the hope of profit.

"No *bagajul*," he answered.

"Then what the hell is your lordship doing in this dump?" seemed to be the next question.

Bernardo pulled himself together and tried to explain that he had been misunderstood. He had come from Cluj and was waiting for the train to Bucarest. He was English and he did not need a hotel.

The policeman got it, again saluted and escorted his Englishman to the station — more as a guard of honor than with any suspicion.

When the midnight train was due, Bernardo tried to buy a ticket. He couldn't. Perico's wad of money was all Hun-

garian except for some small and filthy Romanian paper. He
might as well have offered an old sock; nobody knew anything
of Hungarian money. At last the dreaded word came out.

"*Pasaportul, vă rog.*"

Bernardo looked through his pockets, pretended horror,
called the stationmaster to witness that he had been accompanied by a friend who had gone north to Czernowitz and
explained that this friend had both their passports. Most of
it appeared to get through, but meanwhile the Bucarest express had come and gone.

No baggage, no usable money, no passport, but the smart
coat, boots and breeches of the landed gentry still proclaimed
that, though a half-witted foreigner, he was respectable and
perhaps rich. The policeman led him to the hotel. It was at
the entrance to the main street, and Bernardo in happy days
when he had never heard of that blasted Zita would have liked
the look of it: half a dozen green-shuttered rooms above a
little restaurant shaded by a vine.

The policeman hammered on the door, yelling for Gheorghe.
Gheorghe opened up, naked to the waist and remarkably
hairy. His two round, expressionless, brown eyes and considerable belly suggested a sleepy brown bear on its hind legs. There
was a long conversation. Bernardo nodded and smiled, tried
French, got a slightly better result from Spanish, but could
not dispel the general air of stern duty whenever the word
pasaportul was mentioned. He gathered that he was welcome
to stay the night and that there was a *jidan* — probably a
Jew, for Gheorghe spat in the street — who might change his
money in the morning.

So it could be worse. Gheorghe was unshaven and unwashed
— as who wouldn't be when woken up from sleep? — but the
white-washed room was clean. A fine green and black rug hung
on the wall; a red and white one was spread on the divan

bed. Wine, bread and an admirable cold fish were served to him. Gheorghe, invited to share the wine, managed to put over his opinion that the policeman was a crook who only wanted money and that Bernardo needn't worry about him. *Englez — boum, boum!* They had won the war. Romanians were grateful. And there was their St. George! So indeed he was, a gallant, armored, dark-browed ikon over the bed. Bernardo undressed and slept magnificently, seeing nothing whatever wrong with Romanians except that all classes were very poor and ready quite rightly to get their cut out of anyone richer, that they had an objection to Jews and abused their police who seemed at first sight most reasonable chaps.

The reasonable chap called for him while he was breakfasting and accepted a glass of pale yellow spirit. Bernardo's credit appeared to be good, so he had one himself. Kovacs, he thought, would have enjoyed it though never admitting that this plum gin — *tsuica* they called it — was better than apricot brandy.

Daylight revealed that nothing more than a large village had grown at the junction, its houses mostly of timber and puddled clay under white plaster. All down the long main street the inhabitants stared at their policeman's conspicuous bag. The majority wore conical hats of sheepskin even in full summer, their shirts outside their trousers and rubber shoes — What in God's name did they wear before the coming of the automobile? — held on by thongs to the knee.

On the edge of open country was a two-story house, whitewashed to conform with the rest but built of brick and standing in its own garden. The policeman rang the bell and — since this was too mild and courteous a summons — shouted for Mihai Toledano. The door was opened by a darkly pretty girl in embroidered blouse and skirt. Bernardo noticed that Romanian national costume did not include the many petals of petticoats. Petticoats — Magda — hell! Minds must be kept on money.

Followed by his shadow of the law, he was led to a room overlooking the garden where a man in his fifties with fine-drawn, angular, Semitic features received them with dignified reserve. When he had heard the policeman out, he addressed Bernardo in German. Bernardo shook his head and tried Spanish, encouraged by the name of Toledano.

Instantly he was at home. Toledano's Spanish was clear, slow and very exactly grammatical. The brown uniform stared, apparently surprised that this well-dressed anthropoid could make itself understood.

"Of course I will change your money. I will also telegraph the police at Czernowitz to get in touch with your friend and return your passport. I'll explain all that to this fellow and tell him he can call on you at the hotel at any time. Give him a hundred lei and shake his hand!"

It was evidently a generous tip establishing Bernardo as a land-owning *boyar*. The cop saluted once on the spot and again at the door.

"Your friend has your baggage, too?"

Bernardo laughed. He must have spread some sort of radiance from outer space into that house so lonely among its neighbors.

"What do you think?" he asked.

"That perhaps I should not send the telegram."

"You are very kind. What part of Spain do you come from?"

"My family left Spain over four hundred years ago."

So that was it! Bernardo had never before met a Sephardic Jew. He only knew the history of their expulsion from Spain and that they had settled in the East.

"Are there many of you here?"

"Very few. Here in Moldavia they are all Ashkenazim,

speaking their own German. I was glad to hear my language. You are not a Jew, I think, but tell me what I can do for you."

"After five minutes, Don Mihai?"

"You remind me of my son."

"I'd like to meet him."

"You cannot. God's will be done!"

"I am so sorry. The war?"

Toledano nodded. Bernardo impulsively decided to trust him. He cut his story short, leaving out the privacies of Magda, and answered a few acute questions. Across the desk grave eyes seemed to accept his adventures as believable.

"This Perico — he has no chance at all. He is sure to be arrested."

"He won't talk."

"That may be. But they can trace all his movements. And what questions will they ask you then?"

"Nepamuk?"

"He doesn't count. You will hear no more of him if you do not mention him. But to the police you are bound to appear either a Russian or a Hungarian agent. What did Count Kalmody intend to do with you?"

"I don't know. Keep me till it all blew over, I suppose."

"It will not blow over easily. Much depends on that cliff. If it was as terrible as you describe, no one will believe you climbed it. So in Spain there must be a warrant out for your arrest. Even Kalmody will now be thinking you only told half the truth."

"Can you help me?"

"No, for the sake of my family. All I know of you is that I was asked to change your money and did so."

"Well, what's your advice?"

"You cannot be more than an hour or two ahead of the police. Go to your consul at once, but try to find out how much he knows without giving anything away. It's a pity that you do not speak Romanian. If you did, you could disappear until, as you say, it all blows over."

"The trouble is I'm too innocent for anything like that."

"Don Bernardo, you have lost your virginity and now you will learn only too quickly. Go with God! If you remain at liberty in Bucarest and need a job, go to my cousin Mitrani, a banker in the Strada Lipscani. I cannot give you a note to him in case you are searched, but I will tell him about you. With your languages he could use you."

Bernardo returned to his hotel, lunched and paid his surprisingly small bill. He was indeed learning quickly. His old self would have confidently taken the night train to Bucarest with a sense of relief; his new self realized that it was on the run and unlikely to reach Bucarest openly. He took a long and careful look at the countryside. As seen from his bedroom window as well as from Toledano's garden it was bare and poor with little cover for a fugitive. He could not simply stroll out of the village for a walk; his lonely figure would be far too conspicuous.

When the policeman dropped into the hotel, partly for a free drink, partly to keep an eye on his customer, Bernardo — using gestures and experimental scraps from Latin languages — asked if there were any news of his baggage and passport. No, there was not, but he had already telephoned to Czernowitz without waiting for filthy Jews who could never be trusted. That clinched it. Perico would by now be picked up for questioning in the frontier town itself or caught behaving suspiciously on his way to the banks of the Dniester. The description of the pair of them as men wearing boots and breeches who spoke no Romanian was conclusive.

Waiting till night was a crazy risk. He was certain to be detained — courteously if Perico had invented a credible story,

forcibly if he had not. He must get clear by the next afternoon train and hope to disappear somewhere along the line.
And it would be wise to look a little smarter. He bought a
shaving kit and a hairbrush and cleaned himself up.

Bernardo was escorted to the station, shook a number of
hands and settled down in a second-class compartment. There
was only one other passenger who smiled at him with
irrepressible admiration as if he had been a startlingly pretty
girl. Bernardo said good afternoon in Romanian — he had got
that far — and the coldest possible voice. Life in this complicated east end of Europe was already difficult enough.

His companion was immediately talkative in sound international French. He was a classic Mediterranean type with a
triangular, dark face, gleaming teeth, four of them gold, and
an anxious, lost-dog friendliness.

"One sees that you are not going very far, monsieur. For
my part I regret it."

Bernardo made noises of politeness. He realized exactly
what women meant when they complained of being undressed
by a stare.

"Village to village — you have no doubt your duties?"

Something had to be invented to satisfy this impertinent
curiosity. Evidently he was being taken for a sort of foreign
Nepamuk.

"I am returning after delivering a horse."

"Of course! And without doubt you are English."

He fondled Bernardo's arm with affection. The intention of
the embarrassing fingers was at last clear. It was the cloth
rather than the flesh below which was causing the excitement.

"That coat, those boots, those breeches! And still as fresh
as from the fitting rooms of Savile Row! Ah, monsieur, before
the war I could import such quality but now nobody can pay
for it."

He lectured Bernardo on the poverty of the country. The great landlords had all been expropriated and their property distributed to the peasants. It hadn't worked — no, it hadn't worked. The ignorant peasants were as poor as ever, and the compensation paid to the landlords had been reduced to nothing by inflation.

Sighing and shaking his head, he handed Bernardo his business card, printed in French and of excellent, simple taste: MIRCEA NICULESCU. Tailleur. Fournisseur d'Equipements. Etoffes de Luxe.

One would not have guessed at any luxury stuffs. Mr. Niculescu was himself dressed in wretched cloth — though, on a second glance, admirably cut.

"While you are in Bucarest, do me the honor to come and call on me. My shop is on the corner opposite the royal palace."

Bernardo was stuck. Since he had to leave the train at the first opportunity he could not say he was going to Bucarest nor could he say he wasn't because he did not know the name of any other station on the line. He thanked Niculescu for his invitation and added vaguely that he was going straight through to the sea.

"Ah, to Galatz! You are a seaman? You brought the horse by sea?"

"A naval officer," Bernardo said, thinking that he might as well have a social position worthy of the Kalmody clothes.

"Now I understand! No doubt you delivered it to Prince Ghika?"

"How did you guess?"

"Who else in Moldavia could have a horse sent by a British warship?"

Bernardo reproached himself for entering into the spirit of things too impulsively. On the other hand he had established an identity for himself which seemed to be convincing to this eager Mr. Niculescu.

"Prince Ghika is a customer of yours?" he asked.

"Alas, no more! I cannot compete with Paris and London. But one never knows. He has formed himself into a company and may again become as rich as he was. If only I could put a dummy in my window with such clothes as yours. Tone — it would add tone!"

Lord only knew whether the idea had entered Mr. Niculescu's head, but it was worth trying.

"Well, if you think it might bring in Prince Ghika and company, I shall not want this outfit till my ship is back in Portsmouth."

"You would sell it?"

"At a price — and if you have anything else I can wear as far as Galatz. We are much the same size."

"But I have no other suit in my bag. I have only been away from home one night."

"We might exchange now before anyone else gets in. I can't very well stand in the corridor outside the lavatory and hand my breeches through the door."

Haggling was fierce but went as fast as a hand of poker since the next station was not far away and one was as keen to buy as the other to sell. They arrived at a price of six thousand lei which Bernardo discovered was about seven and a half pounds and at last had an accurate valuation of the unknown currency. He regarded Mr. Niculescu with admiration. By a tug at the lapels and half a dozen pins from his bag the tailor had succeeded in looking like a very shady racehorse trainer compensating for his morals by his clothes. As for himself, he was a middle-class Romanian in a dark suit of cheap Czech cloth, with coat too tight and trousers too short. The shoes were much too small, considering that feet were going to be

91

important. But presumably he could buy another pair somewhere.

The train stopped at Pashcani. It was the junction for Jassy,
the chief town of Moldavia, and Mr. Niculescu could not resist
showing himself off to a public of some standing. He climbed
down to the platform on the pretense of buying a paper and
strolled up and down clicking imaginary spurs. It was a good
chance to disappear. Mr. Niculescu would assume he had
gone to the restaurant car.

Bernardo hurried down the corridor, got off at the rear of
the train and crossed to the opposite platform. No trouble
there. Just enough people idling or watching trains to prevent
his being conspicuous. The ticket collector, if any, was occupied elsewhere. He strolled out of the station and took cover
behind an ox cart as the Bucarest train pulled out and revealed
Mr. Niculescu being led away between two brown uniforms
with a superior blue one following behind.

By God, that had been a close thing! Provided he left the
town at once speaking to no one he had a chance of vanishing
into — well, wherever in Romania one could vanish to. He
hoped that he could count on a good hour before the unfortunate Civil and Military Tailor managed to prove his identity
and the hunt for the real boots-and-breeches was on. It might
start in the wrong direction. Mr. Niculescu had jumped at the
port of Galatz as soon as the sea was mentioned. A railway
map in the corridor had shown that it was a natural assumption; one changed for Galatz further down the line. The police
might well accept that bit of Niculescu's story while rejecting
the naval officer. That the wanted man could be a seaman on
the run without baggage or papers was possible.

Bernardo had no plan at all except to put so much distance
between himself and the town of Pashcani that he could safely
buy food and drink. He started out more or less southwest

with the intention of returning to the forests and valleys of the Carpathians and then taking a train to Bucarest. Once in the mountains he hoped to pass as a casual hiker whose baggage and passport were at his inn; and the language difficulty, insuperable on the Moldavian plain, must surely be easier where tourists were less rare. So far as Bernardo remembered, it would mean a tramp of about eighty miles. Perico had retained the map since at the time his need appeared the greater.

He made a rule of speaking to no one. It was hard to follow and of doubtful value. He was aware that he was leaving behind him a trail of curiosity about this self-centered man, dressed as if he ought to have money for travel, who shuffled through the dust of country roads responding to greetings with only a mumbled good day. He was also limping. After a few miles he slit open the uppers of Niculescu's shoes and moved more easily.

Marching at night for as long as he could see what he was doing and laying up by day seemed the best way to avoid the stares of the curious. It didn't work. Since there were no walls or hedges it was easy enough to circle round the villages but difficult to regain the right road or any road in the dark. When he came across a wattle shack roofed with rushes and floored with hard mud he decided to give up this random wandering and sleep there till dawn.

He woke up on fire with itching and dashed out into the open. Even the half light was enough to show that he was crawling with fleas, hungrier and more active than the occasional Spanish flea. Those had been a mere annoyance; this swarm was a humiliation, driving home the fact that he was a helpless outcast in the chill of dawn at the wrong end of Europe. He shook out his clothes as best he could and hobbled off. The slits in his shoes had freed his toes but badly blistered them.

Sanctuary

No one in the dreary fields was near enough to bother him. Evidently there was little to do once the maize had been harvested. He followed an earth track across country to a hazy line of willows in the distance and came at midmorning to the banks of a considerable river where the water was low, swirling gently between sand banks. He took off his clothes and waded across with a sense of freedom as if the river were an obstacle cutting off the immediate past as well as telephone lines between police stations. A mile upstream was the bridge he would have crossed if he had stuck to the road; downstream was a pool in which was a small herd of water buffaloes — wicked-looking creatures with back-swept, black horns, but plainly as tame as cows in a meadow.

After a swim he lay and sunned himself on the hot sands with his feet in the water, trying to forget hunger in the meticulous job of catching and drowning fleas. He did not dare dip Niculescu's suit in the river in case it shrank to something unwearable. The desolate feeling that he belonged nowhere fell away as he remembered the kindly estuaries of the Basque coast. There too his feet had often ached and been cooled.

But there the countryside flowed with food and wine. In this poverty-stricken province of Romania it certainly did not. After recovering the road he stopped hopefully at a lonely cottage with a bottle of *tsuica* in the window, an iron table outside in the dust and no other customer. Nothing to eat, however much he pointed to his mouth! He gathered there was not even enough for the peasant proprietor. He took a stiff glass of very bad *tsuica* to disinfect the river water he had been drinking and tramped on.

The next place on the road was more than a mere village. A church and a public building showed above the low, white houses and guaranteed that there would be police. Hungry though he was, he stuck to his rule of avoiding the public. It was not so much from fear of being asked questions — whether kindly or suspicious — as that he had had enough of continual stares at his clerk-out-of-work, Chaplinesque figure with the broken shoes. He might, he thought, have done better in boots and breeches after all; at least they would allow him just to wave a lordly hand as if the groom and the horses were just around the corner.

The only handy cover was a sparse hedge of shrubs surrounding the garden of a house which seemed to have its entrance on one of the first side streets of the town. He waited till the road was clear, half circled the garden and took refuge in a dry ditch under arching branches. It was a good spot in which to sleep and wait for darkness. His way on was clear enough and convenient; one of the usual earth tracks, more a boundary between fields than a road, passed outside the houses and ran westwards.

He was woken up by music. The garden was full of colored lights which twinkled through the hedge. He saw a long table at which a dinner party was just sitting down, and other diners in a few dim corners under trees. A birthday or a christening was being celebrated at the town restaurant and — if it was anything like Spain — all the notables would be there. They might ask him to join the party, and half of them were sure to speak some French. What would happen if he limped in and ordered a meal? Hell, but he was too tired and dirty to account for himself! He lay in his ditch, listening to the wail of the leading violin and the speed of the cimbalon. Lawless music and of infinite pity. Hungarian music had been on the whole happy, suggesting wine and dancing, wild in triumph of what is today; but these Romanian gypsy melodies were an aching for what never was. They tore the physical body out by the roots leaving a spirit, lonely as his own, with no comfort but birdsong.

Bernardo cautiously followed the hedge round to the lane at the front of the establishment, prowling in hope of food which could be bought and eaten without committing himself to a table. Over the gate was a string of lights. A path led to the front door which opened into an empty passage with a lot of shadowy activity at the end of it. He saw no chance of getting anything to eat unless he appeared in the full light of the kitchen.

Just inside the gate was a horse, saddled, bridled and hitched to a tree by the reins. Temptation was overwhelming. The respectable shipping clerk contemplated his first crime. Old Mr. Brown insisted that his fall from grace was due to the mood of self-pity induced by gypsy music even more than to the pain of his blistered feet.

In any case he was learning quickly, as Toledano said he would. Since he had no existence, it would be nearly impossible to trace the thief once the horse was abandoned. He patted its neck and unhitched the reins, keeping one eye on the house. Everybody seemed to be busy with the party on the other side of it. The lane was empty and his partner in crime was a docile gelding, not caring who rode him or whether he was ridden or not. Bernardo led him quietly away, ready to jump into the saddle at the first sound of any excitement. As soon as he was on the track to the west and the beat of hooves over dust was unlikely to be heard he mounted and cantered off, hoping that with luck and the help of a half moon he would have covered a good twenty miles by dawn and that the first foothills would be in sight. Mountains obsessed him. There he would never be far from woods and water and free of the suspicion that he was being watched.

He kept riding westwards till well after the sun was up — an amateur criminal on edge with the risk he was taking. It was now time to get rid of the horse, but there was never a convenient patch of cover where it could be left while he himself continued on foot and unremarked. At last he saw ahead of him a tumble of mounds and ridges uncultivated and dotted with bushes. There seemed no obvious geological reason for its existence: no connection with other high ground, no rocks, no water. As he rode closer he was sure that such a barren, untidy mess could never have been made by nature. It must once have been a town of this melancholy Moldavian plain swept clean by one invasion after another.

Over the first rise was a long, shallow depression. Its sides gave the impression of a rubbish heap with old tarpaulins and tattered carpets spread out to dry in the sun. At the bottom were a few canvas shelters over hoops, showing that the place was after all a ragged human settlement though lacking even the comparative cleanliness and order of aboriginal huts.

As he appeared on the skyline there was a clamor of dogs; the rags suddenly pullulated with men, women and children as if a fork had disturbed the riper depths around Nepamuk's feet. Some of the men, much darker than Romanians, ran up the slope to meet him, at first whining and respectful, then for no apparent reason aggressive. One seized the bridle and led him down to the dry bottom.

It was a gypsy encampment. Bernardo recognized the familiar race of Spain, but this branch of the family were still demoralized scavengers from Asia, rejects of civilization rather than decorative strangers within it. However, gypsies in his experience always had something nourishing to eat and some of the men were fat. Bernardo smiled, chattered hopefully in a fair imitation of Spanish gypsy dialect and pointed to his mouth. There was no response whatever.

His first impression was right. This had once been a town. There was a well of good masonry and it was in use. Here and there fox holes had been burrowed between scraps of stone walls, as likely as not leading to dry, paved dens. A couple of appalling old hags shoved their heads under the flapping entrance to one of these holes and screamed.

A most unexpected personage crawled out. He was dressed in a white shirt and black trousers with a red sash at the waist. His round, yellowish face was completely devoid of expression. He lounged up to Bernardo, took a close look at the horse and said something. Bernardo was at once dragged to the ground and held there when he tried to get up. He protested. Gypsies, as he knew them, were consummate petty thieves but never went in for open robbery. Nobody paid the least attention to his remarks. Meanwhile the leader in the red sash picketed the horse and returned at leisure.

Finding that his captive spoke no Romanian, he broke into passable French. It was more astonishing than ever to hear the language of decent society in such a setting.

"You stole this horse last night," he said.

"It's yours?" Bernardo asked, for it was no use denying.

"It is the mayor's. We spent the night looking for it."

"Then how did you get here before me?"

"You think we cannot afford a taxi?"

"Monsieur, I am a foreigner in Romania for the first time," Bernardo said politely. "I would not know how or where to sell a horse. I only borrowed it to go on a little faster. I was going to leave it here among the mounds and walk."

"Leave it here? So that we would be accused of stealing it?"

"But I did not know you were here. How could I? One cannot see your camp."

The blank, dark-brown eyes considered this while never leaving Bernardo's face.

Sanctuary

"True," the gypsy said. "But I must hand you over to the police."

"Couldn't you let me go and say that you just found the horse?"

"No."

The man in the red sash had a point; it would certainly be better for the clan's reputation if they handed over the thief as well as the horse. Bernardo shrugged his shoulders and accepted the position. The men and women were gathered round, listening to the foreign language. Wild hair, wild clothes, eyes without meaning. He felt that the sooner he was in the hands of police, the better, and that meanwhile polite conversation should be kept moving along.

"Where did monsieur learn French?" he asked.

"In Bucarest. From foreigners and soldiers."

"So you don't live here?"

"When I wish."

"And the rest of the time?"

"I have my band."

It all became clear — all, that is, except for the fact that a musician who had played in international society often enough to speak some French should ever desire to return to this revolting squalor.

"Was it your violin I heard last night in the restaurant where I permitted myself to borrow a horse?"

"That could be."

"Maître!" Bernardo exclaimed, his sincerity inspiring a stroke of genius. "Never in my life have I heard anything so moving. And to think it was you who spoke to me with your violin when I was lying in the ditch! In the salons of Bucarest they are too occupied to listen with the heart as I did."

"Have you no money?"

"A little, but not much."

99

"Take it off him and send him on his road!"

Bernardo understood. *Drumul* — the road — was already a familiar word. And gypsies — well, one couldn't expect them to leave a man his cash when there was no chance of being accused of taking it.

They stripped him of every cent. Bernardo turned to the violinist of two lives.

"Will you give me at least a pair of peasant shoes?" he asked.

Yes, willingly. For some reason the request aroused crazy laughter — perhaps because middle-class clothes and rubber sandals with their thongs crossed outside the trousers were so incongruous or because the foreign horse thief was so innocent that he had set out to tramp the road in shoes too small for him. Two of the men led him out of the camp and indicated that he should take a cart-track to the north and hurry. Why the north? Why anything? He obeyed.

It served him right. Stealing the mayor's horse was nothing, but he accused himself of never even thinking that somebody else might be charged with the crime. He trudged on, his feet not so eased as he expected. Why he had been directed north was understandable. There was a dark line of forest on the horizon. Those homeless nomads were all right in the open plain themselves but recognized that for a solitary outcast the shelter of trees was the answer.

So it might have been, temporarily, for an individual able to return to the herd whenever he wished. But Bernardo had no herd. He was stripped of morale as he had been of money. He lost his courage, his assurance, his sense of past and future. For two days he lived on blackberries, preferring the privacy of the woods to the shame of being a pariah who could not communicate intelligibly with his fellows. He despaired of reaching Bucarest or of finding an end to his troubles if he did, certain that no consul could help him, that a Romanian jail would be followed by a Spanish jail and that it would not make two hoots of difference to Kalmody if the father of his grandson — and God damn eternally that lovely obsession of a girl for whom he would be perfectly willing to die! — were garroted by the public executioner for the murder of Bobo who, if there were any justice, should have had his skull blown in by the Bolsheviks.

"I also had dysentery," old Bernardo said. "Nothing like that for the final destruction of a respectable shipping clerk! Continuous wiping of my arse with leaves and wandering nowhere looking for something more solid than blackberries."

Sheer misery was its own cure. He could stand no more of it and padded off through the forest, sometimes in circles, until he came out into the open not knowing or caring where he was. The midday sun, before it was swallowed by towers of cumulus, showed him that he was walking east not west. It didn't matter.

He was out on bare, rolling swells of ground when the storm caught him — a thunderstorm of the hot steppe rejoicing the earth and itself by a display of Old Testament ferocity. The only shelter was an unharvested patch of maize where he was instantly as wet as if he had fallen in a river but the stalks were useful to hide his nakedness — Romanians presumably had a law against it — while his clothes were spread out to dry. The storm returned as he was about to put them on. When that happened a second time he gave up and flapped through the rain regardless. His feet began to give trouble again in spite of the rubber shoes. It occurred to him that peasants wore some kind of foot-cloth wrapped around their feet, not the silk socks of the Hungarian aristocracy.

In the last of the sunset he came to the banks of the River Moldova. His aimless, obstinate plodding to the east stopped there — a final destruction of his will to keep moving, leaving such a blank that he could only concentrate on trying not to faint from exhaustion. He must have done so, for he found himself lying on the path with the light fading. Ahead of him a large town on a hill fortified the sky; beneath it he could make out a peculiarly compact and isolated waterside village, close to the town but entirely separated from it without any connecting suburb. He dragged himself towards the dimly lit windows, perhaps towards a fire. At least in a Christian country he would be fed and given some kind of roof over his head. They could send for the police in the morning if they liked.

He collapsed on a bench under the shelter of a walnut tree. Villagers gathered round him at a safe distance. Another lot of grotesque Romanians. Some were dressed more or less as peasants; some had beards, whiskers in ringlets, black hats and frock coats. He could not imagine what he had landed in this time — presumably an odd sect of the Orthodox Church. The men seemed to treat him as something unclean, which indeed he was. They questioned him in Romanian and what sounded like German. On top of his weakness the mental effort of trying to understand was the last straw. He rolled off the bench.

When he came round he was cradled in the arms of a big man who was speaking with all the authority of his gray beard to the dubious villagers. With only the stern voice to go on, Bernardo expected to meet the uncompromising stare of a hard-boiled village headman who would do no more than open the parish lock-up for him, but the face when he looked up to it was more like that of a kindly headmaster in the flower of his age with very gentle eyes and a generous twinkle in the corners of them. He had at last a feeling that language was unnecessary.

The headman took him home, helped him to wash his feet,

undressed him and put him to bed. After feeling his forehead and taking his pulse he assured Bernardo with smiles and a gesture that there was nothing wrong which food and rest would not put right. Bernardo thanked him in Spanish which his savior obviously recognized but could not speak. Two motherly women came in with porridge and wine and a pot of broth with a wing of chicken in it. He thankfully resigned himself to this confident charity and slept.

In the morning his host and doctor allowed him to sit in a chair but not to move around. It still seemed remarkably easy to talk to him without words. There would be breakfast shortly, he said, and after that an interpreter. He was to put his trust in God that all would be well.

The interpreter arrived in the course of the morning. He had much the same fine-drawn face as Toledano. Evidently anyone who spoke Spanish in Romania was a Jew. Bernardo, bursting with gratitude, got in first with his questions: Where was he? Whom was he to thank for such kindness?

"In this village all are Jews," the man replied. "And this is our beloved leader, Rabbi Kaplan."

Bernardo had no idea that there were whole villages of Jews, and to his dazed eyes the night before they had not been at all recognizable. Fair hair was as common as dark, and there were as many squashed, broad noses as prominent beaks.

"I don't wonder your people were alarmed," he said. "I must have looked like a drowned dog."

"They are very simple," the interpreter explained, implying that he himself was a townsman. "They did not know what they should do until Rabbi Kaplan told them."

"So that was it! I thought he sounded annoyed. What did he tell them?"

"When a beggar stands at your door, the Holy One, Blessed be He, stands at his right hand."

Bernardo was still very weak and emotional. His eyes were inclined to swim at the sudden beauty of the phrase. It must sound even better in Hebrew and whatever dialect of German they spoke. He tried to remember some scrap of Hebrew in which to answer. Nothing came to mind except the First Commandment and a bit of some Jewish family prayer which his Jesuit teacher much admired. He always showed the other side at its best before shooting it down. And, by God, the phrase fitted!

"We lean back on our chairs in comfort and are no longer . . ."

"Servants" was the word he wanted but he could not recall it. He substituted "wanderers."

The interpreter's expression completely changed. Kaplan's could not fairly be said to change, but it was more joyful.

"What else do you know?"

Bernardo fired off the First Commandment to which the Rabbi replied with a blessing, though unintelligible.

There was a slight discussion between the two. The interpreter said that the Rabbi would like to be sure that Bernardo was circumcised.

"Since he undressed me . . ."

"He covered you with a blanket."

"What delicacy! But why should I mind? Here you are, friends!"

Mr. Brown explained that they were not really so credulous as they appeared. In the countries of Eastern Europe, where a Christian took pride in distinguishing himself from Moslem and Jew, the foreskin was a trademark. Even in Spain circumcision had been pretty rare. A Moldavian Jew, limited to his own space and time and ignorant of Gentile customs outside it, could not be expected to know that among the British, due to obsession with the Old Testament and venereal disease, circumcision was common. His English father, familiar with germs and funguses of seamen, insisted that it should be done regardless of the tearful reproaches of his Spanish mother.

He had felt a twinge of conscience. But, after all, he had never claimed to be a Jew; they jumped to the conclusion that he was. And since that splendid fellow, Kaplan, was prepared to treat a Christian with the same generosity there was some excuse for leaving matters alone.

"But the real clincher," he remembered, "was my Jesuitical Hebrew. I was thinking only of Kaplan's comfortable chair, and damned if I hadn't come out with the only bit of Hebrew which every Jew must know! I had not got it quite right, but near enough. Near enough."

Now the questions followed fast. He gave his name as David Mitrani — the only Sephardic surname he was sure of besides Toledano — and said truthfully that he had come from Hungary. He realized in the same breath that he should never have mentioned it in case someone spoke Hungarian. Fortunately nobody did.

Was he Hungarian then? David Mitrani pulled himself together and did some quick and instinctive thinking. Whatever was going to come of all this, he must do his best to ride his luck. Better not be English. Surely no English Jew would leave his own comfortable chair to wander round Romania wet and starving until he fetched up in Rabbi Kaplan's. He thought of Greece or Turkey, but they were too close. The interpreter was sure to ask what other Sephardic families he knew.

"From Africa," he said.

That seemed to go down well without any sophisticated inquiries as to whether he had French or British or Egyptian nationality. Details of Gentile government were considered trivial.

"And what happened to you?"

"I was robbed."

He had an uneasy feeling that he had lied again. But it was the literal truth though he had never quite pictured it as that. The late Bobo had robbed him of his identity and the gypsies of his money.

"And where were you going? We will help you on your journey."

"America," Bernardo said, vaguely remembering stories of shiploads of Jews decanted onto the quays of New York.

"Impossible! There is a quota. You cannot go from these countries any more."

"Well, I might go to Palestine."

To Eretz Israel! His suggestion aroused instant enthusiasm. He gathered that emigration to the homeland was so new that even Kaplan had little idea whether it was easy or not. But certainly young men had left Moldavia for Palestine. In Bucarest they would know how it must be done, and that was where he must go first.

Bernardo remained in the village by the banks of the Moldova for a week. It was the ghetto of the provincial capital, Roman, which stood above it on the hill. By observing his fellows and doing whatever the next man did half a second later he had no great trouble in conforming to religious and social customs. Only the ultra-pious students of the Torah remained aloof up some back alley of mysticism though he could read Hebrew quite as well as they. The workers in the fields who supported the lot were much the same as peasants anywhere else, and in talking with them he began to get on terms with Romanian. Rabbi Kaplan he loved. When a man was plainly a saint and followed all the Christian precepts, one could take it as a mere matter of words — a sort of donnish eccentricity — that he should still await the coming of the Messiah.

Whether Romanian authorities could not be bothered with despised Jews or whether quiet bribes continually sweetened hungry and insignificant clerks he did not know; but an identity card in the name of David Mitrani appeared from nowhere — proof of Romanian birth so long as no one ever questioned it. With that safely in his pocket he was given a third-class ticket to Bucarest, some introductions to co-religionists, a few lei for the journey and a pair of shoes to go with Mircea Niculescu's black suit — shrunk but still good enough for a poor *jidan*. Conscience worried him. He privately considered all this as a loan to be repaid whenever chance allowed.

He was accustomed to the uncleanliness of poverty in the open air, but hard to endure was the concentration of smells — mostly old frieze trousers, sweat and pickled cucumber — from the crowd of peasants crammed into a closed carriage for seven hours. He climbed down to the platform of the North Station of Bucarest and washed and shaved as best he could in a trickle of cold water. Morale improved. The bustling station of a capital city was a familiar, comforting environment. East European spaces had at last contracted to something he understood.

He set out for the British Consulate with growing confidence. Kalmody and Pozharski could have invented all this nonsense of extradition just to keep him quiet. Among his own people his appearance and story would only arouse pity; and, so far as the Romanians were concerned, his only offense was to have crossed the frontier illegally. There was no need to mention the horse or the dubious identity card supplied by Rabbi Kaplan.

It was a city of contrasts. Down by the station were low, white houses which seemed to have escaped from the country carrying a few chickens and pigs along with them; in the center was an air of Russian opulence with cupolas, heavy porches and over-decorated stone and plaster. He asked for the British Consulate and was directed by mistake to the Legation — a squarish town house of dignity with a noble iron gate. He hesitated in front of it. The Consulate would be more businesslike with competent clerks and an uncomfortable waiting room occupied by messengers with briefcases who would get what they came for and shabbier citizens who probably would not.

On second thoughts he considered that the Legation, pursuing its leisurely course beneath a Union Jack of gentlemanly size, might be the better choice. Someone would have time to listen to his complex story and might have heard of Count Kalmody and Zita.

A uniformed porter contemptuously asked him his business in Romanian. So that was what he looked like, did he? Bernardo slightly raised his eyebrows and answered in English, explaining that he had called on an affair of international interest and would like to see one of the secretaries. The porter suggested that the military attaché's clerk might be the chap for him. Bernardo denied having any military interests whatever and filled up a form.

Either his good accent or confident manner got him received, though he never knew whether it was the first, second or third secretary whom he saw. At any rate he was ushered into a very formal room on the ground floor. There was a desk with a large leather chair behind it and a similar chair, but without arms, in front of it. Around the wall were a number of third-class chairs, presumably for the reception of deputations. However the secretary himself was standing up — an indication that he did not judge this Mr. Brown to be of enough interest to justify a chat across the desk. He was wearing a black coat and striped trousers. His dark hair with a slight gray streak in it was immaculate. He had the strong, manly, virtuous face, the wide, thin-lipped mouth of the pre-war Establishment and could have been a distinguished barrister or an aspiring, young bishop.

Faced by this pillar of state, who was regarding the too short trousers and sleeves of Niculescu's suit with extreme distaste, Bernardo did not know how to begin. The consul, he now felt, would have been more used to objects deposited on his carpet by the cat.

"You are a British subject?" the secretary inquired.

"Yes, but I can't prove it here and now. My passport is in Bilbao in Spain. I was kidnaped."

"Kidnaped?"

The perfectly modulated voice suggested that such things really did not happen to holders of British passports.

"It was none of my doing."

"One would indeed imagine not."

"I was walking along the beach, sir, in Lequeitio. That's not far from Bilbao and the ex-Empress Zita lives there. A chap called Kalmody — Count Kalmody — was staying with her."

"I have had the honor of shooting with him."

"Oh, that's good! That will help to get things straightened out."

"What things, Mr. Brown?"

"Well, I don't know exactly. That's the worst of it. But there was a man who tried to burgle the Empress and another man called Bobo who . . ."

"Bobo?"

"That was what Count Kalmody called him. He said he was a Russian refugee or something."

"And you yourself have just arrived from Spain?"

"Well, with a bit of a gap, yes."

"I see. I should tell you at once, Brown, that this is not a matter in which His Majesty's representatives wish to be involved."

"You mean, you know about it?"

"I take it you are able to read. Really one can hardly be concerned in the violent death of a Russian grand duke without arousing some comment in the sensational papers."

"I haven't seen any papers and I'm innocent," Bernardo protested, desperately aware that his agitation must look like guilt. "And Count Kalmody knows all about it."

"It is very conceivable that he does. But Hungarians, I need hardly say, are not in very good odor at the moment."

"I don't see why. I think they have had a dirty deal."

"No doubt you will have opportunities later to give your opinion on foreign policy, Brown. But the game, as you people would call it, is up. You are wanted by the Spanish Government on a charge of murder. The French also wish to talk to you about the shooting of another of your accomplices. You will stay within these four walls while I telephone the police."

It had simply never occurred to the man, old Bernardo said, that his perfection was vulnerable. Mere consuls might sometimes have an inkpot thrown at them, but a diplomat within his own sacrosanct enclosure — unthinkable in those days. Unthinkable!

"But all changed now — both those exquisite dummies and our respect for them. They have become too human. That's the trouble. Oh dear and damn, I'm ashamed to admit what I did! But I hadn't got a knockout punch. In spite of the movies, I doubt if any amateur has with the bare fist. So if I hit him, he'd only spit out a tooth and yell for help, or perhaps ring a bell if that was more in accordance with protocol. He was still standing up, with his legs apart and his hands behind his back, looking down on me in every sense though I was only a yard away. I've never done such a thing before or since. I kicked him in the balls, if he had any, and walked out while he was doubled up gasping. The porter saluted, but no lordly tip from me! As soon as I was through those iron gates and round the corner I ran like hell and resumed the identity of David Mitrani."

He kept going, now walking fast, and arrived in the Calea Victoriei, the main street of Bucarest, where he was lost among the crowded, bobbing heads on the narrow pavement. Crossing a boulevard into what was apparently the business district, he saw the name of Strada Lipscani which Toledano had mentioned and thought of calling on the unknown cousin whose name was now his, but decided it was far too dangerous. The only chance of safety was to find some obscurer Spanish-speaking Jews and disappear among them. It looked as if he might be fated to remain David Mitrani for the rest of his life, and he relieved that depressing thought by a moment of optimistic daydream. He could become an international banker with a white slip to his waistcoat and offices in Bucarest and London. Hell! How did one eat meanwhile?

Till dusk fell Bernardo wandered about in short streets which had neither the rich-peasant quality of the inner suburbs nor the solidity of the center. The houses had an air of being closed to the street rather than opening onto it, and this Levantine effect was enhanced by a few small antique shops, poorly lit but glowing all the more mysteriously with Persian and Romanian rugs, ikons and silverwork. Hanging about the entrance to a café — for he had too little money to risk going in — he heard plenty of Yiddish and what was probably modern Greek, but none of the hoped-for Spanish.

He cheated hunger by a roll of bread and a slice of sausage at an unswept underground tavern and allowed himself half a liter of coarse wine. The problem now was where to spend the night. It was warm enough and a doorstep would do, but he was afraid that vagrants might be picked up by those sallow policemen occasionally glimpsed under the lights. Some kind of description of him must by now have been given by the Legation. It could only say that he had dark hair, brown eyes and a black suit too small for him: a description which covered a good half of the citizens. However, it would also emphasize that the wanted man almost certainly could not speak Romanian, which meant that he must avoid the Law until he did.

As he moved aimlessly onwards, this senile quarter of Bucarest began to decompose. The drains smelt. Here and there houses were decayed, just habitable or half empty. Often a two-horse cab trotted into the district with a man and a woman in it. He noticed more couples on foot. Evidently this was a colony of prostitutes — not beckoning from doorways or hanging out of windows to attract customers, but carrying home to their nests the prey they had scavenged in the gayer center of the city.

He heard the trade using scraps of French. The language always turned up — an inheritance from cultured circles of the Ottoman Empire reinforced by the French divisions which had liberated Bucarest. He entered into conversation with a motherly looking soul who had just got rid of a blue-uniformed officer — the cab had waited — and was slinging a basin of water into the street. Was there anywhere nearby where he could stay the night? She had the experience of her profession and after a glance at him must have known that this shabby clerk meant what he said and no more.

"*Entrez donc, mon petit, et on parlera.*"

She had one room on the ground floor where a weak electric bulb under a worn, red velvet shade gave just enough light to show the color of an expensive, purple wallpaper of the nineteenth century, its cracks forming an imperial home for the bed bugs which had blotched her arms. There were a mahogany wardrobe, a tousled bed with a half-filled pisspot beneath it, a full-length mirror and a table smeared with the filth of years of heavy makeup. Sordid, yes; but at the same time the light, the paper, the rugs on the floor and the cover of the divan bed which lay crumpled on top of them gave an impression not — God help us! — of any romance, but of some cavern where a destitute refugee had left the remains of wealth to rot.

"What are you?" she asked.

"I come from Africa."

"A Jew?"

He could not guess how she had jumped to the right con-clusion, or temporarily right. Perhaps the half-starved wage slaves of Romanian offices usually were, especially in that district which was some sort of distant relative of the business quarter.

Bernardo said that he was.

"Me, too."

She tried him with Yiddish, apologizing for speaking it badly. She had been brought up as a servant in a Gentile family, she said, omitting all other details.

"I do not speak it at all. In Africa we speak Spanish."

"There are not many of you here. But I know one. *Tiens!* She could use you if you're a decent fellow and as strong as you look."

All this while she had been busy with repairs, having re-moved the red velvet shade. It was a hasty job with powder, mascara and lipstick in order not to be late for further busi-ness. Out of it all emerged a woman with at least magnificent hair and eyes — presentable if the next customer liked a reasonable amount of fat and had drunk enough not to care how it was distributed.

"This is the Crucea de Piatra. Turn right into Strada Bradului and opposite the church of Saint Spiridon is number fifty-two. One goes up a ladder at the back. Ask for Susana, but wait at the church till she is free. Tell her that Eva sent you."

Bernardo thanked Madame with great respect and found the church of St. Spiridon — a solid, little home for him with a green, onion dome. From the dark angle of the apse he watched the narrow front of number 52. Nobody came out. Nobody went in. It was impossible to guess whether Susana was at the moment earning her living or not. He decided to risk it and entered a passage under the house. This gave onto a courtyard where he saw Eva's "ladder" which turned out to be an outside stair with carved balusters leading to a balcony with a single door on it.

He went up and knocked. From within there was an alarmed squeak and somebody double-locked the door. Bernardo explained in Spanish — good, pure stuff without the heartiness of Basque ports — that Eva had sent him and that he begged a moment of Susana's distinguished presence.

The door opened. In the half light the girl, clinging to a green wrap, was an attractive vision. She had red hair, fine, high breasts, a wasp waist and the most exaggeratedly wide hips, though fairly slim before and behind.

"Come in, *señor!* Eva is a good woman and very wise."

Bernardo was inclined to agree — leaving aside her profession and her taste in interior decoration. Susana's room was bare and clean, reminding him faintly of the inn at the junction. It was possible that the image she wished to create for herself and her clients was that of a modest girl from the country, whereas Eva had gone for the Balkan *femme fatale.* They would have been more in character the other way round.

He gave some account of himself, making his birthplace Morocco. Feeling too tired for any original invention, he stuck to his story of delivering a horse, saying that he had come by ship as groom to an Arab stallion, that nobody would have anything to do with him when he arrived and that he was penniless.

"You know what I am?"

"Very beautiful," Bernardo answered.

"That's as may be. But original, true? So there are difficulties. I ask you, what do they expect for their money? I am not an animal."

Bernardo did not altogether understand and played for time.

"That can be seen, *muy señorita mia*," he replied very courteously. "Where do you come from, if I may ask?"

"Galatz. But I was born in Salonica. The family of Marguliesh."

"It would be an honor to serve any of them."

"It's that I need a protector — one I can trust of our own people."

A ponce, Good Lord! Bernardo was appalled but preserved his formal manners.

"I am very innocent. Tell me a little more!"

"Look! Some men are brutes. And there is something about me" — she patted her strange body — "which sends them mad. The things they want me to do!"

He could vaguely see it. From the front her figure-of-eight shape had some resemblance to that of a Stone-Age goddess. Apparently tastes had not changed much in twenty thousand years.

"There is an attic. You can sleep there. And if you hear me call for help . . ."

"But I am no *valiente!*"

"Who wants you to be? Show yourself — that will be enough. Remember that a man without his trousers is at a disadvantage! Stay with me, David! I will give you a share of what I earn and myself when you wish."

Bernardo considered the proposal. He was at the very bottom of society and ready to think kindly of others who could never leave it. After all, the only revolting thing about a ponce was that he shared his woman with the town and lived on her earnings. Leave out all that, and he might manage — with an effort — to think of himself as a poor knight errant up in the attic.

"Look, dear Susana! I accept on condition that you speak Romanian and nothing but Romanian with me and give me a meal on days when I cannot pay for one. I will not share your money, and I am your cousin from Africa so it would be wrong to sleep with you."

"Well, man, if you don't want to, you don't have to," Susana replied touchily. "I've enough of it without you. But you must come down when I call and look fierce and swear if a client says he has no money."

"I will swear in French, and they will think I am an Apache. That will give us both a position in society."

Bernardo moved into the attic where he became the owner of an old bed, a dirty blanket and a basin to catch drips from the roof; it could also be filled at the tap downstairs for washing. He needed no more; a week was enough to accustom him to medieval poverty. As for the business of protecting Susana, it was seldom pressing. He extracted a watch from a Bulgar who wouldn't pay and was too full of liquor to do more than goggle at the blast of French, and he escorted down the stairs as far as the nearest cab a very respectable old gentleman whose tastes had proved too exotic for Susana. He had to wait many minutes listening to reminiscences of far-off youth in Paris, together with complaints of the callousness of the younger generation, and received a handsome tip for his courtesy. He gathered that his behavior was in the finest tradition of the ponces of the Second Empire.

Susana was really too innocent for her profession. She demanded speed and simplicity and was offended by any attempt to add a bit of artistry to the proceedings. For this Bernardo was thankful. As it was, the straightforward sounds from below poisoned his memories of Magda. Meanwhile by the light of a candle he read old newspapers scavenged from the street and during the day held Susana to her part of the bargain so that he learned Romanian fast. Only one sound gave him trouble until he realized that it was identical with the murmur which the English used for almost any vowel, itself exceedingly difficult for a foreigner to imitate. If you spoke with mouth open instead of Englishly shut, you had it.

The local policeman interviewed him and accepted his identity card without question, showing no surprise that a Moroccan Jew, though born in Roman, should speak Romanian badly. A pious member of the Orthodox Church, he only interfered with the activities of Christian ponces and obtained his occasional satisfaction only from Christian whores. So long as Susana paid him a small weekly subvention and Bernardo caused no complaints, he was uninterested in both of them.

"I look back with reasonable tolerance," Mr. Brown said, "but when I do I can still smell the Crucea de Piatra. Never mind the drains! One gets used to last year's urine. It was a smell of unaired rooms and spilt, trodden food and the female animal. All half-lit. Always. The cheerfulness of a brothel is far less shaming — I'm talking of the shamefulness of poverty, not the false shame of sex — than those women fornicating away for a living, swabbing themselves with drugs and disinfectants which had gone rotten and calling in the old midwife with her knitting needle when all else failed. I was celibate as a hermit. That crawling of randy maggots from flesh to flesh between one street lamp and another — it put me off. I wonder if a continuous, insistent, sexual environment isn't nature's way of reducing overpopulation."

Susana was attractive enough for an afternoon stroll in the fashionable Calea Victoriei which sometimes resulted in an invitation to spend the night in bachelor apartments. She insisted that she could act a show of reluctance convincingly. A really conscientious ponce should, Bernardo felt, persuade her to display her Stone-Age allurements in a town where she was less well known and to get herself set up in a flat by some mature merchant or local politician who would be quite content with her modest accomplishments. Whenever he knew she would not be home he was free to explore the city, always careful to be part of a moving line of ants, never loitering by himself, and avoiding contact with any sort of public servant, even a tram conductor. The loneliness of it all did not greatly affect him. He was sensitive to the life of Bucarest just as he had been to the sea and mountains of his home.

On one of those days when he knew his services would not be required he set out through the straggling suburbs into the meadowland of Wallachia — richer and more welcoming country than the blank and endless spaces of the northern province of Moldavia. He could not stride out as steadily as in days when he had plenty to eat and more than plenty to drink but covered enough ground to get the flavor of this greener land of streams and lakes, willows and buffalo, all basking in the heat of September.

Sanctuary

In the distance, above the scattered shanties and desert spaces where the main road entered Bucarest, dust hung like a thunder cloud, its underside lit by red flares; out of it came a faint, inexplicable racket in which he could occasionally distinguish the hooting of a cornet or the boom of a euphonium. The noise suggested the practice ground of a municipal band but was too all-pervading for anything of the sort.

It was Bucarest's annual fair, the Mosh. Bernardo, like some ten thousand of his fellow citizens, was primitively excited by the size of it, the deafening row and the ceaseless activity. The wide central alley, half a kilometer of it, was lined on both sides by tented shops, shooting galleries and amusement booths, separated by bars and cafés each of which had its own band of musicians. Bernardo fortunately had something left of the tip given him for his poncial assistance to the aged, and the cheap quenching of thirst seemed to be the main industry of the place at night. He sat down and ordered a large glass of *pelin*, a delectable Romanian drink with which he was temporarily in love, consisting of new white wine treated with much the same herbs as vermouth. One ear enjoyed the traditional violin, double bass and cimbalon of gypsies while the other was blasted by a village band playing what might be Lehar on leaking instruments including two brass-bound leather serpents. A cross-section of Romania paraded gaily through the dust, from peasants in their best embroidered shirts to Bucarest society monopolizing the shooting galleries and hoopla stalls, paying a band for the loan of instruments during the rare intervals and trying to do better until incapable with laughter.

Bernardo had no money to waste on sideshows, none of which, anyway, could have given him so much entertainment as merely watching. He realized that he had moved back a

119

hundred years to the time when there were few shops in rural communities, when a man's need for hard ware or a woman's for soft ware could only be satisfied by setting out with horse and cart to the nearest fair. He wandered off into the narrower alleys where the booths were smaller and poorer and the peasants did their shopping within sight of their carts. Here the sideshows were tuned to an agricultural community: gypsy fortunetellers, small circuses and monsters, of which he could manage to catch a glimpse without paying whenever the curtains of sacking or canvas were pulled aside. A calf with an extra leg, a piglet with two heads — stuffed, that one — and sheep with spectacular deformities were carefully kept for exhibition. They stood in their straw, tame and apathetic.

At the top of the fair on a cross alley serving both peasants and more moneyed townsmen were some slightly superior booths with fat ladies, acrobats and the odd crocodile or dancing bear. One shabby tent had an announcement of "Interesting Deformity" over its arched entrance and a colored placard of a vaguely oriental beauty which underlined the adjective. "Interesting" in that trade — or his, for that matter — invariably implied some sexual abnormality.

Double canvas flaps with the pay box between them prevented any onlooker seeing what was inside. The public were admitted a dozen at a time. Bernardo observed the merry faces which went in and the more solemn faces which emerged. Whatever deformity was being shown was so grotesque, so unacceptable to the subconscious that it changed the mood even of a rich peasant being supported by his fellows. He was so mystified by the reaction of the public that he paid the ten lei demanded — five times the price to see a five-legged calf — and went inside.

A young girl, looking about fifteen, sat on a divan behind a red rope, quiet and expressionless like some sexless guardian angel in a nursery picture. She had an oval Slav face with huge, gray eyes and fair hair in long plaits. Below the waist she was dressed in floppy trousers which conformed to the popular idea of an inmate of a Turkish harem and justified the placard outside the booth. Over her shoulders she had a short, crimson cloak held together by one hand — a slender hand which fitted the delicacy of her face.

When the requisite number of voyeurs were assembled in front of the rope she threw open the cloak twice in quick succession: once to startle, once for a rather longer interval so that the audience could believe their eyes. She had four breasts, all normal except that the lower pair were slightly fuller and irregular.

Bernardo exclaimed, "Good God!" — half from surprise, half from indignation, for the quality of that glorious, stained-glass face descending from high cheekbones had fascinated him. It was withdrawn, but one thought of it as alive and accepting rather than apathetic. The gray eyes, set wide apart, looked straight into his own.

"I can't help it," she said in English.

"Of course you can't, but . . ."

"There was nothing else."

As he went out he glanced back at her. She was still motionless in her absurd costume but responded with a slight half-smile. English? He thought not. He had detected in her few words a slight accent. What then? And how? And what were the police doing to allow it? Or did anything go at the Mosh so long as the exhibition was limited to a second and five seconds? He walked off in a rage, aware that it was a form of the same reaction as that of those too solemn spectators emerging from the booth and arguing. He should not have been shocked. After more than two weeks of living in a colony of apes his view of the erogenous zones of the female was as clinical as any doctor's. But this hit at something deeper; there was more to it than the pity and indignity of the exhibition. A degradation of motherhood, perhaps. Apes? But presumably they would not notice the deformity at all, such curiosity being the very essence of humanity. "Know thyself" was without limits — though, thank you very much, he'd had about enough of it down in the stews.

The Englishman in him recommended calm, reminding him that the exhibition of deformities was certainly in the worst of taste but no business of his. How about cripples showing their sores on the steps of a church? The Spaniard replied furiously that the cripple was an opportunity for Christian charity and a reminder that there, but for the Grace of God, go I. The position of this unfortunate child was entirely different and an outrage, and something must be done about it. That something might well be easier for him, at the bottom of the dregs of society, than for a more respectable citizen using respectable and probably futile methods. At least he knew the full, bitter meaning of "there was nothing else."

It was going to be difficult to talk to her. There must have been a number of kinky people, satiated with normality, who wanted to talk to her. But she did not look as if her proprietor sold her services at the market price for curiosities, whatever that was. Her passivity was not that of a prostitute, nor had she the drawn face. He had by now a theory that the recognizable features of a hard-working whore were not in the least due to supposed licentiousness but to sheer boredom, together with the effort and the cosmetics necessary to disguise it.

Bernardo, being no innocent, put himself in the confessional box and inquired whether he himself was not attracted by two extra breasts. He easily gave himself absolution on that score; his sin, if any, was in being revolted by them. No, he was not thinking of the girl in any way as an object of desire. The nursery-angelface made him feel more like a father than a lover. Preposterous! Well, say, an elder brother.

Could the showman be her father? He had only noticed the top of the man's head at the pay box and a round face when he drew the curtain. All he remembered was that the chap, unlike most Romanians at that hour of night, appeared very clean-shaven. Had there been any other woman about? Not at the booth, but possibly in the caravan or whatever vehicle they used for traveling. He was tempted to go back in the early morning while Susana slept. The Mosh without its roar and excitement would be worth seeing.

Next day he walked down the interminable length of the Boulevard Elisabeta against the stream of packed trams and pedestrians going to work. He could smell the Mosh half a mile away — an odor of dust and animals and rotting straw. The main alley was fairly empty with the air of a night club or café being cleaned up on the morning after. The side alleys, however, were busy with buying and selling in the cattle markets and the shops. It was the time of the peasants, rich and poor, some of them with steps already unsteady after too much *tsuica* for breakfast.

He joined a thin crowd of onlookers round the horse market, where he could keep an eye on the front of the "interesting" exhibition deserted and sordid in the morning sun. For half an hour there was nothing to see except the collection of undersized animals which were being sold — a wretched lot to the eye, though any pair of them were able to draw a laden peasant cart through a long day on a diet of maize stalks. All heads turned as a cavalcade of Bessarabian horse dealers cantered out of the main alley, well mounted and flaunting cloaks of black and red which reminded him of those left behind in the station restaurant of Oradea Mare. The owner of angelface popped out of his booth and exchanged greetings with one of the riders. The language, melancholy on one side, hearty on the other, was Russian.

The man's high voice drew Bernardo's closer attention. The face was not clean-shaven; it had no hair at all and was spider-webbed with fine lines. A eunuch, by God! He would have been recognized for what he was by all Bucarest since the town was proud of its sect of cab drivers whose smart *trasuras* and well-paired horses stood in the rank outside the royal palace. The drivers belonged to a heretical sect of the Ortho-dox Church who were so appalled by the sins of the flesh that a man was only allowed two children from his marriage. He then submitted to castration, thus preserving his soul from the devil, the family from extinction and himself — Bernardo thought bitterly — from the hell of a lot of misery.

The discovery confirmed his opinion that it would be fatal to appear in the guise of a pimp. Whatever the beliefs of these pervertedly pious fellows, it was most unlikely that they would sell their daughters. But she couldn't be his daughter. One surely didn't learn English in remote Bessarabian villages.

He tried to open conversation with the showman in his very limited Romanian.

"Beautiful!" he exclaimed, pointing to the riders.

"Blestemat!"

Bernardo knew that word — damned — for it was a com-mon curse. Possibly the chap was using it literally.

"Why?"

Some of the answer was unintelligible except for nouns with Latin roots. Bernardo gathered that he was being lectured on the iniquity of horse dealers who would all go to hell. Dear old Kovacs would have agreed, but for different reasons.

"I do not understand. I am English."

An impulsive bit of lunacy that was from David Mitrani, Sephardic Jew! But it worked.

"Come inside!"

The eunuch had not recognized Bernardo as one of the quickly passing spectators of the previous night. He led the way through the exhibition booth and out at the back into a canvas extension with a divan, a table and a chair in it. The girl was there, dressed out of business hours in embroidered peasant blouse and skirt. She only appeared to have a clumsy figure, very round with puppy fat. She knew him at once, but was careful not to give it away. Her eyes met his with no more than a lighthouse flash of intelligence, almost mischievous intelligence.

The eunuch made a commanding speech to her in Russian. She looked at him with eyes which were now abstracted, wide and luminous like those of a cat withdrawn into its own thoughts.

"Mr. Stepanov wants me to explain to you that no one can be a Christian who does not avoid the sins of the flesh, and that one must feel pity for riders who only want to attract women. Now, we must talk very seriously as if you believed it," she added without any change of tone.

Bernardo realized without the need for more analysis what it was which had forced him to return. Not her startling beauty. Not curiosity. Not even her impulsive recognition of him as a person to whom some explanation was due. It was her youth. One couldn't call it a radiant youth when, under the circumstances, it was only able to radiate into itself; but, seeing her dressed with the normal gaiety of a Romanian girl, the sordidness of the show and the abnormality no longer disturbed him. Youth triumphed over the lot and held out some sort of invisible hand for companionship. He was young enough himself to receive the message and old enough to respond considerately. She was in no way comparable to charitable objects on the steps of a Spanish church. It was evident that she expected a social equal — leaving out for the moment whether the Crucea de Piatra or a Jesuit College was responsible for the equality — to have some manners, neither repelled by unfortunate accidents of birth nor stickying the place up with the spilt milk of human kindness.

"Hallelujah!" Bernardo answered piously. "What are you?"

"Russian."

"A refugee?"

"Of course."

"Can I help? I didn't come back because . . ."

"I know that."

"But what is a girl like you doing here?"

He could have kicked himself for the appalling banality of the compliment. She must have heard it dozens of times before.

If she had, she ignored the futility of it as irrelevant.

"I told you. There was nothing else for me."

Stepanov broke in suspiciously and she replied to him at length.

"What was that?" Bernardo asked.

"He wanted to know what your religion was. I said you were a Lutheran."

"How do you know?"

"My governess told me all the English were Lutherans."

"Tell me quickly — how can I see you again? He's not going to be taken in by this much longer. I am very poor and out of work, but I will try to do something."

"The Mosh is over on Saturday and then we go to Craiova. Perhaps you can find us on the road. He may go out drinking. What is your name?"

"David."

"I am Nadya. If I never see you any more, God be with you, David!"

Old Mr. Brown remembered how easily that could have been that. He dared not risk taking to the road penniless and drawing attention to himself by bad Romanian. It only needed one policeman suspicious enough to check the antecedents of David Mitrani, and then the trail led straight back to the station of Pashcani, the crossing of the frontier and Bernardo Brown, assassin and assaulter of diplomats.

No, he was not as mad as all that. He might have committed any folly for another sight of Magda, but his quixotic impulse to get young Nadya out of there had not the drive of sex behind it. His helplessness emphasized indignation. To that extent she was an extra spur. He had to restart his life landing any honest job on the way towards Mitrani & Co., Merchant Bankers.

He spent a further two weeks in Susana's attic, bullying her into conversation, reading his old newspapers and getting by heart a Romanian grammar which had been kindly stolen for him by a colleague.

"I got on all right with the other fellows," he said. "A flashy lot of bullies they were. Living on a woman gives a man such a vicious inferiority complex that he has to dress and behave like a professional thug with a dummy gun. Very understandable. Proof that we find it right and natural that a woman should be supported by a man. If it ever comes to real equality of the sexes we'll be paying the head-shrinkers overtime."

Everyone in the Crucea de Piatra knew the pleasant-mannered Sephardic ponce who was forcing himself to speak the language decently. He was a joke, rather like the office clerk who takes business as a farce but is twice as efficient as anyone else when he puts his mind to it. He was often called in to interpret when there was some row with a foreigner flaming enough for a whore to screech and the cockroaches to take cover. That brought in a small personal percentage of any money extorted and occasionally a few tips, so that he was no longer dependent on Susana for a meal ticket and could sometimes take her out to a tavern and pay the bill. When he had to speak English, he said his few words in so uncouth an accent that no one could ever suspect it was his mother tongue.

These diplomatic efforts to calm down excitement and oil the wheels of fornication led to the approval of the local cop who easily accepted Mitrani's story that Romanian was coming back to memory from babyhood in Moldavia. It never occurred to him, naturally enough, that a well-trained mind stocked with two Latin languages could get on terms with a third in a matter of weeks.

"Why doesn't a decent fellow like you believe in Christ?" he asked.

Bernardo was quite prepared to put up a convincing defense of Jewry, but the technical terms of theology had not turned up in local conversation or the newspapers. The cop was unlikely to understand them anyway and content to leave spiritual matters to St. Spiridon.

"One believes what one is brought up to believe," Bernardo answered. "There is no way out."

"There is, Mitrani. There is."

"When I pass your priest, he does not see me."

"Why should he? But English priests are different."

"What have the English got to do with it?" Bernardo asked, alarmed.

"There is a Mission to the Jews, so that they may go to heaven like the rest of us. But in my opinion that is not certain. Salvation is only through the Orthodox Church."

"Not the Catholics, too?"

"They worship images and are doomed in the next world."

"Then they'd better stick together in this one like the Jews."

Sanctuary

"The Mission knows that, Mitrani, and sees that converts are looked after."

"Who told you?"

"My sister is the concierge."

He gave Bernardo the address of the Mission to the Jews, which was across the River Dâmbovitsa in a district of old-fashioned Romanians, tactfully secluded far from the business quarter.

Bernardo at once appreciated the possibilities. If he allowed himself to be converted, it would reinforce his identity, always assuming he could remain in the shadows and not be a public pet of priests. It seemed probable that he could. The Mission was one of the kindly eccentricities of the Church of England and of no interest to the Orthodox.

He cautiously reconnoitered the place, was received by the sister with obvious distaste and directed up to the flat of the Reverend Jacob Polack. He expected some muscular and belligerent Christian, but found instead a neat little figure with a white, pointed beard, himself a converted Jew and earnest as a hen sparrow gathering scraps for her nest. There was something odd and endearing about his Anglican dog collar above a dark gray suit. The Semitic features would have better fitted the robes and whiskers of an Orthodox papa, but could never have given such an air of sincere humility.

The missioner was pleased to be asked for instruction by a Sephardic Jew. He said that they were normally too proud of their history; perhaps if he had spoken Spanish, not Yiddish, he might have had more success. His own background was the Lithuanian pale and Manchester. Seeing that Bernardo's Romanian was faulty, he asked if he had any English. No, none at all. They settled for French which Polack spoke fluently with a strong German accent.

Bernardo attended four times a week, pretending to be

eager and in fact hurrying to get it over before he was caught out. Polack was shocked by his ignorance of Jewish religion and assumed it was the fault of Morocco and his parents. Bernardo, as a former pupil of Jesuits, was also shocked. His new teacher stuck closely to his evangelical brief, regarding as irrelevant the logic and mysticism of this most complex of religions. At home in the attic, as a distraction from Susana's bed shaking like a honeymoon hotel with varying standards of skill and enthusiasm, he wondered what kind of traitor he was — at any rate no worse than the odd dozen of Polack's other converts whom he strongly suspected of changing their beliefs for material advantages. He decided that Rabbi Kaplan would have doubtfully forgiven him, even smiled perhaps. That was a comfort.

He was duly rebaptized in the presence of a small congregation consisting of some hand-picked converts and ageless Englishwomen — governesses, secretaries and still unmodified wives of Romanians — triumphantly dabbing pale eyes with lace-trimmed handkerchiefs. His godfathers were Polack himself and a clerk at the Legation who had fortunately been busy behind his desk at the time of Bernardo's visit. And now conclusively and officially he became David Mitrani. Rabbi Kaplan's dubious identity card was surrendered to the Prefectura which — in these gratifying circumstances — did not question it and issued a new one stating that he was Christian and a Romanian citizen by birth.

He had hoped to keep his conversion secret in the quarter, but that was impossible. The cop, seeing himself as an instrument of divinity, proclaimed his success. Nobody else approved, the Jews being disgusted and the Christians resentful that an outcast had managed to get into the club by the back door. Susana did not care what he chose to call himself, but saw right through him as a ponce. He had despised her, she said, and all that stuff about not being her lover because he was her African cousin was as false as he was. She turned him out in a passion of tears and fury; he was temporarily put up in a bare and tiny hostel kept by the Mission for similar family troubles.

The Reverend Jacob Polack in spite of his humility was no fool when it came to disposing of his converts. He had his lines out in many unexpected quarters, chiefly shops, where the energy of the Jew was most welcome provided he was Christian. The exact nature of Mitrani's former employment had never been specified. Certainly he had been earning a living in a regrettable district, but a man does what he must. Both the cop and the priest of St. Spiridon — who now felt able to say good morning — bore witness to his comparative honesty and good influence. On the strength of his languages and his experience — as Polack delicately put it — of certain social evils, Bernardo was offered the job of night porter at the Hotel Principesa. It was a hotel for cabaret artistes and — which Polack had not perhaps realized — of stern respectability. Gentlemen, unless themselves in the profession, were not admitted.

4. Dniester to Danube

MR. BROWN described his new employment as one step up in the entertainment industry. But no monkey business at all. Any enterprising night porter at the Ritz would have far more chance of making a bit of money by keeping his mouth shut. Still, it was useful experience, he said, and not without its lighter side.

The artistes left the hotel about ten at night and back they came at four in the morning. What they did in the afternoon was nobody's business but they couldn't do it at the Principesa. Bernardo gathered from their squirts of conversation that most of them were neither more nor less respectable than a bunch of honest seamstresses saving up for an eventual husband and only unfaithful to that rather shadowy figure of the future when a customer became so infatuated that he might possibly be it.

And he could become infatuated. They were a handsome lot on the top near eastern circuit, passing from one Balkan capital to another, then on to Istanbul, Beirut and Alexandria and back on the same route to Budapest. That was the exchange station where the scouts were, the center of a figure of eight. If a girl were really irresistible in person or performance she might be engaged for the western circuit — Vienna, Brussels, Paris, Madrid and other productive spots where the champagne was not white wine injected with carbonic-acid gas and most of the customers would be wearing dinner jackets and stiff shirts.

While in Bucarest many of these deliciously second-rate cuties stayed at the Principesa. They were of all nations, from Hungarians with the proud bearing and panache of the race to Russian refugees of exquisite manners and melancholy whom one longed to comfort. A most expensive process. So far as the floor show went, they were none of them remarkable; they sang or danced appealingly but the limit of originality was an English hornpipe or a Dutch clog dance, both appearing reasonably exotic along the lower reaches of the Danube.

Male guests in the hotel were few: generally husbands or dancing partners. Occasionally there would be a well-paid entertainer from the western circuit engaged to pull in new customers who normally preferred a bird in hand to a bird at a cabaret table. The Romanian public did not think much of acrobats and comics but appreciated conjurers. The invisible transfer of property from one person's pocket to another appealed to them.

Perseus, Prince of the Rosicrucians, had taken a room at the Principesa for the three weeks of his engagement. Bernardo met him while washing down the men's lavatories — a tiled and dignified ensemble when first installed but still suffering from the playful habits of German soldiery billeted in the hotel. The girls' establishment next door had not helped. In spite of notices they were inclined to get rid of unnecessary objects, shut their eyes and pull the plug. It was this problem of disposal which now occupied Bernardo. With a bucket and mop at his side he was manfully driving a plunger down into the unknown viscera of the hotel where male and female elements were united. He had two hours of the night ahead of him in which to clear the system before the little dears returned. Failing a charge of dynamite he doubted if that would be enough.

Perseus, a dark and romantic figure in a Chinese dressing gown, hesitated at the outer door across which Bernardo had built a dam of sacking.

"I think that I had better borrow your boots," he said in excellent French.

"For a personage as distinguished as monsieur," Bernardo answered, "I hesitate . . ."

"Well, what would you advise me to do?"

"May I suggest a hotel of more modern comfort?"

"It is my first visit. I was told this was the right place for a performer. One's needs would be appreciated."

Bernardo could well understand that the Prince of the Rosicrucians, his doves, his goldfish and the secrets of his trunks might be out of place in the first-class hotel which he could easily have afforded. He was at the top of his profession: an amazing fellow, able to stop and talk at any table, remove a watch or cigarette case undetected and then accuse some innocent member of the public on the other side of the cabaret which he had never visited of having it on his person. He was equally good at arousing gasps of disbelief and yells of laughter.

"And I am not talking of tomorrow, *mon brave*. This is pressing," Perseus added sternly.

His eyes were becoming fixed and desperate. Bernardo realized that in such a situation magic was no help and gratitude would be generous.

"If monsieur would have the goodness to follow me," Bernardo invited, proceeding up the passage in his socks.

There was only one private bathroom in the hotel which would undoubtedly have been allotted to Perseus if it had not been already occupied by Mme. Hortense, a French contralto of opulent middle age and magnificent shoulders who had once been described — and had the newspaper cutting to prove it — as the Nightingale of Milan. Her voice was still true but its power had so faded that it could safely be exploded in the limited space of a cabaret. She, like Perseus, was not required to sit at tables and so retired early to the Principesa. It was necessary for her to calm her nerves before going to bed. She had explained this dramatically to Bernardo when sending him out to buy a bottle of brandy.

Bernardo opened Mme. Hortense's door with his pass key. The inner door to the bedroom was safely shut; the bathroom was half open. Perseus eyed the excellent sanitary equipment with the same expression of delighted relief which he used when a goldfish flung into his empty top hat appeared a second later floating comfortably in a a bowl of water.

"Our guest sleeps very soundly, monsieur," Bernardo said. "But may I recommend a certain discretion?"

It was most unlikely that the Prince of the Rosicrucians had any money in the dragon-embroidered pocket of his dressing gown; so Bernardo waited to accompany him back to his room and wish him pleasant dreams. Meanwhile he stayed on guard in the passage, a trusty figure in his black and yellow waistcoat.

Perseus was in no hurry. He might be merely meditating or possibly considering all the magic potentialities of an unwinding toilet roll — though in those days that would have been thought intolerably vulgar. Bernardo was appalled to hear Mme. Hortense open her door, a fierce contralto oath

135

as she bumped into the handle, a rattling at the locked bathroom and what sounded like a heave of the immaculate shoulders.

Pretending to have been attracted by the noise and just arrived, Bernardo inquired through the door if there were anything wrong. Mme. Hortense flung it open. She was attired in a vast and virginal cloud of whiteness as if for a belated first communion.

"There is some sort of dirty pig in my bathroom!"

She was swaying a little and, Bernardo hoped, incapable of lucid observation. He declared with confidence that the door must be stuck and rattled it cautiously.

"*Fais pas l'idiot!*"

"Madame?"

"One shits. I heard it."

"It is perhaps a chambermaid, Madame. I will report the matter to the manager. Meanwhile if Madame would be good enough to accompany me . . ."

There was only one refuge and that was the manager's private bathroom. It was kept locked, but Bernardo knew very well that the key was over the door frame. He had not offered its facilities to Perseus since the manager was awake and working and might come up from his office any moment.

Madame cheerfully rollicked behind him from side to side of the corridor, entertaining herself with the "Soldiers' Chorus" from Faust. Bernardo quickly shut the door on her and returned to the Prince of the Rosicrucians to report that the coast was clear. Perseus had decided that for himself. Five minutes later Mme. Hortense, now prettily baby-carolling "*Sur le Pont d'Avignon*" returned to her room. Bernardo locked the managerial bathroom, returned the key to its hiding place and resumed his menial occupation.

When the day porter took over, he went to bed with an

untroubled conscience. He had done his duty. There had been a sense of satisfaction when with one tremendous gurgle the waters of Yin and Yang had simultaneously returned beneath the earth. It was the first time he had been of honest service to his fellows since gallantly agreeing to cause no embarrassment to Zita.

He was roused soon after eleven by the manager, sternly inquiring whether he had been awake all night and what his movements were. It appeared that some petty thief had got into the hotel unless it was an inside job. Bernardo accounted for his time, but was ordered to proceed immediately to the bedroom floor.

The whole corridor was enjoying the excitement. Doors were half open with unmade-up faces, pale yellow from lack of sun, looking out and twittering. A chambermaid was in tears. The Nightingale of Milan was in full voice.

"But I tell you they are not lost. They are not in the laundry. They were laid decently upon a chair. They have disappeared while I slept as in my mother's arms. I have been robbed, I tell you!"

Bernardo asked exactly what was missing.

"Mon caleçon!"

He could of course have stolen her drawers while she was out of the room. So could the supposed chambermaid, who must be cleared at once. He was about to confess the incident of the night when it occurred to him that she herself had never mentioned it. What was the catch? She must surely remember.

"Madame, I hope, does not accuse me?"

"I accuse no one. Give me back my drawers and not a word more!"

"Perhaps the maid may be allowed to search Madame's room?" the manager suggested.

"On no account!"

She slammed the door. Possibly she was embarrassed by the empty bottles at the bottom of the cupboard, yet the chambermaid knew as well as Bernardo how the Nightingale calmed her nerves.

It seemed unlikely that the Prince of the Rosicrucians was a type to steal female underclothing. But in spite of the racket not a sound came from behind his closed door. That was suspicious. When the passage had cleared, Bernardo knocked on his door, knocking more loudly when there was no answer.

"Who's there? Who's there?"

"Only Mitrani."

"Ah, it's you. Wait a minute!"

Perseus' brazenly innocent face left no doubt who was the culprit.

"Sit down, my dear Mitrani, sit down! I am glad to have this opportunity of thanking you. What was all the noise about?"

"Madame Hortense. It appears she has lost an intimate garment."

"Her spirits were a little elevated. Is it possible she threw it out of the window?"

"If she did, no doubt a conjurer such as monsieur will be able to return it to her room. I will be his stooge."

"You suspect me, Mitrani?"

"I am sure."

"But what motive could I have?"

"If monsieur would prefer to tell me rather than the police . . ."

Perseus sighed and dived into his trunk. From its depths he hauled out the missing garment and spread it wing and wing with one flick of his conjurer's wrist. It was a pair of knee-length drawers of remarkable size and elaboration with lace insets and frills, threaded with blue and pink ribbons.

"You ask my motive, Mitrani. You are a man of imagination. Conceive, I implore you, the enthusiasm, the laughter when I produce these from a hat. I could search for years without finding such a property."

Bernardo saw his point; it was impossible for Perseus to resist the temptation. Doves and goldfish were trivial. Some delicate article of female underwear — well, it would only produce a polite titter. But this now unobtainable *caleçon* presented by itself the pre-war world of Empires, the luxury of archdukes. It belonged in a *chambre privée* of Maxim's where — culmination of supper after the opera — it had been respectfully removed by some Paraguayan papal count and laid upon the velvet of the day bed while its owner parted noble, Edwardian thighs and whispered — if she didn't sing it — "Excellency, my resistance is at an end."

Yes, the Prince of the Rosicrucians must have it. Mme. Hortense would have to adjust herself to the shorter silken fantasies of the nineteen twenties. Bernardo regretted that money had to enter into the transaction, but he was in no position to be charitable.

"I will do my best to arrange the matter with Madame Hortense, monsieur. What's it worth to you?"

"Five thousand lei," Perseus suggested, a little too hastily.

It was more than Bernardo expected, equal to about seven pounds and double that in what it would buy. No need to jump at it, however.

"It is a pleasure to serve monsieur. But there will also be the police."

"What would you recommend?"

"Another five thousand. They are very poorly paid."

Perseus handed over the money at once and asked if he could safely hang on to his prize.

"We will see. If you hear nothing from me, we are safe."

He cautiously slipped out of the room. The row at the other end of the passage had started up again, and the manager was evidently on the point of sending for the police. That could be the end of David Mitrani who dared not be questioned about his past and that arrival with a horse from Morocco. Perseus would have to unstick at once from Mme. Hortense's property. He assured the manager that it would be found.

"To hell and the devil with her *caleçon!* Someone has stolen my bath salts."

It was a most expensively cut crystal jar which had been presented to the manager by a grateful client. He kept it in his bathroom cupboard and valued it highly. Nobody in the hotel would have dreamed of telling him that the luxurious jar with its Coty label had been empty and that the client had refilled it with Romanian bath salts from the nearest chemist.

All was now plain to Bernardo. That was why Mme. Hortense never mentioned that she had left her room and why she objected to anyone searching it.

"May I suggest, sir, that you leave the matter in my hands till lunchtime?" he said. "I am sure I can clear both myself and the chambermaid. After all I know more than anybody else of what goes on in this hotel between ten at night and seven in the morning."

"You are a scoundrel, Mitrani! You have all the vices of Jew and Christian in one!"

"And so it is unnecessary to call in the police. Calm, dear sir, calm! By lunchtime I will tell you where your bath salts are."

The small gathering dispersed. The big eyes in the little lemon-colored faces vanished behind their doors. It was nearly time for Mme. Hortense's *petit déjeuner*. Bernardo had no trouble in persuading the waiter to let him take up the tray.

"Well, you! So you have the impudence to bring my coffee in person! Where is my *caleçon?*"

"I do not know, Madame. Perhaps some admirer . . ."

"You disgust me. I await the police."

"Madame may not have to wait long. The manager has lost his bath salts."

"His bath salts? What story is this? Who was using my lavatory last night? He is the thief. Two jolly presents for his girl! My *caleçon* and a little something to freshen her up where she needs it most!"

"But whoever he was, he did not enter the manager's bathroom."

"Insolent! You dare to accuse me?"

"Unavoidable, Madame. We are all under suspicion."

"Is it true that he is sending for the police?"

"I doubt if I can prevent it. I only hope I shall be able to keep my mouth shut."

"Would you care for a little drink, Mitrani?"

"Willingly, Madame."

"You will find a bottle in the cupboard. Serve yourself, and a little in my coffee if you would be so good."

Bernardo took a quick look round the cupboard. Meanwhile Mme. Hortense allowed her bedjacket to slip back. It was only too evident that she would have won the red ribbon at any dairy show with Eva only a Highly Commended.

"The needs of beauty excuse everything, Mitrani."

Bernardo politely agreed but remained the passive servant of the hotel. Mme. Hortense, realizing that there was no alternative, pulled out a neat little purse and presented him with a hundred lei. Bernardo gave it a cabman's cold look and said nothing.

"But that is for you on condition . . ."

She put one finger to her lips.

"I have my duty to consider, Madame."

"And there is another!" she declared with an air of splendid generosity.

"The police will be here shortly, Madame. Shall we say five thousand?"

"But this is blackmail! I will report it. *Tiens!* I'll give you a thousand. There!"

"Five thousand lei, Madame."

"Two."

"Four or there will be a scandal."

"Mitrani, I was told the Romanians were gallant. I will give you three. Or, naked and defenseless as I am, I will consent to be dragged to jail."

Bernardo gave up. It was impossible to bargain with a Frenchwoman. He took his three thousand and removed the tray.

He threw on his uniform coat and shot into the manager's office, feeling that he had not done badly for one whose commercial experience had been limited to shipping and Susana. But his nerve was going. The manager was furiously throwing papers from the Out tray to the In tray with the fateful telephone far too near his hand. He turned his temper on the night porter.

"Well, Mitrani, well? Where are my salts, half-wit?"

"I have warned you, sir, not to leave the key over the door of your bathroom."

"And I told you that the girls were not tall enough to reach it."

"But Mme. Hortense? On tip-toe? You must remember that when she returns at two she is almost alone in the hotel."

"Why should she? She has everything she needs."

"Like Bluebeard's wife — merely because the door is locked. And a cupboard! Wherever she is, she is incapable of not rummaging in it."

"She'd never take the risk."

"Excuse me, sir! The jar was full. So there was a chance that you never used it and would not miss it. And soon she leaves for Belgrade."

"At her age can one be a thief?"

"Impulse, dear sir. The needs of beauty excuse everything."

"Beauty, my backside!"

"One must be charitable. The years pass so quickly."

"You learned that from your English papa?"

"It's in the works of Saint Spiridon."

"And her pants, clown?"

"Obviously, sir, she invented this story of a thief in case the salts were missed."

"But how can I get them back without a scandal?"

"There is a large doll in her room in our glorious national costume and its stuffing is on the floor of her wardrobe among the empties. I suggest that before she leaves we put something of similar shape in its belly."

"Mitrani, you should be in the police!"

Bernardo took the opportunity to remind him that the help of the police was always expensive. No tip was forthcoming, but he did get the genial promise of a rise in pay. The precious bath salts must have been of great sentimental value.

With a total of thirteen thousand lei earned — when one came to think of it — solely by helping his fellows in their distress Bernardo jumped into a higher orbit of optimism. Another wad of this easy money and he might get a sight of Magda again. Meanwhile there was that child on his conscience. An abomination! God only knew where she could fetch up and what more indignities she might have to suffer.

He made some inquiries about fairs. Craiova was finished. There was no regular route for the sideshows and amusement stalls which moved according to the hunches and preferences of the owners. Up in Moldavia were two possibles, besides some sort of grubby affair at Giurgiu on the Danube and a probable at Târgu-Jiu in Transylvania which seemed the easiest run from Craiova. Bernardo called up the police station at Târgu-Jiu, pretending to be the manager of the Alhambra, Bucarest's smartest cabaret, to ask if the Stepanovs were at the fair.

He struck it lucky at once. He was warned to have nothing to do with them. An impossible show for the Alhambra — did he understand the nature of the exhibition? There had been complaints from some impertinent Protestant League of the Magyar minority. As men of the world, the police could see no harm, but they had had to shut the Stepanovs down and move them on. Bernardo asked if it was known where they had gone. Well, that filthy eunuch had asked for a Bulgarian visa and got it, so it was very likely that they were working the Giurgiu fair and would cross over to Rusciuc by the ferry when it closed.

Giurgiu was easy to reach. On his day off he was free from seven in the morning till ten p.m. the following day, thirty-nine hours if he did not sleep. He told himself — having no clear idea what sort of quixotry he intended — that he was killing two birds with one stone. He had always wanted to see the Danube.

After a couple of hours in the train, there it was: a majestic river of silvers and browns rather than blue with a swirling, noticeable current although the water was at its autumn low. Barges and tugs seemed to be the main interest of the port, and two ocean-going tramps were alongside the quay with its familiar line of warehouses and consulates including his own. For a moment he was tempted to go in. But better David Mitrani than that badly wanted Bernardo Brown, that unspeakable outcast who had assaulted His Majesty's representative.

The fairground was on the flood plain, upstream and well inland. He found it half dismantled with traveling carts packing up. He could see no sign of the Stepanovs, but did not explore too closely in case the man should spot him and become suspicious at his second appearance. It looked as though they had left. The timetable of the ferry to Rusciuc showed only one crossing early every morning.

Recognizing a small menagerie which had been close to the "interesting" exhibition at the Mosh, he stood around waiting for a chance of casual conversation. The mangy animals, each in a cage hardly bigger than itself, were being hoisted onto an open truck: a leopard, a lion and a bear at the bottom, wolves, snakes and monkeys together with the empty exhibition cages on top. Short lives they must have, with hardly room to lick their sores. The bars of the wolf cage broke, but it made no attempt to escape, cowering utterly uninterested while the lid of a packing case was nailed in place.

"Going to Bulgaria?" he asked the showman.

"Not me! A cruel lot the Bulgars are — no better than Turks!"

"Does anyone go over there?"

"Only if the show is big enough to put on rail. That's too expensive for most of us chaps."

"What about putting a cart on the ferry?"

"No room. But it will tow a boat. There's one dirty dog is

going that way. Next to me he was, exhibiting his own
daughter. Pfui!"

"What's the matter with her?"

"Four tits."

Bernardo showed a proper disgust, asked a few questions
about the animals and strolled off. "Is going" not "has gone."
So Stepanov must be waiting somewhere till next morning.
There was no sign of him on the waterfront, on waste ground
or in back streets, and so, after searching for a couple of hours,
Bernardo settled down at a café table from which he could
watch most of the activities of the port. His professional eye
observed that it was difficult to load a showman's cart from
the quayside; it would have to be lifted by crane. In the barge
basin anything could be wheeled on board, but there the
lighters were too large, built for strings behind a powerful tug
and probably unmanageable behind a small steam ferry in a
current.

The thing to do was to ask questions, though his Romanian
was not yet up to nautical technicalities. However, in a busy
port it did not matter if he gave himself away as a foreigner.
He got his answer at once. No, the ferry could not tow a
barge, but at this time of year, if there were cargo which could
not be accommodated, it would take a flat-bottomed boat
picking it up from a hard beach above the town. The steamer
had to go upstream anyway to Rusciuc.

It was now evening. Bernardo walked out of Giurgiu along
the Danube towards the marshes at the mouth of the River
Vedea. A rutted earth road led him along the embankment
to a distant maze of rushes beyond which a golden gleam of
water reflected the low sun. He left the road and wriggled his
way through the reeds to see without being seen.

Just below him was a gravel bank with one flat-bottomed
boat, plainly rotten, drawn up for repairs and another moored

to two posts with only its stern aground. The current of either the Vedea or a backwater of the Danube rippled against the starboard beam. The ferry boat could go astern, take a line and tow it off with a minimum of delay.

The eunuch's traveling cart was on the hard, loaded with the poles, canvas and furniture of his booth. Nadya and Stepanov were eating something out of a pot suspended above the ashes of a fire. The pair of horses rolled on the gravel, shook themselves and stood hopefully over Nadya waiting for a piece of bread. An idyllic picture if one did not know the physical misfortune behind it all.

While it was still light, the boatman came out from Giurgiu passing close to the invisible Bernardo, and after chatting with the Stepanovs let down the stern bulwark of the boat to form a ramp. Stepanov harnessed the horses, backed the cart onto the boat and helped the boatman to lash it down to ring-bolts so that all was ready for the morning. He then locked Nadya into a tiny, inconspicuous cabin between the driver's seat and the load and strolled off into town with the boatman, leaving the horses picketed and munching at a pile of maize stalks.

The flimsy cabin seemed inadequate protection for a lonely girl. However, there was nothing else worth stealing but the horses, and since Stepanov did not bother about one essential half of his livelihood, it was natural that he would not feel much anxiety about the other. Bernardo went on board the boat and knocked on the wooden side of the cart's cabin.

"I am David. Do you remember?"

"Of course I remember."

"Can you get out?"

"Easily. I have another key. He does not know it."

She climbed down to the boat where she took his hand, not right to right but right to left like a child. He led her up

to the bows where they sat in half light and silence except
for the derisive racket of the frogs.

"If you can get out, why don't you escape?"

"Where to?"

Without knowing more of her history it was irresponsible
to try to answer such a question. If like the wolf which would
not leave its cage she had never known any other life, apathy
would be understandable. But at some time, seven or eight
years earlier, she had left a civilized world which included
governesses.

"You are not really his daughter?"

"No. That is only what our papers say."

"When will he be back?"

"Not for a long time. He has gone to drink with the boatman."

"And you are off to Bulgaria in the morning?"

"I don't want to. It's a frontier. I don't want to."

So there could be emotion in those calm eyes. He had
been on the right lines thinking of the wolf. But it looked as
if her cage were larger than the cabin and the exhibition
booth; it could be Romania which she considered safety.

"Well, I suppose you needn't," he said doubtfully.

"No. Not now. I shall come with you."

Bernardo was appalled. He had intended to talk, to give
her advice and all his money if it meant a hope of freedom
for her. This sudden trust out of the blue was completely
unforeseen. Or perhaps subconsciously it had been foreseen;
perhaps it was just her instinctive trust which had compelled
him to return, like turning back to pick a starving kitten out
of the gutter when a cat was the last damned thing you
wanted. And there it was! He couldn't temporize. He couldn't
hand her over, like a decent, chivalrous *caballero* to a home
for — for what? For four-breasted showgirls? He could only

148

take action himself and alone without even a Sancho Panza to plead common sense.

"What papers have you, Nadya?"

"None. He has a passport with me on it."

"I suppose that as a Russian refugee you could get a Nansen passport," he said, more to himself than to her.

"I don't know what that is. But if I'm found he'll have me brought back to him by the police."

As his daughter. Of course. Seduction of a minor — or, if she was not a minor, some other Romanian offense — was still another crime about to be added to the list. He considered his hours in Giurgiu. He had been very careful and left no trail of curiosity behind him. Good enough for himself, but not for her. She would be picked up by the police in no time at all. He looked at the figure sitting on the side of the boat opposite to him with the stained-glass face and pretty feet and the hunched peasant blouse. Would it be possible to dress her as one of those grossly overfed boys one saw about Eastern Europe? And what happened afterwards? That was up to her with a bit of help from him. From him? It was only a few weeks since he had begun to be able to help himself.

The sudden flash of hope and trust had died right out of her eyes.

"You stared at me like they do. It's not my fault."

"I was only thinking about dressing you up as a boy, Nadya."

"But I can't! I mean — less than most."

"No, more than most. A fat boy."

"Oh, I see."

"You might want a bit of — er — stuffing — well, in the middle," Bernardo said, very embarrassed, "if you could, I mean, manage it."

"I do already. I'll try. We could forget it then."

That possibly settled that, but nothing else. The boat quivered and creaked at its moorings as if the hand of the river could only reach out to it after darkness had fallen. It was a bloody awful boat, Bernardo thought, not at all what he would choose for crossing the Danube to Bulgaria. Presumably it had taken the tow in safety scores of times, but it would certainly have been condemned by the Port of Bilbao even for the simple run down the River Nervion to the sea.

"Can you forget it? Can you?"

"I wasn't thinking about it at all, Nadya."

He saw that he would have to be very careful with her. None of his usual silent thinking and dreaming. Silence meant to her amazement and disgust.

"What were you thinking then? About Bulgaria?"

"About making you disappear so that no one would ever look for you."

"But how?"

"Drown you."

A bit abrupt, but there was enough light from the water for her to see his smile, and she had this extraordinary habit of finding eyes as communicative as words.

"There would be no body."

"I don't see why there should be. If you fell off the boat you'd fetch up in the Black Sea or the Danube marshes. Let's go back to the hard."

From there she could watch everything he was doing. He did not want to disappear behind the loaded cart and leave her wondering if he would ever reappear.

He inspected the small lighter bit by bit, entirely absorbed by the short-term consequences of his plan; long-term consequences he refused to think of. The starboard bollard to which one of the mooring ropes was attached turned out to be bolted to rotten wood. It was bound to go sooner or later, and any inspector would see that. What he must not detect was that it had been helped with the sledgehammer which Stepanov used to drive in tent pegs.

"Have you got a file in the cart?" he asked Nadya.

"What is a file?"

He explained, and she brought out a tool box from under the driver's seat. Bernardo filed irregularly through the two ropes which lashed down the cart so that they would appear to have broken. Whenever the lighter hit anything on its career downstream and heeled over, the cart would be tipped out with Nadya supposedly locked in the cabin.

His conscience worried him. The poor were the poor, however vilely they earned a living.

"I hope this won't ruin him," he said.

"He has plenty of money. He sends it home every week. And he had three days' takings under my bed. I'll get it."

"It will look as if you weren't drowned."

"No, it won't, David. It floated away — it floated away!"

She laughed gaily and naturally without a sign of strain. Her face had never before revealed any likelihood of breaking into laughter.

"And I shall set fire to the cabin."

"That is not necessary at all," he said firmly.

"But God sent you, so God wishes it."

It was impossible to equate the juvenile delinquent with the pious angel. He told her to go ashore at once and hide in the rushes in case something went wrong.

"Let me fetch the money and my wallet first!"

She disappeared into the cabin for a moment, locked the door when she came out and then did as she was told, trotting — almost skipping — up the hard and into darkness.

Bernardo took up the sledgehammer and swung at the starboard bollard on the stern of the boat, hitting the loop of the rope so that no mark would be left. It didn't work. He then used a tent pole as a battering ram, which went straight through the rotten wood of the strake. He levered the whole bollard off and did his best to efface the marks of the pole by picking away with the file. With luck all the wood would be spongy when the wreck was found.

The lighter swung to the stream as he expected, so that the stern was now afloat and held only by the rope round the port bollard. He had not decided on the least suspicious method of dealing with that. Meanwhile he concentrated on his work with the point of the file. When he looked up, at last satisfied with his arrangements of splinters, he made a jump for the hard. The mooring post was bent over and pulling out; a moment later it oozed clear of the ground. The boat, turning round and round in the main current and dragging rope and post most convincingly behind, was clear so far of shallows and on its way to the Black Sea.

Footprints, now. Nadya's did not matter. She had been about for hours and must often have gone to and from the boat. What of his own? He could not see any, but perhaps a detective would be able to spot something in the dust of the hard. He walked backwards up to the rushes, sweeping Mr. Niculescu's coat over the ground as he went. That would have to do.

Bernardo collected Nadya from cover and hurried off on the road to Giurgiu. There was no other way, and Stepanov with or without the boatman might return at any moment. Fortunately the night was black so that they had only to take a few paces off the track and lie down to be invisible. He told her not to talk above a whisper and held her hand to give her confidence although she seemed in fact to be bouncing with it. He wondered what time the shops opened and where in this unknown countryside she could be hidden until he came back from town with boy's clothing. They had the Danube on their right and, so far as he remembered, blank, open flood plain on their left. His short-term planning had been ridiculously short-term.

Out on the river somebody appeared to be fishing fairly close to shore with a lit torch. A violent torch. It grew and flamed up. Cart, cabin, tent poles and canvas were all blazing on their course downstream.

"That's you?"

"Yes, David. Only a candle."

"I didn't see any light."

"I put it under the bed in the box where he kept his money, and some straw from my mattress for it to burn down to."

"You were supposed to be drowned."

"Yes, David. But you forgot the cabin was locked, so I couldn't have jumped overboard. So I had to be burned up."

Bernardo did not argue. It was true that he had quite forgotten that Stepanov locked the door. Nadya and God were right. The calm, feminine simplicity of it was more effective than all his meticulous work. The boat had come much closer to the shore than he expected; its dark bulk could well have been spotted when passing the lights of Giurgiu and towed into port intact with no Nadya in the cabin.

The flames lit up the whole riverbank, sending them stumbling away from the water in a panic until Bernardo realized that they were quite safe in the rough grass a hundred yards inland and that it would be wise to lie there and watch exactly what happened. Already nothing was left of the cabin. The bonfire was of poles and canvas. Some of the load had fallen into the river; some was burning alongside the cart and reasonably sure to destroy the wheels on that side. It was difficult to make out black outlines among the flames and smoke, but there was no mistaking an audible splash. The remains of the cart had gone overboard.

"So I'm burnt," Nadya said with satisfaction. "And now nobody will ever look for me."

A launch put out from Giurgiu and extinguished small spurts of flame before the boat had burned to the waterline. Then a shadowy line of men came running along the river-bank with bobbing lanterns. They would have no trouble in reconstructing the disaster. The starboard bollard was on the beach still attached to the post by its broken line; the marks where the other post had worked loose from the ground and dragged could not be mistaken. The fire — well, after all, was it so unlikely? Nadya might have lit a candle before going to bed. With a lurch of the boat it fell over and her straw mattress caught fire.

An hour or so later the procession returned with the horses, all talking at once. Their tramplings over the gravel must have wiped out every trace of earlier movements. Nobody, as Nadya had said, was ever going to look for her, but what if she could not be hidden and was seen?

They moved cautiously over the plain, crossing dry or muddy ditches most unlikely to give adequate cover in daylight. There was nothing for it but to wait till the first gray of dawn when with luck nobody would be about and they could see further. Nadya curled up and dozed. The girl's faith was all that prevented Bernardo, brooding in the damp dark over his lunacy, from advising her to give herself up. She would be quite safe. She had only to say that she jumped in time and lost herself in the featureless landscape. Then she could face the winter with at least a roof over her head and enough to eat, neither of which could be provided with any certainty by a suspected murderer.

The light grew, showing a considerable expanse of gray water ahead without a stand of long rushes anywhere. To the west this lake or backwater looked as if it joined the Vedea, in which case there was no way round it; the eastern end was dotted by a few cottages where suspicious movements were bound to arouse curiosity. He woke Nadya and hurried towards the water. At the worst she must sit in it wherever there was a patch of vegetation to hide her head. In another half hour a standing human figure would be seen a mile away. The black raft of duck floating well out from shore was perfectly safe from gunners when they took off.

A muddy path led westwards, apparently going only into a network of waters although deep prints of heavy boots showed that it was used. One set of prints turned off to the left. Bernardo ignored them for there was nothing in that direction but a small scattering of brushwood which would not have hidden a rabbit. He plodded despondently on, only turning round at a shout from Nadya. She wasn't there. She had vanished. He walked up to the brushwood — since she could not be anywhere else — suppressing comment on childish and futile pranks in an emergency and found a pit with a foot of water at the bottom. Nadya looked up at him, her eyes luminous with her usual air of finding something already prepared for her. It was a hide for duck hunters, she said, and a safe spot till the evening because it was too late for anyone to walk out and get into position for the morning flight.

It was also a perfect lady's fitting room if one threw down turf and twigs to keep shoes and skirt hem out of the soup at the bottom. Bernardo guessed at her height and length of leg, but waist was a problem. The front of the fat boy had to have an even slope all the way. The obvious solution was to use her skirt as extra padding. He fussed over how she could fold it and tie it while she listened patiently, at last reminding him that she was not inexperienced and that he should remember to buy a packet of pins.

It took him an hour to get into town, following the shore of the lake and entering the first street from nowhere via a rubbish heap. No one had reason to be inquisitive about his presence there, for the rubbish heap was also a popular public lavatory. A back-street café provided breakfast and a place to wait till the shops opened. Choice from their windows was far from easy; anything would do to get her as far as the railway station in safety, but he had to think of the future as well; in case money ran out, whatever he bought must allow her to circulate in Bucarest without being noticed.

A ship chandler's on the waterfront offered some cheap, rough clothing, and he collected shoes, socks and trousers but could find no suitable coat. Passing up the main street, he came on a shop with a window assigned to children's outfitting in which was a dummy dressed in a high-school tunic which buttoned up to the neck, with a peaked cap on its smug head. That would save buying collar and tie. Yes, they thought they could fit his little brother. Yes, in their experience all that precocious development would disappear in a year or two. Ah, and a packet of pins. He damn nearly forgot that.

With the two parcels under his arm and a thick sandwich for Nadya in his pocket he walked back along the lake, now sunlit but still deserted except for a flashing pair of kingfishers. He was utterly unable to think of any story to account for what he was doing there and kept nervously searching the horizon until he dropped into the pit and could unwrap his purchases.

"My God, your hair!" he exclaimed when he came to the schoolboy's cap. "What are we to do?"

"But you told me I'd be a fat boy, so I took my scissors from the cart. Cut it off for me!"

All that luscious pale gold. He felt that it was an outrage, a crime like plucking the blue iridescence of the kingfishers. He said he was sorry he had to do it as if he himself had insisted on it.

"I hate my hair."

Of course. All one with grubby crimson cloak and the Turkish trousers. Just another of Stepanov's stage properties. He had already forgotten that brutal vulgarity and the pity which overwhelmed him. There was no time for the past of either individual in this urgent present.

He chipped away inexpertly. The back and sides were tolerable; the top was a mess, but the cap would cover it till one or both could have another go at leisure. She stamped all the cuttings hard down into the mud at the bottom of the hide, asking him to get rid of the two long plaits and come back when she called him. Obediently he kicked out a trench at the lake side and buried them. Indignation returned in a rush as he imagined her combing out that Slav glory and hating it.

She did not call. She came out and paraded herself in front of him with the impersonality of a mannequin. He was beginning to understand her now. She was not going to smile until he did — or until she saw the quality of his smile. She must have found nothing but admiration and amusement in it, for she giggled happily. She looked more like a Salvation Army bandsman recovering from alcoholic dropsy than a schoolboy, but the disguise would pass.

"A bit too pink and white," he said. "What about a streak of mud?"

"Wait till we come to some dust, David."

When they did, she rubbed a handful into her face and

brushed it off. The result was definitely more masculine. They had no trouble with the only person they met: a fisherman with a net over his shoulder who asked where they had come from.

"This little bastard ran away from school," Bernardo said.

"People who have enough to eat," the fisherman replied, looking pointedly at the well-filled tunic, "owe it to the rest of us to learn their lessons."

"You speak Romanian well," Nadya said as they continued on their way to Giurgiu and its railway station.

"Enough for us to speak it together, I hope. And we can always use French. But we must never, never speak English from now on."

"Aren't you English?"

"I am David Mitrani and I was born in Roman. I only know a few words of English."

She switched to Romanian then and there without question. It was far more fluent than his own, spoken with a slight accent which slurred the clarity of Latin vowels. She would probably be recognized as coming from the former Russian province of Bessarabia and it was credible that she could be his brother or cousin.

"But you could not have done anything wrong."

"Not to start with. I'm improving daily."

"So I shall make everything more difficult for you."

"No, you won't. I think you are lucky like Joan of Arc."

"Why Joan?"

"She always did the right thing and then said that God told her to."

"Well, if he hadn't, it would not have been the right thing, would it?"

By four in the afternoon they were in Bucarest unremarked and unquestioned. He gave her a solid meal with what was left of his money and then took her straight to his room at the Principesa. That would be all right for a day or two since their times for sleeping did not coincide. He was not allowed to bring in women but a boy was permissible. The highly heterosexual Romanians did not jump easily to scandalous conclusions.

Having comb and mirror now, they made a respectable job of the hair. When it was brushed back from the center parting she had always had, Bernardo found that he had given her the fashionable cut of the time, right for a Romanian officer but not a schoolboy. He let it stand. There soon ought to be some way of returning her to her own sex without risk. Nadya Stepanov was undoubtedly dead and nobody was going to look for her in Bucarest.

He asked her what her real name was. Nadya Philippovna Andreyev, she answered and then, as if to prove it, undid the top of her tunic and pulled out what she had called her wallet: a small, flat box of soft leather with traces of gold and red stamping now worn away by sweat and friction. She extracted a black-creased document and two photographs: one of a tall, robust man in his forties so bearded that it was hard to distinguish any features but large, kindly eyes, the other of a lovely young woman in ancient Russian costume.

"My father and mother," she said. "And that is my birth certificate. I have nothing else."

She was seventeen, older than he had thought.

"Tell me how you came to Romania."

"All of it?"

"What you like."

"I want you to know everything, but there is so much. Little bits will come out day after day. You must fit them in."

Day after day. Put like that, the prospect of being stuck indefinitely with an adopted sister disquieted him. Yet any breath of permanency was somehow soothing when he could not even use his own name and had no real existence outside himself.

She sat on the edge of the bed, elbows on knees, her hands clasped under her chin, trying so earnestly to preserve a sequence of time when all that mattered most came last or in the middle. It was, with personal variations, the story of hundreds of thousands — the beginning, old Bernardo pointed out, of our Age of the Refugee. Those Russians had been the flower of the people, indistinguishable from the rest in blood and religion. A diseased flower, certainly, when it came to the Bobos. But the vast majority was of squires and merchants and government servants passionately in love with the great sweep and culture of their country, eager to reform its society and guilty only of hesitation.

Her family was one of old-fashioned, prosperous merchants with a house on the Povarskaya in Moscow. The Andreyevs were too content with their solid position in this life and assurance of the next to run after the landed nobility and the court of St. Petersburg. They imitated high society only in speaking French at home and English in the schoolroom — not that they despised their native language, but they were very conscious, trading as they did from Riga to Pekin, of the world of empires.

In 1917 they couldn't believe it. Holy Russia could not behave like that. No, they couldn't believe it until towards the end of the winter the Povarskaya house was invaded by anarchists and turned into a nest of murder and loot. Some of the servants were shot for no reason but sport; those who escaped barricaded themselves upstairs with the Andreyevs. The rioters collapsed, rolling drunk, before they could break in, and the Andreyev party were able to escape at the back of the house, lowering themselves by knotted sheets with all the jewelry and furs they could lay hands on.

Nadya's recollections of the months which followed were empty. They lived with friends. Friends came to see them. But she was never allowed out of the house. And then, without warning, her father, mother, brother and sister were all in a boat going down the Volga with their papers in order.

Trotsky in April 1918 at last had the time to impose discipline on Moscow. The anarchists were cleared out of the Povarskaya by the army and their corpses removed. Though his house had been burned down in the fighting, Andreyev called on Trotsky in person, saying that he knew he could never expect compensation but wished to congratulate the Commissar for War on the return to order. No, Nadya did not think it daring. Her father's goodness and patriotism had always made him welcome in government offices. Bernardo could imagine Andreyev facing the great man with a sturdy innocence like Nadya's own, idealist to idealist.

In that short interim when the Bolsheviks appeared to be firmly in the saddle, commerce had to be restarted. Andreyev, coming in like that out of the blue, must have presented himself — to the snap judgment of an exhausted man — as a gamble which would do no harm and might do good, for he was known to everyone and genuinely understood that the Government was going all out to restore administration. He was chosen to travel down to Astrakhan reassuring the merchants on his way, and allowed to take his wife and children with him.

They had not gone far down the Volga before her father saw that no reassurement was possible, and as often as not nobody was left to be reassured. Orders from Moscow were meaningless to the local Soviets on his route, feverishly organizing nothing into less than nothing. Andreyev decided to get out and remake his life and business somewhere between Persia and Bokhara. They sailed in a lugger owned by an Armenian straight down the Caspian to the Persian port of Enzeli.

Nadya was then ten years old. She remembered the week on the empty Caspian as if it had been a glimpse of heaven between a past which was unintelligible and a future of terrifying helplessness. The Andreyevs were at last out of trouble and still together. She welcomed Enzeli, low-lying and warm, with longed-for fruit in the market. It was the first foreign land she had ever seen, the first of her three frontiers.

For one last day heaven carried on as they rode up the pass through the fresh green of the Caspian forest where the roadside was carpeted with fairy-tale flowers. Movement was all the other way, of straggling, hungry troops drifting without discipline from the Turkish front down to Enzeli. Most of them did not know what the revolution was all about, but they had had enough of war and were going home.

Andreyev loved his fellow countrymen, right or wrong, and this jovial sense of fellowship compelled him to stop and talk with the soldiers they met. Though peace of a sort had been concluded with the Germans, he argued that Russian armies should still be defending Christian civilization against the Moslem. With one weary band of deserters near the top of the pass he might have been too positive. An officer, till then neglected and ignored, was suddenly overcome by this kindly voice speaking of duty and tradition. With Russian abandon he leaped into the discussion — if it was a discussion — and stood by Andreyev telling his men to listen. A bored soldier picked up his rifle and shot the pair of them dead.

Nadya, weeping over her father, appreciated little of what happened then and only knew what she was told afterwards by her mother who continually blamed herself for not taking the children on into Persia. The soldiers themselves were shocked. They had finished with killing, or thought they had, and this was so unnecessary a crime. When they had lightly buried Andreyev and their officer in the woods, they swore to look after mother and children and start them on their way back to Moscow.

Started they were; but the corridor which still connected the Caspian with Moscow was narrowing all the time. The Turks were advancing; the Germans were in the Ukraine; and the Whites were threatening the Volga and already into the Crimea. In spite of their government pass, the family spent nearly a month on the way, sleeping rough, arrested, released, always trying to keep clear of officials and the military. Her brother, five years older than Nadya, wanted to try the adventure of joining the Whites, but their mother would not hear of it. She insisted on keeping to territory firmly controlled by the Government where at least there was no fighting.

When at last they did reach Moscow ragged and half-starved, no one took them for anything but members of the proletariat. They found shelter with their former cook: a formidable woman whose word ran in her street. She swore that Mrs. Andreyev was her daughter from whom she had been parted ever since the war began, and obtained for them rations and a permit to live with her. Nadya said she might still be there if her mother, now desperate for the future of her children, had not listened to an old friend.

He was in hiding after the attempt of the Social Revolutionaries to take over Moscow, and had a plan for a mass escape to Finland. It must have sounded convincing to her mother. Nothing so dangerous as slinking across the frontier or rushing the wire was involved. The plan depended partly on bribery and partly on political sympathizers among the guards who would themselves escape.

The first move was to a village near the shores of Lake Ladoga, dressed as peasants. Their Social Revolutionary friend was sure of his organization, but there were other strangers in other villages and presumably the discreet movements into the area were noticed by the police. When the party was united in the forest and very near the frontier, it was surrounded. The young children were taken out and marched away. Before they had gone very far they heard the machine gun and the isolated shots which followed. They did not belong to anybody any longer. Back at Leningrad they were questioned but obviously knew so much less than their interrogators that they were turned loose to live or starve as they liked.

Nadya and her sister continued to exist, joining a gang of children who scavenged and slept and died as casually as young wolves after the poisoning of the main pack.

"But did nobody care?" Bernardo asked.

"Only the police."

"What did they do?"

"When they could catch us they beat us and let us go again."

"Without food?"

"If I cried, they gave me tea."

Inexplicably her eyes were dancing. Bernardo, appalled at the sufferings inflicted on a cultured, eager, little girl, could not account for this dash of humor in a nightmare. He supposed that it was due to sheer pride in staying alive or perhaps that she was reliving the secret ambition of every child to make fools of the police — real police or just the policeman-like qualities of clumsy adults.

But details were unobtainable. She was reticent over this part of her history, jumping to the first signs of winter when their only hope of life was to get back to their old cook in

Moscow. They hung shivering around the railway station, feeding on any scraps they could steal or were given.

Jammed and unnoticed in a stampede of Russian skirts, trousers and baskets, they were swept on board a train. It was a good train. They even had room to sit on the floor. But unfortunately it was bound south and not going to Moscow at all. They stayed on it because it was a better home than unknown stations, and were well on their way to Kiev when the police threw them off in spite of the efforts of a peasant family to claim them. They were pitied and protected by those who were more used to suffering. Nobody seemed to believe that children who once belonged to the capitalist class had only got what they deserved.

Anywhere was the same as nowhere. The railwaymen had no advice to give and could only point out the road to Moscow. So they took it, shuffling on with bare feet through mud which had not yet frozen until they ran into the Red Army in the form of a company of engineers bivouacked around their trucks in the open. They showed themselves cautiously, ready to turn and run for their lives; but instead of being machine-gunned or beaten up they were stuffed with good soup from a field kitchen and kindly asked what they were doing. They always had the same story which left out politics. Father had been killed on the Turkish front and mother had died of typhus and they wanted to reach Moscow where they had relations.

The soldiers were sorry they could not help, for the detachment was going to the Ukrainian front — if the battered trucks held out and if there were no patrols of White cavalry out across their route. Having a passion for pets like any other army, they took the two sisters along with them in the back of a truck, deloused them, fattened them and kept them warm until ordered to get rid of them in the course of incomprehensible advances and retreats across the western Ukraine. Nadya remembered that they had a cousin at Balta which was not far away. Yes, they could be driven to Balta. The two proletarian cherubs were delivered to the cousin by a sergeant major with the warning that he had better take care of them or else.

But God, according to Nadya, decided that they were too fortunate.

"Fortunate? You?"

"Well, we had lived through the winter. Fresh fish, David! Lots of it! And we were so used to death, like the soldiers."

So it was time for her to face her third frontier. The cousin, appalled by terror and counter-terror now that the defeated Germans had gone home leaving a vacuum behind, was determined to escape to Romania. He had useful friends down the River Dniester at Tiraspol. The French were holding the right bank of the river. The Reds, having abandoned Bessarabia, were in force on the left. Both were bogged down by the March rains and were leaving each other in peace. While that lasted, any local man who knew the reed beds and backwaters should be able to get across unchallenged.

The cousin, the two children, a fisherman and his friend managed to cross the main stream in darkness and pouring rain, and were poling silently down a narrow channel between tall reeds. They were very near to the Romanian side when a star shell went up. Nadya remembered thinking how beautiful it was and how the boat and the faces were suddenly striped by the black shadows of the thin screen of rushes — too thin or else the French only spotted the bending and waving of their tops. A blast of fire, first from the right bank, then from the left, hit the supposed raiders before they could jump into the water. Nadya was the sole survivor. When all was silent she swam ashore and must have passed between French posts without ever seeing them. Her luck was nicely balanced. On the one hand she was unhurt; on the other, if anyone had made out a Russian girl crawling out of the mud into Romania she might have become a pet again and eventually joined her compatriots in Paris.

Not that Romania treated the new arrival badly. When a kind-hearted family, ten miles back from the river, found her on their doorstep, she was hardly distinguishable as human except where the interminable rain had washed her. How she could have got that far without dying of shock and exposure she did not know. Her saviors quickly nursed her back to health and would have kept her if their own children had not been faced with hunger, for nothing but bits of men and horses had been sown on their land the previous autumn. Through the village priest a place was obtained for her at an Orthodox convent which was caring for the waifs and strays of Bessarabia. In that remote province which had been Russian and was now Romanian the bankrupt state had to leave it to charity to clear up the aftermath of war. The rescued girls were all alike in speaking Russian as their first or second language. What had happened to their parents it was pointless to ask.

The Orthodox nuns sounded to Bernardo more worldly than Catholics but more distant. In their stiff, well-bred way they were equally kind to all their orphans within the limits set by crowded plank beds and scanty food. Education was severely practical. Those who could sit still were taught to sew and embroider; those who couldn't tended the garden. Nadya and a few others into whose houses somewhere had come governesses and spectacled professors were taught by the abbess herself, a tall, unbending lady of Byzantine family who

in the vanities of the world could justifiably have called herself a princess. Later on, Nadya was encouraged to give simple
lessons in French and English.

"And were you happy?" Bernardo asked.

"I was grateful. And it wasn't bad among ourselves till I
was twelve."

"Yes, I see. Your mother must have known?"

"Of course. But the doctors were sure they would not grow,
so we had no need to worry."

"And the nuns?"

"They were distressed, David, and whispered. And if they
didn't, I thought they did. They wanted me to stay with
them and become a nun. It's hard to explain to you. As if I
were a cripple. I was no use and could only serve God."

"Not much of a compliment to God!"

She stared at him as if trying to work out this little squib of
impiety where there should be none.

"I could give praise like anybody else," she said. "I don't
mean hymns. There was so much in the open air I loved."

And not much inside the nunnery, he supposed. He could
fill in a lot of what she had felt and was trying to express. At
her age he had not been aware of missing anything of value.
But in Spain why so much lonely and sometimes ecstatic
walking over coast and mountain when he had plenty of
friends with whom to appreciate a rich, very ordinary life?

"How did you get out of the place?"

She gave him the facts very honestly but was evasive about
her motives. He had to put some solid flesh on her privacies
when he was alone to think about them. There had been the
usual black-robed, hairy, Orthodox priest wagging his whiskers
at the nuns, and he had a son. Bernardo imagined — with little
more than a scatter of exclamations to go on — a not too
flashy, straight-haired Romanian youth with fine eyes and one

of those wide, mobile mouths which could gain sympathy even for an irresponsible liar. He must have been fascinated by her face, for her shape was odd however tight the nuns packed her, or perhaps any sort of body would do and he was just taking advantage of her longing to be loved again. At any rate he got her away most romantically in a motorcycle and sidecar borrowed from a friend. When they were beyond easy recovery and on the willowed bank of one of those laughing Romanian streams, he made the first idyllic exploration of her body. Up to then there had been only passionate words and brown eyes married to gray over the wall of the convent. He was shocked beyond measure. He panicked. He drove off and left her.

She stayed where she was. At least when she crawled ashore from the Dniester she carried with her the one certainty that she was a child who had been loved. Now she was a horror to herself. So far as the destruction of a human personality went she would, Bernardo thought, have been better off, for a time at any rate, if she had been a normal girl, seduced, abandoned and finishing up in the Crucea de Piatra.

Though ashamed of it, he found that he could understand that hysterical Romanian lad. Why on earth hadn't she warned him that she was different than other women? Starry-eyed innocence? Or an assumption that he must know what all the convent knew? Or could she conceivably have thought that what was a slightly prurient indelicacy to silly nuns offered an extra richness to the love of a man? And one might fairly safely guess that, added to any one of these, her experiences of death and filth and starvation had taught her too thoroughly that the state of the physical body was unimportant where there was deep affection.

What happened then was that Stepanov found her. How did he find her? She couldn't face that question. She said it was a coincidence. It was very obvious to Bernardo that the priest's son, either from remorse or in hope of profit, had let Stepanov know of her existence and that the eunuch had at once gone off to search for her. At any rate Stepanov, who up till then had earned a poor living exhibiting fetuses in bottles, took her home to his village unresisting as if death had once more refused her.

When they started on the road together in the spring she was Stepanov's daughter. His village headman must, like Rabbi Kaplan, have had the ear of a police officer who could not be bothered with the peculiarities of pious Jews and voluntary Russian eunuchs and was ready to hand over any papers required if the hand were greased.

"He was kind to you?"

"Yes. He used to say it was a punishment for the sins of the flesh."

"Yours?"

"No. Lots of generations. It wasn't my fault at all."

"You mean — it was almost as if he had caught a devil in a trap and was exhibiting it?"

Again she gave him her shocked look which this time brightened into amused comprehension.

"Something like that. Yes, with a tail! We could have poked it down my trousers."

For that night Nadya occupied his bed while he was on duty and then cleared off to buy clothes. Stepanov's three days' takings, she said calmly, would easily pay for her return to femininity as soon as she saw what townswomen were wearing. One wouldn't have believed there was so much lecherous curiosity in Giurgiu.

Bernardo slept till midday and then jumped to his feet with a nagging sense of guilt before he had made up for his sleepless night. He did not know what the hell to do with his acquisition. He had no money to feed both of them; he was as irresponsible as her disgusting boyfriend; and he knew nothing about Russians except for a few second-rate dancers at the Principesa who claimed, often with truth, to have been trained at the Imperial Ballet School and were all big eyes and sorrow. Nadya was a bit like that herself, except that she never showed sorrow. Acceptance was quite a different thing.

There should be a dying swan in her hotel bedroom at the moment. She never got up till the afternoon. Bernardo had no right to wander upstairs when off duty, so he waited in a bar at the end of the street till the clients began to drift out of the hotel alone or in couples. A damned flashy, vulgar lot, he decided. The Nyroubova was different. She looked like any young working girl going home from the office in a neat black coat, a white fur hat and a little scarf flowing at the neck. He bowed respectfully and asked if stars of the ballet had any objection to taking a drink with the night porter. Not at all, she replied, with this particular night porter.

He told her of a refugee he had come across, stateless and destitute. He wanted to help her, but had no idea what he ought to do and nor had she. Nyroubova just laughed at his innocence. Surely he, a cosmopolite, didn't believe that Russians were incompetent? She could not tell him offhand what committee was looking after refugees in Bucarest, but since scores of them had entered Romania when the Turks decided that Istanbul had enough of them, there must be some efficient organization. He was to send Nadya Philippovna Andreyev up to her room just as soon as he could get hold of her and not to worry any more. She gave him a kiss on both cheeks and thanked him. He left her in a daze of relief, never having realized the free masonry of White Russians or that it would be so easy to return Nadya to her true identity. He wished to God there was something similar for English refugees from Hungary.

5. Despina

IT WAS due to Mme. Hortense, of all the unlikely people, that Bernardo was offered the job of stage manager at the Alhambra. He had never realized that she was a great lady of the cabaret world. As a Frenchwoman of past fame her prestige on the near eastern circuit was matchless. She knew how things were run in Paris and flatly refused to be engaged by any establishment which was full of *putains*. Her associates could be as spectacular as they pleased at lunchtime, but when the show was over their movements must be seemly.

Mme. Hortense had been impressed by Bernardo. He had saved her with courtesy from a minor scandal; also she had beaten down his price and was always generous in victory. His French was much too good for a mere night porter and could be listened to without flinching. In fact he was just the sort of scoundrel who could be trusted to behave like a gentleman in a frequently disgusting profession. There was also the question of his kindness to that adorable, fat, little Russian always in and out of Nyroubova's room whom Mme. Hortense overwhelmed with chocolates and embraces. Nadya had spoken of this to Bernardo with some alarm, but it was needless. In such an emotional flurry of bosoms, double the normal size could safely be mixed with double the normal number.

Ion Stelian, owner of the smart Alhambra, wanted a foreigner for the job but was not allowed to import one; he had to employ a Romanian though he had no exaggerated opinion of his own countrymen when in charge of a menagerie of attractive girls. It was natural that he should consult Mme. Hortense. Had she by chance run across anyone who would be acceptable to distinguished artistes such as herself? She had, and could recommend him.

Bernardo Brown, badly wanted by several countries and known to have reached Romania, should never have accepted so public an employment; but he was not in the forefront of David Mitrani's mind as often as he had been. The fact was that Bernardo, once out of immediate trouble, was always inclined to dream of the future — in some ways an excellent habit for a criminal, preserving him from depression though offering golden opportunities to the police.

But the job seemed as safely obscure as that of night porter at the Principesa, so he took it. He supervised the back rooms and the back door and rarely had reason to go into the hall when the show was on. His duties were in fact quite lowly, not to be compared to those of a true stage manager, for there was no stage, only one and a half dressing rooms, and Stelian himself together with the maître d'hôtel ran everything of any importance.

Inquiry into his antecedents was perfunctory. The Principesa was obviously sorry to lose him, and the Prince of the Rosicrucians gave him a magnificent reference for tact. Bernardo stuck to his story of coming out to Romania with a horse, said nothing of the Crucea de Piatra and admitted his conversion. Again it was considered a recommendation that he was a Jew so long as he was a Christian.

A very bold move, especially since he was required to use far more broken English than he had dared so far. But he had to earn more money in order to settle Nadya. Nyroubova had at once booked a small room in the hotel for her and started the process of establishing her identity. That had been far simpler than expected. The abbess confirmed that she had been picked up in Bessarabia after escaping across the Dniester, adding that her character was not recommendable and that she suffered from a physical disability. The good Russians were not impressed by that. Which of them after years of poverty could claim a spotless character and which had not some disability? As to what she had been doing since she left the convent, that was easy to answer; she had been assisted by a certain David Mitrani. Mr. Mitrani wrote highly of her in impeccable French, emphasizing that his relationship with so defenseless a girl had always been that of brother and sister.

In the hotel Nadya had had difficulties and very narrow escapes. Apart from her own natural shyness it was essential to avoid gossip leading inevitably to the tragedy of Giurgiu. So Bernardo found a ground-floor room for himself with a bedroom above for her, and no questions asked about their sharing of a bathroom. She would have to wait a long time for her Nansen passport, but so long as she remained in Bucarest her civil status was clear and no authority was likely to bother her. The only essential precaution was to avoid being seen by any fashionable cabmen from Stepanov's village.

The short ferocity of Romanian winter was soon on them, the chill, clear December days suddenly changing to a north-east blizzard straight from the Urals which seemed to Bernardo to cut him lengthwise into two halves of a frozen carcass; he huddled over the tiled stove of his room trying to unite them by draughts of hot *tsuica* while Nadya laughed at him. She was working as a waitress in a newly opened Russian restaurant where the squareness of her figure and the saintly beauty of her face fascinated Romanians and foreigners alike who saw in her the typical peasant of Russian literature and were generous with their tips.

In summer the land belonged to the Europe of the Danube. In winter it was unique: a Latin Russia. When the blizzard was over, the main streets and boulevards were cleared but the outskirts of the city were silent under the snow. The smartest of the eunuch drivers substituted runners for wheels and waited to be hired beyond the boundary of the sweepers where the *trasura* and its pair of black horses could take the fur-coated passengers — usually one of each sex — hissing over the roads to the inn or restaurant of their choice. The gaiety of indoor life was less languorous than the willow-patterned ease of summer. The gypsy bands were wilder. Game, from bear to snipe, was abundant even in the cheaper restaurants. The winter season at the Alhambra was lavish with women and song.

The stars were a pair of French twins, weighing together little more than Mme. Hortense and bringing to Bucarest the latest hits of Josephine Baker. Most exotic of all — from the Romanian point of view — was Miss Lou, an angular but graceful American in a short, Greek tunic who sailed round the floor from pose to ecstatic pose expressing the joys of spring — or it might have been summer — in well-meant imitation of Isadora Duncan. The rest of the artistes were Hungarian with only one Romanian, employed for her tall, calm loveliness rather than her dancing which was of little more than graceful ballroom standard.

Despina

Bernardo enjoyed himself backstage, not in the least jealous of the oilmen, minor diplomats and foreign businessmen on whom the Alhambra depended for its profits, since it was too expensive for all but a few Romanians. He was ironically amused by the facade and its complete falsity and remembered both with pleasure.

"Inevitably at my age," he admitted, "one feels a certain *nostalgie de la boue*. They were all floating and feminine then — none of this tedious nakedness designed to give the salesman the illusion that he can still feel the same excitement as he did at sixteen. Or perhaps he does. I can see the time coming when we'll get more kick from dressing a girl than undressing her."

It was a night soon after the Orthodox Christmas when David Mitrani, idly watching the show from the obscurity of the artistes' entrance, was suddenly backfired into the torments of Bernardo Brown. The band was changing its music for the Viennese froth which suited Despina Vladimirescu, the Romanian dancer, and only the yappings and hummings of conversation sounded in the hall. Over this background a clear tinkle of high-pitched laughter easily carried. It must be Magda. Nobody else could manage that crystal note of provocative enjoyment. The sound came from a shaded box on the dais which ran round half of the Alhambra. Across the glare of top lights over the floor he could not see with certainty who was in it; a quick dodge behind the band gave him a better view. The pair were Sigismond Pozharski and Magda. She was leaning forward, murmuring something to the distinguished white head and altogether too close to it. The air of intimacy, of flirtation even, could not be mistaken. Bernardo told himself fiercely that a reasonable warmth was to be expected when she was being taken out by one of her father's old friends.

He dared not show himself to Pozharski, but surely there must be some chance of a word alone with Magda. He went round the back into the kitchen and stopped the maître d'hôtel at the swing doors, asking if the couple were enjoying themselves. God, yes! They were crazy Hungarians lapping up French champagne like water and no fooling them with labels. What was in the bottle had to be really French. Any idea who they were? No, but the man was staying at the Athenée Palace Hotel and the girl at the Austrian Legation.

So Bernardo's suspicions were scandalous and wrong. On the face of it that was confirmed after Miss Lou's act. Pozharski invited her to the table and was distributing gallantry quite impartially between Magda's midnight-blue silk and Miss Lou's flowing daffodil-cum-batik. Magda must have seconded the invitation, for she was chatting gaily with the American in English and not in the least ruffled.

They were nearly the last to leave, all in high spirits including Miss Lou — who had every right to be, considering her commission on the champagne. Pozharski and Magda waited for her to change; he must have asked her round to the hotel. No other bar or cabaret was still open. Meanwhile they were chucking money about and taking a last drink with the gypsy band leader.

Bernardo nipped over unseen to the front entrance where a *trasura*, already called by the doorman, was waiting. From the safety of the cab's street side he beckoned to the driver to lean down. The hairless face poked out like a tortoise's between the conical cap of astrakhan and the collar of the vast, fur-lined, dark blue coat.

"The police want to know where you take these Hungarians," he said. "Report to me on your way back! I'll still be here."

"Tomorrow. They won't run away. Got to sleep, haven't they?"

True enough. The cabman brought him back to common sense. He couldn't possibly intercept Magda. Pozharski would certainly see her back to the Austrian Legation and then take Miss Lou home, and good luck to him! When engaged she had insisted on a small, private apartment which Bernardo had been able to arrange for her. The plumbing was more reliable than that of the Principesa and there was no inconvenient night porter to turn away her wealthy compatriots from the oil fields.

He agreed to meet the driver in a cabman's bar at ten and went home. He slept happily. It was all useless and dangerous, but at least he would find a way of coming face to face with Magda again and telling her that no other woman could ever take her place.

The pair of horses were tucking into nose bags outside the bar — horses that were glossier and blacker and more than horses because they had carried Magda. The cabman was on a bench in the steaming room and as Bernardo entered quickly downed his glass of hot *tsuica* in order to be paid another.

"Well?"

"I took them to Sixteen Strada Spâtarului."

"What's there?"

"Nothing. Little house at the back of a courtyard with a tree in it. The man lives there. Opened the door with his own key."

"All three went in?"

"All three."

"They didn't tell you to wait?"

"What for? They were in a hurry, *domnule director*."

"How do you mean, in a hurry?"

"Running round the tree and kissing each other. The fair

one — pawing away at them, she was! The flames of hell, *domnule director*, that's where they'll finish. The flames of hell," he repeated with satisfaction.

"Anything else you know?"

"Yes. Friend of mine over there fetched the two whores away between seven and eight — one to the Austrians, one to Strada Lahovary."

Right! Now for that bastard, Pozharski, and damn the consequences! He must be suffering from a well-deserved hangover and couldn't protect himself and was going to confess why the whole of Europe was against Bernardo or be beaten up. It sounded as if he might be alone. If there was a valet, he'd be dealt with too.

Bernardo went back to his room and took the precaution of changing into Niculescu's suit. Then, if Pozharski set the police on him, they would have exactly the same description as before and no evidence that he had come up in the world. Without an overcoat he was very cold but did not notice it. He strode down the Boulevard Carol to Strada Spâtarului in a murderous temper.

A nice little love-nest number 16 was, not too far from the center, inconspicuous, giving nothing away about its occupant. It was the sort of doll's house which would perfectly suit a young married couple without children. He wondered in how many capitals Pozharski paid the rent of something equally discreet.

The narrow front had a large, shuttered window on the ground floor and another above. The upper window had the shutters slightly open. Pozharski's bloody English schooling — he liked to sleep in freezing fresh air. The front door was up a short passage at the side, with a small lavatory window, also shuttered, to the left of it. Burglary in full daylight was impossible — though he was nearly mad enough to try it — for the courtyard and passage were in full view of any passerby and overlooked from the other side of the street.

He tried the door, found it locked and stood by it listening. Somebody was bumping about inside — housekeeper, valet or cleaning woman. One could not imagine Pozharski getting his own breakfast. When he heard the living room door shut and movement in the hall beyond the front door, he jumped back and pretended to have just arrived and to be walking up the courtyard. The door opened. A respectable female in a black dress and a severe cloche hat came out and turned as if to shut the door behind her. Bernardo asked if Mr. Pozharski was awake yet. She regarded him with disapproval, no doubt partly due to his shabby appearance and partly because he knew that Pozharski would be sleeping late, indicating that he was some pimp or waiter with a bill from the previous night. She herself was obviously a superior servant, probably from one of the German districts of Transylvania.

"What do you want?"

"I've got a message for him."

"Mr. Pozharski has left orders that he requires no breakfast and will get up when he pleases."

Bernardo, with the open door under his eyes, saw a chance. Beneath the Yale lock was a large, conventional latch worked by the door handle. If he slipped back the Yale lock she might not notice it when she shut the door behind her.

"I will write it down and leave it if you can get me a piece of paper and a pencil."

She went into the room on the left. Bernardo fixed the lock and when she returned was standing with his back to it. He scribbled a few words of English, folded the paper and gave it to her. As soon as she had put it on the hall table he held the door open for her with a little bow of disarming courtesy. Then he followed her out and shut it.

"You work for Mr. Pozharski?" he asked as he strolled up the street with her.

"I look after the house once every week when he is not here and attend him in the morning when he is."

"Does he often come to Bucarest?"

"Mr. Pozharski's movements cannot be foreseen."

"Depends on the opposite sex, I suppose."

The remark seemed to release all her indignation at clearing up every time that Pozharski booked in at the Atheneé Palace Hotel and did not sleep there.

"A pigsty! That's what it is. A pigsty! And goodbye to you!"

She stalked up the Boulevard Carol, outraged but no doubt well paid for it. Bernardo went off the other way. As soon as she was lost to sight, he returned to 16 Strada Spâtarului and let himself in.

To the left was the large living room, expensively and darkly decorated in the style of Bakst and the Russian Ballet with the usual tiled stove in one corner roaring happily away. A double divan occupied most of a curtained alcove. The staircase faced him and he tip-toed up. There were only three doors — bedroom, bathroom and a small service kitchen.

Pozharski was fast asleep with an infantile smile on his face. His bedroom, in contrast to the living room, was of almost military simplicity and blessedly warm from the tiled flue of the downstairs room which continued up to the first floor. Bernardo drew back the curtains, shut the window and slammed a hairbrush onto the dressing table.

Pozharski started straight up in bed and looked at him with amazement. He then snuggled down again with his hand under the pillow. Bernardo stood over him with the water carafe.

"Take your hand out from under the pillow or I'll crown you," he said, remembering Pozharski's speed and accuracy with the champagne bottle and fearing that he might have learned a trick or two for dealing with unwanted visitors in bedrooms.

"Dear Bernardo, you will spill that if you aren't careful. I thought you were a nightmare — assuming one can be said to think with a slight hangover."

"Sit up!"

Pozharski sat up. His white hair and emerald pajamas radiated geniality. He was incorrigible.

"That dressing jacket, if you would be so good, and a hairbrush . . . thank you. And now, Bernardo, how did you manage to find me?"

"You have been watched since your arrival."

"Nonsense! If you were ever anybody's agent you'd have been dropped like a hot potato by now. God knows how you have managed to beat the cops without a word of the language! I shall have to tell them you called here in case they know it, but if a few thousand lei are any use to you meanwhile . . ."

"You can stick your money up your arse! And if it's the last thing I do I shall tell Kalmody you've been fucking his daughter in Bucarest."

"What a word to use of the Baroness von und zu! You remind me somehow of far-off days at Eton. Fucked his daughter, gave her twins and stopped her water. Unlikely, don't you think, dear boy? Though these recent researches in gynecology suggest that almost anything is possible."

"For you it is. And you have to be helped out by an American! I suppose you need it at your age."

"I do not. But I remind you that Americans are famous for their sandwich fillings."

"Haven't you any decency at all? A Prussian military academy is where you should have been sent."

"I was never good-looking enough to get the best out of it. Bernardo, do you think I could be allowed a brandy and ginger ale? You're the boss."

"And don't you forget it!"

"Well, if you go downstairs, you'll find all the doings in the ice box. That's the what-not which looks like an altar."

"And leave you up here? No bloody fear!"

Pozharski sighed and rolled out of bed.

"All right, we'll both go. How's that?"

Bernardo walked close behind him down the stairs. He was finding it harder and harder to deal with this intolerable Magyarized Pole as he deserved. Truculence consistently appeared as bad manners.

Pozharski politely pulled up a chair for him next to the stove, removed candles and altar cloth and poured out two pints of brandy and ginger ale.

"Bernardo, didn't I once ask you if you wanted to be cured?"

"You did and I am."

"Well, that clears one awkward problem out of the way," Pozharski said cheerfully. "Any other favor I can do you?"

"You mentioned certain circumstances . . ."

"The circumstances, dear boy, were removed in good time. Her inside, she said — or perhaps I said it — was not going to be a mere collecting box for the Church. You had something obscure to do with her change of mind. She respected you. An excellent reason for bearing your little Pforzheim I should have thought. But one never can tell with Magda. She carried on as if it was she who had put you in the family way."

"Perhaps you were able to take over from me."

"You suggested that before, Bernardo. When you were so very hard hit, I could not attempt to explain. My relations with dear Magda are as frank as they are complex. If this gullible Viennese professor we hear so much of tried to analyze them, he'd blow a fuse. But let me assure you that the entrancing American was between us like a Statue of Liberty, open, practically everywhere, to the desires of the down-trodden."

Bernardo tried hard to suppress a chuckle.

"What were you both doing here anyway?" he asked more cordially.

"We came — myself as her cicerone — to arrange a visit to Pforzheim from a specialist. And Romania has the best. Here they have so much experience denied to others."

"Same chap you got for the Emperor Franz Josef, I suppose?"

"Bernardo, your attitude to crowned heads is far too flippant for the dirty little agent you are believed to be. I cannot understand it."

"I did not kill Bobo."

"Well, the Spaniards say you did. If I were you, I should surrender to the Romanians. You can't be extradited to Spain for crimes there while you're doing time for crimes here."

"But the whole thing is absurd! My life in Bilbao was an open book."

"It was not. The police would like to know where you slipped off to alone every weekend and what you did there."

"I was praising God. Or that's what a friend of mine would say. But you won't understand."

"Oh, won't I? I, who stood in my youth upon the top of Ararat? And what about the first time some perfection of a woman gives her mouth with all her desire behind it?"

"I am sorry. Of course. How much have I got to answer if I give myself up?"

"The biggest mistake you made, my boy, was in not taking a look at that cliff. It can't be climbed. So they say you were on the top with Bobo all along looking out for the chap who tried to burgle Zita's villa. And Bobo was about fifth in succession to the Russian throne, damn it! The Romanoffs ought to give you the Order of the White Eagle for services rendered."

"Count Kalmody believed I climbed the cliff."

"Istvan is in a black fury and incomprehensible. When I last saw him I listened to the most vituperative, obscure, classical Hungarian since the sons of Arpad were converted by Saint Stephen. So far as I understood him, you and Bobo had been circulating forged French francs on behalf of the Vatican."

Bernardo had read in the Romanian papers a sensational account of members of the Hungarian aristocracy being arrested for forging francs: column after column of excited Latin journalism on the former Hapsburg monarchy, the persistent criminality of Hungarians and mysterious enemies in general. It was so hysterical a story that he had not believed a word of it.

"Somebody really did forge a lot of francs?" he asked.

"Somebody did indeed. Not Istvan, but he's in the soup, too. The police dug up Nepamuk who was so shaken that he forgot to use his influence, and your escape became front-page news. The Romanians know that you and that groom crossed the frontier illegally and that you were both Kalmody's people. Then out comes some connection between Zita, Bernardo Brown and the pancake that was Bobo — just the thing Istvan was trying to avoid by quietly removing you. And that leaves our young Bernardo either a Hungarian agent or a Bolshevik agent or both, with the French and Romanians very eager to pull out your toenails till you squeal."

"Where do the Bolsheviks come in? And may I have another drink?"

"With pleasure. They come in because of your horsy friend."

"You mean, he got clear?"

"The traditions of the conquistadores were too much for the effete frontier guards of Europe, Bernardo. When they arrested him, he set the guardhouse on fire, escaped in the excitement and crossed the river with the help of a Romanian officer. Nobody dared shoot."

"A traitor?"

"Not at all. Success with Nepamuk must have given Perico the idea. He ripped the officer's sword from its scabbard and swam him across the Dniester like a water buffalo with a goad at its rump, then delivering him to the Reds as evidence of good faith. So there's a second motive for you assassinating grand dukes. You're down in the books as a brutal thug, my boy. Look at the way you burst into my bedroom, intent on treating me as you did His Majesty's representative! He has had to be sent home on leave."

"I didn't kick him that hard."

"It was the shock to his public image rather than his private parts, dear boy. But never mind! They'll probably appoint him minister plenipotentiary in Albania to make up for it. That's the least of your worries. Look here, I've got a spare fur coat! If you rip my name out, it can't be traced."

"I'm not quite as down-and-out as I look."

"Oh, I see. Yes, very wise. Well, now that you don't think any longer that I'm going to shoot you on sight, how about a gentleman's agreement? You keep your mouth firmly shut on the sandwich and I won't say a word to the police."

"O.K. It's a deal. Are you going to tell Magda?"

"God forbid! She's just enough of a democrat to have some disastrous question asked in the Hungarian parliament and make matters worse."

"And Kalmody?"

"I'll see whether I tell him. Not yet. He's still flaming angry with you about Nepamuk, though everyone else is delighted. And nobody can go frigging around with the crown of Saint Stephen and retain Istvan's good will."

"About that attempted burglary, is he sure that Zita never missed anything?"

"Yes. Why?"

"If you get a chance, remind him that the suitcase was full, not empty. He didn't seem to pay much attention to that."

"We've been inclined to assume that you knew what was in it."

"If you could get it into your heads that my story was true . . ."

"Up to the cliff it might be."

"For Christ's sake, if you believe in the boat you must believe I climbed the cliff!"

"The bloody gendarmes swear there was only one man in the boat — the chap Istvan shot."

"Because they couldn't see as far as the end of the Lequeitio causeway."

"Bernardo, whatever you have to put up with, don't get caught yet! Now may I without embarrassing you withdraw some money from my arse?"

"If you're sure you have plenty."

"I think there must be some left from the revels. When next you see a chance of calling on me safely, dear boy, give me time to go to the bank!"

Bernardo walked home with his identity and its purpose in a chaotic muddle. At last he had Magda in perspective; there was no longer any doubt about that. But having been Bernardo Brown for an hour David Mitrani was out of focus. Mitrani might not become a merchant banker — or was it now a cabaret impresario? — after all. He might vanish, as if by a trick of time, into a personality which had never yet existed, leaving not a soul to miss him but Nadya. He pulled himself together. The daydream of resuming his true self by stages was extremely dangerous. When Pozharski had impressed on him that he must not get caught, he was warning him not to let their cordial meeting arouse any false hopes. No, he had to stick very firmly and with absolute conviction to David Mitrani. Garroting in Spain was a most unpleasant end, though said to be just as quick as hanging, if the public executioner was sober and his wrists in form.

Pozharski had insisted on giving him all the money he had, amounting to twenty thousand lei. He must have had a packet on him when he started on the Alhambra's champagne. If young Nadya had not left for her restaurant, it would have been fun to take her out on the town. She was always a quaintly original companion. He did not see enough of her except on afternoons when she had a few hours off and he had finished sleeping.

As it was, he changed his clothes, gave himself an excellent lunch and then, well fortified against the cold, strolled over to the Alhambra to see what could be done — cheaply — about the girls' complaints of the dressing room lights. He found Despina Vladimirescu on the floor, practicing dance steps to a gramophone, and stopped to watch her. She was, he thought, more attractive without makeup — a graceful creature with fresh, ivory skin and gently classical features who ought to be decorating some fashionable drawing room rather than earning a poor living in cabaret. It occurred to him for the first time that there were the devil of a lot of tall Romanian girls of distinguished appearance. His eyes must have been in the sulks too long. He asked Despina if she was working out a new number.

Despina

"I am trying to wake it up," she said. "I ought to have a partner."

"If he's good enough, Stelian will give him an audition. Have you anyone in mind?"

"No. I need a man who can really dance. But if he can, he'll either be a pansy or want to sleep with me."

"Well, who wouldn't?"

"That's as may be. I want a purely professional relationship."

"Shall I find you a cabman?"

"Please be serious, Mr. Mitrani!"

"Well, I can't see what's wrong. You look like a Hollywood star when you swing those marvelous skirts of yours."

"Up the straight, but not on the corners. Now, dance with me and I'll show you what I mean."

Omitting some intimate movements with Magda which at once became more intimate still, Bernardo had not danced since Bilbao where his flamboyant tangos had been known to clear a magic circle on the floor while equally cheerful friends applauded his cavortings from the safety of the perimeter. He mentally spat on his hands and embraced Despina. She was superbly light and flexible. It was like dancing with a willow wand from one of those Wallachian streams. He decided that, by God, he had missed his profession and sent a chair crashing into its table.

"Not so much contact," Despina said. "Your trousers are far too rough."

"It would be all right if you had a skirt on."

"And this is not a Danse d'Apaches. Now, start again! Imagine that I am a débutante and this is the coming-out ball in Vienna."

"I don't think they had tangos."

"I'll put on a valse. . . . You needn't be as far away as all

189

that. . . . And that's too close. . . . God, what did you have for lunch?"

"Ginger ale. You're not used to it, that's all. And you look delicious with your head turned away like that — straight from the convent into the arms of the archduke!"

"That's just the effect I want. Swing me gently round the corner and into the middle! Now take me right off the ground and don't hit anything! I'll do it all for you if you simply keep moving."

She did. He saw her point about the partner. One couldn't do that ecstatic swirl without something to hang on to.

"Now slow! At half the time! And lean forward while I look up at you!"

That was too much. The head thrown back, the half-closed eyes, the full-lipped, mobile mouth, small only when in repose, were irresistible. Bernardo got disappointingly little response, but at least the willow wand curved in all the right directions.

"That is not professional, Mr. Mitrani."

"Well, you shouldn't have done it. I'm not made of iron."

"We thought you were."

"Who the hell is 'we'?"

"The artistes."

"They all look as if the sun had never touched them."

"Do you expect to find Pavlova on the near eastern circuit?"

"No, and I don't expect to find the flower of all Romania either."

"We will start again, Mr. Mitrani, and remember my face is all part of the act. Don't think about it!"

"I assure you I am not, *fetitsa mea*."

The pretty Romanian diminutives were hard to speak — not that they had been left out of his vocabulary like the terms of theology, but all had been fouled in the course of passage through the ceiling above Susana's bedroom. He tried French, of which Despina understood enough for the purpose. She listened with a half smile and her head on one side — an adorable mixture of the derisive and the provocative — and had to accept what was coming to her.

She disentangled herself and spun off to the dressing room to change for the street, firmly locking the door in spite of Bernardo's pretext that he only wanted to look at the lights. When she came out, elegant and self-possessed, kisses were as if they had never been. No, she could not come out for dinner. Her aunt was expecting her. Bernardo knew the aunt since she always called for Despina at four in the morning when the Alhambra shut. She was a respectable, straight-backed, old grenadier of uninhibited speech. She might or might not be open to offers for her treasure. Despina, he knew, had run away from her husband and taken refuge with Aunt Floarea.

At night she was the same as ever, well mannered and distant. Bernardo was puzzled. He had no doubt that the interlude of the afternoon had been entirely her doing and probably due to curiosity. In the past he had been inclined to put down his occasional successes to his own irresistible approach. He observed that he was cured of that illusion, too, though still able to be intoxicated by outstanding physical loveliness as any alcoholic by the taste of liquor. Remembered Spanish beauty seemed to him hard and a little coarse compared to the Byzantine serenity of this distant Latin cousin.

It was difficult to get a moment alone with her in all the comings and goings of the Alhambra. Two nights later she at least had the decency to arrive a little early for the show, and he had time to tell her she was cruel.

"I do not know what sort of man you are, Mr. Mitrani."

"We have met every night for weeks."

"But all you gave us was indifference. One night — the night before you came bursting in and made me dance with you — you were so pale and angry that we all thought you had got the sack. Nobody could guess what was the matter with you. That's it! Yet nobody dislikes you. All I know of you is that you shout foreign languages at me and try to break me in half."

"I've never made love to anyone in Romanian."

"But you were born in Romania, they say?"

"When you were born, the stars sang for joy. Let me see you home tonight."

"You know my aunt calls for me. But I will ask her if you may come to lunch with us tomorrow, and afterwards you can take me to the Alhambra for rehearsal."

Miss Floarea Luca turned out to be a great-aunt, as Bernardo might have guessed since Despina herself was only twenty. It did not take him more than five minutes and a second shot of her admirable *pelin* to see that she had never dreamed of using the girl as a source of income. Perhaps a scion of one of the princely families might be considered as an unofficial protector, but money would be an insult.

Obviously Aunt Floarea herself had very little, though no one would have guessed it from the variety of delicate patties set out with the *pelin* and the lunch of aubergine salad, a boiled fish straight from the river, creamed chicken and the honey-tasting Tâmâioasa wine — a lady's drink but the old girl saw that his glass as well as her own was continuously full.

The flat was on the second floor of an ancient commercial building, showing bald brick where the plaster had fallen off, with a saddler's workshop underneath. It was furnished with a tremendous weight of oak made by some long-dead provincial joiner who depended on glue and dove-tailing and never used a screw. The windows looked onto a corner of the Central Market where peasants in their embroidered smocks eddied among oxen and undersized horses. Beyond were the lines of the rug sellers along the Dâmbovitsa embroidering the riverbanks themselves in red, black and green.

This was Bucarest as it had been in the last century and a proper setting for Miss Luca. Over the coffee she talked severely at both of them, praising the stern morality of her girlhood when there had been no Romania, only the two principalities of Wallachia and Moldavia governed by native princes under the suzerainty of the Turks. She recalled a land of waving corn and gross *boiars* who owned it and Greek traders, pestered by invading Russian armies and popular bandits. She prided herself on descent from Tudor Vladimirescu, a peasant hero who had impartially led revolts against Turks, Hungarians and landlords in general.

"I should have liked to show you his portrait, Mr. Mitrani, but during the German occupation of my house they used my grandfather as a lavatory seat."

Bernardo, startled by this demure, eighteenth-century frankness, made enquiring noises.

"He was in an oval frame, you see. One would not have expected such a thing even from Turks."

"They don't use seats," Despina giggled.

"I am well aware of that, my dear," Aunt Floarea replied stiffly, as if such discussions were perfectly proper at her age, but not at Despina's. "My father, I may say, had a most lucrative offer for me to join the Sultan's seraglio."

Yes, there had been the occasional, spectacular Turk trying to buy their lovely Christian virgins for the court. She considered her niece's profession was altogether too close a parallel, especially since her last engagement had been in Istanbul. Brothers, Bernardo gathered, were what Despina needed, who after protecting her honor from all those nasty foreigners with whom she had to sit at table would have fled, blood-stained and respected, into the mountains.

Miss Luca evidently approved of him. Although he was engaged in the same vile trade as Despina he was presentable and of good Moldavian descent. She went so far as to remark that her treasure had been married to a brute and that the Church would give her a divorce whenever she wanted it. He was permitted to pay a formal visit and to return hospitality at a restaurant of her choosing where the food was somewhat oriental and the gypsy music superb.

She still took Despina home from the Alhambra herself, but Bernardo was now allowed to call for her at the respectable hour of nine p.m. A fortnight passed which was enough to disinfect for him all the Romanian words of affection and to arrive at the exasperating limit of what could be effected on a public street in an open cab. Nadya remarked that he looked less worried and that, whatever he might say about the winter, it was doing him good.

He was getting fond of Great-Aunt and — for just a moment — was more sympathetic than excited when one early morning she did not turn up to take Despina home. He asked if she were ill. No, Despina said, but they had quarreled. Someone had proved to her that the name of Mitrani was Jewish. Aunt Floarea stormed that she had been grossly deceived by both of them; they had allowed her to think that he was of good family. His accent and the little mistakes he made in the language had reminded her of the *boiars* of her youth who were educated abroad and spoke more French than Romanian. Neither she nor Despina would have anything more to do with him. Turning Christian just to get a job!

"What did you say?"

"That you'd have got a much better one by remaining a Jew."

"But then I should never have met you."

"I believe you never had any religion at all, David. But it takes courage to leave one's past. It was not easy to leave my husband, but he could think of nothing but money."

"Well, Aunt will be over it very soon."

"Maybe. But I shall not. I am not going home."

Old Mr. Brown looked back through the fog of the years. Probably there was little to be seen through it but the ivory pillar of Despina and the mixed appeal and decision of autumn-colored eyes of which the expression rather than the shape remained.

"Neultata Despina! Unforgettable! I can see the comedy of Magda — that febrile, overwhelming actress. But Despina: no comedy, no bitterness, just a divine simplicity fit to be worshiped. I did, by God! And always the exquisite, drowsy response. You don't expect acrobatics of Aphrodite."

The only thing which interrupted the undiluted worshiping was a slight inquietude about Nadya. He vaguely felt himself in the position of, say, a widower living with his daughter and reluctant to parade an affair too obviously. Her room was far enough away on the next floor, and she had no chance of observing his return from work unless she deliberately looked out for him. There was, however, the common bathroom which she used when he was still fast asleep. He got up once and inspected it with the care of a detective until sure that there was no trace of Despina.

In the long run he reckoned that it would be easy for Nadya to accept the position. Her work at the restaurant and his at the Alhambra only left a couple of hours in the afternoon for him to keep an eye on her. Despina's private rehearsals would still allow time for that. Nadya in any case could hardly be shocked. In the aftermath of the revolution the back-street search for any kind of sexual satisfaction must have been as familiar to her as the back-street search for bread. Bernardo had never discussed the matter with her. Considering Stepanov's dismal exhibition and her disillusionment after eloping from the convent, delicacy precluded the subject. He was inclined to think that Nadya would never have any sex life or, if she did, that it would be some detestable affair in which the man's part would be limited to a short-lived curiosity.

For three days he congratulated himself on getting away with it. Nadya left for her restaurant while he and Despina were still in bed, and by the time she came back for her free hours of the afternoon, the pair of them had gone out for their breakfast-cum-lunch, after which Despina went off to the Alhambra. Twice he cleared his throat with the intention of having a fatherly chat with young Nadya and both times she seemed too abstracted for him to get anywhere. It was absurd and distracting that he should have difficulty in reconciling two plain and easy relationships.

It was Despina who broke the spell of inaction by asking if the girl upstairs was a servant. Bernardo said she was a Russian refugee who worked as a waitress.

"What a curious figure!"

"She didn't have much to eat for a long time. Perhaps she can't help making up for it."

"And such an exquisite face! We ought to do something for her."

Bernardo, wriggling on this unforeseen hook, asked what.

"We could tell her she would be lovely if she took more care and exercise. Or is she pregnant?"

"Not by me."

"As if I think you'd take a roly-poly pudding to bed unless you were drunk! And then a girl as sweet as that wouldn't look at you. How like a man to live under the same roof and not ask questions!"

"I can't go asking strange girls if they are pregnant."

"But I can."

This was the devil. He went up to Nadya's room that afternoon and warned her that a — um — friend of his was likely to ask awkward questions.

"She has, David."

"Already, you mean?"

"Yes. You were still asleep and she was going out when I came in. So we talked and she came to my room."

Bernardo suspected that Despina had not been quite so sure as she sounded about the roly-poly pudding, but she could not be accused of duplicity. She never said that she had not talked to Nadya, only that she intended to.

"What did you tell her?"

"What I tell everyone — that my bones are a little deformed. I don't think she believed me because she asked if I was pregnant and if she could help."

"The darling!" Bernardo exclaimed enthusiastically.

"Yes, she is. I thought that when she came home with you she was just here for the night."

"You knew?"

"Of course I knew."

"She might be here for some time, Nadya."

"She must love you very much."

"I don't think so. Just a little."

"Then God does not like it."

"But I do."

"Do you want me to find somewhere else to live?"

"Of course not! What for? This place is just made for you until you get your passport."

He knew at once that he should not have mentioned "un-

til." Always in talking with her he tried to avoid any forecast
of a future from which David Mitrani and his moral support,
such as it was, might have to vanish without warning.

"Are you going to marry her?" Nadya asked. "If you marry
her, I shall not lose you."

That took a bit of working out until he saw what she
meant. She knew very well that he was English and compelled
for some reason to hide it. That lovely Romanian girl who
could afford to be generous represented possible permanency.
If there were anything which could settle him firmly in time
and space it might be Despina.

Thereafter Bernardo's home life continued in peace, though
he heard Nadya's laughter less often. When Despina, apparently seeing more of her than he did, repeated the sad story
of her life, he observed that Nadya had given nothing away of
her essential secrets, managing to slide without any perceptible
break from the convent to the restaurant and keeping up a
pretense of meeting Mr. Mitrani for the first time when he
took the downstairs room. Bernardo had never suspected that
she could use her angelic simplicity as an impenetrable cover,
never complicating anything unnecessarily. She would have
made a much better secret agent than he.

Despina had not forgotten her need of a partner. Bernardo
made no effort whatever to find one for her but Stelian did,
engaging — of all unlikely nationalities — a Norwegian known
on the near eastern circuit for uninspiring competence and
astonishing good looks. He had been dancing with a German
girl in Athens when the partnership was broken up by a
monumental row in which the lady had thrown a whole crate
of empty bottles at his head, leaving the young martyr
chivalrously passive but out of a job. Bernardo gathered from
the reports that he was of Arctic rectitude and not over-
sophisticated — in fact that it wouldn't have much affected

his intelligence if his partner had hit him with a sledge-hammer. To judge by the manliness of his photographs he and Despina — if they could hit it off — would be an outstanding couple, compelling admiration however well or badly they danced.

Though the pair had no common language but bad French, Despina was delighted with Holgar Johannsen and had high hopes of contracts in Vienna and Paris. He was put up at the Principesa where his manners and little formal bows created as favorable an impression as the Prince of the Rosicrucians. Bernardo was at first inclined to agree with Aunt Floarea that dancers were too open to temptation, but soon saw that he had no need to be jealous. Holgar was a model of correctitude with no secret Nordic passions which might break surface at the afternoon rehearsals.

He was even *persona grata* with his consul who had once turned up at the Alhambra. It was doubtful whether this dilapidated Viking had ever been in a civilized cabaret before since he tried to take Despina on his knee and demanded beer. In view of his diplomatic status the maître d'hôtel had sent out a boy to get it for him and he had then disputed the bill. Holgar apologized for him, saying that he was a most worthy, clean-living man and a fine influence upon such Scandinavian seamen as found themselves stranded or in trouble in the Danubian ports. The consul had, Bernardo judged, the inno-cence of his native north plus the hearty, filthy mind which went with it.

Holgar of course did not sit at tables, but neither did he go home to bed at the Principesa. Still magnificent in his tails, he considered it his duty to keep an eye on Despina in case she was insulted, which she never was. Her excited admirers were always allowed to think that she was so overcome by their charm and champagne that they were ready to wait an hour for her at the front door when she had long since gone home with Bernardo from the back. Bernardo found this misplaced chivalry incredibly comic and encouraged Miss Lou, outwardly the other saint of the Alhambra, to invite Holgar to take tea in her apartment. Stelian discovered the result, though the dressing room knew nothing. Holgar had indignantly removed a slender hand. He was sure, he said, that it had strayed accidentally but told his few male acquaintances all the same.

It was a month or so after Holgar's arrival that Bernardo had a curious conversation with Stelian, who of course knew Bernardo's background from his conversion on but had never shown any interest in Bernardo's story that he had been taken to Morocco as a child. Stelian asked him to have a drink in his office before the first customers arrived and talked vaguely of opening up another establishment in the oil town of Ploeshti.

"You ought to speak German, dear Mitrani."

"I can learn if it's worthwhile."

"It should be easy for you since you speak Yiddish."

"I don't. My family was Spanish-speaking."

"Then how was it you were born in a village of Ashkenazi Jews?"

Bernardo was immediately wary. His boss was a pure Romanian from the west of Wallachia where there was only a scattering of Jews. He would certainly have picked up in cosmopolitan Bucarest the difference between those of Spanish and those of Central European origin, but he was unlikely to know that the former were uncommon in Moldavian villages.

"Why not?" Bernardo replied to see what he would say.

Stelian seemed to cover embarrassment by pouring out two more glasses. It was obvious that he did not know why not. So somebody else had put him up to asking the question and that somebody else had better be answered. Bernardo explained that after the Kishinev pogrom of 1907 refugees were all

mixed up. Anyone who could emigrated to America. Others
settled down in Moldavian villages. He had no idea whether
there was any truth in the explanation but it would be difficult
to deny.

The question smelt as if it had been prompted by the
police. They liked to work discreetly. He himself had occasionally been asked to find out personal details of an artiste.
This interest in his past was probably of no importance but
should not be ignored. For some reason or other he had
emerged from safe obscurity.

He asked Despina whether anyone had been showing
curiosity about him.

"Only chatter in the dressing room."

"What do you tell them?"

"Whatever comes into my head," she laughed.

"Have you ever heard questions about Nadya? I don't mean
from the girls. They have never seen her."

"From Holgar I have. He has only met her once but she
made an impression. Do Russians like Norwegians?"

"Russians like everybody to start with. For God's sake
don't try to fix them up! That fellow hangs around enough
as it is."

"He only calls for me in the afternoon, David."

"And sits and sits."

Bernardo loathed her partner. It was intolerable to watch
Despina floating round the floor with half-closed eyes in the
arms of such a spectacular half-wit. He could never resist returning Holgar's little bows and heel-clickings with more of
the same.

"But you mustn't tease him."

"He doesn't see it. He thinks the vulgar Latin who takes
you home is gradually picking up the manners of a gentleman."

"Worse than vulgar, *iubit!* You're a bad influence and he would like to protect me. I am a beautiful shepherdess from the mountains in your evil grip."

Well, that was all right. If the police were seriously interested, they would have put the screws on Despina and found that she could tell them no more than Stelian. A shopworn lot, the Bucarest police! They had the Slav enthusiasm for reporting vague suspicions, corrected by the Latin insistence on a complete dossier before action. The easiest way of combining the two for underpaid, underfed cops was inaction.

But the next little pointer was not long in coming. The Alhambra doorman handed him a letter which had been left for him, he said, by a fat, dark woman. They were both used to that. Half the prostitutes in town thought the Alhambra was a showroom and wanted to be allowed to sit there. The note was anonymous and asked him to turn up at a café in the Calea Budeshti about six o'clock — an invitation which he would have ignored if it had not been written in badly spelt French.

This was almost certainly a voice from the Crucea de Piatra. Since he had left only good will behind him — except for Susana — and he was not earning enough to be worth blackmail, it could do no harm to keep the appointment.

The place was the usual bar-cum-grocer's, serving local residents of any class with good wine at a few bare wooden tables. It was too far away to supply the simple needs of the Crucea de Piatra, but near enough for varicosed legs off duty. He arrived early and sat at the table closest to the door. It was opened a quarter. Eva peered cautiously into the café, hesitated and joined him. She was even more appalling than he remembered her, in a sagging dress of royal blue velvet trimmed with so much decaying rabbit that she suggested a gamekeeper hung with cleaned carcasses; yet her eyes were still magnificent and — so far as any thought was in them — kindly.

"I did not recognize you, David."

"Another suit. That's all. What will you take?"

White wine and red carp caviar and a vast grocer's sandwich — all very cheap but enough to keep her going till some other irregular cheating of hunger.

"I am always grateful, dear Eva. Tell me what I can do for you."

"Nothing. I am not for the Alhambra. I have come to tell you that you have an enemy. Perhaps you have taken a girl who belongs to some big man."

"No. There's an old lady who is annoyed that her niece is a dancer."

"She should be glad! Well, if it's her she must have friends in the police. One of them has been asking me when I first saw you. How should I know? One year is like another. Some time after Easter, I said."

"That's right. Did he ask Susana too?"

"Yes. She sent him to me. She has not forgiven you and would do you all the harm she can. So she said you had been living on women for years."

"What about our cop? He knew when I came."

"He's dead. The sewer overflowed and he slipped on the ice and cracked his skull. Some of us went to the funeral. He was a good man. They get kind when they are too old for promotion."

That was a bit of luck — God rest his soul! Susana, if she was believed, had proved his presence in Bucarest long before his real arrival, and Eva had put it four months too early.

"Did the man ask what languages I spoke?"

"Yes. I had forgotten that. We all said the same — that you spoke French and Spanish and bad Romanian and that was all."

Bernardo went home uneasily considering what he had learned. The inquiry could not have anything to do with Giurgiu and Nadya, and was most unlikely to have been started off by Aunt Floarea. However unforgiving, she was too experienced an old bird to give Despina a bad reputation with the police. So Bernardo Brown was the chap they were after. It had occurred to somebody that he could be David Mitrani.

There must be conflicting reports in the dossier. The evidence from the Crucea de Piatra, for what it was worth, clearly indicated that Mitrani did not speak English and had not crossed the frontier in September. On the other hand somebody must have repeated his weak story that he had landed in Galatz with a horse from Morocco. That could be checked with the port, though wrong dates would complicate the inquiry.

But meanwhile why not haul David Mitrani up to the headquarters of security police for a — to start with — friendly talk? Bernardo could make a disturbing guess at the answer. They might not be inefficiently shuffling papers; they might be leaving him at liberty inside a net that was closing. Bernardo Brown, to be extradited to Spain on a charge of murder, was an ordinary, unimportant criminal. Bernardo Brown, forger of bank notes for political motives, secret agent of Hungarians or Russians or both, was far more interesting. Mr. Mitrani had better get out of the country while the going was still good. But where to and how? To try to obtain a passport was hopeless. His application and the documents to be signed would force the issue and compel the police to act at once.

He had to run. Over which frontier? He dared not risk a return to Hungary. He was certain to be picked up, and if Kalmody was busy lying his way out of trouble he'd do his best to see that the awkward witness was slapped into Spain as soon as identified. Yugoslavia? Bulgaria? The Danube at least offered a slim chance, using his knowledge of shipping, to stow away and reach Istanbul.

It was hard to tear himself away from his proud and gentle Despina, but he knew it was not going to hurt as much as the parting from Magda. Anyway it had to be, and without a word. She was bound to be interrogated by the police and the less she knew, the better. She had never bothered about his past. He could not remember telling her anything much except fantasies of camels and palm trees and answering questions about the prospects for a cabaret dancer in Tangier.

Mr. Brown looked back upon his Unforgettable, silently weighing up the particular crossroad of his life which she represented and what might have happened if he had been free to take it.

"Despina taught me that one can love without agony. Not the highest form, perhaps, but a step on the way, a step on the way. The perfect, lasting honeymoon. Sad to think it would have ended in sheer boredom like the harps of heaven. She? Well, soon she would have been off with that damned Holgar on a round of engagements. She knew there could be no permanency for us. And permanency — does a woman ever give her whole soul without at least a dream of it? Standing among the smoke of the burning bras but still at heart invincible monogamists! She was no girl to be in tears before the ikon of the Virgin. A Lilith, not an Eve. I had no restless anxiety about her future. I was able much later, anonymously, to do a little something for her."

What he did worry about — and the sharpness of it surprised him — was Nadya. He wanted to see a life for her, not a living. She was all right for that; her face and her nature and the help of her compatriots would carry her through. But all those difficulties of privacy which he had settled for her were insistent. A slipup could easily lead to the question: Are you Nadya Stepanov?

The next day he decided to go up to her room to prepare her, but just to sit on the edge of a bed was too callous for what might be a last meeting. It was spring, warm enough to laze outside in the afternoon. Russia had receded into its melting snows and the Mediterranean, out of barracks, was feeling for the empty space beyond the Balkan Mountains. He walked to her restaurant, taking for the first time precautions that he was not followed. When she appeared, he suggested that they drive — choosing a hairy cabman — out to the chain of lakes which formed a crescent around the north of Bucarest.

They walked off into the silent world of the rushes, she ecstatic at the ending of the cold which, all the same, she had so much enjoyed. Her people had learned to live happily with the seasons of the year, he thought, unlike the English who sulkily tolerated winter or the Spaniards who cursed the discomfort.

"Nadya, I want to talk to you seriously," he said. "Come here and stop dancing around!"

"About Holgar?"

"Holgar? What's he got to do with it? No, I may have to leave Bucarest suddenly."

"With Despina?"

"Not with Despina."

She took his arm with a quick little gesture of sympathy.

"This is to do with the reason why you won't speak English?"

"It is."

"I told you my life, David. Why don't you tell me yours? You know I can keep secrets."

He did. She had kept theirs perfectly. And there might be others. For example, what the hell had Holgar been up to that she should think him a reason for driving out to the lakes? She had a right to be told why he had to disappear. Despina would learn some of it from the questions which the police asked her. Nadya, however, being merely a Russian refugee whose only known connection with him was that she happened to live in the same house, was unlikely to be bothered.

"Yes, I'll tell you all of it."

They sat on the water steps of a deserted summer tavern with the brown lake at their feet, motionless as it had been under the ice but already with green spears sprouting from the shallows. He gave her the story quite shortly from Lequeitio to the Principesa, though reliving all the past with the speed of thought. When he began to speak of Romania — omitting for her the Crucea de Piatra — he realized for the first time how his affection for country and people had grown. Partly it was due to Despina, coming in as an epitome of the tall and lovely women so much more competent than their men, but it had begun with music in a ditch, the roar of the Mosh and Nadya herself, the dripping orphan received in a war-ravaged country with such pity and kindness.

It was the plain he loved, not the mountains. Mountains were the same everywhere unless they had the sea at their feet. Willows and reeds, birds and buffaloes and wine, the low chant of the rivers as they glided from the rim of Transylvania to the Danube — those would be his memories. Yes, it was a country where a mooring post was quite likely to pull out under strain, which would seldom happen in Hungary. That was an example of the difference, of the reason why that romantic and aristocratic people should despise the mixture next door, ignoring the fact that the mixture had its roots in the Eastern Roman Empire. There were no counts and barons, only peasants with a stake in the land and a middle class, with melancholy and intelligent eyes, nearly as poor as they.

Beyond exclamations of sympathy Nadya's only comment was that he should never have denied his religion.

"I did not. I denied a mere formality. Leave out names! You should have known Rabbi Kaplan. He looked as fierce as Moses and was as gentle as Christ. His religion was the same as yours."

When he came to the end and his certainty that the police were making inquiries about him, she said that he must go at once and that she would come with him.

Bernardo was alarmed. The last thing he wanted was to be responsible for her as well as himself.

"You can't. You have no passport. You must never go away from here until you have it and are safely Miss Andreyev."

"I can get one now. Tomorrow if I like."

"How? What for?"

"Like the Mosh. But worse, I think."

"Who found you out?"

"Holgar."

"Before I go I'll leave him in the Crucea de Piatra with a knife in his back."

"It was an accident. You mustn't blame him."

"How did it happen?"

"He came in while you and Despina were still at lunch and while he was waiting he went to the bathroom. You know how the door sometimes jams. I suppose he was in a hurry and thought it had. So he gave it a kick and broke the lock and I couldn't get out of the bath in time."

"Did he say anything to Despina?"

He was sure that Despina would have kept the secret even from him, but equally sure that she would have discussed it with Nadya.

"No, but he must have told someone. There's a man who knows and he talks to me at the restaurant."

"Who the hell is he?"

"I don't know his name. A Belgian. They say he is going round the cabarets."

Bernardo could identify him at once — a nasty bit of work called Henri Scheeper with an air of false distinction entirely due to an unlined, massaged face under dyed hair and a white mèche in it. He was scouting for turns sufficiently exotic to interest Brussels. Despina had been interviewed by him and had at first been impressed. He offered good money but would not consider a partner in what he described as intimate cabaret. Holgar had hopefully called at his hotel and spent some time over drinks with him, receiving only vague promises that his name would be kept in mind.

"He wants me to travel with him. He says he can fix it," Nadya went on. "I wouldn't do what I think he wants. But I should be out of Romania and we could find each other somehow."

Bernardo lectured her. Didn't she know how many of her dreaded frontiers she would have to cross to reach Brussels? And how could she ever find him when he was on the run? He had never heard such blazing, artless lunacy. She must promise him never to speak to the man again.

"I must, David. You forget I am a waitress," she answered meekly. "But I promise I will never go with him if you will promise me something too."

"What's that?"

"Swear you will see me again before you escape and tell me

where you will try to go. Come at once to the restaurant or wherever I am!"

"I promise."

He had no doubt what had happened. In talking with Scheeper that simpering ass Holgar had emphasized his gallant sense of responsibility for Despina and had spoken of her lamentable attachment to a degenerate Romanian — shepherdess in his evil grip, as she had put it! Scheeper, finding this threw a new and more promising light on the cool beauty he had interviewed, encouraged details, and out came the shocking Sunday-paper revelations. Mitrani had been a ponce in the most disgusting quarter of the city. Mitrani was a mercenary louse on the face of the earth. Mitrani kept another girl upstairs with four breasts.

Bernardo was sure this had something to do with the inquiries about his past, though there seemed no obvious connection. Giurgiu, perhaps? But not a soul had known of his visit; he had got clean away with his rescue of Nadya. What was it Eva had said? Such intelligence as she had was confined to rat-like scufflings through garbage, but there she was a reliable guide. She had asked if he had taken a girl who belonged to some big man.

Got it! That precious pair! Holgar had also whispered the secret of Mitrani's bestial enjoyments to his dear friend, the consul, who had licked his lips in lecherous horror. And then Holgar had pressed him to act. Surely a consul could protest to the police and get the fellow removed as a public disgrace?

The police of course would not give a damn whether the floor manager of the Alhambra was ten times more infamous in his pleasures than Pozharski. But since it was a consul — Eva's big man — who complained that Mitrani was keeping monsters and possibly procuring minors, they had at least made some routine inquiries about his background. And then some knowledgeable cop, unshaven for two days and at the blissful stage when *tsuica* inspired imagination just before imbecility, had wondered how a Spanish-speaking Jew could have been born in the ghetto of Roman.

So they had duly established that Mitrani had indeed been a ponce in the Crucea de Piatra and was no doubt as revolting a character as the consul described. But that was no crime. They were not after Bernardo Brown at all. Far more likely than arrest was a blackmailing approach inviting him to report on any likely artiste who might wish — or be persuaded to accept — the protection of a captain of police during her engagement in Bucarest.

Bernardo was satisfied. The future, after all, was still worth dreaming about. He could look forward to a further step in his profession as manager of the proposed new establishment in Ploeshti, where he might well make so much money that Despina could retire and their delightful affair need not be interrupted. He had thought that it would be their last night together and intended to implant in his memory every downy, delicious half inch of her. That could equally well be done as a thanksgiving service. The only definite action that he was determined to take was to arrange an accident for Holgar, not fatal but ensuring a longish stay in hospital. It might be profitable to ask which of them had the highest record for septicemia.

It was not surprising that he was a bit drowsy the following night at the Alhambra, paying no attention to audience or artistes. Shortly after Despina's turn he had business with the maître d'hôtel and walked round behind the band to the service door. From that angle the shadowed box on the dais, where Pozharski had sat with Magda, was in full view. There were two Romanians in it. One was Mircea Niculescu, the tailor who had exchanged clothes with him; the other was gray-faced and baggy-eyed with the plumply satisfied air of a politician or a colonel.

They were looking away from him, perhaps deliberately, but they must have seen his face again and again under the lights at the artistes' entrance. David Mitrani had been identified as the man on the train in riding breeches. It was no good making a bolt for the street until he saw what the setup was, so he continued on his way to the maître d'hôtel, spoke to him and casually returned as if he had noticed nothing. He looked out of the back door. Across the street were two brown-uniformed policemen who had never been there before.

The front door was bound to be guarded, but one might as well see. This time he passed round the other side of the hall directly below the dais. As he passed the box Niculescu pretended to be hunting for something under the table. The other man looked through him with a complete absence of expression.

Stelian was in his office. Nothing was to be lost by trying to guess whether the police had warned him or not. Bernardo asked him who the two fellows in the box were. They saw few middle-class Romanians unless a foreigner was paying the bill. Stelian answered that one was a Major Vlaicu of Military Security and the other his tailor.

"How long have they been here?"

"Since about half past eleven. Yes, that's it. Mircea Niculescu didn't look at all happy. I reckon he wanted his bill paid instead of being softened up with champagne."

At first sight the front door did not appear to be guarded. Bernardo was tempted to jump straight into a *trasura* which had just delivered late arrivals, but the doorman simultaneously engaged it for a customer who emerged from the cloak room slightly unsteady on his feet. Fifty yards up the street the cab was stopped by a municipal policeman accompanied by an apparent civilian, and the passenger was asked for his identity card. The other end of the street was blocked as well; now that Bernardo knew what to look for, he could distinguish two figures in the shadow of a doorway. It was plain that these outside operators did not know his face, though they were bound to have a detailed description. Major Vlaicu had not ordered his men to come inside so that he could point out the suspect.

So much caution was alarming and could not be just for the sake of avoiding a scandal. Straight police arrests had been carried out before in the Alhambra, usually of some young fool who was spending someone else's money in the place; he was asked if he would take a drink in Stelian's office and he went and nobody was any the wiser. No, Bernardo Brown, the international agent and assassin, was such an important catch that nothing was to be allowed which could put him on his guard.

The game was up, but it was impossible for Bernardo to guess how the end would come. He might be grabbed when the cabaret emptied or, if that was too long to wait, whenever Vlaicu thought fit to send a waiter quietly out to the doorman with a message to his operatives. Perhaps Vlaicu was wondering if Niculescu could possibly be wrong, since the suspect must have noticed him and had not shown a sign of agitation. It was lucky that Bernardo had been dreaming on his feet. If he had been more alert, he would have been out of there as soon as the tailor walked in and run straight into the net.

He returned to the artistes' entrance. Despina had changed and was just floating out in a new dove-gray evening creation, filmy as a wisp of cloud and calling for a pair of fat cupids to play tag on top of it. He managed to whisper for the last time that she was the flower of all women and then she was immediately invited to Vlaicu's table where there was now a third man. Poor Despina! But she could come to no harm. She knew nothing, and it would not take them long to be convinced of her proud honesty. Bernardo drew back into the shadows to watch.

She played her usual hard-to-get trick of standing by the table as if charmingly uncertain in what company she found herself. She must have genuinely disliked Vlaicu or else she was saying that she would fetch another girl to join the party. At any rate she turned to go and then suddenly collapsed into a chair. Vlaicu had grabbed her wrist and pulled her down.

Her face was set hard in indignation. The third man said something, possibly identifying himself as a police officer. Police or no police, Despina was not standing such treatment. She shook her head disdainfully and looked round for help, but everyone was watching the last turn: a splendid Georgian leaping about and throwing knives from his mouth. Again she tried to get up, and Vlaicu's assistant held her down with a hard hand on her thigh. Nobody noticed except Bernardo and the ever officious Holgar.

He advanced upon the table — the Galahad of the near eastern circuit in his shining armor of white tie and tails. The hand was very high up on that thigh in its tempting mist of dove-gray, and Holgar evidently misunderstood the situation. He remonstrated with those coarse-looking Romanians. The highly improbable had happened at last; this was the chance Holgar had been waiting for to show himself a man, cleansed of the disgrace of Mitranis and four-breasted ladies and the mercenary trade. He was told quietly to go away and shut up. Despina managed to rise to her feet and also appealed to him, perhaps telling him not to be a fool, perhaps trying to create a diversion as if she had guessed or been told that it was David Mitrani who was in danger. And then Holgar produced an almost professional left and right developed in some innocent

Oslo gymnasium. The right hooked the third man over the table which broke under him. The left landed on Vlaicu's straining fourth waistcoat button. Everyone turned round at the crash. The Georgian dropped a knife and loosed a blast of thunderous Russian as it quivered point downwards in his boot. Mircea Niculescu had vanished. Vlaicu was vomiting champagne.

Bernardo saw a wild outside chance and took it. He dashed to the back door. All depended on what orders the two uniformed cops had received — with luck the simplest for simple men: just to prevent anyone leaving by that door.

"Help! Help!" he yelled. "Major Vlaicu is attacked. Quick! Draw your guns!"

They didn't hesitate. They dashed into the Alhambra fumbling with their holsters. Bernardo grabbed a hat from the pegs and ran.

The street at the back of the Alhambra was long and narrow, with the first crossroad over a hundred yards ahead. When he reached it, the pursuit was momentarily hesitating at the back door and about to race after him. Vlaicu might be out of action, but his Number Two was efficient. As Bernardo turned left, sprinting for the Calea Victoriei, he saw that a second lot was on his track led by the two fellows who had stopped the cab near the front of the Alhambra. If they had known of his escape half a minute earlier than they did, he would have been intercepted at the crossroads.

It was after one and the Calea Victoriei was nearly empty, offering no chance of mingling with passersby. He crossed the street at a fast walk since there were three policemen on normal duties in sight, and then ran down the first available side street regardless of the stares of a few pedestrians. He had sacrificed his lead and was stranded in a blank quarter of public buildings without any alleys or courtyards. Having put two

215

corners between himself and the pursuit, he saw ahead of him a pool of white light outside the back of a newspaper office where the last of the bundles were being heaved into waiting carts. If he dared to slow down and approach at a walk he might be able to bluff his way in and disappear.

But there was not enough time and he knew it. Another desperate chance offered. At the back of the Military Club were a couple of garbage cans — the large cans with wheels and shafts which the municipal collectors pushed from house to house. He jumped into one and crouched down. It had no lid but it was the only hope. A moment later a rush of feet went past succeeded by other, heavier, more conversational followers like a blown field pounding along behind a pack of silent hounds. They ignored the garbage cans hypnotized, as he had been, by all the activity around the pool of light. It was so obvious a place for a fugitive to mix with other human beings and be lost.

What to do now? Just down the road was the Cismigiu Park. He believed it was not open at night, but a desperate man could surely find somewhere to climb in. Before he could make up his mind, he heard enough whistles and shouts from that direction to make it certain that the police, the military, the secret service, the Hapsburgs led by a side-saddled Zita and any other enthusiastic members of the hunt had had the same idea. They had gone for the Cismigiu.

Bernardo decided to remain where he was, though it was agonizingly risky. There must be a party still searching among printing machines and delivery chutes; when they came out they might take a look in the garbage cans. Alternatively a kitchen boy could appear from the Military Club, where a ball or reception was in progress, and heave a load of sturgeon bones and mayonnaise on him. It was bad enough as it was. He seemed to be squatting on the remains of teatime pastries.

Despina

He waited nearly an hour until the door of the newspaper building clanged down. Valses at the Military Club were still in full swing, but the street was deserted and it was safe to move if there was anywhere to go. On two sides were the Cismigiu and the wide Boulevard Elisabeta, both of which must be avoided. Just to the north was the Royal Palace. Solitary and suspicious night-walkers, whether wanted by the police or not, had better keep clear of that. The only hope was to the east, and that meant crossing the Calea Victoriei again.

It had to be done, though he would land in the smart diplomatic quarter with well-lit streets and a sprinkling of police about. They could probably be bluffed, for he looked respectable apart from whatever was sticking to his trousers. Patrolling only their routine beats, they need not necessarily have been alerted. The main cordon would be between the Cismigiu and the Crucea de Piatra — a very likely spot for the ex-ponce to go to ground.

Bernardo scraped his trousers with half a broken plate and then took a very cautious look at the Boulevard Elisabeta. Not a ghost of a chance there, as he had thought. The police had gone all modern. There was an open car stuffed with them down by the railings of the Cismigiu and another close to the intersection with the Calea Victoriei. He tried the opposite direction, passing round the north side of the Military Club. This was more hopeful. At the end of the street he could see a few guests leaving the club on foot. A bunch of them must sometime cross the vital main avenue and he could join them. Or could he? All the bastards who were civilians had overcoats over full evening dress. He would be more conspicuous accompanying them than crossing alone.

He waited, feeling exposed and unconvincing. The tendency of Romanians to stand and chat before doing anything saved him. Half a dozen post office clerks drifted out of the telephone building on the other side of the street and stood talking on the pavement. He joined them as soon as they started to move, crossed the Calea Victoriei alongside four of them and dived into the opposite side street. There were now more people about, going home from whatever late entertainment they fancied, and he felt less noticeable. He was on the route by which he had escaped, and away to his right was the gaily lit front door of the Alhambra — the last place, he thought, where anyone would be looking for him.

Wrong again! A cop some way off shouted: *Asculta, domnule!* Listen, sir! implying that he must wait and be questioned. He ran again. It was the end of safety and any possible bluff in that respectable district. The only thing to do was to break out across the Boulevard Carol which was a continuation of the Elisabeta but possibly not yet patrolled. It soon would be when that cop reported a running man.

He crossed the wide, empty boulevard, forcing himself to walk steadily like any good citizen with nothing on his conscience. On the other side were older, darker, less fashionable streets. He felt that the pressure on him had lost immediacy. There was no particular reason why he should be in this quarter more than any other. The cordon round the Crucea de Piatra, if there was one, would be further south.

After exploring several small parallel roads for possible cover and escape routes he came to a dark space with a church in it. Though paved and open, it seemed a good place in which to wait for morning. From the shadows of dense black thrown by a bright half moon anyone approaching could be seen in plenty of time to take evading action. If he could hang on there or thereabouts till full daylight he might join the crowds going to work in the financial district and somehow get clear of the city.

Meanwhile all was silent except for two cats melodiously mating over low roofs and in and out of the square. An older Bucarest, ignoring the vulgarities of police, cars, cabarets and the agitated military, slept in peace by the protecting dome of its almost village church. On the cobbles, outside the entrance, was a poor, single-horse *trasura*, driver and horse exhausted, one asleep in the passenger seat, the other on its feet. All was rest. Rest at last.

"Idyllic!" Mr. Brown remembered. "Idyllic, I say. They maintain — or used to — that the fox enjoys being hunted. Nonsense! But there may be a moment, when hounds have lost his line, of triumph, of peace exaggerated by what has gone before."

The snores of the cabdriver were audible but gentle. Bernardo envied his peasant tranquility and then realized that, as so often, his troubles had been lulled away by alcohol. Poor devil, working late, swilling *tsuica* — it was not worthwhile driving miles down the Boulevard Carol to some miserable hovel on the outskirts of the city. He could sleep it off where he was and perhaps pick up a fare, someone who had missed his tram, in the early morning. The Boulevard Carol. . . . The last time Bernardo had been down it was his furious march on Pozharski's love-nest.

By God, that was an idea! No place could be safer than the discreet and shuttered house. He could stay there unsuspected till the hunt died down. But he dared not break in during daylight. It had to be done at night, at once, taking the chance that no one would pay particular attention to the crash as he broke the side window and the shutter.

Strada Spâtarului was less than ten minutes' walk away, but the odds were a hundred to one against reaching it unchallenged. That cop who had seen him run must have reported the incident by now and the Carol would be just as hot as the

Elisabeta. Bernardo had the wild idea of removing the cabman and driving the *trasura* down the boulevard. It wouldn't do. For one thing the driver might wake up; for another, he could not expect to get away with driving a *trasura* — if he could drive it at all — sitting on the box in a respectable suit and no overcoat.

He took a closer look at the driver who smelt of stale alcohol and pickled cucumber. He would sleep through anything so long as he remained sprawled in the back of the cab. So the horse at any rate was available, though its trot was probably slower than that of the fattest Bucarest policeman. But why bother about its speed? Bernardo perceived that a walking horse was all he needed, plus the driver's hat and any other handy garment.

He had never had time to notice the hat he grabbed as he rushed out of the Alhambra. It was not his own. It was very expensive black astrakhan lined with silk and probably belonged to the Georgian knife dancer. Such a fine hat would be ample recompense for the driver if he had the sense to keep quiet about it. Very gently he removed the pointed, gray-mottled, sheepskin hat from the driver's head and substituted the astrakhan. There was an old rug on the box seat — filthy, but a driver who left his cab surely would not leave it for anyone to steal.

With the rug over his shoulders and the literally lousy hat on his head he slipped the traces off the horse's collar and quietly lowered the shafts to the ground. The horse woke up with a general air of resignation and seemed quite willing to be led anywhere by anybody. Bernardo was about to start when he remembered that Pozharski's house was modern; there might not be any slat of the shutters so rotted by snow that it could be knocked in or torn out by the bare hand. After

casting round among harness and springs and with a side
glance at the church — but lead piping would not do and
there was unlikely to be a chisel in the vestry — he opened the
lid of the box seat. Inside was a rusty biscuit tin with needles,
waxed thread and leather patches for repairing harness together with a worn, sharp knife. He took it, and finding himself unable to steal from someone fated to be permanently
wretched — as indeed he might be too, but not yet — left a
few notes in its place.

The choice of a route was tricky. It was essential not to
draw attention to Strada Spâtarului by entering or stopping
near the street; on the other hand he dared not go far beyond
it since he would have to walk back without the cover of the
horse. He decided to put all to the test at once and not to mess
about suspiciously in side roads. He led the animal into the
boulevard and proceeded straight down it as if bound from
the center of the city to a stable.

He plodded along from light to light, himself and the horse
the only miserable traffic. A policeman wished him good
morning, to which Bernardo answered gruffly with some vague,
wine-sodden curses at whatever disaster had forced him to
leave his *trasura*. A car, full of military this time, cruised past
him with hardly a glance. When well past the Strada Spâtarului he spotted some sort of lane serving the backs of
houses. Nobody was in sight. It would have to do.

Leaving the horse in the lane, he slouched off. With
trousers still stained from the garbage can, the rug over his
shoulders and the driver's hat he felt fairly confident that he
could not be recognized as a possible David Mitrani. The
horse gave him an unexpected bonus. It saw no food, water
or comfort in the lane and took off at its regulation trot,
carefully keeping to the right of the road until the next inter-

section where it turned out of the boulevard, presumably towards the distant stable where it ought to have spent the night.

He passed no more than two or three very early risers who glanced at him suspiciously, but it was only suspicion of the homeless poor. At the top of the Strada Spâtarului was a bored and lonely policeman who exasperated Bernardo by refusing to get on and patrol his beat. When at last he hunched his shoulders like the cab horse and dejectedly moved somewhere else, Bernardo wasted no time. The sky was already lightening in the east, and it was all or nothing.

Sliding into the Pozharski courtyard he attacked the shutter of the lavatory window. The knife broke in half, but he had time for experiment. The willow tree now was opening its buds and the branches covered him from easy observation. With the half blade he hacked out a slat, wrenched off the one above it and could then get at the catch. He waited uncertainly, dreading the crash of glass to come when he broke the double window. But he was in luck; it was not necessary. The first window, opening outwards, was not properly shut and the stump of the knife dealt with it. The inner window gave to continued pressure on the frame, backed by the leverage of his feet against the passage wall which he could just reach at full stretch. He was in without a sound but the splintering of wood.

Bernardo closed up everything, bolted the front door and collapsed into a chair, of which the broad, soft arms themselves suggested security. It took him a few minutes of relaxation before he remembered Pozharski's altar bar. Except for ice it was still lavishly stocked. A pint of brandy and soda restored him enough to go upstairs and take a shower in the dark, carefully soaping the cabman's companions — if he had any — out of his hair and sponging his trousers. His respectability had to be impressive if by bad luck he had hit one of the days of the Transylvanian housekeeper's weekly visits.

He went to bed in Pozharski's pajamas feeling gloriously safe — or at least too intolerably tired not to feel safe. At intervals he woke uneasily but murmured, "to hell with it!" and slept till eleven. Morning brought reaction. His impulsive imagination had saved him, but what steady course did one take from there? The time one could live on alcohol was presumably limited, and there was nothing to eat in the house but a handful of stale biscuits. He breakfasted on them with warm champagne.

Having restored the slats of the shutter with gummed strips from envelopes so that at least they stayed in place, he idly returned to the champagne and its reviving influence. Pozharski's telephone, which he had at first regarded warily as if it were an incalculable intruder from the outside world, became a possible ally. He ought to call Nadya at her restaurant. She had so seriously made him promise to tell her before he disappeared. The risk was slight. There was no reason why the authorities should detain for more than five minutes the innocent little Russian refugee who happened to live above David Mitrani.

She recognized his voice at once, but made no indiscreet exclamation. He told her quickly to come to 16 Strada Spâtarului and to bring something home for dinner, dear, because the butcher had not delivered the meat. He wished he had risked adding that she should take care not to be followed and then realized that the advice was unnecessary. Her experiences as a child had left little mark on her character but had developed an instinct for secretiveness. He had noticed it more than once ever since her brilliant and disobedient burning of the lighter.

With the help of more dozing, three hours passed in the

darkened room. He did not dare open the shutters or show a light; from the opposite side of the street the house must continue to appear a *pied à terre* very occasionally visited by its wealthy tenant. From four o'clock onwards he sat by the front door listening for Nadya's footsteps, nervous lest he should open the door to a stranger. He recognized them without a shadow of doubt, puzzled that he could be so sure when they were so faint.

"The house belongs to that Pozharski I told you about," he explained. "I knew it was very unlikely he would be here, so I broke in."

"And you're not hurt?"

"Never better."

She had brought a loaf, butter, cheese, sausage and a liter of good red. Adorable attention to his tastes! It would remain a secret forever that wine for once was what he needed least.

"What happened at the Alhambra?"

He told her. When he came to the horse she gave one of her rare gurgles of laughter. Bernardo himself did not think it funny. Memory of the night was altogether too close.

"And you're sure no one saw you come in?"

"I can't be sure, but it's the least of the risks. Have the police annoyed you?"

"No. They only searched my room and asked a few questions when they brought Despina home."

"She's all right?"

"I think so. She told me that she felt you were trying to say goodbye to her and couldn't. She has gone to her Aunt Floarea."

Trust Despina to sink her pride and do the right thing! Bernardo could imagine Miss Floarea Luca protecting her treasure, insisting on accompanying her to police headquarters and impressing those fragile, new-fangled fellows with the authority of a generation which in old Romania had policed itself.

"And Holgar?"

"In jail. Despina said they had to turn the fat man upside down to save his life. He was choking."

Nadya smiled, quite unconcerned that Major Vlaicu had nearly died. Damn it all, the man had only been doing his duty! She had certainly moved on a lively distance from that statue at the Mosh.

"I must leave now. I will have you out of Romania to-morrow, dear David, and you'll have to take me with you whether you like it or not."

"You're not to dream of it! If it's that crook Scheeper . . ."

"Wait and see! I have told the restaurant that I have to go and see a Russian at Cluj who might be my cousin. They won't expect me back for a day or two. I shall come here again this evening whenever I can."

It was no use arguing with her. The funny, little, fat thing — he always thought of her as little, though really she must be of full average height — walked determinedly out of the house. She again reminded him irresistibly of a cat with her air of soft, appealing innocence and God only knew what capacity for terrifying folly when desperate.

After sunset it was depressing to sit in the pitch darkness of the house with nothing to do. He drew the heavy curtains across the living-room window, but still would not risk a gleam of light. At last he remembered that the alcove with the big divan in it was enclosed by a second curtain and a lamp behind it could not possibly be seen. He had been in-clined to avert his eyes from that alcove — an astonishing bit of prudery from one who had lived his life of the last six months. Undoubtedly it was due to last fragments of the Magda affair. Once admitted, they became genuinely the last.

Since he could not know when Nadya would return, it was a bore to sit at the door listening for her. He decided that there was no danger in standing outside, blotted against the wall at the end of the passage where he could not be seen and at the same time could observe anyone who passed the court-yard or showed interest in it. No one did, but there were more police patrolling the street than on the previous night. It was easy for them to guess who had pinched that horse on the other side of the Boulevard Carol, though they must be very doubtful whether he was still in the district.

He saw Nadya's unmistakable figure pass the house; she did not even glance at it. Nobody was trailing her on either side of the street. He never spotted her arrival until she was actually in the courtyard. She must have slid from the pavement into a dark patch at the corner. Even so it was not her roundness which gave her presence away but the little square case she carried. As she entered the passage he detached him-self from blackness and quickly opened and closed the door, leading her by the hand until they were in the alcove and its light could be switched on.

"There!" she exclaimed, laying down on the divan between them Henri Scheeper's Belgian passport and two sheaves of tickets from Bucarest to Brussels. Her eyes were dancing with mischief.

"Didn't I tell you I could get a passport for both of us? Look what it says! Accompanied by his niece, Marie-Louise Chrétienne Scheeper. Born 1910. I can look as young as that if I try."

She could. But what use was it? Bernardo was touched by her innocence.

"Scheeper's photograph is on it, my dear, and he must be at least fifteen years older than I am."

"But he looks like you. That's what put it into my head."

"He does not look in the least like me," Bernardo said indignantly.

"Yes, he does. Your faces are the same shape. You have only to get that white mèche in your hair."

There was something in that. Their complexions were utterly different, but Scheeper's carefully massaged matt and Bernardo's tan which had become yellowish after so much night life could not be distinguished on a passport photo. Eyes, nose and height corresponded. Nobody could possibly mistake one for the other in reality, since Bernardo was broad and muscular and Scheeper slimly built. But that did not show on a head and shoulders photograph especially as Scheeper padded his shoulders.

It seemed to Bernardo that his chance was slender but so were the odds against stowing away on a Danube barge. And how long was it going to be before Scheeper missed that passport? Poor, loyal darling, he hated to disappoint her. Very gently he demanded explanations.

"But it's simple, David! I told you Scheeper made me an offer. So I went to his room at the Athenée Palace and showed him."

"No!"

"What did it matter? You don't expect him to buy the tickets when he doesn't know what he's getting for his top-class brothel, do you?"

"Nadya!"

"Well, that's what he wants me for, I think."

"Nadya, you are playing with fire like a baby. How did you get hold of that passport?"

"When I told you my story, I left out the bits which you wouldn't like. You're so easily shocked, David."

"Only by you."

"Oh, no! You think you aren't, but you are. I found that

227

out long ago. Now, you remember that my sister and I were living on the streets after my mother and brother were shot?"

"I always wondered how you did it."

"We were a gang of starving children together. One of us had been trained as a pickpocket and he gave me lessons. He said I looked so sweet and innocent. I'm really very good."

"What on earth does God think of that?"

"God is not interested in petty crime. And I've never done it since or only once or twice. And He may have let me learn just so that I could help you."

"But Scheeper will report it to the police," Bernardo almost shouted.

"No, he won't. I told him that, if he did, I'd say why he wanted me and that I was Nadya Andreyev and not his niece at all."

"Will you please tell me exactly what happened?"

"I have."

"The details," Bernardo said, "could be important."

"Oh well, if you want to talk about them! I went with him to buy the tickets and saw him put them in an envelope with his passport. So I asked him to buy me an ice cream at Capsha. And then I went to the lavatory."

"With the envelope?"

"No, no!" she answered as if everybody knew the technique. "With the menu of course."

Bernardo was lost. He just looked at her.

"But it's so simple! You see, the envelope was thick. He was bound to notice he had lost it whenever he moved his arm. So I folded up the menu card till it was about the same size. And then he offered to walk home with me so I took him down a dark street and he seemed to get a bit excited because I was walking very close to him. And when I had swapped the envelope for the menu I pretended he was frightening me and ran away. He followed but he couldn't see where I had gone."

"Where had you gone?"

"Up a tree. He looked such a fool standing there and he couldn't make a scene and he couldn't stop me dropping into somebody's garden. And that was when I told him what I would do if he complained to the police. And tomorrow we'll be over the frontier!"

It was not good enough. Bernardo had to disappoint her. Yes, they might get clear of Romania, given luck and a sleepy passport-control officer. But when Scheeper had time to think it over he must surely see that he had only to deny everything. He could say she had been pestering him to be taken to Brussels and that her accusation was blackmail. The second ticket was for — well, there must be a girl or two in Bucarest with whom he had opened negotiations as he had with Despina. He had never had any intention of passing her off as his niece, Marie-Louise. Why should he? She had a passport of her own. And that was the end of Nadya's story.

"We'll go right through to England," Nadya said.

Tempting if it could be done. In England there was no need for identity cards. Both she and Bernardo Brown could disappear.

"It's a hard climate without money."

"You always bother what you are going to live on, David. England is your country. You're bound to find something."

He examined the tickets. They were for the Arlberg Express, first-class without wagon-lit. Scheeper had not booked on the Orient or the Simplon because he could not share a sleeper with Nadya and could not let her share with anyone else.

"We'd never get as far," he said. "We have to cross six frontiers — Hungary, Austria, Switzerland, France and Belgium to England. It takes four days and a telegram from Bucarest will have us arrested at one of them."

Was there any way of making Scheeper wait confidently for the return of his passport from Friday to Tuesday? A confederate was needed to keep him quiet, and that was impossible. He could not drag Despina into this; it might mean a black mark against her forever. That ass, Holgar, would have swallowed any story if it was romantic enough to fit his ice-bound conception of chivalry. But Holgar was in jail and likely to stay there for weeks unless that beer-sodden consular friend of his could get him out on bail.

He wondered how much Scheeper would know of the row in the Alhambra — not more, surely, than that Holgar had winded a security major and been run in. Stelian could not tell him a great deal, only that it all had something very secret to do with Mitrani. Scheeper spoke fluent English; so did Holgar with a strongish accent and his unmistakable, constipated delivery.

It was worth a try. Bucarest telephones were not good enough for any very clear analysis. Mitrani could not be suspected since he was known to speak very little English. He called up Scheeper at the Athenée Palace Hotel.

"This is Holgar Johannsen speaking. . . . No, I am not calling you to worry you more for a contract. . . . It is something else. . . . No, I am not in jail. My noble consul very much protested. But I am forbidden to go forth until they catch that dirty pig Mitrani. . . . No, it is my duty to speak to you about the girl, Nadya. I did not believe a gentleman would do such a thing. . . . You know what thing. I will not mention it. . . . But her behaving was most wrong. When she confessed to me, I was very much in dudgeon. I will not allow blackmail. I addressed her severely, Mr. Scheeper, until she was on her knees to me. So I have your passport and the tickets. . . . Yes, she regrets very much her sin. . . . No, the police do not know, Mr. Scheeper. I was by good fortune able to hide your property in a safe place. . . . How much? I beg your pardon, but I do not understand. . . . I am indeed insulted. . . . Ah, just a reward! Is it so? Then I will ask you to give it to the Mission to Seamen, Mr. Scheeper. . . . No, I am not in the quod. I am honorably treated by the military but I may not go forth till they find me guiltless. . . . Four or five days. So they have assured my consul. . . . I shall then visit you at your hotel, Mr. Scheeper, and deliver to you the passport and tickets. . . . Your foreign money? Tchk, tchk! This is a bad mischief indeed. She has not told me all the truth. She will be on her knees to me again. . . . At three o'clock on Tuesday. Yes, I will make it convenient, so I give you my knightly word. . . . And I must ask you not to prosecute the erring child. . . . That is most Christian, Mr. Scheeper. Till Tuesday, Mr. Scheeper."

Bernardo put down the telephone, wiped his forehead and collapsed on the divan kicking his legs in the air. Nadya was in fits of laughter. She threw her arms round him and kissed him. It was the first time he had ever felt the deformity close against him. She too realized the effect of her impulsive gesture and drew back. He held her close, but shoulder to shoulder, expressing wordlessly that his affection for her was — leaving aside desire — all that one human being could feel for another.

She kissed him again and rolled lazily off the divan. The gray clouds of her eyes were luminous and transparent. A broad smile was back as if she were just recovering from laughter without any interval.

"What was that about money?" Bernardo asked.

"Oh, he must have meant his wallet."

"You took it?"

"Not the one he used to pay his bill at Capsha. This one was much flatter and came out with the envelope. I couldn't put it back, could I?"

She plunged a hand into her blouse and took out a smart, thin folder of black leather meant to stand upright in a breast pocket. It contained a few new notes of high value — Hungarian, Austrian, Swiss and Belgian — all ready for the journey and the restaurant car. Mr. Henri Scheeper was evidently a neat and experienced traveler.

"Weren't you ever caught at this?"

"Yes, David. But by then I had passed on whatever I got. So they were ashamed and gave me something to eat. Russians are kind. Now I will do your hair."

She opened her bag and took out a bottle which he recognized. It had put the fear of God into him for weeks. Despina in one of those irrational, fairy-tale urges of women for metamorphosis had decided to become a dazzling blonde and could only be dissuaded from the sacrilege by Bernardo's repeated protests. With the aid of Pozharski's brush and comb Nadya went to work on him. First she peroxided the whole head and made him wash it off after an hour; then she did a streak, assuring him that when he woke up in the morning he would have a white mèche very like Scheeper's.

"And I've got an idea. Don't shave and I'll do the bristles every day."

"Will it work without taking my skin off?"

"Of course it will! It's what these Romanian women use for their moustaches."

In case Scheeper or the police should call on her, Nadya had to remain in the house until it was time for them to go. She had decided that for herself, leaving her few clothes behind and buying the cheap, square case to carry toilet necessaries and lingerie. More baggage was essential for the journey to avoid suspicion and give the customs men something to stick their white-gloved hands into. Search of the house produced a battered suitcase of crocodile leather but few contents which could produce a casual impression that it was shared by uncle and niece.

For the female side of the family there were an alluring, flouncy peignoir, one stocking, the housekeeper's overall and two pairs of Pozharski's silk pajamas which might be anything. A neutral pile of freshly washed laundry added bulk. All that Bernardo could find for himself was a splendid old Norfolk jacket with a fur collar, dating from shooting parties before the war, plus the equipment of Pozharski's dressing table and bathroom. He chose to wear the jacket, though it was too small, and pack his own coat. That would make him look like some impoverished country gentleman, German or Austrian, who stuck to his pre-war clothing because he could not afford any more. A hat to go with it would have to be bought on the way to the station.

He put Nadya in the upstairs bedroom with instructions to climb down the drain pipe and run if police were busily occupied with his arrest. Himself he lay on the divan sleeping little. It was excitement rather than anxiety which kept him awake, for there was no halfway house in this escape. If they were stopped at the station or on the Hungarian frontier it was the end; if they were not, they would go all the way through undisturbed. He was more worried by the problem of Nadya in England. She would not fit into his dreaming, now more resigned than optimistic. She could not expect much help from any refugee organization as soon as Scheeper found out that he had been robbed and fooled. And she was only seventeen, without experience of the normal solidities of life.

Up a tree! How perfect and how young! He would have loved to know at what point on the way from the travel agent to Capsha to her chosen dark street that tree had occurred to her. It did not simply grow when she needed it, though to hear her talk one might think that she was confident that it would. She had this gift of committing an irrevocable act of audacity and, if it failed, of lifting her head from her paws, as it were, and blinking at an angry world with surprised and innocent adoration. If only the girl were not handicapped she could capture any man she set her heart on, and he couldn't do much about it against divine approval.

They were up early. Bernardo shaved, refusing to allow chicken fluff to grow on his face. The light brown hair and its white mèche were perfect. He disliked himself in the mirror — a sleek, shady customer old enough to know better. Nadya made the bed and smoothed the divan, meticulously cleaning up to remove all evidence of their presence. What she had done to herself was impossible for an honest man to analyze. She did not look a day more than fourteen and clumsy with puppy fat. Her face was scrubbed and pink. Her hat was more on the back of her head than usual and she had tucked her hair into it untidily so that one ear showed and the other did not. A few pins — she seemed an expert on the use of pins — had transformed the plump and simple gray coat and skirt in which she had arrived into something schoolmistresses allowed you to wear when uncle asked you out to lunch on Sunday.

He telephoned for a taxi. Its arrival set a seal of quiet normality on last-minute fussing. Bernardo shut the front door and tried to walk down the courtyard with the air of a responsible householder under the eyes of a maid shaking her mop out of a window on the other side of the street. He hoped that she had never seen Pozharski. He hoped she would not gossip about a strange gentleman without a hat.

On the way to the station he stopped to buy a tweed cap

which he put on severely straight instead of flopping over in the English manner. He did not, he supposed, look particularly Belgian, but would pass as a sound Continental traveler without money to waste on the luxury of the Orient Express and enough to sit up snoring in the dignity of the first class.

He whisked Nadya into the waiting room and then looked carefully round the platform for Scheeper or any abnormal number of police. The coast was apparently clear, so they went straight to their compartment where he took off his cap to show the color of his hair. He wondered which of the passengers drifting up and down the corridor were security police in plain clothes. Some of them must have been. He talked unceasingly to Nadya in French. Their relationship had to be manifest.

Looking back, Mr. Brown was amazed that they got away with it.

"That touch of peroxide — the first thing any detective would think of! The real disguise was Pozharski's coat and his crocodile leather, plus my angelic young niece with her wide-open eyes drinking in everything in the funny, foreign station."

The half hour before the train pulled out was interminable. Even when they were away they dared not face the restaurant car though breakfastless and very hungry; so long as they remained where they were the charm might hold. At Brashov, three hours out, he found the courage to buy some food from the station buffet. Then they sat on and on, glued to their corner seats. The compartment itself carried an aura of respectability. In the other two corners was a middle-aged Hungarian couple of obvious integrity with whom relationship was limited to safe nods and smiles.

In the middle of the night they reached the frontier at too familiar Oradea Mare. Bernardo sank into his corner pretending to be asleep and praying that Lieutenant Mureshanu left the examination of passports to his underlings. Meanwhile Nadya gazed out of the window at the first peaceful frontier she had ever crossed. He watched her out of half-closed eyes, noticing how she was at first controlling nervousness and then beaming with the expression of a child patted on the head by her dentist and told there was no work to be done. The joint passport was stamped without question, the joint bag unexamined. The Arlberg Express clanked off into Hungary. It was a pity that the restaurant car was closed till morning. Bernardo was in a mood to celebrate his niece's birthday.

6. Nadya

"NOTHING else to report! Mr. Scheeper's black folder provided for us amply. So I remained in a pleasant sort of limbo between the extinction of David Mitrani and the birth of someone who hadn't yet been christened. That nameless person only began to wake up when we got to Basle and were about to cross northern France into Belgium. It occurred to me that if Scheeper often traveled to Central and Eastern Europe his face might be well known to Belgian officials and we had better leave the train before the frontier. So we got off at Nancy — no trouble about that — and spent a pleasant day cleaning up and refreshing ourselves. You couldn't have asked for a more fascinating companion than Nadya once the pressure was off — that preposterous faith in the future and more than a touch of Russian extravagance! Damn it, she actually encouraged me to spend money!"

At Calais Bernardo strolled into the British Consulate to find out whether a Belgian needed a visa or not. He was received with a cordial interest which seemed to him more friendly than official. The vice-consul asked him twice whether he was sure that he and his niece really wanted to go to England. Bernardo said that of course they did. She was joining her mother in London and could not be allowed to travel alone.

The white cliffs of Dover produced no tear from the exile. They seemed to him forbidding — a white wall with a narrow hole in it. Mr. Scheeper and niece were going to get in but he would have preferred to know what welcome they would receive and how they would get out again if it became advisable. However, the damp quay, the porters, the trains, the immigration control were comfortingly safe and familiar. He presented his passport. The officer stamped it, looked at it again, looked at Mr. Scheeper and passed the pair of them through.

On the way to the train a respectable citizen who had the neutrality of a bank cashier or insurance clerk touched his bowler hat and asked:

"Mr. Scheeper?"

Bernardo agreed that he was. The greeting was so natural that he wondered — though his heart was doing overtime — whether it could not possibly be a friend deputed to meet Scheeper on arrival.

"Would you mind stepping this way?"

He stepped, followed by Nadya. At the door of an office marked PRIVATE the unknown friend remarked, "Perhaps the young lady would like a cup of tea."

Whether the young lady liked it or not, a female, equally neutral, materialized to back up the invitation. Nadya, caught between two very professional smiles, was led away and Bernardo waved to a chair in the office.

"Well, Mr. Scheeper, we didn't think we should see you again."

"You were expecting me?"

"Since you were kind enough to call at the Consulate. . . ."

"Do you want me for anything in particular?"

"Come off it, Mr. Scheeper! The police want you for keeping a brothel and skipping bail. Who's the lady? Bit young for a new recruit isn't she?"

Bernardo's mind became an absolute, terrifying blank. Whatever he said would be wrong. He preferred to be jailed for brothel-keeping rather than extradited to Spain, but what would happen to Nadya?

"The lady is really my niece," he said. "There was nobody else to escort her to her mother, so I — er — had to take the risk."

"I see from your passport that you left Romania on Friday. Your niece was living there?"

Bernardo explained that he had picked her up at Zurich where she was at school. The immigration officer rang a bell, wrote something on a slip of paper and handed it to his clerk.

"A cup of tea, Mr. Scheeper?"

Bernardo silently blasted the tea and accepted it. In any decent European country he would have been offered — if offered anything at all — a drink which might have inspired imagination.

"How long do you think I'll get?"

"Well, I see you pleaded Not Guilty. No faith in the jury, Mr. Scheeper?"

The clerk returned with another slip of paper.

"Miss Marie-Louise says she was at school in Belgium."

"Well, so she was."

"She also states that you both left Brussels this morning."

There was nothing more to be said, and Bernardo did not say it. Henri Scheeper and niece were despatched to London by a later boat train. Bernardo retired behind a newspaper, trying ineffectively to read it and ignoring the pale green dance of spring all over the Kentish countryside. He commented that although it was May the rain had stopped and it was not freezing. Nadya on the other hand prattled away to the escorting constable. She soon had him in a fatherly and tender mood, telling her all about his daughter of the same age and wishing the pair could meet. It seemed most unlikely. Encouraged by this love-fest Bernardo began to consider whether anything could be gained by getting the constable to take her hand and lead her to the lavatory. But the train stopped nowhere and offered no chance of escape. He felt helplessly imprisoned by the compartment and the miles and miles of uniform London suburbs now streaming past the window. Since the State would be supplying board and lodging for some time, he told Nadya in Romanian to remove and keep Scheeper's black wallet without the constable seeing.

They were delivered to Vine Street for further inquiries. Nadya was taken away for still another nice cup of tea. Bernardo was shown into the superintendent's office by a constable who had an unpleasant air of knowing all about him and finding it offensive.

"Well, well, Scheeper, isn't this an unexpected visit?" the superintendent began and then stopped short and stared. "And what have we here, may I ask? I knew he'd never show his face in this country again!"

Bernardo said weakly that it was a longish story and feverishly began to compose it. He explained that he was English and lived in Brussels. He gave a false name and address, though well aware of its futility. Still, there might be a chance of vanishing before the facts were checked.

"I shall hold you on a charge of illegal entry. Anything you say may. . . ."

"No, you won't," Bernardo answered boldly. "I'm British. I don't need any passport."

"Then why did you see fit to use someone else's?"

"That's the Belgians' business, not yours. You can't hold me on any charge at all."

"I can think of half a dozen, my lad. You may or may not be British, but your Scheeper's niece isn't."

Bernardo saw a gleam of light. Wherever it led, it would do for the moment.

"She's a White Russian refugee and hasn't got a passport. That is why I borrowed Scheeper's. I wanted to get her into this country, you see."

"Your young lady?"

"You could put it that way."

"Fourteen years old?"

"That's Scheeper's niece. This lady is over the age of consent, if that is what you mean."

"I understand you to say you are not Henri Scheeper?"

"You know I'm not."

"I know nothing of the sort, sir. You answer his description, and it is my duty to keep you in custody until you can be identified or otherwise by the police officers who carried out your arrest."

A mean and ingenious fellow, the superintendent! There was no arguing with that one.

"Well, can Mr. Scheeper talk to his niece then?"

"No. But you have no need to be worried. She seems to have mislaid that mother of hers in London, so we will see that she is put up at a respectable hotel for the time being. Now come on, Romeo, and take it easy!" he added with a grin.

Bernardo was duly locked up. The experience was not so

bad as he imagined it would be throughout the months when he had daily awaited it. Supper was edible for a hungry man and the cell clean, as indeed one would expect if gilded youth were frequently locked up at Vine Street as that amusing young fellow Wodehouse seemed to think. He could not remember exactly what happened if a man was charged with a criminal offense and skipped bail, but certainly he would have to come before the magistrate next day. And what the hell to say there? The only hope was to expand the Romeo and Juliet romance which the superintendent apparently had half believed.

Next morning appearance in court was delayed — if, that is, the beaks kept business hours. It was after eleven when the superintendent himself opened the cell door.

"Good morning, Mr. Scheeper."

"I am not Mr. Scheeper."

"In the same trade perhaps?"

Bernardo denied it with an indignation which must have been impressive, for the superintendent smiled.

"If this was a rescue operation, wouldn't you be wise to make a full statement?"

"Rescue?"

"Her movements were very quickly traced and they were waiting for her at the Belgian frontier."

"You must have got the wrong girl."

"There will be no trouble in identifying her. Our information is that she has four hum — ha."

So the game was up for Nadya. Bucarest police seemed to have attended to their In trays a lot more rapidly than usual. But of course they need hardly have been brought into it at all. As soon as Scheeper discovered that Holgar was firmly in jail and could never have telephoned him, he would have reported the theft of his passport to his consul. Then routine inquiries quickly established that Nadya had crossed the frontier on the Arlberg Express with a Scheeper who wasn't Scheeper. It might still be some time before anyone guessed that the companion was David Mitrani.

"For all I know she may have as many as Diana of the Ephesians," Bernardo replied with pretended impatience.

"Disgusting what they will allow abroad! The Ephesians — yes, I've heard of it. One of those so-called theatre clubs, I believe."

Bernardo saw another possible line of defense. It had the advantage, considering Scheeper's reputation, of being plausible.

"Would the police consider a rescue operation justifiable?"

"It might assist us to overlook irregularities. Now, I advise you again to think it over and give me a full statement as soon as you are returned."

"Returned from where?"

"Never mind that! Just an informal talk with a certain person, I understand."

The superintendent led him to a handsome limousine standing outside the station. There was a chauffeur in the front seat and a burly fellow in the back, quite big enough to frustrate any attempt at vanishing into London. Bernardo was firmly shoved in alongside him. The car headed along Piccadilly and down the Haymarket.

"Where are we going?" he asked.

"The Admiralty."

That was a puzzler. Arson on the Danube? The port of Bilbao? That fictitious horse delivered at Galatz? Or had Mr. Scheeper a concession for providing naval conveniences in Malta?

He was escorted through a maze of passages and into a small office stacked with filing cabinets. His companion sat down at a desk with a typewriter on it, refusing conversation and leaving him standing; he could not be anything but a retired chief petty officer with a full appreciation of his own importance. There was another door opposite that through which they had entered. A bell rang sharply in the room beyond it. The petty officer jerked his thumb in that direction and said the admiral would see him now.

The room was carpeted and restful and resembled a bachelor's study rather than a government office. Standing in front of a comfortable coal fire with his hands in his coat pockets was a genial, gray-haired, old cock who was presumably the admiral and looked it.

"Good morning, Mr. Mitrani."

"Good morning, sir."

Bernardo found that he had very slightly peed himself — not enough to show, he thought. The naval bloke asked him to take a chair, which Bernardo did in a rush, and himself remained in his fatherly position in front of the fire. His constant smile varied and was nerve-racking. Sometimes it seemed to reflect inner amusement; sometimes it would do very well for raising morale in an Arctic gale.

"You've given those fellows over on the Continent a long run, haven't you?"

"In Belgium, sir?"

"In romantic Romania, Mr. Mitrani. Now, what could have made them think that you are really Bernardo Brown?"

"Who's Bernardo Brown?"

"A quite remarkable crook. I could do with one or two of him. Arranges an accident for his accomplice, disreputable but after all a grand duke. Makes a getaway into Hungary — you will tell me how he managed it — and then appears in Bucarest where he calls at the Legation to explain that it was all clean fun at the seaside and does not improve his case by doing what I have always wanted to. While living off women from one end of Bucarest to the other he learns the language perfectly in one winter. And you still say he isn't you?"

"I admit I am David Mitrani. But I am not this Bernardo Brown."

"Mr. Brown, what a whopper! Your hair is very badly dyed. You must have done it in a hurry."

It was futile to go on denying. If the truth had to come out, this was the man who should have it. Bernardo felt that it was better, roughly speaking, to be eaten by this tiger with the bared teeth of imperial security than to be worried to bits by the pack which was after him.

"Their police exaggerate, sir. I have never lived on women in my life."

"I am glad to hear it. So that brings us to the subject of your real income. Who was paying you?"

"Who is it supposed to be?"

"Cards on the table, Mr. Brown? All right! My report from Romania states that you were working for Hungary."

"I had no need to spy for anyone if that's what you're getting at. The Alhambra paid me enough to live on. And the Romanians are inclined to see Hungarians under the bed."

"They are, are they? Well, they needn't be. Hungarians always conduct their dirtier business in a jovial blaze of publicity. Then they get caught like you and have to lie their way out of it. What do you know about those forged francs they were circulating?"

"Nothing beyond what I read in the papers. It sounds crazy."

So there was the mysterious crime again! He expected better of the admiral. Forgery of francs seemed a stock accusation against any suspected international criminal. It left him almost indifferent.

Old Bernardo chuckled at the memory, saying that it was the most incredible example of post-war intrigue in Central Europe but absolutely true. The State Cartographical Institute of Hungary had printed in their cellars thirty million French francs in thousand-franc notes. The main distribution was done by half-witted, young, idealistic Hungarian agents who were caught in possession of the forgeries in December 1925.

"And that had a lot more to do with me than I knew," he went on. "In the first week of January, about the time Pozharski warned me, Prince Ludwig Windischgraetz — a very prominent figure, he was, at the old Hapsburg court — was arrested in Budapest with, God help us, the chief of police! Both of them got ten years penal servitude. Windischgraetz swore that none of the proceeds had been used for personal gain and that he had done it for patriotic motives. Hungarian character being what it is, that was enough to make him into a national hero. But nobody to this day knows what the patriotic motives were: probably to finance a putsch, either nationalist or monarchist. The only defense their prime minister could put up — he was on the edge of it as well — was that thirty million francs, say £230,000 at the then rate, was not nearly enough to finance an internal plot, let alone an international one. And that was true, too. So you pays your penny and you takes your choice. But there were France and her allies of the Little Entente roaring bloody murder against the Hungarians, and everyone else's Central Bank more than a little nervous about what might really be going on."

The admiral agreed that the plot was crazy, but added that it must have been profitable or Bernardo and his accomplice would not have been such fools as to have anything to do with it.

"Why did you bump him off?"

Nadya

"I did not. He fell. And I never knew who he was."

"The Hungarians did."

"I think Count Kalmody was trying to avoid any suspicion of that, sir. So he drugged me and had me flown out to his estate. If I wasn't around to answer questions, the two dead men could not be connected with the Empress Zita at all."

"You killed them both?"

"Count Kalmody shot one when he broke into the villa, and I tell you the other one they call Bobo fell."

"That's for the Spaniards to decide when we hand you over to them. When did the Russians first contact you?"

"I don't know any except White Russians."

"Just as bad as the other lot! What about that groom of Kalmody's?"

"Have you run across many Spanish-Americans, sir?"

"Of course I have! Excellent fellows when they aren't building castles in the air!"

"Well, that was Perico. He just wanted to live where there were no big landlords and lots of horses. And I couldn't stop him."

"I see. This Russian girl you arrived with — did you pinch Scheeper's passport for her or did she pinch it for you?"

"I did. For her."

"Another lie, Mr. Brown. Who is she?"

"A very unfortunate refugee, sir, earning an honest living. She made herself look young, but she is really seventeen. Her name is Nadya Andreyev."

"In love with you, I suppose?"

"No. More like brother and sister. I was able to do her a favor once, and when she knew I had to clear out of Bucarest she helped me. That's all."

"Remarkably generous for a sister. What was the favor?"

"I will not answer that."

His interrogator refreshed memory by a glance at the file on his desk.

"Believed to be a certain Nadya Stepanov, drowned off Giurgiu. Well, there could not be two answering her physical description. A background of traveling fairs, Mr. Brown — is that where you usually recruit your agents?"

"I suggest you question her yourself, sir."

"What for? This is not a Waifs and Strays Society. She'll only tell me a lot of gypsyish lies about the pair of you."

"But with your long experience I am sure you can tell which are lies and which are not."

"Ha! Only seventeen, eh? She'll be easier than the usual run."

He rang a bell for the petty officer in the adjoining office.

"Tomkins, ask the Vine Street superintendent where he has put Mr. Scheeper's niece and bring her here!"

"And if she won't come, sir?"

"For Christ's sake, boy, then get a constable and make her come!"

Bernardo was dismissed to a waiting room where the morning paper and the usual cup of tea were provided. When all was quiet he opened the door and looked out. A naval rating in uniform was on guard outside. The window was barred. There was nothing for it but to wait in patience.

After three-quarters of an hour the faithful Tomkins escorted him back to his chief's office. Nadya was curled up in an armchair by the fire. The admiral was in his usual position in front of it, looking down on her with indignant, paternal eyes. She smiled at Bernardo tenderly, her eyes brimming with tears. It occurred to him that he had never once seen her cry for joy or for sorrow, whatever she might do in private. She had undoubtedly been editing the truth with some emotion. He had been right ten times over to draw her in to defend herself.

"I'm glad there is at last something to be said for you, Brown," the admiral growled. "The poor child! Good God!"

"Yes, sir," Bernardo answered noncommittally.

"If these Belgians make any fuss, I think you both have a perfect defense to the charge. Not that it matters to you personally — well, we won't disillusion the child. Now, I have a Captain Walinski in my department. Late of the Imperial Russian Navy. I know he and his wife will be delighted to look after Miss Andreyev till her case is settled. I'll get him over here."

He jiggled the telephone without any result.

"Damn that switchboard! If I hadn't got feet under me, we could be at war for a week and I wouldn't know it. Come on, Miss Andreyev!"

"And David? Mr. Mitrani?" Nadya asked pathetically.

"That's in the hands of the police, my dear. A sad business. Nothing to do with Scheeper. A sad business. But there you are. These things happen."

"Can't he come too? I'm frightened all alone."

"Well, no reason why not. Tomkins!"

The confidential clerk jumped to it as to an imaginary bosun's pipe.

"Tomkins, tell 'em I'll want the car in five minutes to take this fellow home to Vine Street. You've no need to come back. I'll send him down to you under guard when I've finished with him. Close up at your end!"

The admiral took them out through the other door of his room into a far grander passage. He carefully locked the door behind him, put the key in his waistcoat pocket and led them down the corridor and round a corner with Nadya timorously at his side.

"Did you drop something, my dear?" he asked.

Nadya glanced at her bag and the floor.

"No, I don't think so. I expect it was the heel of my shoe. It's so worn."

Bernardo's thoughts were wandering in a linked daydream from the majesty of an Admiralty corridor to a chill Spanish courtyard. He could not remember whether the condemned man stood with his back to the garroting post or sat. At any rate this Walinski would look after Nadya. She had always said that Russians were kind.

Nadya felt for his hand as if to comfort him. The little darling seemed to know instinctively what he was thinking. He pressed the hand and found the key of the admiral's office transferred to his own. That was the last straw. What the hell was he supposed to do with it? He'd have to drop it unseen if there were any trouble. But of course! That slight noise which the admiral had heard made sense. She had covered them both.

Captain Walinski was not in his office. The admiral left a message for him and returned to his own. Bernardo waited, deep-frozen with apprehension, while he searched his waistcoat pocket.

"Where the bloody hell did I put that key? I beg your pardon, Miss Andreyev."

He searched all pockets without success.

"But it's automatic, damn it! Same every day. When I leave the office I lock it and I put the blasted. . . . Oh, that must be what we heard drop!"

He trotted down the corridor and round the corner.

"No time! No good!" Bernardo hissed as Nadya prepared to bolt. "He'll see at once it isn't there."

They had just time to unlock the door and stand back looking lost and lonely. The admiral reappeared with a giant, bearded Russian who suggested George V and Nicholas II piled one on top of the other.

"Some ass must have picked it up," he exclaimed and introduced Walinski to Nadya.

"Are you sure you locked the door, sir?" Bernardo asked. "I don't remember you doing so."

The admiral roared that of course he did, violently turned the door handle and nearly pitched head first into his room. Walinski followed him in and was at once overwhelmed by an embarrassed, incoherent explanation of keys and waistcoats and down the passage. Both had their backs to the door. Bernardo quietly shut and locked it.

They ran, stopping at the head of a fine, curving staircase. One floor down they could see a hall, a door to the outside and a glass box with a porter in it.

"We have to walk this whatever happens," Bernardo said. "Innocence — dignity — only chance."

Before they reached the bottom he could hear the distant thunder as the Royal and Imperial navies attacked the door. He hoped to heaven that the Admiralty switchboard was living up to its reputation.

"Pass, sir?"

"We were told to look for Tomkins who has the car ready."

"Other side of the courtyard, sir."

As they passed through the door and hesitated a taxi drew up. Bernardo waited in agony till it was paid off, then threw Nadya and himself into it. The racket upstairs had stopped, showing that the prisoners had broken out or been released. He told the driver loudly to go to the House of Lords. The porter who was walking towards them returned to his box.

"We can't have more than a minute," he said as the taxi moved off. "Got any English money?"

"Yes. I changed some."

"We must get out before the Lords."

"Why did you choose it?"

"The only swell place I could think of. And who but a lord would wear this coat?"

At the bottom of Whitehall he spotted the Westminster underground station, paid off the taxi and they vanished into the station. There was no time at all for thought. He was obsessed by an impulse to get clear of London. That ancient shooting jacket of Pozharski's made him as distinctive as if he were walking around waving a flag, and no coat at all would be nearly as bad. He grabbed tickets to Charing Cross, the nearest railway station, and three minutes later was back in the open air on the Embankment. But he had forgotten that the main-line terminus was a fairish walk from the underground station and that both were far too close to Whitehall. If the Admiralty porter had taken the number of the taxi it could have been traced already. He dragged Nadya back into the underground and glanced at the map in the booking hall.

"Two to Marylebone."

They were away again and perhaps safe, for at Charing Cross underground one had a choice of all four points of the compass. The ticket clerk could not fail to remember so odd a pair and would remember their destination if the police got on to him soon enough. But would they? Say that they spotted at once the dash from Westminster to Charing Cross. Then the search would be concentrated on the Strand, the Embankment, the mainline terminus and adjoining streets. It might be an hour or more before it occurred to somebody that the fugitives had bounced straight back into the underground.

Marylebone. A station of modest size and far too empty. As they ran up the steps into the open, Bernardo saw a constable coming out of the gents' lavatory and another wandering loose. Both had the professional faraway look in their eyes calculated to assure the innocent public that it was not being watched and the criminal that he was. Both came to life and stared at them. He told himself that naturally they would stare; it didn't mean that Marylebone Station had been alerted yet.

A train for Rugby was leaving in a minute. He dashed into the booking office and bought tickets for Brackley, the first stop. They might not have enough money for the fare to Rugby and anyway it did not matter where they went. They drew still more attention to themselves by running for the train and jumping into the last carriage as it pulled out.

Walking up the train they found a compartment to themselves and drew breath.

"We've done it, David! We're safe!"

"Safe? With the admiral roaring his head off? What did you tell him?"

"It was wonderful. God put the words straight into my mouth."

"Good for him! It's this damned coat which will sink us. You're all right. There are lots of little, fat girls about."

"I am not fat or little, David."

"Well, you know what I mean. I've made a mess of it. They'll be telephoning every damned station you can get to quickly from Charing Cross. Those cops at Marylebone will get a medal for putting them on to us and there'll be more of them waiting at Brackley."

"I can go back to Captain Walinski if you like."

Bernardo recovered his calm and said it was what she ought to do.

"You've got the old boy in your pocket and he told you himself that there was nothing against you. You have only to swear I lifted the key off him and you didn't know till it was too late. Nadya, little darling, take that line and you can't go wrong!"

"When you say 'little darling' do you mean *dragutsica?*"

"Yes, I do."

"The sort of little you used to call Despina?"

"Damn Despina! Will you listen? It's all in character. Just look at my history of violence! Bobo — Nepamuk — that pin-striped sod. And the bleeding barge, which is bound to come out. And now I've locked the head of the British Security Service in his office. Oh, my God!"

"Yes, David. Do you think that was what he was?"

"Well, it would be just like them to have their dirty work done by Rule Britannia in this blasted country."

"It's a beautiful country. Look at that!"

The wide valley spread out like a river of green as it flowed down into the Vale of Aylesbury. In Bernardo's mood of resentment he saw it as a self-satisfied land with its cattle and fat sheep placed exactly where a child with a toy farm would place them, all segmented by pretty hedges rising in a blaze of white hawthorn to the orderly stands of beeches on the skyline. And where was the water rushing down through the woods and narrow meadows of Vizcaya or silvering the Romanian plain? Water in this country ran tidily underground.

"It's all so loved," Nadya said.

But of course it was. Everyone loved the country in which his eyes were born. Even the Russian refugees ached for their birches and rolling lowlands. He sulkily said something of the sort.

"But this *looks* as if it were loved. Like an animal."

She had gone deep there. Tame it was, but tame as some glossy, splendid animal conscious of love and answering it.

She went on to say that her first impression of his country was its peacefulness.

"Peaceful? But there's a chap wandering round every half acre all day. Nobody can feel alone."

"Not that kind of peace, David. That's for explorers and monks and sometimes you. This is peace for everyone. Did you notice the gardens?"

Yes, he had noticed the gardens, and the English half of him had inevitably longed for one of its own. But safety was what he wanted first, and there was none.

They had crossed the Vale of Aylesbury when the brakes went on and the train pulled up in a cutting. The sudden silence was absolute except for the faint voices of travelers in the next-door compartments. Dense scrub covered the thirty-foot slope. The new shoots and new leaves made it appear thicker and taller than Mediterranean maquis. Turned soil left alone for sixty or more years had re-created a primeval England.

"Why don't we jump out and run for it?" Nadya suggested.

She gave him no time to protest again that she herself was in no danger if she played her cards right. She had the door half open already, turning to him with a smile of invitation as if to get out and pick cowslips. Another of those unaccountable feline pounces from a nothing to a possible something. At any rate the result could not be worse than meeting police on Brackley station or, if they were not there yet, exhibiting themselves in a small market town and sticking in the memory of every passerby.

She had already slid into cover when he hit the ground. They heard the guard shout at them, but they had vanished. The train slowly clanked into life again and left silence and the scent of hawthorn behind. Nadya actually did pick cowslips — one for him and one for herself.

On the level ground above the cutting was open grassland with no adequate cover. Speed in getting away was more important than any halfhearted attempt at concealment, so they stepped out boldly, crossed a road and followed a green track up to high ground until they came to a junction of footpaths in a desolate space between hedges.

Till then Bernardo had only known that he was half an hour by train from Brackley, which was far from helpful. From the high ground he could see what sort of country lay below and make a vague mental map of it. To the southeast was the Vale of Aylesbury; to the north miles and miles of the rolling Midlands, so full of tall, hedgerow elms that Nadya thought she looked down on forest. He had seen enough of England to know that there was none, but all the same this toy landscape could be safer than Hungary or Romania for anyone who needed to avoid the public. While he had been dreaming of wild distances, Nadya had instinctively recognized the privacies of an utterly foreign land though she had only a short railway journey to go on.

But even assuming they could disappear into those privacies, where then? His mind ran as usual to a port for himself, provided some sort of refuge could be found for Nadya. The longer she stayed with him, the more she was going to be tarred with the same brush. The admiral might be no longer well disposed, furiously suspicious of that sob story and fuming because he had let one suspect and one established criminal slip through his fingers in the most humiliating way when the police had only passed them over to him as a favor. Money was going to be their worst problem. Apart from a few foreign notes which could not be changed in a country bank without attracting curiosity, they had only fifteen shillings and some coppers.

It was exasperating not to know how much time they had

— till next day, perhaps, if their departure from Marylebone was only discovered as a result of routine inquiries; none at all if the police were waiting on the platform at Brackley and the guard reported a man and a girl jumping out of the train. He remembered past experience. The right game was to stock up with food at once, while he could still risk showing his face in public.

From their miniature plateau they looked down on a village half a mile away. It had a church; it would certainly have a pub; it might or might not have a shop. He told Nadya to stay where she was and left the deadly Norfolk jacket with her. A man in his shirt sleeves on a warm May afternoon would pass in a village though not in London.

With his cap covering Scheeper's white mèche there was nothing much to single him out from his fellows. He passed a red-brick cottage marked Police Station with a notice board outside entirely concerned with abortion in cattle and a by-election for the rural district council. The walls were covered by a climbing rose in leaf and a fine broom in flower. It was difficult to be afraid of anything so far removed from the usual barrack-like building of Europe.

The village did have a shop with a little food and a surprising stock of buckets, brooms and fly papers. He bought a loaf, butter, biscuits, tins of bully beef and a cheap, sturdy knife, and as an afterthought two pint bottles of lemonade in case clean water should be hard to find. The old lady who kept the place spread the lot out on the counter and asked, "On 'oliday, be yer?"

"Camping with some boy scouts."

"Don't yer 'ave nothing to put all this 'ere in?"

"Not unless I go back for it."

"Oi can give yer an old sack if yer don't mind bein' seed with it like."

Bernardo was all for being seed with it. The sack with some lumps at the bottom provided protective coloring; he would appear to be just slipping out, coatless, from cottage to field with vaguely agricultural requirements. When he left the shop he saw that the police station at the other end of the street had lost its picture-postcard innocence. Standing outside was a police car which he approached slowly, not daring to stop or turn back in case he drew attention to himself. The car drove off fast with four men in it, two of them in uniform. At the same time the village constable came out, jumped on his bicycle and rode straight past Bernardo without looking at him. He gave the impression of being absorbed by the urgency and importance of his task.

So that settled the question of time. They hadn't any. He returned to Nadya and found her sitting in the sun and contentedly messing about with the Norfolk jacket. When she held it up for him he hardly recognized it; she had ripped off the fur collar and turned it inside out to show the silk lining. It looked like the ultimate wreck of something cut by a ladies' tailor in the eighteen nineties.

He told her what he had seen in the village and insisted that they had to move at once.

"They can't catch us down there," she said, pointing to the vale, all dark green on light green and dotted with brown jets where oak and ash were still in bud.

But they could, and without anything so drastic as watching crossroads. Two or three of those constables on their silent bicycles could be just as effective. A man and a girl carefully avoiding villages, forcing their way through hedges, inevitably getting mixed up on tracks which only led to farms, would soon be reported.

"We shall be safe at night, but there are six hours of daylight left."

"Why don't we go back quickly to the cutting?" Nadya suggested. "They'll never look for us there."

A gamble, but a fair one. The fugitives would be expected to bolt away from the railway as far and as fast as they could. The search would fan out from their starting point, but the hinge of the fan was not worth bothering with. The trouble was returning to the cutting. Across the open fields it was no longer safe. The only way was to risk walking along the road as far as a bridge which crossed the line.

The coat inspired him. She, not he, ought to be wearing it. And if she wore his cap as well . . .

He explained to her that tramps, male and female, were a common sight on the by-roads of England and that they looked as abandoned and disreputable as anything out of Gorky. He helped her into the coat which came nearly to her knees and was completely shapeless. He added his cap, squashed and twisted, and rubbed her face with leaf mold. The result was convincing. If a cop passed her on the stretch of road he was more likely to stop and ask her if she had seen the wanted pair than to suspect she might be one of them.

"When you get to the bridge," he said, "see that there is nobody in sight and no train and nip over the wall. Find a good place in the cutting and wait for me."

"But what about you?"

"I'll try the same trick afterwards under cover of the hedges. Leave me your own coat and I'll carry it folded over my arm. And your hat can go in the sack."

She set off down the green lane and reached the road unobserved. She was then out of his sight until she was within a hundred yards of the bridge. There a farm cart passed her, its driver paying no attention. She was over the wall and into cover and nobody any the wiser.

While he was planning his own route, a car stopped on the road, dropped two men and drove away. To his alarm they took the track up to the open space where he was. Bernardo looked frantically round for cover. Hedges were windswept and thin, and ditches shallow. The only hope was a low, thick holly standing by itself in a corner. So long as the new arrivals did not separate he might be able to keep moving round it.

The two could see at once that nobody was at the top of the green lane. They were about to search the ditches when one of them came across the fur collar which Nadya had ripped off. He had no doubt what it was and declared that Brown and his popsy must have dashed up that promising lane and then gone round or through the village below. The roads out of it were under surveillance, and if they tried the long, bare slopes on both sides of the railway they were sure to be seen. Either way they would be caught before dark.

They trotted down to the village on the same route that Bernardo had taken; he gathered that the car was waiting for them there. In another five minutes they would have picked up his trail at the shop and learn that he was going about without a coat. It was an easy deduction that the popsy could be wearing it, inside out or not. The only comfort was that Nadya had been right; it never occurred to the two detectives that the wanted couple had gone back to the cutting.

The mention of Brown showed that his true name had now been passed on to the police. Bernardo Brown alias David Mitrani alias Henri Scheeper, an international criminal if there ever was one. No wonder the village constable had gone charging off on his bicycle with his eyes on promotion instead of the pavement. Bernardo ran down the green lane. The road was empty. So long as he stayed between its high hedges he knew he could not be seen. He decided to get it over, walking fast and chancing the traffic. He had to race a goods train to the bridge but was into cover by the time the locomotive came abreast.

It was far from safe to walk along the track in full view of the bridge. While the casual passerby would take him for a railwayman any of those plain-clothes cops cruising round the district would be after him at once. He moved by short dashes in and out of the scrub, looking and listening before he showed himself. He felt like an inadequate, young rabbit always moving when he shouldn't, and was thankful when Nadya called from above and he could dive into the railway jungle for good.

The spot she had chosen was so thickly overgrown that he could not see her till she moved. There was a small patch of vegetation to sit on and a view through an elder bush of the line below. He told her how he had been nearly caught and asked if she had been seen. She didn't think so. She had pushed her way along the top of the cutting between the fence and the scrub.

After some cautious work with the knife had produced a roomier den they opened up the sack and ate. In spite of bottled lemonade Bernardo was at peace for the first time in twenty-four hours. The passing trains emphasized their security as if occupying the same space but a different time to theirs. In the evening a couple of linesmen walked along the track, occasionally inspecting the cutting for signs of erosion.

Bernardo wanted to get clear as soon as it was dark. Nadya was for staying where they were; and since he could not specify exactly what was to be gained by hurry he had to agree. She had a good point, saying that since their train had been held up on this stretch of line it was probable that another would be; if it was a goods train they could slip into any convenient truck and go wherever it took them. She added that anxiety had kept her awake all the previous night, that she was sleepy and there was room to curl up.

For a long time he sat up with knees to chin dozing, depressed and thinking about her. The adventures of her childhood and life with Stepanov must have accustomed her to sleep anywhere. The ground was damp and it would be vilely cold at dawn, yet she appeared content to accept the present for what it was without looking forward to the hopeless complexities of their situation. Partly it must be due to her blind confidence in seizing an opportunity although, when one came to think of it, her instinct would get her nowhere unless he took over and built on what she had created. That seemed to be the pattern ever since their eyes had first met at the Mosh. A good partnership, but could it continue? It was impossible to avoid capture, to eat or get a roof over their heads so long as they remained together.

"I am cold," she said.

There was no room for more than one of them to lie down, but he had the support of yielding branches at his back. He took Nadya on his knee and threw over her Pozharski's jacket on which she had been lying. She evidently found the arrangement a lot more comfortable than he did and wriggled into position with her head on his shoulder. In sleep her voice sometimes purred in unintelligible Russian. The common warmth brought on some stirring of excitement, and he rebuked the offending instrument; it had no business whatever, he told it, to think that this child who trusted him and would not leave him was Despina in a similar position. Memories of the Mosh huffed and puffed in two opposite directions. Her hair tickled him. He retired to a mentally neutral corner and decided that someday she ought to let it grow again to the length it had been then.

Day came with a promise of still more fine weather, though
the sun on the east-facing slope of the cutting was more cheerful than warm. When they had stood up and shaken the
stiffness out of their limbs, cold seemed of less importance
than continued freedom. The lemonade was finished at breakfast but an ample supply of food remained. They lazed away
the daylight hours expecting a train to stop. None of them
did.

They were impatient for the long twilight to end. The
obvious game then was to follow the railway, lying down or
taking cover whenever a train or a railwayman was approaching. Since the first could be heard far off and the other
carried a bobbing light, they had little fear of being caught.
In single file they crunched on over the ballast at the side of
the line, easily avoiding trouble except on long, bare embank-
ments where twice they had to dive over the edge. Before
midnight they came to a complicated junction with a lit
signal box and no station. The right-hand line seemed to have
the least traffic so they followed it, vanishing at once into a
primeval England where the sight of man was rare and the
wild life was accustomed to the passage of a fiery dragon which
did no harm. A badger waddled across the line showing his
white streaks in the darkness like a phosphorescent little
bear — which Nadya thought he was. The sides of cuttings
were busy rabbit warrens. The scent of hawthorn mingled with
half a dozen faint unknowns in the heavy night air. Toy
landscape? By God, it wasn't! If only one could build a hut
and light a fire one could live on the bounty of the railway
indefinitely.

They came to a small station where no one was on duty but
a barn owl. Not far away a stream was flowing under the line.
The ripple of water and the timber platform suggested to
Bernardo a forgotten quay on some remote Vizcayan estuary;

even there one could find no wilder seclusion. The station was called Wotton Underwood, but more important than a mere name was the discovery of a station tap. They could drink and fill the lemonade bottles.

After another hour they crossed a bridge over a main road running east and west — a perfectly useless piece of information provided by the Pole Star. They walked on in a void of friendly, mysterious darkness, not knowing what was in any direction or what would be the result of arriving there. At any rate it was most unlikely to be a place where police were waiting for them.

The first red streaks of the early dawn hung over wide patches of woodland to the right of the line. They cut across the fields and pushed through a belt of hazel into true forest, silent in its age as soon as the clatter of disturbed wood-pigeons had disappeared. The wind was getting up from the southwest, reminding Bernardo of weeks in the two English Mays he had known which would have soaked an Eskimo to the skin and then frozen him. They had had luck with their weather, and now it was over.

Low clouds swept over the trees which at first gave shelter from the driving rain and then very little. Both were already dripping when they discovered a fallen elm under which they squatted, she huddled in the Norfolk jacket, he with her coat over his shoulders. Even Nadya was for once dejected. The rain underlined their helplessness — no more food, no money except for the foreign notes which remained, no certain destination, no possibility of ever getting dry. Bernardo was haunted by a disquieting sense of continuity as if a steady state of desperation had endured from a Moldavian wood into an English one and his existence between the two had been illusion. And illusion it was — he couldn't get away from that — maintained only by the ridiculous optimism of an unsustainable David Mitrani. Nadya was the only reality.

In the afternoon they moved miserably on, more for something to do than in any hope of a solution. Once out of the trees, they were in the usual meadowland and walked, bundled into themselves, along twisting country lanes. Caution seemed a waste of time apart from reconnoitering the bends before committing themselves. Bernardo doubted if the public had been given any general warning to look out for them as if they were a couple of dangerous thugs escaped from prison. To the rare passerby on foot or in a farm cart they appeared huddled, harmless tramps well used to bad weather.

On the outer edge of a straggling village they came to a small, thatched pub standing alone by the side of the lane. It was called The Rising Sun, and it was the cheerful gold of the inn sign which made Bernardo take the risk and damn the consequences. He quickly took Nadya through a gate and behind the hedge before they could be spotted.

"You're going to stay the night there if you can talk your way in," he said. "We daren't go together."

"But what about you?"

"I shall find a shed or a barn or something. Then you can slip out with a hard-boiled egg and a bottle whenever there is a chance. How much of Scheeper's money have we got left?"

It came to about five pounds in French francs and bits and pieces of other currencies.

"Will they let me pay with that?" she asked.

"Not a hope! But they won't ask you to pay till tomorrow or whenever you leave if you look fairly respectable. And by then I will have found a way of changing money."

The first task was to convert her, so far as it was possible at all, back from a tramp into a simply dressed young lady

265

who had been respectfully beamed at by waiters at Nancy only five days before. She washed her face in the water racing down a field ditch, arranged her hair, cleaned some butter off her hat and shook out her own coat. When she had finished she looked as if she had been caught in the rain and perhaps slipped in some mud; but it was really the seraphic, oval face which dressed her. Such a girl could not be anything but ingenuous and well brought up.

She was unsure of it in this very foreign country.

"What am I to say?"

"Anything except that you are Russian. Go straight in and ask if they can put you up. The man will say he doesn't know and that you'd better ask the missus. God will give you the right story to tell her as soon as you see her face. Remember they are the same in England as anywhere else. A pretty girl who looks honest and lost — they'll take you in."

Mr. Brown remembered how he had watched her, always so curiously neat and alluring when seen from the back, walking up the lane to the pub and in at the door and how he had blamed himself for a confidence which might be wholly mistaken.

"Lord, it's so much easier today!" he exclaimed. "Look at these gallant, young creatures wandering with a bedroll over half the world and putting up at youth hostels or cottage rooms and no questions asked! But they've lost something worth having. Today you'll seldom get a bed at a village pub. Then nearly all of them would take you in — or if they couldn't they would send you to the next one — and charge you five bob for bed and all the breakfast you could eat, beer and supper extra."

Nadya disappeared inside, and a little later he saw the land-lady throw open a small lattice window hidden under the deep thatch. So that was all right. The next thing was to find some shelter for himself which would be warm and dry. There was a Dutch barn half a mile back along the lane with a haystack and a couple of wagons inside it. He was by no means sure of English agricultural practice, but surely nobody was going to need hay at a time when the grass was growing almost visibly.

Warmth at last. He scrambled to the top of the stack under the corrugated iron roof and took off all his clothes to dry, undisturbed by men or dogs since the farm was up a drive on the other side of the lane. Though the hay prickled, scent and softness were an opiate. In the early morning he was woken up by some activity below, but it was so obvious that nobody could have any reason to climb to the top of the stack that he went to sleep again. This excellent lodging was one which — with care — he could use as long as he pleased. Food had to depend on Nadya.

He knew she would be out looking for him, but it was difficult to find her in that closed country; so he tucked himself away in a thicket of tattered, ivy-choked saplings alongside the lane where there was also a spring and waited, sure that at some time she must pass. At last he saw her walking slowly and stopping at intervals to listen. When he called to her she came running with open arms, a parcel dangling, and gave him one of her impulsive kisses from which, as before, she quickly drew back. It occurred to him that the odd position she had adopted when he kept her warm in the railway cutting was the only one which would avoid any frontal contact.

"Yes, it's lovely and so clean — sheets, everything. I like it, David. If only we could both stay there! The woman is very clean, too, and rather stern. She told me she had been a parlormaid in a big house before she married. She took me for a *boiar* in spite of what I look like and was quite respectful. So I played it from there. There was a calendar from an Oxford brewer in the bar. Is Oxford far away?"

"I don't know. It must be all of twenty miles."

"Well, I said I had walked from there. I was at the university and they made me wear black because I didn't know any Greek."

"Of all the . . ."

"Well, she didn't know any better. And I said I was so angry that I had telegraphed to my father in Hungary and walked straight out."

"Why Hungary?"

"Because it isn't Russia and it isn't Romania and according to you it's full of counts. So I'm a countess."

"Did she believe it?"

"She wanted to, but all she said was that there was a bus from Oxford and I needn't have walked. So I told her that the family never took buses. We walked or we rode. Why are they so impressed by horses, David, when there are some in every field?"

"I think people only ride for fun. It means you have money."

"Well, anyway here are bits of my breakfast and I asked them to pack me some lunch and there's that, too. The only wine they had is called whisky, so I brought some. They were a bit doubtful about that and the lunch. I hadn't any baggage, you see, and I might never come back. I pretended to be very much surprised. You remember you told me the Kalmodys never used money."

"You didn't have the face to tell them that!"

"Not quite. But it gave me the general idea. Now, here are two cold sausages and half a loaf from breakfast, and bread and cheese and cold mutton sandwiches for the picnic. And cherryade for me because it looked so pretty and whisky for you."

Bernardo took a hearty swig at the half bottle and filled it up with doubtful water from the oozing spring. Nadya remarked with surprise that she had never known him take water with his wine.

If she was to continue to get away with it, father in Hungary had to telegraph some cash. The ex-parlormaid was evidently a romantic, but there would be a limit to her trust. Bernardo determined to change money and did not think it too great a risk if only he could avoid appearing in the Norfolk jacket or his shirt sleeves. He asked her to find out what time a bus ran to where and to keep her eyes open for an old coat. Even a coat off a scarecrow might do.

"And pinch the boss's razor if you can," he added. "He can't possibly need it while he's serving in the bar."

Nadya returned after dark with scraps of her supper, a bundle and the news that a bus went to Buckingham at eleven in the morning and back to Oxford in the afternoon when banks would be closed. The bundle turned out to be a farmer's long, brown, linen coat. It had been, she said, in the cupboard of her room along with other old clothes and was unlikely to be missed. She also had the razor. He shaved painfully and inadequately at the spring.

Bernardo started off in the morning knowing nothing of Buckingham but reckoning that since it had given its name to a county as well as some dukes it ought to have a bank which knew French francs when it saw them. After he had paid his bus fare he had twopence left in the world. Observation of his fellow passengers assured him that he was not conspicuous; he could be taken for a garage hand, say, or a salesman visiting farmers. Nobody showed any curiosity about him when he got on or when he got off.

Buckingham turned out to be only a small market town, but had two banks of which he chose the more imposing. He had intended to appear as a Frenchman with a marked accent but decided that as he looked a possible native of the country-side he would play the honest John Bull. He asked what his francs were worth as if he had never seen such nasty things before and mistrusted them. He was told, and they were changed. No suspicion at all.

He bought a map, soap and a cheap razor and then wondered what to do with himself until his bus left. Hanging round the town with no object was dangerous and he did not want to be seen tramping the roads. Further down the High Street was a lot of activity around the cattle market with drifting groups of men, many of them wearing coats much like his own. He joined them confidently, his position allowing him to keep an eye on the main road to the east while brooding over a pen of sheep — not that he expected to gain any useful information from the traffic, but he wanted to get the feel of this society after slinking through it like a nocturnal animal.

He saw buses to Northampton and to villages, the names of which he memorized and could find later on the map. Movements of cattle lorries were worth watching in case it should be possible to slip into an empty one and escape observation when the driver closed the doors. A police car cruised past the market, but there was no reason to suppose that the arrest of Bernardo Brown had priority over other duties. The search for him ought by now to have gone further afield than this tiny patch of the Midlands.

A traffic jam was just building up at the corner where an excited and athletic heifer had broken away from the auction ring and was being doubtfully contained between a bunch of Buckinghamshire farmers waving arms and sticks and a horse box which had drawn up across the road. Half a dozen

loafers, full of market-day beer, were betting on the chance
of the heifer getting a clear run up the High Street. A couple
of women with perambulators had taken refuge in a shop.
Bernardo joined the crowd. At the far end of the line of traffic
he saw a face, tanned and moustached, which he could have
sworn he recognized, above the wheel of a black car so imposing that it ought to have been chauffeur-driven. The heifer
was cornered; the traffic loosened and streamed away. It was
Kalmody. Not a shadow of doubt. And his driving was typical.
The two perambulators, casually emerging into what seemed
safety, were only saved from demolition by his astonishing
swerve.

Only one reason could have brought Kalmody to Buckingham. Bernardo was appalled at his own importance. As
assassin of grand dukes, forger of francs, spy for anyone you
like to name, perhaps he should have expected it. He skulked
towards his bus, hat well down over his eyes. On a sudden,
ridiculous impulse he bought a half-crown bracelet of imitation silver for Nadya to remember him by when she was an
old maid in — in God's name where?

When he arrived back in the village, she was most unwisely
waiting in the street: a sure sign that she felt greater anxiety
than she had ever admitted. They passed each other without
a glance and he strolled off, taking a roundabout route to the
ivy-choked saplings and the spring. She was there before him.

She was absurdly delighted by the bracelet, far more than
by the money which allowed her to pay her bill and gave a
day or two more of security. It was possible, he thought, that
since childhood she had received few tokens of affection,
however trivial. He wanted to go on watching the sudden
vivacity of her face and did not mention Kalmody.

"What have you been doing all day?"

"Out. I can't just sit there."

"Good! Then you can say you got your money from a post office."

"Which one?"

"There are several different Claydons on the map. One of them must have a post office. Just say Claydon if anyone asks. Where were you really?"

"In your haystack. I left some food and beer there in case we missed each other. And then I stayed. It was so comfortable."

He waited till dusk before returning to the haystack himself in case her visit had been noticed. The puzzling presence of Kalmody showed that the hounds were too close on their scent for any risk to be taken. He might have been called in to identify the criminal or — a more disturbing thought — he might have come over to keep in touch with the case and to ensure that Bernardo Brown disappeared finally and forever before he could be interrogated in more depth. But it was near impossible for Kalmody to find him before the police did, since they must be his only source of information.

He slept a third night in his haystack, thankful for the bread and cold meat which Nadya had left. Over at the inn they must think she had an astonishing appetite. He left the barn at dawn before the unseen laborer could arrive and do whatever he did do. Suppose the fellow brought a dog which started to bark at the stack? His instinct for self-preservation had become much sharper in the night and compelled him to spend the early morning lying on the reverse slope of some rising ground from which he could see the backs of houses and sections of the road where it entered and left the village. Nothing out of the ordinary appeared except some young Hereford bullocks which came up and sniffed at him and jumped away. His own forebodings seemed just as senseless, but there they were. Though it was much earlier than Nadya's usual time of arrival at the rendezvous, he decided to go down and wait for her.

She turned up ten minutes later. Something was badly wrong. He thought he knew all the moods of that exquisite face — resignation, calm, mischief, affection — but this was new. It was the face of the woman she was becoming, not that of the child he was always too inclined to think her. The skin was tightly drawn over the high cheekbones, masking the soft oval.

"Let's go away, David!" she said. "Anywhere — but away!"

"What's happened, *dragutsica?*"

"That woman! And she couldn't even bring herself to say why!"

"The police?"

"No! She was looking at me very queerly last night. I think it was the post office. They all know each other round here. I think she may have telephoned and caught me out in a lie. Afterwards I heard them counting the cash in the till and it wouldn't come right and then it did and she said something about that girl. If people like that see they have been fooled, they never forgive it. I'm sure she suspected that when I was out all day I was stealing the money to pay my bill."

"Well, but it doesn't matter."

"She must have watched me through a hole in the wall or something to see what I did or what was in my bag."

"She wouldn't have got much change out of that."

"But you don't understand! I haven't any night-dress or dressing gown and I hate sleeping in my clothes. And this morning, not a word! She just told me to get out as if I were unclean. Oh, David, pity me — pity me! Can I never have what I want? They'd be kind if I were a hunchback or a cripple. But I'm like a leper used to be. I'm an animal — a bitch with teats, inhuman, horrible. Men, yes, I know. But a woman? Shouldn't she feel for me?"

Nadya was dry-eyed and for the moment beyond comfort, looking past him and hardly listening. She would not let him touch her beyond the hand which he held.

"Do you think she will talk?" she asked.

To console her Bernardo said he did not think so. But he knew the type of that ex-parlormaid though he had not set eyes on her — respectable, suppressed and, worst of all, with a false, romantic view of the world which, when she was faced with reality, left her as helplessly resentful as a beetle kicking on its back. One didn't find so many of them in Latin countries where women — at any rate after marriage — were conditioned by common sense and sorrow to extend their natural generosity.

Yes, the ex-parlormaid would be up in the village already, whispering to her cronies and appalled as if she had given hospitality to Dracula's Hungarian daughter. And soon the men would know. He could imagine the nods and murmurs in the bar and the sudden guffaws. Prurient curiosity was inevitable to start with, but it would not be long before those healthy agriculturalists were disinfecting the whole story with humor, and humor was never far from pity.

"What did her husband say?" he asked.

"She kept him off. I could see that. When I caught his eye, he shook his head in a sad sort of way. He wanted to help, but he didn't dare."

This was the end. The village policeman would get it from his wife or the first friend with whom he downed a pint; after a couple of questions he could be sure that this was the wanted girl and that her companion had been hiding close by. Common sense told Bernardo that they must separate at once. Love and blazing anger prohibited anything of the sort. She would have to be left to her own bitter loneliness sometime, but not yet. Meanwhile the risk of traveling together had to be taken.

These little closed communities among the elms had become too hot for them. They had probably been wrong to leave the anonymity of city streets though it had seemed the most certain way of escape with only desperate minutes to spare. The best bet now was to try to return before telephones could ring in police stations and the cars and bicycles converged on them.

He explained to Nadya that if only they could reach London they might be lost for good. They could live as they had in Bucarest and perhaps he could get a job under still another false name.

"Look here!" he said, tracing the map with his finger. "We daren't try Aylesbury or Brackley, but there are trains to London from this place called Bletchley and we can get there on this cross-country line with lots of little stations. They can't be watching all of them."

She paid no attention, not even reacting to the deliberately cheerful reminder of Bucarest.

"I'm going to let them catch me. I can't come to any harm, David."

That was true enough; she had committed no crime in England. But what would become of her? Suppose no refugee organization would have anything to do with her now? In her present mood he could imagine her curling up in some corner and simply collapsing like a deserted, misshapen kitten.

"I'll tell them you left me days ago, and have gone I don't know where."

"You will not. Who threw up everything to help me in Bucarest when she had a safe, peaceful future?"

"I don't deserve gratitude. I don't want it."

He tried to impress her with the vital importance of hurry.

"Just forget all about that blasted woman!" he said. "She doesn't matter and we haven't time for a lot of baby talk."

"You put up with it from Despina."

"I did not. She was always calm."

"Because she didn't love you."

"I hope she didn't, but she pretended remarkably well. Now, listen!"

She was to walk alone to Claydon station and he would walk to Marsh Gibbon. Both were about the same distance. They would take the next train to Bletchley unless it was due within ten minutes of arrival at the station. They would travel apart and leave the train apart, always keeping in sight of one another. He would look out of the window at Claydon to see that she had got on safely.

"And at Bletchley," he added, "just cross to the London platform wherever it is and wait while I buy the tickets. I'm the least likely to be recognized. I'll leave the Pozharski jacket in a ditch."

She agreed and at last produced a set smile. He gave her a quarter of an hour's start and then set off for Marsh Gibbon. The farmer's linen coat gave him confidence, and he did not attempt to avoid the occasional cars and pedestrians. It must be difficult for the police to put out any really conclusive description of him so long as he kept his hair safely under his cap.

He waited nearly an hour for the next train to Bletchley. Arriving at Claydon, nine minutes later, he looked out of the window. She was not there and she did not get in. This was the devil. He jumped out just as the train started, explaining to the stationmaster that he wanted to break his journey and see a friend, and walked back along the route she ought to have taken, afraid that she had not been concentrating on his instructions and had lost her way.

He was halfway back after casting right and left at all cross lanes without any conviction that he could overtake and find her. If she had really lost herself, she might be absolutely anywhere and he had no hope of picking up her trail without continually asking questions. But she couldn't have lost her way; the lanes were well signposted. She might of course have been arrested. It seemed the least likely explanation. They had hardly seen a cop since arriving in the district, and it was too soon for police headquarters, wherever it was, to have got the news.

He sat on a stile despairingly trying to work out what she could have done. It took him a lot of intelligent, logical analysis, dismissing one alternative after another, before he turned his thoughts from geography to the girl herself. It occurred to him that he had been obsessed by the effect on their escape of that prying into her privacy rather than its effect on her. His impatience could have been nearly as devastating as her elopement from the convent. Not only had she been reminded by a cruel fool that she was a monster at a fair, but she had been overwhelmed by a sense of guilt.

There was one place worth trying. It could be her temporary refuge from loneliness. Great caution was necessary in broad daylight, but she herself had managed it the day before.

He strode out for their usual rendezvous, followed the hedges and approached the Dutch barn from the back. As he began to climb rustling up the haystack he was agonized to hear passionate sobbing which stopped as soon as she detected the intruder. This time he would not allow any turning away from him. Four breasts, twenty breasts — why should she think it mattered? She was his sister, his beloved friend. He was very careful to speak only English, avoiding all suspect Romanian endearments.

"I did start," she told him, "but I knew I mustn't. So I turned back."

"I don't believe that was what God told you."

"God has left me."

"Because he is talking to me now. He said: Try the haystack!"

"Don't make fun of me! . . . What else did he say?"

"That Mr. Bernardo Brown should be ashamed of himself."

"I don't know him. I only know David. For ever and ever David."

"Then don't you run away again! We'll try it together and after dark. There's a late train. I looked them all up while I was waiting. And there must be something on to London."

It was always the same with Nadya. When she had comfort in mind and body she went to sleep. She must have formed the habit as a waif in Russia, putting her tail round her nose when it was the only refuge. Bernardo disengaged himself, retaining her hand, and considered the chances.

First, they had to walk together to Claydon station. He knew that he could now trust her to walk far behind or far ahead of him, yet they might so easily lose touch in the darkness and he was not going to risk any repetition of that. Her desolation had not been so very different from his own, though at the time he had hidden from himself what he felt by damning and blasting the lanes, his stupidity and her incompetence. It was on the trains, not on the road, that they needed more than a fair share of luck. They could have counted on it earlier in the day.

Never was the night of the leafy Midlands more placid. They passed no one in the lanes. There was no one on the two platforms of the station — a horizontal dimness, lit by a few oil lamps, among the greater, vertical darkness of the elms. He told Nadya to go on alone, buy her ticket to Bletchley and cross to the far platform. When he saw that she was over and inconspicuously waiting for the train, he too went through, saying good night to the stationmaster.

A large and venerable locomotive rocked in out of the night, hauling two almost empty coaches. There seemed no point in traveling in separate compartments since anyone interested in the passengers could spot them both at a glance. One station after another was passed with little sign of life beyond the friendly scatter of lights from villages in the distance. Four passengers got on; nobody got off. Then the line curved round an embankment suddenly carrying them out of rural England and into the white light of Bletchley station.

The train docked in its own bay. On the left was the exit and booking hall; on the right, a main-line platform with an empty train standing at it. Two uniformed police were alongside the ticket collector. A man in a bowler hat had started to walk towards the new arrival, leaving no doubt what he was and whom he wanted. Bernardo opened the door on the wrong side, ran round the locomotive and the train on the opposite line with Nadya alongside him and raced down the track.

They were shouted at by railwaymen, but only when they were clear of the empty coaches did the police see them. They crossed a road bridge and then bore to the right, instinctively choosing the spur by which they had arrived rather than the signal lights and shining metals of the main line. With the pursuit a train's length behind them they slid down the embankment and climbed a fence. Close to it was the privet hedge of a suburban garden through which Bernardo crashed, making a gap for Nadya, then over a wooden fence into another garden with police now closing up. Gardens evidently stretched away for house after house and unless they could get out of them into the wide space or field which separated the row from the curving embankment they were bound to be caught. Either the gardens had no gates leading to railway property or they could not spot them in the dark. The only hope was a greenhouse in the next garden up against the boundary wall which might give a possible way over if they could reach it in time.

"No!" Nadya whispered. "Better way!"

She picked a flower pot out of a pile and handed it to him. "Throw it!"

He saw at once what she meant. The flower pot smashed into the greenhouse low down. While they dropped flat, close under the wall of the house, the chase — two bowler hats and three uniforms now — passed within yards of them, over the next fence and over the boundary wall by way of the greenhouse, smashing more panes.

"Back, David!"

He obeyed without question the greater experience of a juvenile delinquent. He could understand Scheeper and that tree now. She was keeping up with ease, running lightly and fast. It was the first time he had seen her run, for never before had it been essential. A revelation for him. Her dumpy top half postulated clumsy legs so that his subconscious continued to insist that they were although his eye was well aware that they were slender.

They crept back along the route they had taken, reached the foot of the railway embankment and began to follow it round the curve. Ahead of them the party had broken out of the gardens and was combing the rough land where the elusive pair might have dropped to the ground hoping to be overrun in the dark. Two figures were up on the embankment itself, throwing powerful beams along the track to spot the fugitives if they tried to cross it. In the houses more windows were lit where the inhabitants had been stirred up by the crash of glass or police knocking at their front doors.

They had to stay where they were, crouched at the foot of the embankment close to the station but well outside the range of its lights, while their pursuers were casting back and forth over the rough ground. Then the pack crossed the railway to beat out whatever cover there was on the other side. It was safe to move very cautiously forward.

Immediate danger was over except for a cop on the line itself whose figure could just be made out against the sky. It was doubtful if he could see them when they passed below him but he would certainly hear them, for it was impossible to move quietly through the weeds and tufts of grass at the foot of the embankment. Bernardo scrambled up and wriggled across the line to see if the other side offered an easy passage round the sentry. It seemed to be very broken ground sprinkled with low scrub which was being thoroughly searched. The number of lights showed that the police had been reinforced.

Their own side of the embankment was safer as the search of the strip of field between houses and railway had been abandoned. They silently followed the boundary wall of the gardens and were very nearly spotted by some officious citizen who popped his white face over it and searched the neighbor-hood with a powerful acetylene lamp. The greenhouse, two gardens back, was the obvious method of dealing with him. Bernardo crawled along the foot of the wall, found half a brick and produced another satisfying crash. The white face disappeared. The beam of the lamp was thrown across the gardens, and someone yelled, "Oy! Got 'em! Police!"

The cop on the line shouted something down to the other side but his companions were uninterested, probably ac-customed to being thrown off the right scent by too enthusiastic members of the public. Bernardo and Nadya crept on under the shadow of the wall and returned to the foot of the embankment as soon as they were safely past the sentry. They could now be fairly sure that there was no trouble ahead of them, so they trotted along the metals for a mile before stopping to rest and think.

The night was utterly silent. There was no pursuit. Bernardo again found it difficult to accept his own importance. He was not a bank robber, merely a desperate and suspicious character with a record of comparatively minor offenses. It was an effort to remember that he was wanted in Spain for the murder of some princely crook. But there it was, and the police were not at all likely to give up. They seemed to ignore railway lines but one could bet they had blocked all likely roads. And what about bridges over the railway which would allow them to keep an eye on both?

The first bridge loomed up after another mile. He treated it with proper caution, taking to the fields in order to circle round it. When they had slipped across the road which the bridge carried, he stealthily reconnoitered the approach. He could make out a car standing just short of the parapet. A few more yards along the line and it would have been all up.

The railway itself had proved too risky, so they ploughed across the damp meadows alongside it until they came up against a wood surrounded by a low barbed wire fence. The moon was now getting up in a clear sky; the wood offered a return to the darkness which nerves, badly shaken by their narrow escape, demanded. It might be a belt of trees with little cover or it might offer refuge for a day or two.

After worming under the wire they pushed their way through a tangle of ash, thorn and overgrown laurel. The center of the wood was open, but too rough to be called a glade. The moon showed a sandy waste of mounds, holes and bramble bushes with knee-high growth between them. There was a strong smell of fox. A startled roebuck bounced into cover.

Stumbling and tripping across the moonlit mess they found on the other side a stand of larches. Beneath the trees was pitch darkness and a soft, dry bed of needles. They had a place to rest and — up the easily climbed trees — a possible hiding place in emergency. Beyond the larches a rutted, overgrown track led out into the open past what looked like a disused hut.

Both were enchanted by the copse and its promise. Inexplicable England! On its own small scale the place was wilder, more tangled, more full of hidden life than any Romanian forest Bernardo had seen, yet it was within four miles of a busy town and bordered by the railway. The damp and warmth of May had accumulated in a mere thicket — so far as he could judge it was not more than twenty acres — lush growth and a concentration of animal life which would be scattered far and wide in the great woods of Europe and seldom seen.

They settled down under the larches, prepared to spend the rest of the night there and explore ways of escape in the morning. Anyone entering the copse could be heard and avoided. Even half a dozen searchers would think the place empty while the pair they wanted was hidden among the dark stems of the laurels or with bodies halfway down a badger sett and head and shoulders invisible unless stepped on. It was futile to look forward to London or anywhere else, but for the moment they were safe.

Sometime after one they heard movement through the bushes too clumsy to be that of an animal. Then there was a thud followed by a string of curses which Bernardo recognized as Hungarian. He signaled to Nadya to remain under the larches and crawled silently forward until he could distinguish anything moving in the open center of the wood. Moonlight caught on white hair. The intruder was undoubtedly Sigismond Pozharski mopping his forehead. He sat down in full view on one of the little tumps thrown up centuries ago by the spade of man or quite recently by the claws of badger.

"Bernardo, dear boy," he remarked to nothing, "if you are roosting here along with somebody's pheasants, will you kindly come out?"

He lit a cigar and remained squatting on his tump like an amiable troll.

"The police, so far as I know, are nowhere near the bridge where you so wisely avoided them. The car was Kalmody's. He picked you up with night glasses."

Bernardo preserved complete silence. The glasses were now hanging on Pozharski's chest, unpleasantly reminding him of Bobo's.

"Whenever we meet, you always assume I am ill disposed. I am not. Nor is Istvan. It's a long story how we were able to trace you. Meanwhile I may point out that my housekeeper was seriously alarmed by an absolute procession of lice hatching out from a Romanian cabman's hat."

Bernardo rose to his feet and strolled out into the open.

"My dear fellow! It was only a fifty-fifty chance. How glad I am! And now present me to this clever Miss Andreyev."

Nadya came forward uncertainly and suspiciously, for Pozharski must be aware of her history as far back as the Mosh. He took both her hands, treating her at once as if she were the daughter of an old friend.

"You never told me what she was like, Bernardo."

"I have hardly had a chance."

"Istvan will be as enchanted as I am. He insisted on ex-

pecting a Russian refugee all pearls and tears and sensibilities.
I told him we should find a muddied little oaf at the bottom
of a bramble bush. How wrong we both were! To see you, my
dear, is to wish to serve you. Never be afraid again!"

"I am sorry I never noticed the hat when I cleaned up, Mr.
Pozharski."

"And she can laugh! Was this the face that launched a
thousand ships, swiping the key from Whitehall's waistcoat
pocket? Sweet seventeen against sixty odd is not fair, Nadya.
I wish it were up to you to get us out of this one, but only
Kalmody can."

"I saw him in Buckingham the day before yesterday," Bernardo said. "Obviously on my trail! I don't trust him."

"Well, you're wrong. Having convinced himself that you
are innocent, he is now furious with the Romanians for daring
to harass a guest of his. A typical Hungarian, dear boy —
arrogant, illogical and quixotically gallant! You couldn't be
in better hands. And by the way — in case we are suddenly
interrupted — you had better know that I am the foreign
correspondent of *Az Ujsag*, an excellent Budapest daily in
which his party holds fifty-one percent of the shares. Anybody
who fools the Romanians is a natural hero. So the Hungarian
people must have the lowdown on you before you get extradited to Spain. That's our story and we're sticking to it."

"I don't see how it helps."

"Later! Later! What I'm afraid of is that the police may
guess your movements just as we did and borrow a dog off the
nearest farmer. Come on!"

By way of the dark avenue of larches they entered the track
which led across a long open field to another copse. As they
passed the dilapidated hut, one corner of it quietly detached
itself, swept off its hat to the startled Nadya and kissed her
hand.

"I am at your feet, Miss Andreyev. To you, Mr. Brown, I owe a thousand apologies. My correspondence with the Vatican . . ."

"Damn the Vatican! Come out of the eighteenth century, Istvan, and tell us where you left the car!" Pozharski interrupted.

"Off the track in the wood over there. All's clear. What's the hurry?"

"The hurry is that I don't want to go to jail."

"Oh, they'd only put you inside for a couple of months. Mr. Brown, the futility of apologies . . ."

"Why don't you call him Bernardo? We always do when we talk about him."

"Well, if he will accept it from an older man whom he has no reason to like."

"But I did like you, Count Kalmody. Who wouldn't? Only that vast place of yours was a nightmare."

"Of course. I should have seen it. I thought you would be so impressed that you would stick it out. But I could not cage hills and the sea along with you. I also thought — my very worst mistake — that you were too experienced to take very seriously — well, er, such distractions as were provided. Again I apologize, Bernardo. Now, to settle an argument with Sigi here. Did you or did you not have a fine toy railway at an early age?"

"I did. And my father made a quay for it. And cranes."

"You see, Sigi?"

"Yes. And I think I saw a blink of headlights in the trees there."

"Off this track then! Bernardo, you take Sigi and go round by the right-hand hedge! Miss Andreyev and I will go by the left. We meet in four minutes precisely where the track enters the trees. Don't cross it and keep in cover!"

Kalmody's manner had changed completely. He had taken Nadya's arm and both were already indistinguishable against any background. Bernardo and Pozharski trotted straight down towards their hedge, quite content not to improve on darkness.

"I still don't see the newspaper correspondent," Bernardo said.

"Simple, dear boy. What the police know, we know, given Istvan's introductions and — not to put it too crudely — his lavish entertainment of them. I think they assume that Magyars live in tents and on mare's milk and are easily offended. We make them feel like the Bunga Bunga colonial police arsing about in khaki shorts and condescending to take the native gifts. So Istvan's special pal calls us up and says he has got you cold. We shot down to Bletchley to see if we could help but came too late. They said you had both broken away and taken to the brickfields."

"Aren't you talking a little loud, Mr. Pozharski? And keep into that hedge!"

"Thank you, Bernardo. Experience teaches. Now I know why Istvan split us up like that. His only real passion in life is stalking animals. Sometimes he is so pleased to have outsmarted one that when he gets him in his sights he lets him go. He didn't believe in the brickfield. He said he knew your mind from your movements. You used the railway to escape from Hungary. You bolted for it in London when they were minutes behind you. What you did then nobody knows, but somehow it must have been the railway. So he was sure you had gone up the line and betted me you had played with puff-puffs as a child. We looked at the map, made a beeline for that bridge and his hunch paid off. Then we scouted around on foot and he swore you would have made for that copse and stayed there whether you had four legs or two."

They dived into the ditch as headlights flickered over the grass. A police car bumped out of the trees with four men and a dog inside it. When it had crossed the meadow and stopped somewhere near the hut, Kalmody stood up on the other side of the track. He held up a hand for silence and beckoned them on, himself leading the way with Nadya. About a hundred yards from the end of the wood and the good, metaled road which bordered it he turned into a rutted opening in the undergrowth where timber had been hauled out. His black car was there, invisible under hazels.

"I'll go forward and see if it's safe to move," he said. "You stay here."

He was back quickly, moving over the grass of the ride as if he knew where to put his feet in spite of darkness, and reported that there were two men on the road. They could easily be rushed, but the car would be recognized.

"I'll try and draw them off to the north corner. Once they are rooting about in there we can risk it."

He vanished again. In a few minutes they heard a man rushing desperately and clumsily through the hazels to break out at the north corner. The reaction was two piercing whistles: one from the direction in which the count was creating his diversion, the other from the junction of road and track. Kalmody was an exasperatingly long time returning. Meanwhile they heard the police car start up far away across the meadow.

"Drawn off one of them," Kalmody reported, appearing at the bonnet of the car. "The other fellow must have had strict orders. He never moved from his post."

The police car had already entered the track and stopped. It sounded as if some of the men in it had got out and were beating half the wood — the correct half — towards the two stops on the road.

"Get us out of this, Istvan!" Pozharski exclaimed. "Damn it, you were once a captain of Hussars!"

"Of course. One forgets. Covering fire!"

He draw an automatic from his pocket and checked it.

"For God's sake, this is England! You'll get us all twenty years."

"Nonsense! If I hit one I can always give him a pension."

Bernardo protested that they would accuse him, not Kalmody.

"Well, they can't prove it if you aren't here."

"We used to draw off the police by starting a fight," Nadya said.

"What sort of a fight?"

"If they thought someone was getting killed, they dropped whatever they were doing and broke it up."

"She's got it. Quick!" Kalmody whispered.

He disappeared with her across the track into the other half of the wood, racing against time and not caring whether the advancing party of police heard them or not. Then there was a silence, suddenly broken by Nadya screaming:

"No! No! Help! No, don't!"

A shot cut the scream short. A few seconds later there was another shot — the cold finish of something still alive.

Old Mr. Brown said that never in the whole of his Grand Tour had he been so frightened. It had been utterly convincing. One could be sure — after a moment of agonizing doubt — that Kalmody was reproducing the scene from past experience. Nobody had ever said much about the recovery of the estate from the Communists with Nepamuk's loyal assistance.

"It worked like dynamite," he went on. "The beaters changed direction. One of them nearly ran into us in his hurry to get to the other side of the wood. Orders were shouted. The two fellows on guard in the road came charging

up. And then Istvan Kalmody and Nadya were at the car.
Don't ask me how they got there! Nadya and I were bundled
into the back under a rug and two suitcases and we were out
of the hazels and in the track with one awful moment when
the wheels wouldn't grip in a rut. Then into the road and a
right turn and Kalmody cornering through the lanes like a
snipe he'd missed with the first barrel."

Bernardo and Nadya disentangled themselves and sat up on
the car floor, braced between front seats and back. Hedges
loomed up and were miraculously avoided. Pozharski was helplessly trying to read the map on his knees.

"I don't think they are on our tail," he said.

"Of course they aren't. They can't leave until they are sure
there is no corpse and no Bernardo."

"They'll suspect it was the foreign correspondent of *Az
Ujsag*."

"Yes. Tomorrow. When they can't find us in the district
any longer. But you'll be all right when we have gone, Sigi.
They can't prove a thing. You were after your story and you
lost your nerve when you heard the police begin to shoot."

"The police are not armed in this country."

"Well, you're what they call a bloody foreigner and you
don't know it. Not armed when chasing a desperate character
like Bernardo? It's incredible."

Pozharski made him stop at the next signpost while he made
some sense out of the map. He said that if they kept going
they must hit Watling Street somewhere and then would have
a civilized run to London produced by Romans, not Saxons
driving pigs round angles.

"Then that's where we can expect a road block, if any.
Cross it and work east as soon as we are well clear."

The two Hungarians might be clear, but it did not seem to
Bernardo that he was. There was no frontier he could safely

cross, no identity he could safely take, and the rescue which Kalmody had mounted could only lead to another tactful imprisonment.

"May I know where we are going?" he asked.

"Spain. Both of you."

"They'll arrest me as soon as we arrive."

"They will not know you have arrived. I may need your knowledge of the coast, but leave the rest to me!"

"You mean the plane?"

"Sitting on the River Crouch, full up with oil and gas. The pilot came over to look for a new engine. No connection with me at all."

"They'll work it out eventually," Pozharski said.

"So what? Let them fine me for taking off without clearance. All Europe knows I can't be bothered with papers."

The journey was cramped and painful but without incident. Two hours after dawn Kalmody, with something of a conjurer's pride in his voice, told them to sit up and look out of the window. They were on rising ground above Burnham, and there downriver was the seaplane sitting on the water. He said that they would not take off till nightfall when he hoped they could get out to her unseen. All that must be arranged. As it would be unwise to leave car and passengers in the town while he talked to the pilot, he would leave them in the safest place that could be found and go back to Burnham alone.

Kalmody drove out into the marshes, twisting at random among tracks which only served isolated farms. It was a gray day without color in grass or sedge. Beyond the sea wall the ebb tide was baring mile after mile of gray flats. Bernardo thought their exposure far from ideal after the closed country of the Midlands. The car could be seen from far off; on the other hand, so could a constable on a bicycle. A half empty, hidden creek with a hard bank above the mud offered perfect cover. There Kalmody left them with a bottle of champagne for breakfast and a stale sandwich apiece.

Nadya was silent and restless. Had memories of the bare spaces of Russia anything to do with it? Bernardo could only guess that she had not resigned herself as he had, and distrusted so sudden a leap into an uncontrollable, pointless future.

"I am hot and uncomfortable and bruised, Mr. Pozharski, and I am going to walk to the sea."

"Come then!" Pozharski invited. "Bernardo should stay in his accustomed ditch. But you and I? Father and daughter bird-watching on the Essex marshes? There's no one to show curiosity unless it's a Dutchman with a telescope."

Rather to Bernardo's surprise she answered his smile and seemed grateful. He lay on the edge of the bank and watched their two figures diminishing as they plodded towards the sea wall. The dull flats of the North Sea were depressing, infinitely far away from the sunlit reeds and lively frogs of the Danube marshes. He could tell from the poise of Nadya's head and shoulders that she was talking eagerly. A gust of the easterly breeze carried the music of laughter. The last time he had heard it was also in answer to Pozharski. One had to admit that the old scoundrel's love of women was instantly perceived by them. Kalmody's extreme and formal courtesy gave nothing like so much confidence.

The count was still not back when they returned, flushed with sea wind and exercise and on the best of terms. Bernardo remarked that they should have shown more interest in birds.

"Our Nadya was anxious about both your futures, dear boy. When Istvan is operating at speed he is not easy to understand. Naturally she wanted to know what he thought of all the Scheeper escapade."

"How did he come to hear of it at all?"

"I was in Romania while you were still there, instructed by Istvan to find you at all costs. Mountains and plains, the Danube and the Dniester — all blank, absolutely blank until I returned to Bucarest and visited the Alhambra for post-graduate studies. It's extraordinary how a little relaxation is often more productive than the stern voice of duty."

It certainly had been. He heard of one Mitrani who had escaped from the police by, it was said, driving a *trasura* down the Boulevard Carol in the middle of the night. His house-keeper reported that the house had been burgled, a case, an old coat, toilet articles and some laundry stolen and a cabman's fur hat left behind. Was it possible that this Mitrani was young Brown, especially since the burglar had known where the drinks were?

"You should never again be rude to diplomats, Bernardo. Their parties are tedious, I admit, but a marvelous source of information. I heard that Mitrani was indeed you. I heard of this adorable Nadya and Scheeper's passport. And then Istvan — with all the suppressed energy of a lifetime's idle-ness — charges into action mounted upon political influence with his squadron of letters of credit galloping behind."

It was another half hour before they saw the car threading the marshes. It was obvious that Kalmody was not driving it with any kindness. He got out, followed by his pilot, and walked quickly down into the cover of the creek. He was in a rage of controlled temper, his face two shades lighter than usual.

"I told him never to go out of reach of a telephone," he said.

"Wouldn't he look a bit conspicuous, Istvan?"

"That has nothing to do with it. My orders should be obeyed, right or wrong."

"I can't see a stake anywhere."

"What in God's name do you want one for?"

"For you to burn him at."

The pilot, a Frenchman who spoke little English, observed the conversation with a look of stolid irony. Except at Spezia airport, Bernardo had seen almost nothing of him but his back. His face suggested that he might be genial company when not submitting to the incalculable whims of his employer.

"I repeat that six hundred and fifty miles across open sea is lunacy, *monsieur le comte*."

"You can make Spezia from Pasajes."

"Unwillingly. But in case of engine failure there are ports within easy reach."

"So it can be done!"

"Not against the prevailing winds."

"The wind is east, my friend."

"It will change tonight."

"I pay you to take risks."

"On the contrary! You pay me not to take risks."

"It is not my safety that is at stake. It is my honor."

"I permit myself to doubt whether that will affect the oil gauge."

Kalmody was all ice in his manner, all fire in the way he held himself with one hand on hip and the other gripping the edge of some imaginary and barbaric robe. The pilot remained immovable in his equal professional pride.

"If we're in trouble there's bound to be one of the fishing fleets in sight at dawn," Bernardo said.

Kalmody jumped at this highly speculative suggestion.

"You see? I even give you a Biscay pilot."

"Well, I will risk the two of you if the wind holds."

"Two? There are four of us! Two in the seats, two on the floor."

"Utterly impossible! I will not even allow you to take off."

"Two is enough," Pozharski said in English. "It will be a pleasure for me to look after our Nadya."

"But suppose she is picked up?" Bernardo protested.

"I will make her disappear."

"Where?"

"Into a very private hospital. With all my faults, Bernardo, I am a man of taste. My duty in this world — if I have any — is to assist its creator to perfect it."

"It can't be done."

"Then they will tell me so, David," Nadya said.

"Need I remind you of delicate missions, dear boy? I have my trusted specialist. And if he does not put me on to the right surgeon instanter, he's seen the last princess with the clap I ever send him."

"Bernardo, I promise you that Sigi will cherish your Nadya as if she were my own daughter," Kalmody declared.

Bernardo and Pozharski caught each other's eye and looked away before a smile could break.

"I observe, Bernardo, that being only human we trust each other for the worst possible reasons."

"What about the car?" Bernardo asked.

"We must chance that. Straight from here to Harley Street. Quarter of a mile to the Legation garage. Leave it there for a month and change the tires in case of polite curiosity."

"God tells me not to go, David. But I shall."

"And God says every bloody minute counts. Kiss him, child! And look forward to the next one!"

Old Bernardo was very reticent about that parting. He had felt damnably ashamed of himself. Bond after bond had grown up between them since that first meeting of eyes at the Mosh, but any physical bond had been, with trivial exceptions, out of the question. Until that kiss he had refused to suspect that Nadya's own emotions might be more desperately involved; or, if he had suspected it — well, a passing girlish enthusiasm was no tragedy.

Kalmody gave the pilot his last instructions. He and his anonymous passenger did not wish to be seen and would swim or wade out to the plane after dark. He must get as close to the shore as was safe wherever the chart showed a hard and use the regular light signals as at Lake Balaton.

When Nadya and Pozharski had gone, taking the pilot with them as far as the main road, the count and Bernardo settled down to wait out the day in their slit-trench of a creek. He was a little nervous of the great man, for they had not been alone together since the Arabian Nights entertainment. However, Kalmody's ease of manner, presiding over the breakfast for four which he had brought back with him in the car, was perfect as ever.

"I was so wrong about you, Bernardo," he said. "I realized your intelligence but thought it not very practical."

"It was not. I remember telling my story to a very kindly Jew and saying I was too innocent for the mess I was in. He told me that I would very quickly learn. I did."

"If only you had not run away!"

"I am sorry about Nepamuk."

"Oh, no need to be! He was getting above his station in life. Of course I could not keep him on after he had been made ridiculous, but he is very well provided for."

"And Her Majesty?"

"Blessed are the pure in heart, Bernardo, for it is the duty of the rest of us not to bother them. I believe I told you during your short stay in the villa that for once she had something worth stealing?"

"So after all the fellow got away with it?"

"Not exactly. Exchange is no robbery. A few days before my

arrival at Lequeitio Her Majesty had been given a million francs in cash by a Viennese gentleman who claimed to be a loyal Hapsburg sympathizer. He was impressive, and she is easily impressed. He warned her not to change his gift immediately as questions might be asked by the French Exchange Control. She hadn't got a safe, so she locked up the suitcase containing the francs and put it away in the downstairs office.

"Now, when that chap whom we both thought was French had got away over the wall, and you were swimming to the island, I allowed myself to interrupt Her Majesty's reading and asked her to see if anything was missing. Of course she rushed at once to her francs and found the case still full up and where it ought to be. So we thought no more of it. As I told you, I believed I had merely interrupted a burglar before he could get to work. I only realized when you turned up that the affair was likely to be far more complicated.

"Soon after that dear Zita was inspired. She decided that what had been given by God should be returned to God, and she sent half to the Pope and half to the Little Sisters of St. Margit. She gets back a silky letter from His Holiness giving her a rather cagy blessing and his thanks for the pious thought. Same sort of thing from the Little Sisters! The letters were so alike that I could guess the Mother Superior had asked the Vatican what she should say. I assumed that His Holiness, knowing Zita's poverty, had considered that charity ought to begin at home.

"Meanwhile the Spaniards were very courteously occupying far too much of my time with pointed inquiries about you, Bobo and the late burglar. They would tell me nothing, so I appealed directly to King Alfonso. When he was a boy my father taught him to shoot. He said that the police had found no useful evidence except a few thousand-franc notes washed up at the foot of your cliff."

"Were they forged? Was that the reason why I was mixed up in the Windischgraetz case?"

"No, they were good. I went home, suspecting you of robbery as well as murder, only to find that the Romanians were accusing me of financing international spies. The Romanians! A primitive tribe of revolting catamites who powder their faces and wear corsets!"

Bernardo refrained from comment. One could not defend Romanians to Hungarians or Hungarians to Romanians without risking an explosion. Powder, yes, because of their very blue chins. Corsets — possibly among well-covered staff officers. But catamites was a ridiculous slander upon a country where every man's chief interest was fornication to the limit of his income.

"Then more scandal in January! Windischgraetz and his forged francs! I saw him in jail and told him he ought to have known his young idiots would be caught as soon as they started to distribute the forgeries. He replied indignantly that they had started in July and got away with it.

"July. I smelt a rat. I visited the Vatican . . ."

"I remember Pozharski asking me if I had bumped off a cardinal."

"I visited the Vatican," Kalmody continued impassively, "because in the first place they are well informed and, in the second, because a Kalmody is always welcome. My vague suspicions were confirmed. The francs sent by Zita to His Holiness and the Little Sisters were all forged. They knew she must be utterly innocent. They had also discovered that the distributors did start in July, and that the French had caught them at it and stayed quiet for reasons of their own. So the whole matter discreetly vanished into the private files of the Curia.

"Then, Bernardo, Sigi Pozharski met you in circumstances

which I do not understand and perhaps should not. He came back from Bucarest insisting that all your story was true and that you had told him to impress on me that the suitcase in the boat was full.

"I had a dear Russian friend who would tell me the truth. It was so much easier in old days when, if one had a private question to ask, one could just order a special train and ask it. Now those blasted Romanoffs are never in one place long enough. When I had run him to earth, I asked him if Bobo ever did any jobs for the French Secret Service. Answer: Yes, he did. I was congratulated on having removed him. That is the sort of reputation you have given me, Bernardo. I all but replied that the Kalmodys are an older family than the Romanoffs and have at no time found it necessary to resort to assassination. Now, my dear fellow, again my apologies and I hope all is clear to you."

"I am awfully sorry, Count Kalmody, but I was a small boy in the old days and the Empress Zita and Hapsburgs and King Alfonso are all beyond me."

"Not Alfonso, surely? He will insist on seeing you himself, you know, before giving orders to the Ministry of Justice. A case like yours can't be fixed lower down."

"Oh, God!"

"You'll like him. He'd be the best King of Spain for centuries if he didn't make the mistake of thinking himself the best politician too. But you were asking?"

"I was asking what you were talking about."

"Bernardo, I have again overestimated your sophistication. Could the French and their scoundrelly allies find a better way of discrediting the Monarchy forever than by proving that Zita circulated forged francs?

"They had only to buy two identical suitcases and fill one with forged francs and the other with genuine francs in case some mistrustful servant of the Crown took a handful round to the bank for approval. Then, having thoroughly cased the joint, as they say, land from a small boat and swap one bag for the other! Probably Bobo and his accomplice were told they could keep the good million for themselves if they pulled it off. The plot would have worked to perfection, Bernardo, if there had not been an unexpected stranger present with some experience of handarms."

It seemed to Bernardo that the count exaggerated the effect of his spectacular shot. What had really disrupted the whole operation was a very simple woman better fitted to be a saint than an empress.

He thanked Kalmody profusely for taking such an interest in his fate — an individual who did not matter one way or the other.

"Of course it mattered. Justice is too important to be left in the hands of common magistrates. And now tell me all that happened to you in Romania! Alfonso will want a complete dossier and we shall prepare it for him. He loves people and dislikes documents, so leave out nothing which could entertain him."

His story, together with Kalmody's acute but always courteous questions, occupied most of the morning. When he came to Rabbi Kaplan, the count exclaimed, "A great gentleman of religion! In Hungary, Bernardo, the well-born have no fear of Jews. They tend to marry them when short of money, and often when not."

"In that case may I ask you a favor?"

"It is granted of course."

"A ticket from Roman to Jerusalem to be used by anyone whom Kaplan nominates."

"I shall be delighted. Let's make it fifty of them!"

"I think that Kaplan might be startled, unbelieving. He's not the sort of man to want a miracle to be — well, spectacular."

"If ever you are wealthy, Bernardo — and it's going to be that or disaster — never forget that sometimes, very rarely, one may tend towards vulgarity. Would half a dozen be all right?"

The gray day wore on in silence. Bernardo at intervals raised his head to feel the wind. It was still east and dropping. The count was apparently immune to anxiety about weather. He made himself comfortable and went to sleep. The moustache of brown velvet stirred with occasional snores. It could be dyed. He was much older than Bernardo had thought, and dead tired.

When the sun was already low he sat up, shook himself and splashed his face with the salt water now silently rising towards their feet.

"Bernardo, I need your advice. At Pasajes I am admitted without question though distrusted. A passenger, above all Bernardo Brown, might strain the friendships I have bought."

"Then you had better let me out somewhere else."

"Those civil guards are everywhere. We should be seen."

"Where are you taking me afterwards?"

"Straight to Madrid where Sigi's flat is at our disposal. I could pick you up by car at any rendezvous."

Bernardo could think of one or two beaches and coves where he could swim ashore unseen, but none of them was near a road. A wet stranger walking to a rendezvous with Kalmody was likely to be stopped and questioned as he had been before, especially after a plane landing on the water had attracted attention. He built up images of his beloved coast, superimposing them upon the drab Essex marshes and dreaming of past summer days on lonely beaches: Sopelana, Gorliz,

Mundaca, names like remembered trumpet calls from another life. The Atlantic was still cold in May, but a few of
the heartier young Basques would be trying it already.

"Have you got a swimsuit in your bag?"

"No. But I can do a dressing gown."

It was impudent to return at a point so close to Bilbao, but
the conditions could be met given a calm sea which would
allow the pilot to come close in under the headland opposite
Plencia. A swimmer could not be seen from anywhere. Then
he could go round by the rocks — not before midday — wade
across the river and onto the beach at Gorliz. Nobody would
suspect a young man in a bathrobe unless it happened to be
raining.

"Tell your man to aim at Bilbao Harbor," he said. "When
we are a mile or two off the breakwater I'll give him directions."

They moved off in the dusk, working their way towards the
River Crouch and tying themselves up among the creeks as
the light faded. Kalmody lost patience, swearing that only a
fool entered marshland without a guide. He walked straight
for the lights of Burnham and strolled along the waterfront
with an appalled Bernardo.

"What the hell does it matter? Sooner or later they are
going to know it was you and me. Boldness, boy! There won't
be a cop."

In fact there was. He paid no attention. After all, one had
only to look at Kalmody striding regardless through the world
to feel that he had a right to do whatever he happened to be
doing. Why, Bernardo asked himself, had he ever run? Could
it have been as simple as this? No railway lines, no false religions, no false passports and dyed hair. It was only with an
effort that he remembered he also had no money.

A waterman took them out to the plane. Two boats were

there already, and an enthusiastic garage hand was being taught by gesture and scraps of English how to swing the propellor. It was incredible to Bernardo — this assumption of his peace-loving countrymen that any perfectly open activity must be quite in order so long as nobody in authority said it wasn't. Somewhere — perhaps in one of those softly lit pubs — a coastguard or customs officer was sitting and wondering whether the usual rules applied to seaplanes and if he should not telephone; but meanwhile they were on a straight course down the tideway with the plumes of spray streaming from the floats.

The lights of England fell away behind. An hour and a half later they picked up those of Le Havre. The pilot warned Kalmody, in a voice which was a shrug of the shoulders, that they now had to risk two hundred and fifty miles with no water to come down on.

"*Je m'en fous!* The Loire is in the way somewhere."

"I must keep to the shortest line. We shall not cross the Loire till Nantes and once there we are over the sea again."

Bernardo listened for any faltering of the engine in the mood of poking a tooth to see if it hurt. He wondered how far they would get if the wind changed to the south. Yet the pilot's back was relaxed, the Pole Star was steadily behind them and the night sky brilliantly clear. It appeared that weather, wood and metal were all infected by the confidence of a Kalmody. He went to sleep as soundly as if he had again taken one of Zita's orange pills.

Kalmody poked him. It was dawn. There was no land at all in sight unless the solid and irregular clouds to the south were in fact the Cantabrian Mountains.

"Anticyclone over the Bay. Wind has been pushing us west a bit. Very civil of it! So we are making Bilbao as easily as Pasajes. Here's my dressing gown."

It was of blue silk and not too conspicuous. At any rate there was no collar of sable. Huddled warmly into his fur-lined flying coat Bernardo looked at it with distaste. He was going to be vilely cold hanging about on the rocks at the foot of that north-facing point.

Half a sun rose out of the Atlantic — enough to light up the rusty cliffs of Vizcaya and a faint streak which was the breakwater at the mouth of the Nervion. A haze hung over the shipyard and the foundries. The sea looked calm. Bernardo undressed, left his chair and knelt beside the pilot to give him exact instructions when to turn to port and lose height. The pilot swept round in an easy half circle as if he had picked up a landmark and found himself off course. They were then off Galea Point and flying just above the water parallel to the beach of Sopelana.

"Now!"

The plane taxied gently over the water beneath the next overshadowing cliff.

"Gorliz then as soon as I can get there," Kalmody confirmed. "And keep out of the bars! I'll bring lunch."

Bernardo rolled up the dressing gown, tied it to his body and slipped from the moving float into the sea. It was very cold. He reckoned that he would be the only person on Gorliz beach. When he hauled himself out onto the tumbled rocks at the foot of the cliff, the plane was just lifting from the water like a skimming swallow which had quenched its thirst. He saw Kalmody wave and hoped no one else had.

It was not quite as bad as he thought it would be. He had forgotten that round the point and — if one was careful — still out of sight of the little town of Plencia, the cliffs caught the morning sun. Even so he could not stop shivering. He tried some private cliff-climbing to keep warm and found that he had completely lost his nerve for any height above ten feet.

Nadya

But it was going to be the splendid day that the haze over the Nervion had promised, with the gray and green of the coast and the red and white of houses glittering in the sun. He wondered what Nadya, if she ever came, would make of still another foreign country. He hoped that Pozharski was making her laugh. That faultless oval with, sometimes, the veiled, cat-like eyes! Surely any surgeon must feel that he was clipping the wings of an angel? Wings? He could be giving her wings.

When the sun was nearing south he ventured out and strolled round the point. Back at last in his own world, he sat on the shingle downriver from Plencia. The town appeared to be carrying on its business unconcerned with assassins of grand dukes and seaplanes that passed at dawn, so he waded across to Gorliz beach and lay down on the warm sands, annoyed that he could not take off the dressing gown and dry it.

By midday there were mothers and nannies and children on the beach with here and there a man. Only paddlers were in the water, but passersby readily assumed that he had been swimming and told him he was very valiant. It was a joy to talk and laugh. He deliberately coarsened his Basque accent, remembering with unfair disgust the formal, old-fashioned Spanish of David Mitrani in the Crucea de Piatra.

A car was bumping down the rutted, sandy track to the beach. Even before seeing the coronetted falcons on the door panel he had no doubt who was in it. Nobody else would have a dark red Hispano-Suiza the size of a bus. He walked unhurriedly towards it as if returning to the inn where he was staying. Kalmody pulled him immediately into the warmth of furs, then opened the lunch basket. None of that damned champagne, but the dark purple Rioja from the wood. What a thought and what a man! Who else could have guessed what would be the right wine for his homecoming?

"I'd have been here sooner, but we ran out of fuel just outside Pasajes and had to get a tow in," Kalmody said. "Never mind! The Spanish roads are excellent now and we'll easily do the four hundred kilometers to Madrid in time for dinner. By the way, they are operating this afternoon. The surgeon says it will be a long job but straightforward and she's tough as nails."

"I hope Sigi will telephone."

"What do you think? And give me some of that before you finish it!"

Kalmody made Madrid in five and a half hours in spite of mountain roads and taking a lot more care with oxcarts than he would have done in his own country.

"And a very respectable flat we arrived at, overlooking the Castellana," old Mr. Brown said. "Pozharski really lived there, and it was Arabian Nights all over again. Kalmody thought it best for me not to go out yet, but he ordered in a procession of barbers, tailors and shirtmakers and by the time of our appointment at the Palace I was the best-dressed man in Madrid — the sober cut and color of a Spaniard and just enough of English tweediness. Those suits lasted me for years, and I've still got the morning coat."

He was sweating with nervousness and could not help dreading lest one of all those chamberlains and majordomos might run him in before he reached the royal study, though Kalmody was fairly confident of what was going to happen, assuring him that Alfonso only wanted to see what he looked like. When Bernardo was at last in the presence, he did whatever Kalmody did half a second later just as in the ghetto of Roman; and as for the rest he was allowed to feel merely one *caballero* in face of another with normal manners on both sides.

"He never photographed well, Alfonso. I don't know how

such a lively face could look so sinister. A casual, very courteous fellow, admired by all traditional Spaniards. It was the chaps who took their ideas from abroad who wouldn't hear of him. It's the 'oughts' rather than plain facts which do so much damage in this world. One 'ought' to prefer a republic to a king who didn't give a damn for the constitution. So the virtues of Alfonso were out before they were even considered."

Bernardo was asked to repeat the story of that night at Lequeitio and the climbing of the cliff. He did so in English since Alfonso had decided it was the common language of the three. The king listened with a smile that was wholly charming in spite of his marked Hapsburg lip and told him that his case would be withdrawn from the courts and the extradition order cancelled.

"All the same I think it would be wise to wait a little before you visit England again. What will you do? Any ideas, Kalmody?"

"I will see that he has no need to do anything as long as he likes, sire."

"And you, what do you think?" Alfonso asked, switching to Spanish.

"That it does not suit me to do nothing, *Vuestra Majestad*."

"A job as my vice-consul in Romania?"

"Impossible! Remembering how I lived, they would never honor Spain as they should."

"The yard where your father worked?"

"I do not know enough for them. Ships built on the Nervion are the best in the world."

"Then sell them, *hijo mio*, if that is what you feel! Sell them! I will see to it. Rogue! *Picaro!* You belong to us. And what did you find in your cabaret to amuse us at San Sebastian this summer? Kalmody and I have been known to go out incognito."

Nadya

"Only a dancer, *Vuestra Majestad*, graceful and Byzantine. She has also a great-aunt, outspoken and proud of her descent from a bandit. If she should come as chaperone, ask her about the portrait of her grandfather. I will mention their names in the right quarter. But the count will not be the best of companions. He can see no good in Romanians."

"He does not see much good in Spaniards either, Don Bernardo. But a man of exaggerated nobility! You will not lose by your sufferings. That is more than most of us can say."

So in June Bernardo was back in Bilbao launched on his profitable Anglo-Basque career, dining out on his story and at first somewhat embarrassed by the social consequences of royal favor. He even had a bull dedicated to him and, he said, one could hardly do better than that.

"Nadya. Yes. Her letters were unreasonably reserved and did not tell me much except that God now agreed with her that it was all O.K. I must admit I was anxious. Sigi Pozharski had taken her down to the South of France to recuperate and I was not ready to trust him that far. I would have liked some reassurance from Kalmody, but he was away in Hungary for a couple of months — clearing his name all round, I think — and I heard nothing from him until he called me from Lequeitio out of the blue. He wanted to know the fastest way to get a truck of flowers from Nice. I said it wasn't my job any longer and I was not up to date, but I recommended the normal route of Toulouse–Lourdes–Bayonne, making it worth the while of the stationmasters, and asked him why he didn't get them from Málaga anyway. No, he insisted that Nice was traditional and would I keep Saturday fortnight free and lunch with him at the villa.

"I went in by the back door, this time saluted by the pair of Civil Guards on the road. After lunch we rolled through the villa onto that fateful terrace all decorated with flowers.

Zita's birthday, I supposed. Blow me down, they like fun, those Hungarians, when there is any sort of excuse for it! Such unbelievable generosity! Even today their bloody communism is different to anyone else's.

"They had hired the Lequeitio pipes and drums playing Basque warsongs up and down the beach with a crowd which didn't know what was going on. Zita was there, too. I don't think she had the foggiest notion what was going on either. I was presented to her. All in black she was like Queen Victoria but a damned sight better looking.

"And then Sigi Pozharski brought Nadya round from under the trees with a lovely old Russian headdress dangling pearls down her cheeks and a white Parisian afternoon frock with the top cut very like Magda's when I first saw her. It only occurred to me years afterwards that I might have mentioned it sometime or other on our travels. They had even dug up some ferocious old Hapsburg who was very drunk and couldn't keep his eyes off her. She held out her arms to me and gave one almighty squeal when I hugged her. I'd forgotten about the scars. But no complaints since then on either side. No complaints at all except that she will still call me David."